I0838457

The Path of the Vestal

JD EASTERLING

INDIEOWL
PRESS

300 Lenora Street
STE 1567
Seattle, WA 98121

info@indieowlpress.com
www.indieowlpress.com

THE PATH OF THE VESTAL

Cover Design by Kayla JaQuay
Interior Layout/Typesetting by NightOwlFreelance.com

Manufactured in the United States of America

Paperback ISBN-13: 978-1-949193-11-4

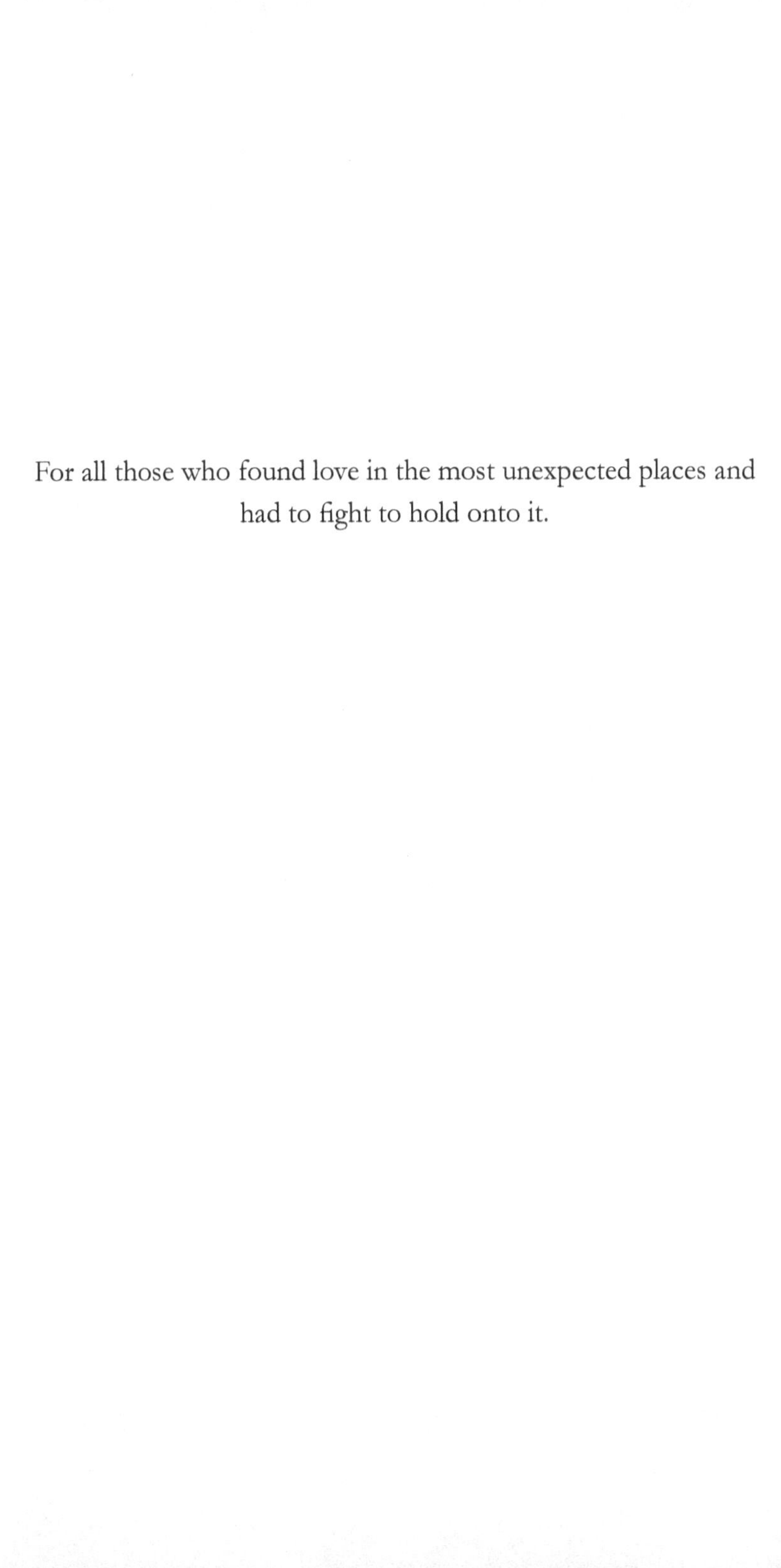

For all those who found love in the most unexpected places and had to fight to hold onto it.

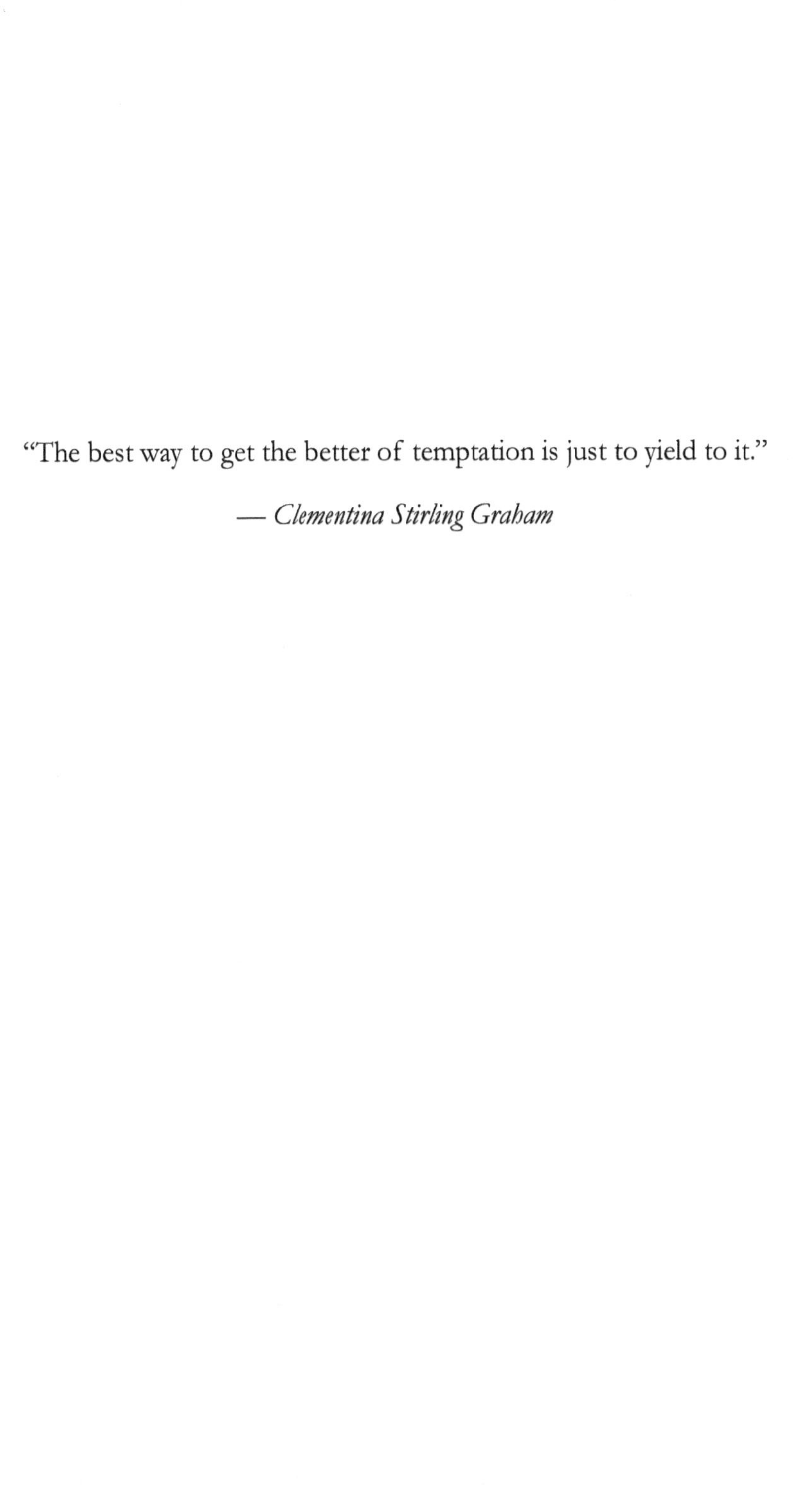

"The best way to get the better of temptation is just to yield to it."

— Clementina Stirling Graham

The Path of the Vestal

There were few sounds Evelyn loved more than the beating of her horse's hooves as they pounded against the earth and swept the miles away beneath them. She held the reins firm in her gloved hands and felt the wind whip her hair around as her mount hit a full gallop. These were the moments she lived for. That one daily opportunity to escape the cold stone walls of Airedale Keep and feel alive.

Somewhere far behind her, Evelyn's chaperones were struggling to keep pace with her. Lord Dalton, her father, was particular about the guards he employed to protect his family and his assets. The large men escorting her wore heavy breast plates and were armed with muskets. They were mounted on strong-backed horses, bred to carry heavy loads. Evelyn never gave them a chance to match her pace as she charged out of the courtyard and sped off on her daily ride. She always selected the spryest horse, looking for the tell-tale glint in the eye of an animal that wanted to run. She preferred the younger and less tame horses, the ones that deep down could never truly be broken in. Somewhere in those hungry, fiery eyes, she saw a piece of herself.

She suspected the guardsmen never told her father that she slipped their sight. She couldn't tell if it was because they were indulging her by letting her have her moments of freedom before returning her to the Keep or whether it was because they were fearful of her father's reprisal. For her part, Evelyn made sure that her chaperones always knew where to find her. No matter which path she took, or how far she deviated from the roads, she always made her way to One Tree Hill.

She let her horse slow to a gentle trot as she approached the summit of the hill and moved under the shade of its one large oak tree. This was her favorite place to come and be alone, even if the solitude was brief. The smell of the ocean made its way from Airedale Port, all the way up the limestone cliffs and rolling hillsides. Evelyn squinted against the afternoon sun, looking out to sea. In the far distance, barely a speck on the horizon, she could see the tall sails of an approaching vessel. As still a day as it was, the ship looked as though it had been painted against the pale blue horizon, scarcely moving as it made its way to port.

She had never been on a ship, or even a boat, and wasn't entirely sure what the difference was—or if there was much of a difference. All she knew was there was something quite alluring about watching them sail in and out of port. The ability to roam and be free was something she envied in anyone who possessed it. For her entire life, Evelyn had always been restricted to the Keep and its surrounding land. She could only assume that when she married, her tether would simply move to another location. She doubted it would lengthen. As a caged bird envies watching others of its kind soar through the skies, Evelyn watched each ship that came and left Airedale port with a deep sense of envy.

The glare of the sun strained her already tired eyes as she gazed at the ship. She had woken early to the sounds of servants hard at work, scurrying frantically about the rooms and corridors as they prepared for the arrival of Lord and Lady Tallisker. No doubt her father was attempting to forge some new trade negotiation or political alliance with the visiting lord. Evelyn had learnt a lot from secretly spying on her father's meetings when she was a child. When she had been small enough to creep around the Keep without being noticed, she had discovered many things about its inhabitants. Sometimes considerably more than she wanted to.

Since becoming a woman, there were certain things expected of her, and hiding behind the tapestries or climbing through the rafters were not among them. Most of her daily activities were chosen for her, as well as what she should wear and with whom she would socialize. She couldn't really remember when it had happened. She supposed it had just been so gradual she hadn't really noticed it. Like the hour hand on a clock moving almost imperceptibly, her life had gradually shifted from carefree to confined. Everyone else had seemed prepared for it, but for Evelyn it had come as a very unwelcome realization.

Now, when it suited her parents, she was dressed up like a doll and paraded in front of potential suitors. Or worse, the parents of potential suitors, who looked at her with judgmental stares and talked about her as if she wasn't in the room. Evelyn had been told from a distressingly young age that she was a particularly valuable asset to the Dalton family. An only child, heiress to a large amount of land and a valuable trading township and, in the words of her mother, she was 'passably attractive'. She had noticed many male servants, particularly the younger ones, had begun to stare just a little longer than they ought. While she herself had no particular views about her appearance, it was becoming increasingly obvious that men did.

She could hear one of her father's guardsmen calling out to her, but she ignored him. They knew where to find her once it was time to turn back. She wasn't in a hurry to get back to the Keep. As cold and distant as he could be, Evelyn had noted that her father seemed to genuinely love throwing a feast. It wasn't just a chance to show off his wealth, Evelyn saw a passion in him that only came out when he was surrounded by food, wine, and company. But her mother, the perpetually dissatisfied Lady Dalton, had a very different view on entertaining, in that she would simply rather not. When Lord Dalton was indulging his guests, Lady Dalton would remain steadfastly in her seat and do her utmost best to engage as few people as possible. She did what was 'expected' of a lady in her position.

For her part, Evelyn landed somewhere in between her parents when it came to hosting events at the Keep. She enjoyed her home the most when it was full of laughter and strangers. Beyond church, events were one of the few opportunities she got to drink wine, and she found it much more enjoyable when the occasion was social and not sacramental. Though she suspected she would be much happier as a guest, particularly one of the less important ones. Whenever there was a feast, Evelyn would be seated with her family, enviously watching the tables furthest from her as they drank, ate, and laughed heartily. The farther the guests sat from their social betters, the more they seemed to enjoy themselves. Evelyn had to maintain composure and make polite conversation when it was required of her and that was where she sided with her mother. She would simply rather not.

"My lady," the voice was much closer now than it had been. Her chaperones had caught up with her, and Evelyn knew it was time to return to the Keep. "We really must return," the guard said, sounding worried. As much as Evelyn wasn't ready to leave, she knew the trouble her watchers would be in if she returned late. The enjoyment of the ride would be considerably lessened if a man was flogged for it later.

"Very well," said Evelyn, suddenly aware that the reticence in her voice had her mother's cadence. "But wasn't it a beautiful day?" she said, hoping the cheery tone didn't sound false.

"Quite beautiful, my lady," replied the lead chaperone obediently.

Evelyn sighed. It took a lot of self-control to stop herself from mimicking the guard as he spoke. As a child she used to mouth the responses she knew the servants and guards would give. It had driven her mother crazy when she did it, which naturally only encouraged the behavior. It was only a stern word from her father that had brought it to an end.

She turned the horse around and made her way back to the Keep without bothering to engage in any further conversation. The sun was hanging low in the sky by the time she returned to the stables. The air in the Keep was filled with the smell of roasting meats and the sounds of furniture being moved around. Knowing time was against her, she didn't linger and made her way to her chambers quickly.

Evelyn had played with dolls as a child but now wished she hadn't. If she hadn't, then the comparison wouldn't have been so obvious. Whenever there was an occasion that called for her to be on display, she found she was living the experience of her childhood toys. She would sit, motionless, as her hair was styled. She let herself be stuffed into dresses that she had no way of getting into herself. She had people tell her how pretty she was and how lovely she looked in her clothes. As it all happened, she would just let herself be moved around without a word leaving her lips or any sign of emotion on her face. She found the process easiest to endure when she imagined herself anywhere else.

This evening had been particularly trying. As she was late, the servants were in a hurry to prepare her, so the process was a little less delicate. Hair pulled, ribs poked, feet squashed, and cheeks pinched, Evelyn was apparently ready. Like a flock of birds taking flight, the servants around her disappeared and she was left alone to study herself in the mirror. Her blonde hair meticulously woven into wide braids stood out against her blue dress. The fabric was heavy, made to withstand the harsh Airedale winters, but it felt like she was wearing a suit of armor as she tried to move in it.

She'd been sprayed with a perfume she didn't recognize, and her nose wrinkled at the foreign floral scent. Not that it mattered of course. As soon as she was in the Great Hall all she would smell of was meat and smoke. A smile formed at the sides of her mouth at the thought, and she felt her mouth water. If nothing else, a feast at Airedale Keep promised good food and fine wine.

Her solitude was broken by an urgent rap at the door. "Your presence is required, my lady." Evelyn's lips moved in sync with the words. She gave herself one last look in the mirror.

"Right," she said to her reflection, "let's see what all the fuss is about." She drew herself up and walked out the door. She could hear announcements from the Great Hall as guests arrived. That meant she was very late. She picked up her pace, forcing the servants in front of her to walk faster, as if propelling them forward with an invisible forcefield. As more guests began to filter in, Evelyn was quickly ushered to her seat. Though she avoided making eye contact, she could feel her parents glaring at her as she took her place.

Once the meat was carved and the wine was poured, the festivities were in full swing. Evelyn let the warmth of the evening wash over her. On occasions such as this, the Great Hall took on a life of its own. The walls glowed with the reflected heat of a dozen open fires and a hundred warm bodies. The air rose hot from the floor, thick with the smells of baked pastries, roasted meats, and the perspiration of the feasting masses. The huge torches that lit the room cast shadows only seen on nights like this, giving the hall new limbs. The hearth fire flickered and pulsed, giving the room a heartbeat of its own.

Evelyn knew this room mostly as it slumbered, as the cold stone lay silent while her father gave council, and the dull-eyed servants busied themselves with their menial tasks. Normally when she passed through it her footsteps echoed off the tall walls and bounced off the ceiling. She felt a kinship to the large room. It needed excitement to bring it to life. The rest of the time it was just an empty shell as it waited for the next opportunity to showcase itself.

Scanning the rest of the hall, Evelyn looked enviously at the guests as they laughed and drank. Her father had fully immersed himself into the politics of the evening with the enormous Lord Tallisker sitting to his left. Her father's guest seemed more preoccupied with running his fingers through his long, twisted mustache than talking about affairs of state. As he caught Evelyn staring, he gave her a warm smile. Evelyn imagined for a moment what a mustache like Lord Tallisker's would feel like pressed again her face and wondered if Lady Tallisker enjoyed it. Evelyn imagined it would feel like kissing a broom, something she was happy to pass through life without experiencing.

Her mother sat drearily to the right of her father; the excitement of the evening lost on her. Despite the vibrant color of her dress, Lady Dalton managed to be the only shade of gray in the Great Hall. Next to her, Lady Tallisker was laughing uproariously at a joke she had told about the lower classes, but the quip failed to elicit a response from her mother. Evelyn realized that she couldn't remember what her mother's laugh sounded like as she cast her eyes away from her parents and across the room of assembled guests. Most of the faces she recognized, though she recalled very few of the names. For the most part, the room was made up of the local gentry taking full advantage of their Lord's generosity and making liberal use of his cellar.

As she surveyed the room, she was caught by surprise. There was one pair of eyes staring straight back at her. Piercing green eyes that locked with hers so intensely she couldn't look away. He was surrounded by some of the coarser looking men at the feast, strong and able-looking gentlemen with weathered skin and stern looks.

He wore a blue captain's jacket, but his sense of style and relaxed pose suggested he was a merchant captain and not a naval officer. A short auburn beard hedged his jawline, contrasting brilliantly with the darkness of his attire. He smiled a rapscallion's smile as he caught her looking back at him. Evelyn ran a hand over her hair and looked away nervously.

Suddenly, she felt betrayed by the Great Hall as the warmth of its walls surged through her. Her veins rose to her skin as the heat seeped into her body. She was no stranger to the leers and protracted stares of men as her body had matured. While most of the servants knew better than to gawk, she often caught her father's guests staring at her. This had felt different, though. He had looked her in the eyes with a confidence she hadn't seen in a man before. She looked back at him, only to meet his eyes again. He rose his glass and very subtly tilted it toward her before taking a sip.

The moment was interrupted as the next course was brought to the table. An entire side of beef was placed in front of Evelyn and a team of skilled servants descended around it. Her view was obscured as they carved and distributed the meat in front of her. Evelyn moved her head to the left and right, impatiently trying to see around the servants who seemed to be expertly trained to obfuscate her view of the green-eyed captain. When the servants had finally disentangled themselves from her presence, she looked back to the table where he had been seated and felt her heart sink as she found no trace of him.

After the bones had been picked clean and the plates cleared from the tables, the dancing began in earnest. Evelyn felt her mother's cold hand on her shoulder as she rose from her chair. "Come, dear," she said wearily. "Let us join the...revelry," she spat the word from her mouth as if it were a distasteful morsel. Evelyn allowed herself to be led to the dance floor. Though she loved the act of dancing, she had always found a certain level of disappointment in the limp or clammy grips of her male partners. Each man on the dance floor seemed intimidated by her. She often mused that her station meant the dancers took extra care with her, as if treading on eggshells around her to avoid a disapproving glance from her father.

Twirl. Curtsey. Move to the next partner. Another limp capture of her hand as she was passed to her next partner. Twirl. Press. Move back. Move forward. Twirl. Curtsey. A new partner, another soft grip of her hand. Twirl. Press. Move back. Move forward. Twirl. Curtsey.

Her eyes widened in astonishment as her next partner joined her. There was no mistaking the navy-blue officer's jacket or the rough red beard. A strong hand with a firm grip clasped around hers. The hand on her waist wasn't placed, it was planted. She wasn't twirled, she was spun. She wasn't pressed, she was engulfed. She was pushed back. She was pulled forward. Spun a second time as a hand lingered a fraction too long on her waist before tracing up her body and lifting her chin. Their eyes met. The heat of the room surged through her body again, as if all the life of the celebrating masses were channeling itself through her. "Magnificent," said a voice she could barely hear over the roar of the festivities. She didn't curtsey. She stood stunned for a moment, then heard a throat clear in front of her.

She awoke, as if from a dream, to Lord Tallisker taking her hand and leading her in the dance. She felt the roundness of his stomach and her feet struggle to move in time as his bulk pressed against her. The rest of the dance was completed in minutes, but it felt like an eternity to Evelyn. She did her best to keep her composure and act appropriately, but she stole every moment she could to search for the captain. Once the dance concluded, Evelyn told her mother she needed a moment to take the air. If her mother heard her, she didn't show it. Interpreting the lack of response as approval, Evelyn slipped through the crowded hall and sought refuge away from the noise and heat of the feast.

The focus of the light on the center of the hall threw deep shadows out to the furthest walls. Here, for a moment, a young lady could be free from the heat of the warm walls and gathered bodies. She breathed deeply, wishing her dress was made of a lighter fabric. Her moment of solitude was broken by a voice behind her. "You truly are quite spectacular, my lady." To her surprise, she turned to find her captivating dance partner leaning casually against a stone pillar a short distance away. She somehow managed to compose herself quickly.

"You should be with the rest of the guests," she said, trying her best to sound playful but stern.

He drew himself up and shrugged. "And you should be seated with your family, but here we are." His tone indicated that her attempts to seem authoritarian had failed. Even in the shadows his green eyes had a mischievous glint.

"What's your name?" asked Evelyn. He opened his mouth to reply but she cut him off quickly, "I just want to make sure that the guards know exactly who to look for when I tell them a strange man thought it was a good idea to approach me alone. Though I suspect if I tell them it was a poorly dressed sea captain in need of a shave, they'd find you easily enough." Her tone was playful, but the threat was deliberate. Evelyn had never felt unsafe in her home, but this was the first time she had ever been isolated with a man. He raised his hands defensively, but the smile remained on his face. "Harper," he said. "Captain Finn Harper. And I mean you no harm, my lady."

"And what are you doing here, Captain Finn Harper?" asked Evelyn, her brow raised slightly.

"I was commissioned by your father and Lord Tallisker to—"

"I meant," said Evelyn archly, "what are you doing skulking around in the shadows away from all of the other guests?"

"Oh," he paused for a moment. "Well, my lady, I suspect I'm here for the same reason you are."

"And what reason would that be?"

"To cool off," said Harper evenly. There was silence between them for a moment. The sounds of merriment from the feast seemed louder as they stared at each other. He took a step toward her, and then another. Then he stopped, a few paces from her. His eyes dared her to take the next steps, and she could feel her heel begin to rise off the floor before her mind had a chance to process what was happening. She knew she was standing on the precipice of a decision. The correct thing to do was to go back to the feast and take her seat back at her family's table, but that was not what she wanted. A thousand thoughts crammed themselves into a fraction of a second, but none of them were able to gain control over her desire. She was surprised at how little hesitation she had as she took her first step toward Harper.

"No one has ever called me spectacular before." It was true. Harper had given her the first compliment she had received (that wasn't directly about her body) in as long as she could remember. Since childhood, she had received comments on the color of her hair or her "growing beauty." While "spectacular" *could* have been a reference to her body, Evelyn felt there was more behind the word when it came from Harper's mouth. "Then I'm glad to have been the first." The distance between them closed. A familiar grasp took her hand, pulling her deeper into the shadows of the Hall. She let herself be led as her heartbeat pulsed through her whole body. She could feel from the coarseness of his skin that this was not a man who led his people from a chair, as her father had done. These were the hands of a man who had spent his life working with them.

"I would very much like to kiss you, Lady Evelyn Dalton," his voice was smooth and soft as his fingers rose her chin. Her lips were close enough to his that she could feel the prick of his short beard hairs. She looked into his eyes. The cheekiness had been replaced by something else. She could tell just from looking at him he was practically bursting with desire as she leaned into him. However, the consequences of being caught kissing a stranger nagged at the back of her mind. Despite the risk, she felt safe in his embrace.

"I would...yes..." was all Evelyn could manage to say. She had expected her first kiss to be demure and ceremonial. This was as wild and untamed as the ocean. The roughness of his beard scratched against her face as she willed his tongue to explore her mouth. She gasped as a hand came to her rear. The thick fabric of her dress padded her body, but Harper did not seem fazed as his hands traveled over her. Her hands pressed against the thick double breast of his captain's jacket, before traveling up to touch his face. Her fingers ran through his hair as they kissed again, her tongue excitedly trying to navigate the new dance she was learning. She pressed her face deeper into his, pushing him back against the wall as the moment consumed her.

The sound of footsteps tapping against the stone floor broke the kiss. Evelyn looked at Harper in wide-eyed panic. He put a finger to her lips, then gently kissed her forehead. The footsteps sounded closer. Harper stepped away and moved out of the shadows. Evelyn held her breath as she listened to Harper approach the footsteps. "Hello there," she heard him call. The footsteps stopped. Evelyn risked a peek. Harper had startled a servant carrying a pile of dirty plates. The poor man struggled to readjust his load as Harper walked toward him. "I must have enjoyed too much wine tonight," said Harper, faking a slur as he spoke. "I can't seem to find the way back to my ship."

The servant looked at him as if he were mad.

"This place is a maze."

"There is only one guest entrance, sir. The way you came in."

Evelyn smiled as Harper threw his hands up in the air. "I never do well at these stuffy indoor events." Harper made a show of hiccupping loudly as he put his hand over the servant's shoulder and turned him around. "I could plot you a course from Portsmouth to Nassau, but once I'm inside one of these stone monstrosities, I'm a lost little lamb." The servant expertly balanced the dirty dishes as Harper leant heavily on his shoulder.

"I would be happy to escort you the rest of the way, sir," said the servant dispiritedly as they moved away from Evelyn. Finally, when they were out of sight, she released her breath.

She took a moment to compose herself and did her best to regain control of her hair. His hands had tousled her blonde strands as they had kissed, and she didn't need a mirror to know how disheveled her hair must look. When she was satisfied that her appearance wouldn't raise suspicion, she made her way back to the feast. She scanned the room before joining her parents but saw no sign of Harper or the men he was with. As she sat at her mother's side, she noticed that her father and Lord Tallisker were embroiled in a deep conversation. When he caught her looking his way, Lord Tallisker gave her a wink. Though it appeared friendly, Evelyn felt something else behind the gesture.

Quietly, she asked her mother if she might be excused for the evening so she could retire to her bedchamber. Her mother gave a disinterested wave, which Evelyn took for affirmation and collected herself up. "Evelyn," called her father as she turned to leave. She froze, turning slowly, her hands bunching in her dress. "Where are your manners?" Evelyn looked perplexed for a moment. "Say good evening to our guests before you retire," said her father, gesturing to the Talliskers. Evelyn felt caught off guard. She had completely forgotten her manners and turned to Lord and Lady Tallisker and gave them a polite curtsey. As her legs bent, she felt her hastily rearranged hair fall out of place. Her mother rolled her eyes and waved her away as Evelyn tucked the wayward strands behind her ears.

Once she had been safely escorted back to her room, Evelyn replayed the events of the evening through her mind. The quiet kiss she had risked blazed in her memory. She felt a rush of excitement, knowing that she acted in defiance of what was expected behavior for a young lady and had enjoyed every second of doing so. As she began the lengthy process of undressing, she imagined how it would feel to have Harper's hands removing her clothing. She remembered how eager his touch had felt on the outside of the thick fabric. She let the dress fall in a heap as she stepped out of it. Catching her reflection in the mirror, shed of heavy dress, she now looked quite petite.

She owed her slender body to the fact she was constantly on the move. She had never enjoyed sitting and was forever roaming through the Keep, searching for new ways to escape the ennui that had long since claimed her mother. Apparently, that would have to stop when the first of her children was born. "You can say farewell to your freedom when you become a mother," her own mother often reminded her. "You can say farewell to those slender hips as well," she would always say with a hint of a smile, as if she were relishing the day when Evelyn's physique took on a more rounded frame. The prospect of round hips bothered Evelyn far less than the thought of losing that last bit of her freedom. She already felt her adult life was constrained enough without the burden of motherhood. She didn't like to think what else there was to lose.

Her nightgown donned, she flopped backward onto her bed. When she closed her eyes, she felt she was back in the Great Hall. The smoke of the fires still clung to her hair, and the smell quickly crept into her pillows. Even through her closed eyes, she could see the piercing stare of Captain Finn Harper. She felt her hands move down her body and pushed her head back into her pillow as she explored herself. She had been warned about pleasures of the flesh at church—but that was one of many lessons from Father Baldwin that she often ignored.

Her brow furrowed as she concentrated on recreating the memory of being in Harper's arms. Just as when she had let Harper take her by the hand, her mind was now overflowing with dozens of distracting thoughts. What if she had been caught? Would she see him again? Did he enjoy the kiss as much as she had? What kind of woman did her actions make her? A frustrated moan left her mouth as she slipped from the brink of climax. Sleep would not be the only thing not to come easily to Evelyn that night.

Captain Finn Harper took in the first light of day from the deck of the Vestal as he enjoyed a rare moment of solitude. The crew were enjoying shore leave and his officers were sleeping off their full bellies after a night feasting and drinking, so he had the deck to himself. Just below his feet, fastened to the bowsprit, hung the figurehead of the Vestal. A beautiful bronze sculpture of a veiled priestess. Some of the crew mistook her for the Virgin Mary while others claimed she was the wife of a past captain, drowned at sea and immortalized in bronze. Harper knew better, but he enjoyed listening to the men as they argued about her origin. He knew she was a priestess of Vesta, ancient goddess of the hearth, placed proudly at the front of the ship as its guardian.

The captain of the Vestal was considerably less virtuous than the namesake of his ship. Even over the damp and salt of the sea, Harper could still smell Evelyn Dalton's perfume. She had infatuated him from the moment he had seen her. There was a spark in her that outshined everyone who surrounded her. She had shone like a lighthouse burning through fog when he first saw her through the throng of the feast. Though he felt he had been bold enough in stealing a moment with Lord Dalton's daughter, he wished their intimacy hadn't been interrupted. He smiled at the rising sun, knowing that in a few short hours he would return to Airedale Keep, and wondered if the day would bring with it any new opportunities.

From behind him, he heard the creak of footsteps on the weathered planks of the Vestal's deck. "Mornin', Captain," Harper turned to Nicholas Webb, the Vestal's first mate.

"And a very fine morning it is, Mr. Webb," said Harper with a nod. Webb wasted little time on pleasantries before moving quickly to the railing and dropping his trousers.

"It's rare to make port in such a comely town," he waited until Webb had finished relieving himself before he continued. "Have you slept off the ale?"

Webb gave a pained look. "Unfortunately not, and I fear I'm the worse for it. What about you, Captain?"

"I was drinking wine," said Harper, tapping the side of his head. "Seems to have agreed with me better."

Webb ran a hand through his thinning hair before rubbing at his temples. "I woke up half mounted to a cannon, couldn't for the life of me find my berth." He stretched painfully, his spine audibly cracking as he did so.

"I swear, Webb, an entire cabin to yourself is wasted. I suppose as long as all you did was sleep on the cannon, then it isn't a bother," said Harper. "Would have been hard to explain if you'd fired one off in the state you were in..."

Webb took a drink from his flask and belched loudly before offering it to Harper, who declined with a shake of his head. "Might not strike the right chord with his lordship if there's the smell of rum on my breath," said Harper. Having arrived in Airedale later than expected, Harper had already taken the opportunity to apologize to Lord Dalton. The benefit of his late arrival meant his passenger had missed the feast, which had, in turn, yielded benefits of its own. "How is our guest?"

"Sleep'n," replied Webb with a shrug. "Otherwise, I'd presume he's still a pompous little mollycoddle, but I can't confirm that 'til he's awake."

Harper nodded. He had little respect for men who didn't know the merit of hard work. He didn't expect that all men should take to the seas and live as he had, but it was his belief that a man should be strong enough to protect his wealth and his people. So far, Edmond Tallisker, the youngest son of Lord Tallisker, seemed capable of nothing other than being underfoot.

The sun had long since set when Vestal had finally crawled into port. Harper rationalized that by the time Edmond was woken, dressed, and escorted to Airedale Keep, it would have been daybreak. So he let Edmond sleep peacefully through the night, made his apologies to Lords Dalton and Tallisker, and then, since he and his officers were there anyway, he enjoyed the feast. Harper knew it was a cruel thing to do to the young man, but as the result had been an unexpected but entirely welcome encounter with Lady Evelyn, he would have gladly done it again.

"Wake him up at six bells," said Harper, striding off to his cabin. "And request he joins me in my cabin once he feels he is sufficiently presentable."

"Expect him around noon then, Captain," said Webb with a chuckle. Harper indulged the comment with a short laugh of his own.

He locked the door to his cabin behind him once he'd entered. It was rare he took the time to manicure himself, but this was an important day. Despite his better judgement, he was going to be mingling with nobility. Once he had delivered Edmond safely, he would then have the unpleasant task of rubbing elbows with the nobility of Airedale. Privateers had made trade more difficult. There were plenty of nobles and merchants looking for a ship as capable as the Vestal to further their own ends, and Airedale provided an abundance of opportunity for commission. Most of his men would have just spent whatever remained of their coin on hard drinks and loose women, which meant Harper needed to turn profit.

He selected his best jacket, a double-breasted naval coat with silver trim, and set to the long task of doing up the brass buttons. As he dressed, he imagined what it might feel like to be undressed by Lady Evelyn. Her soft, delicate hands taking the time to remove each item of his clothing. As he fastened the last button, he remembered the feel of her slender frame under his fingertips. The memory was enough to trigger a physical response, and he soon found his trousers had become far too tight. As the garment struggled to expand with his body, he was sorely tempted to drop them and relieve himself, the image of Evelyn burning in his mind's eye.

As soon as his fingers moved to his belt, however, a timid knock came at the door. "Bugger," Harper mumbled. He moved to his desk and sat in his chair, using the polished oak as a barrier to disguise his arousal. "Enter," he called, doing his best to sound composed. The latch to his cabin jiggled, but the door remained closed. "I'm terribly sorry, Captain, but the door appears to be locked." The accent annoyed Harper. If ever there was a voice to match a body, this was it; pale, manicured, and far too well polished for one at sea. Harper sighed and rose from his chair. "Wait a moment," he said, moving as quietly as he could across the room, shuffling awkwardly in his overly full trousers. Carefully, he unlocked the door and then stealthily made his way back to his desk. "Try again," he called.

The door opened and Edmond Tallisker stepped into the room, with a look of astonishment on his face. "I say, I thought it was locked, but I guess it just needed a bit more brawn to get it unstuck."

Harper nodded. "Always been a fierce opponent, that door," said Harper, not moving from his seat.

Normally, he would stand whenever anyone entered his cabin, particularly a lord, but he chose to remain seated until he regained control of his body. "Good thing you woke with a healthy vitality this morning." Edmond made punching motions in the air as he advanced across the room.

"Fear not, Captain," he said haughtily, "I'm yet to meet any piece of carpentry that can best me…" as he moved forward, he caught his knee hard on one of many chests that occupied the floor, a wince coming over his face.

"So I can see," said Harper, his eyes narrowing as Edmond hopped awkwardly on one foot to avoid falling over completely. "Are you hurt, my lord?"

"Perish the thought, Captain," said Edmond as he hobbled over and took the chair opposite Harper. He couldn't be sure, but Harper could have sworn he saw tears welling in the young man's eyes. "We Talliskers are made of sterner stuff than you might think."

Though Edmond Tallisker wasn't fat, his body lacked muscular definition. Harper suspected that, like most of the Tallisker family, Edmond was mostly made of pork pies and buttered potatoes. "Well, I'm glad you're unharmed. I've sent some men ashore to arrange for the coach. The Keep is a brief journey, but your father expects you delivered before the midday meal." Harper stood, feeling his body had suitably calmed down after his earlier excitement. "Once you feel you're ready, we'll depart."

Edmond rose with the captain, straightening his frock coat and clearing his throat. "I fear if I spend any more time grooming, the townsfolk will slow us down as they spill forth into the streets just to catch a glimpse of me." Edmond gave a desperate smile, and Harper hoped the young man was joking. It was hard to tell through the pomp of the accent. Experience had taught him that laughing at a lord's statement that wasn't intended as a joke was ill advised. Instead, he did his best to force a polite smile and gestured toward the door.

As they made their way on deck, several of Harper's crew readied to lower the gangplank down to the jetty. Edmond took the lead, striding ahead of the captain and taking a firm grip on the railing as he prepared to descend the rickety plank. Looking up, he stared into an exceptionally unfriendly face and took a step back in surprise. He let out a startled "Oh my" as he backed into Harper's chest.

"No cause for alarm, my lord. It's tradition that Blackbeard sees off anyone who leaves the ship."

Edmond looked at the large black cat sitting on the railing. Its missing eye was covered by an eye patch, and its bushy, wild fur formed a beard-like mane around its scarred face.

"He's…hideous," said Edmond distastefully. Harper reached out a hand and scratched at the beast's left cheek, resulting in a deep, rumbling purr.

"Aye, he's hideous," said Harper with a grin. "But he keeps the rats out of our food, and he's got the best set of ears onboard." Edmond regarded the tattered ears with disgust. "Hasn't set foot on dry land in eight years, but he always makes sure he says a farewell to anyone heading to shore." Edmond did his best to shuffle around Blackbeard as he descended the gangplank. He could feel the cold, judgmental stare of the one-eyed cat watching him as he clumsily made his way down to the docks.

"I say," said Edmond once he was on solid ground. "I could swear the ground is moving under my feet."

"Sea legs," explained Harper as they made their way to the coach. "Shouldn't last more than a few days."

"A few days," said Edmond in dismay. "It feels terribly strange. Do you feel it too?"

"Not since I was a lad, my lord," said Harper. Then, to make the young man feel more at ease, he quickly added, "but everyone feels it after their first voyage. Nothing unusual about it."

Harper spent the coach ride listening to Edmond describe everything he saw. Airedale was clearly a far busier and more exciting town than Edmond was used to. His face was practically pressed against the window for the entire trip, only peeled away to excitedly point out interesting things to Harper as they passed. Having walked the streets of Airedale the previous evening, they held little interest for Harper, but as they came under the shadow of the Keep, his attention was piqued. "I say," said Edmond, "look at those guns!"

In the dark, the Keep was little more than a silhouette against the pale glow of the moon. Now, in the daylight, Harper saw a different side to Lord Dalton's home. The thick, high walls of Airedale Keep boasted an impressive arsenal of cannons pointed out to sea. This was a fort that was built to withstand a siege. There wasn't a ship sailing into or out of Airedale that Lord Dalton couldn't turn to kindling. Harper had no doubt Lord Dalton would gladly turn his guns against The Vestal if he knew the liberty her captain had taken with his only daughter.

"She's certainly a sight, isn't she, Captain," said Edmond, gesturing to the Keep as it loomed in front of them.

"She certainly is," Harper agreed, as his mind played out the potential consequences of his actions.

Evelyn breathed in deeply as her corset was tightened across her back. Anna had only been her handmaiden for a short time and seemed to have a poor grasp of her own strength when it came to dressing a lady. Before she could release her breath, Evelyn felt the straps tie fast against her back. She was imprisoned once again. The confining garment forced her to breathe small, shallow breaths while she remained in its suffocating grip. She could hear her father pacing impatiently outside her bedchamber as Anna fussed around her. She felt pushed, pulled, prodded, and probed as her body was manipulated into the garment against its will. Of course, no one had bothered to tell her why she was being dressed up. That would imply that she had an interest in her own affairs. She looked at herself in the mirror with a blank, doll-like expression as her hair was brushed and styled.

Besides her unwitting strength, Evelyn had no complaints about Anna, but she missed her former servant, Madame Bellegarde. The Madame had been a kind and compassionate mentor to Evelyn in her younger years. One day, her mother had decided on a whim that the company of a mature and refined French woman would suit her better and had arranged for Madame Bellegarde to transfer to her service. Anna, an unwed mother, was the daughter of one of Lord Dalton's close friends and, in exchange for her service, lived in the Keep while raising her child.

It had been an important lesson for Evelyn to learn. Though she was several years younger than Anna, she had understood quickly the dangers of falling pregnant outside of marriage. Her mother had also made it clear that if Evelyn ever found herself in Anna's predicament, she would earn her living among the sailors on the docks. Evelyn often wondered if Anna had been kept around just as a daily reminder of the value of being chaste—as if the sermons and homilies from Father Baldwin weren't enough.

Finally, once she was satisfied that Evelyn was ready, Anna opened the door and her father stepped in. He smiled at her, which immediately made her suspicious of his intentions.

"You look beyond magnificent, my dear," said Lord Dalton as he entered the room. "You'd melt the heart of any eligible young gentleman that laid his eyes on you." Evelyn smiled and gave her father a kiss on the cheek as he approached her.

"Thank you, father," she replied. Though she had done her best to sound grateful for the compliment, her heart sank at his words. She knew the inevitable conversation that was coming as he took her hand and led her out of her room.

"You may have noticed last night that I was preoccupied with Lord Tallisker." Evelyn said nothing, but she felt a rising panic forming in the pit of her stomach. She had avoided marriage to several undesirable characters. From the moment she had turned fifteen, her father had used the promise of her hand as leverage in negotiations.

In the past, luck had been the only deciding factor in keeping her out of the hands of men her father would have gladly married her to. Ugly men. In some cases, violent men. Although her hand was a powerful asset to negotiate with, Lord Dalton understood she could only be sold once. For that reason, when the price had not been to his satisfaction, he had withdrawn her from the bargaining table. While Evelyn was certain that he loved her in his own way, she was also certain that he would never let that love get in the way of his own gain.

"The Tallisker family has become increasingly wealthy and powerful over the last decade. So much so that I must now look to them as either a threat or I must take steps to make a more permanent alliance. Lord Tallisker and I have been negotiating the terms under which we might join our families through marriage for some time. We want the region to grow, and by becoming allies, we secure peace for our people and prosperity for our merchants."

Evelyn had heard this speech before, verbatim, though she knew better than to move her mouth with the words. The only difference was the family name. Last time it had been some other family. Greenhorn? Grayhall? She couldn't remember now. Evelyn simply nodded as her father spoke. "Edmond Tallisker is said to be a very fetching young man," her father continued. Evelyn felt insulted that the rumor of a man being handsome was in some way meant to soften the indignity of being married off to a stranger for political gain. "He's the youngest of Lord Tallisker's sons, just a few months older than you. Twenty years old last winter and now the Lord of Dunshire."

She dreaded the idea of being shipped off to an unknown land only to become a prisoner in another Keep. Surrounded by new, judgmental faces and unfamiliar walls. The only expectation she need comply with would be the birthing of as many children as her small frame could produce.

"He was meant to join us at the feast last night, and I had hoped that you would share a dance with him, but the ship he was meant to arrive on was delayed. Captain Harper made the journey by foot last night to apologize for his absence." Lord Dalton stopped in front of Evelyn's mother's dressing room and put his hands behind his back as he waited. He knew better than to pace impatiently in front of his wife's door.

"Captain Harper?" asked Evelyn, her eyes widening.

"Yes," said her father dismissively. "The unshaved chap who sat with a few of his officers on the far side of the hall. He came in person to apologize for Lord Tallisker's absence. He's exactly the sort of person who this union would help, Evelyn. A merchant captain could create a very healthy profit for himself by serving the needs of the Daltons and the Talliskers."

Evelyn smiled inwardly. Somehow, she doubted that Captain Harper would see her marriage to another man as beneficial to his needs. She had only known him for the briefest moment, but she had felt firsthand that he was a man driven by more primal instincts than her father. If he cared about wealth and power, then he certainly hadn't acted like it. He had spent his evening stealing glances from the Lord's daughter instead of attempting to gain the favor of the assembled nobles. From Evelyn's perspective, Harper was a man who prioritized pleasure over profit. She flushed as she remembered the feeling of his body pressed against hers and the feeling of his hair through her fingertips. Her father mistook her red cheeks for embarrassment.

"Evelyn, you have nothing to cower about. Stories may tell that young Lord Edmond is handsome enough, but every man with a name worth mentioning knows that Lord Dalton's daughter is the most beautiful woman in the realm."

"The most beautiful unmarried woman, at the least," Lady

Dalton said, emerging from her room with a dour look on her face.

Evelyn looked at the spectacular dress and jewelry that her mother had adorned herself in. If she would allow herself some happiness, Evelyn thought to herself, she truly would have been the most beautiful woman in the kingdom. Lord Dalton took his wife's hand and kissed it with a rigid formality.

"Of course," he said to his wife. "But not to be unmarried for much longer. Come ladies, let us take our place and prepare for the young Lord's arrival. I suspect by now he will be on his way to the Keep."

Evelyn and her mother walked slowly behind Lord Dalton until he was several strides ahead of them. Behind them, Lady Dalton's handmaids kept a steady pace at a respectable distance. Evelyn had always wondered how servants knew the correct distance to keep. Too far would be inattentive, too close would be overly presumptuous, but somehow, they always seemed to get it right. Evelyn knew she would make a poor servant as she would be forever following too closely, gleaning whatever she could from the quiet conversations of her betters. "So, it seems you are about to start your own family," said Lady Dalton, commenting with the same level of emotion she used to describe moderate weather.

"Apparently," said Evelyn distantly.

"An exciting time," said her mother, without a hint of excitement. "I am sure the wedding will be decadent—if the Talliskers are as wealthy as they boast."

"Exciting isn't the word I would choose," said Evelyn quietly. She was bordering on defiant, and she knew it.

"Oh?" Lady Dalton raised an eyebrow at her daughter. "And what word would you choose, Evelyn?"

Evelyn was quiet for a moment. She couldn't think of a single word to describe what was flooding through her mind. Her mother's impatient look forced her to choose one, though. "Terrifying," confessed Evelyn.

Her mother's face softened, or perhaps more accurately, thawed. She stopped walking. Evelyn heard the footsteps of her handmaidens stop behind them. She felt her mother place her hands gently on her shoulders. For a moment, the woman in front of Evelyn stopped being Lady Dalton and became her mother.

"Yes," she said earnestly, "it is terrifying. Men in powerful positions are capable of terrible things and they can inflict harm on almost anyone they choose—even their own wives. If you're lucky, he won't be a cruel man." Evelyn could feel the panic rise from her stomach to her chest. "Perhaps you'll be luckier still and his indiscretions will be private." Her mother removed her hands from Evelyn's shoulders and returned to being Lady Dalton.

"Indiscretions?" asked Evelyn. "What indiscretions?"

"All men have their indiscretions, Evelyn," replied her mother as she continued walking. "Some just hide them better than others." There was an awkward pause.

"Even father?" asked Evelyn, in barely more than a whisper. The rest of the walk was conducted in a long and cold silence.

ord Tallisker's mustache bristled with anger as his son approached the steps to the courtyard. "Where the devil were you last night!?" The mustache moved with such puissance it looked as though it might leap off the Lord's face and attack his son. Harper thought about attempting to calm the situation but watching Edmond's failed attempt was proving too entertaining to disrupt. "We arrange for an evening to be held in honor of your arrival, and somehow, you manage to be absent! Only you, Edmond Tallisker, could make such a mess of things."

"The ship arrived later than..." said Edmond.

Lord Tallisker looked about to strike his son.

"Oh, the ship arrived late?! Did it indeed?! Sent the captain to apologize for you while you slept like a babe?"

Edmond looked at Harper and then back to his father.

"I..."

"Not another word from you, boy," said Lord Tallisker.

"My lord, if I may?" Harper chose his tone carefully.

"Humph?" replied Tallisker.

"Edmond showed considerable spirit on the voyage over, attempting to work alongside the men so that he might know more of the life at sea. Though the voyage was a short one, he applied himself heavily to the task." It was partially true. When boarding, Edmond had made bold claims about his desire to pitch in and work alongside the "common folk of the sea." Webb had given him some light duties so as not to risk the boy hurting himself. To everyone's surprise, Edmond had applied himself harder than anyone expected him to, though his natural clumsiness meant very little actual work was accomplished. Combined with his aloof demeanor, his unfamiliarity with physical work had been the basis for Harper's initial impressions of Edmond. But now, watching the boy struggle in front of his father, Harper felt a pang of pity for the young Lord.

"He applied himself hard to shipboard duties and completed tasks that even the most seasoned seadogs struggle with," continued Harper.

"Sea dogs..." he heard Edmond whisper with a touch of pride.

"At the conclusion of his labors, he slept heavily. The men tried to wake him, but he slept with as much vitality as he had worked. The ship's physician thought it best to leave him." That part was absolutely a lie, as the ship's "physician" was primarily the cook, and at no point had he even met Edmond. Harper delivered the lie with enough sincerity that Lord Tallisker's face softened, and for a moment, his mustache lay still. "I've always held the man who sleeps deeply doesn't sweat over past misdeeds," continued Harper, leaning in closer to Lord Tallisker. "I'd say that a man who sleeps as deeply as the young Lord Tallisker must have a spotless conscience."

Lord Tallisker nodded gruffly.

"There's certainly truth there, Captain. He's a good lad, for the most part," he leaned in closer still so that only Harper could hear him. "He's always been a wet fish. Takes after his mother. Sailing's not a task I'd have him doing again, but hopefully it helped build some muscle on that round frame of his, ey?" Lord Tallisker chuckled and gave Harper a playful elbow to his side. Harper wondered whether the rather rotund Lord Tallisker was suited to judge the physique of his son but returned the laugh. Edmond shuffled awkwardly behind them, a nervous half-laugh leaving his lips.

Lord Tallisker looked at his son. "Come on then, lad," he said gruffly, as the smile faded from his face. "Let's go meet this young lady you're lucky enough to marry. Captain Harper and I have already had the pleasure of a dance with her, so you've got some ground to make up if you're going to make an impression."

"You danced with her?" Edmond asked Harper uncertainly.

"Didn't I say not another word from you, lad?" Lord Tallisker rolled his eyes. "Now follow me and try not to make an arse of yourself as you're introduced."

The heavy wooden doors were dramatically swung open as the Tallisker men ascended the short flight of stairs and stood at the entrance to the hall. Harper could hear music coming from the hall, the formal kind of music that was only ever played for ceremony and not because it was in any way pleasing to the ear. Harper preferred the music of his crew. A rambunctious chorus with dozens of clapping hands and stomping feet, accompanied by a fiddle or a piccolo. That was the sort of music that stirred the soul. These flat tones added formality to an already formal affair, creating a musical redundancy that offended Harper's ears.

It took Harper's eyes a moment to adjust to the well-lit hall as they stepped inside. Though the tables had been removed, the smells of the feast lingered. He looked down the long walls of the Great Hall, where the shadows were deepest. Somewhere in those shadows, he had kissed Edmond's bride-to-be. In the daylight, shadows didn't seem so deep, and he wondered if he might not have been as stealthy as he had imagined. Around him, armed guards flanked the walls and exits of the hall. If his actions were witnessed, this was going to be the last room he ever willingly set foot in.

Unconsciously, his hand moved to rest on the pommel of his sword. His mind raced quickly to find a logical anchor and stop him from panicking. The light was different by day. He was sure they had been careful. If someone had seen him kiss Evelyn, he doubted that Lord Dalton would have waited this long to do something about it. If an accusation had been made, then the Keep's arsenal would have been deployed against the Vestal and Lord Dalton would now be stoking his fires with her timbers.

There was probably nothing to worry about.

◆

At the feast, Evelyn had noticed that Lady Tallisker was not a small woman, but sitting next to her, she fully grasped her size. Lady Tallisker sat fanning herself as beads of perspiration accumulated on her brow. "Frightfully warm," she muttered to herself. Evelyn said nothing in response. She found the Great Hall to be rather too cool for her liking. When Lady Tallisker had seated herself, her large bottom rested on the side of Evelyn's dress, pulling it tight against her. As if the corset wasn't enough, Evelyn could now feel the blood leaving her legs as they began to numb. Unable to move and barely able to draw breath, she sat as demurely as she could whilst her mother and Lady Tallisker talked over her head.

The assembled guests rose to their feet as Lord Tallisker approached them. As Lady Tallisker's bottom left her chair, Evelyn gathered up her dress and rose to her feet, noticeably slower than everyone else. She felt her mother's sharp glare but kept looking forward. Her left leg had fallen asleep, and she was having trouble remaining still as the uncomfortable prickling sensation ran up her thigh. She looked down at the small flight of steps in front of her, knowing that walking down them gracefully was out of the question. She tried to jiggle her leg under her dress without anyone noticing and winced as her mother stuck her long fingers into her side. "Be still!" Lady Dalton hissed, loud enough for most of the guests to hear. Lord Dalton cleared his throat loudly.

"Lord Tallisker," her father began, his voice bouncing off the stone walls of the hall. As he spoke, Evelyn froze in the most formal pose she could muster. The musicians ceased their playing, and the only sound in the room was her father's commanding voice. "It is an honor to once again welcome you and your family to Airedale Keep. These walls have been home to my family for generations, and I hope that in years to come, the children of our children will come to think of these lands as their own." Lord Tallisker returned the greeting with a bow. Evelyn stifled a smile at the sight of the portly man bending to bow, imagining his weight toppling him over if he leant forward too far.

"Lord Dalton, it is a pleasure to once again stand in the company of your esteemed family. Your hospitality has been warmly received. When I return home, I will have our bards sing songs of the good foods and fine wines of Airedale and the generous nature of the lord who rules there." Evelyn wondered if most of the songs Tallisker bards sung were about food. "I am pleased to introduce my son, Edmond Tallisker. He arrived yesterday evening on the Vestal— so exhausted from helping the men in their labors at sea that he regrettably could not rise for the feast. Now fully restored in vitality and civility, he has traveled far for the opportunity to seek the hand of Lady Evelyn Dalton." A lackluster young man shuffled around to stand beside his father. Though her father had said he was several months older than she, he looked young for his age. He was all smooth skin and soft edges. Literally. The beginnings of the Tallisker proportions were already taking shape.

Then she looked at the man standing behind Lord Tallisker and his son and nearly gasped aloud. There was no mistaking the green eyes that stared right through her, let alone the coarse face she had kissed only the night before. Though his attire was more appropriate for a court than what he had worn to the feast, Harper still hadn't shaved and wore a rougher look than the other men assembled. Despite that, Evelyn found him just as alluring in the light of day as she had in the torchlight of the feast. She tore her eyes away and returned her attention to Lord Tallisker's son, doing her best to keep her composure.

"My apologies, Lord Dalton, for my inability to attend the festivities yesterday," Edmond took a step forward from his father, turned his attention to Evelyn and took a deep breath, "I understand, my lady, that I missed my first dance with you last night. I would very much like to make amends, and I hear the gardens of Airedale Keep are a sight that is not to be missed. I would be honored if you were to show them to me," he stretched out a hand to Evelyn. She swallowed nervously. Her left leg was still asleep, and only partially under her control. If that weren't enough, being under Harper's gaze was deeply flustering as she attempted to gather herself.

Carefully, painstakingly slowly, she made her way down the steps toward Edmond. To those watching, it must have looked like this was the first time Evelyn had ever negotiated stairs. From behind her she could hear Lady Tallisker whisper loudly to her mother, "The poor dear is nervous." Once she was close enough, she reached out and seized Edmond's hand. She heard him breathe excitedly as she gripped it fiercely. The stability it offered allowed her to once again look like the lady she was supposed to be, and she drew herself up. There was a moment of confusion as Evelyn and Edmond looked at each other.

"Which way are the gardens?" whispered Edmond in a hushed panic.

"Oh," said Evelyn, suddenly aware that Edmond had no knowledge of Airedale Keep outside of the room he was standing in. She nodded slightly with her head in the direction of one of the many exits from room. "That way," she whispered.

As Edmond led her away, she desperately wanted to glance over her shoulder and catch one last glimpse of Harper. But she stifled the urge. This was definitely one of those times to act as she was supposed to and not as she wanted to. She could hear footsteps falling in behind her. Presumably her mother and Lady Tallisker, keeping chaperone as their young nobles wandered the gardens. Evelyn had no intention of stealing away with her suitor, but she knew of many isolated spots in the garden where two people could be alone.

Occasionally, when she was younger, she had come across servants fornicating in the garden. Couples that had stolen away from their duties to lose themselves in a moment of shared pleasure. She had watched them in secret while they rutted like animals among the thick foliage. She had never told her parents, or anyone else, what she had seen, but she often imagined similar affairs taking place in many other secluded parts of the Keep. As she walked through the hall, she glanced at the spot she and Harper had shared their kiss and knew that she now shared an intimate secret of her own with the walls of Airedale.

Edmond's hand was clammy, and his grip was much softer than Harper's. She was relieved when he took her hand and placed it on his arm. "Now, Captain Harper," she heard her father say from behind her. "Lord Tallisker and I have some important matters to discuss with you..." she again resisted the urge to turn around and look back. Instead, she did her best to push him out of her mind. Edmond looked like he might burst at any moment, his face becoming taut as the nerves built up inside him. Evelyn wasn't at all sure if he'd taken a breath since they had started their walk. "How was your voyage over, my lord?" asked Evelyn, trying to break the silence as gently as she could.

"Pleasant enough, my lady," replied Edmond. "The weather was clement."

"I've not been to sea before," she confessed. "Though I would very much like to."

"To be honest, this was my first voyage," confided Edmond, leaning more closely so that the procession behind them couldn't hear them. "And it was almost everything I could have hoped for."

"Almost?" asked Evelyn inquisitively.

"Well, it was fascinating being at sea and watching the crew work," said Edmond. "But we didn't get the chance to fight any dreaded sea beasts or nefarious pirates. I was hoping to see Captain Harper and his men in action and join them in battle. He has quite a reputation, and I am hoping to make one for myself." Evelyn did not doubt that a man like Captain Harper had a reputation that preceded him. As burning as her questions about the captain were, she kept them for a later time. If this man was to be her husband, then she did not want her first conversation with him to be about a man she lusted over.

"Why on earth would you want to encounter pirates and sea monsters?" asked Evelyn. From his physique, she assumed Edmond was a poor swordsman, though perhaps he had learned to ride or hunt with a musket. Even still, his polite demeanor didn't seem suited to battle.

"The excitement of it all," said Edmond. "I don't know how it is for you in Airedale but, where I'm from, my days are planned. My servants dress me; Father organizes my affairs, even from afar, and I perform my duties as well as I am able. It's just what's expected of me." Evelyn understood that all too well.

"I know how that feels, my lord," she said earnestly.

"So if I were to see something incredible out at sea or discover some new and uncharted land, then who knows what would happen next? Life could change almost instantly. Suddenly, I wouldn't know what was about to happen next and the thought of the unknown… excites me." Edmond's cheeks flushed with embarrassment. "Sorry," he said. "I know that must all sound terribly silly."

"No," said Evelyn softly. "It doesn't sound silly at all."

"You're a military man, aren't you, Harper?" asked Lord Tallisker. Now that the formalities were over, the Great Hall had a more relaxed feel to it. Harper noticed that both Lord Tallisker and Lord Dalton also seemed more at ease now that their wives had left the room. Unfortunately, that wasn't all he noticed. To his annoyance, the musicians had started playing again, a less formal but no less irritating tune than before. "I have seen combat, my lord."

A knowing smile came over Lord Tallisker's face. "Yes, you have, haven't you..." Lord Tallisker trailed off as if expecting the captain to continue his sentence.

Harper wasn't sure what to read from the response and remained silent.

Lord Dalton cleared his throat. "I believe Lord Tallisker is referring to your years spent as a privateer," said Lord Dalton. "You served with Captain Barnet aboard the Tyger, did you not?"

Harper nodded. "Yes, my Lord. I was a midshipman on the Tyger until 1720, before becoming a commissioned officer on the Falkland. When my father passed, he left the Vestal to me, and I became her captain."

"Your reputation is that of a man who has overcome exceptionally challenging odds at sea," Lord Tallisker's mustache bristled as he spoke.

"I have a good ship and an able crew," said Harper. "Two of the things necessary to overcome such odds."

"Yes, but not everything that is needed," said Lord Dalton as he began a slow walk toward a stairwell at the far end of the hall. "If you'd follow me, gentlemen." Harper looked to Tallisker and gave a nod for him to move first, falling in close behind. The stairwell was narrow, and Harper struggled to see anything past Lord Tallisker's girth, the large man breathing heavily as he ascended each step with a labored difficulty. Stairs certainly seemed to be the man's enemy. After a brief climb, they emerged on the battlements. The smell of the ocean filled Harper's lungs.

The walls to Airedale Keep were impressively thick. Harper doubted that even if a ship could elevate its guns high enough, any damage inflicted would be superficial. Anyone fool-enough to attempt an invasion would have to do so overland whilst under heavy assault from the Keep's considerable defenses.

Lord Dalton stood by one cannon, his foot resting on the wooden bracket that the enormous piece of artillery lay dormant in. "I do love the view from up here," he said wistfully. "Not a single vessel comes into these waters that I don't know about." Harper noted the positioning of the cannon, looking down its length to where the Vestal was moored.

"Quite spectacular," puffed Lord Tallisker, wiping the sweat from his brow before curling a thick finger through his mustache. Harper looked down at Airedale. The township and the port were in clear range of the cannons that lined the walls of the Keep. The outer bailey and main gate were built shorter than the inner walls, giving Lord Dalton's men the ability to fire from both. Though

Harper saw a problem with the arrangement. His expression caught Lord Dalton's attention.

"What do you think, Captain? asked Lord Dalton.

"She's impregnable from the outside," said Harper. "You've nothing to fear from an invasion by land or sea. With a hundred men you could keep back thousands from ever setting foot through the front gate."

"And yet you seem unconvinced..." said Lord Dalton. It was interest, not anger, that sculpted his tone. Nevertheless, Harper pushed on with care.

"Where is the cannon aimed at the moment?" asked Harper, knowing full well the cannon Dalton stood next to was pointed at his ship.

"To sea," said Lord Dalton airily.

"May I?" asked Harper, motioning for Lord Dalton to step away from the cannon. Lord Dalton stepped back to join Tallisker and watched with interest as Harper busied himself making adjustments to the cannon.

"What the devil is he up to?" asked Lord Tallisker brusquely, but Lord Dalton waved him to silence.

"May I borrow some of your men?" asked Harper. Lord Dalton nodded, and Harper called two of his guardsmen to come over. With some assistance, Harper moved the cannon and changed its trajectory. "Now, my lords, please examine where is the cannon aimed." Lord Dalton, a paranoid man at the best of times, recoiled as he looked down the line of a cannon pointed squarely at his own front gates.

"As I said, my lord, you have nothing to fear from the outside." Harper knew he should have just looked at the defenses, complimented Lord Dalton about the Keep's impeccable safety, and just moved on. But he couldn't. He was talking to a man who had a cannon pointed at his ship, and the favor had to be returned.

"You're suggesting that one of my own men might sabotage my defenses?" asked Lord Dalton incredulously, as if the notion were beyond impossible.

Harper shrugged. "Is that so inconceivable? Many men are susceptible to bribery. Or perhaps one of your enemies might plant a spy among your ranks. Both equally potential threats. I trust all of my men, as I'm sure you do yours, but mutiny is a possibility I'm always prepared for."

Lord Tallisker clapped a hand together in delight, "Well, he's certainly a sharp one."

"Yes, he is," agreed Lord Dalton. "And sharp is what we need."

"My lord?" asked Harper. Lord Dalton stared down at the gates.

"Move the cannon if you'd be so good, Captain. I see Father Baldwin leaving for his morning errands, and I'd hate for our chaplain to think we're about to fire on him." Lord Dalton gave a disarming wave to the startled priest. Harper obediently changed the trajectory but repositioned it away from the Vestal.

"Your ship. Is she fast?" asked Lord Tallisker, as Harper busied himself with the cannon.

"Yes, my lord."

"Armament?"

"Twenty guns, my lord."

"Yes, twenty guns," Lord Tallisker seemed to be taking notes in his mind. "Seen combat?"

"She has."

"What about cargo? What can she hold?" asked Lord Dalton, re-joining the conversation.

Harper glanced back and forth as he faced a barrage of questions from both lords. It seemed Lord Dalton was primarily interested in the Vestal's capacity as a merchant ship. His questions focused on the

Vestal's range. Had she made voyages to the New World? How much weight could she hold? Was she available for commissions now? But Lord Tallisker seemed much more fascinated with the Vestal's capacity as a warship. What size were her cannons? Their range? How many ships had she defeated in combat? What was her crew capacity, and did she have a full complement? Harper was quick to affirm that the Vestal was not a battleship, but that she could defend herself in open water or make a quick escape when combat wasn't favorable. Seemingly satisfied, the lords returned to the matter at hand.

"The wedding is to be held at Dunshire, Edmond's lands granted to him recently by his father," said Lord Dalton. "Between Lord Tallisker and myself, we have lost seven ships in the past few years to pirates and French opportunists."

"And the Swedes," added Lord Tallisker. "When they've got the stones for it."

"Yes, and the bloody Spanish as well. We've the whole damned continent arrayed against us." snapped Lord Dalton. "Simply put, I do not want to risk my Evelyn's safety in the passage to Dunshire with a captain that is not up to the task." Lord Tallisker nodded his agreement.

Harper hated himself for even asking, but a question bubbled up inside him. "I don't mean to be impertinent, but why not make the journey overland, my lord? Not that I don't think the Vestal equal to the task, but the journey between Airedale and Dunshire could be made almost as quickly by horse and cart." Lord Dalton glanced at Lord Tallisker. "Evelyn's dowry is...considerable, Captain. I believe an expeditious voyage by sea is the safest way to transport both the dowry and the bride to their new home in Dunshire."

"You could send the bride and the dowry separately if you fear for the safety of both," suggested Harper, cursing himself for even suggesting Evelyn not travel on the Vestal.

Lord Tallisker cleared his throat. "It is my intention that Edmond arrive safely back in Dunshire with both his bride and her...assets. Lady Evelyn will be married on Tallisker land, and once all persons and effects are in place, the wedding will take place in Dunshire. And until the wedding takes place, Lord Dalton..."

Lord Dalton raised a hand. "Yes, yes," he said wearily. "You will not honor our agreement until the wedding. Your terms are steep, and you hold me and mine to ransom Lord Tallisker, but I will uphold my end of the arrangement."

Harper's stomach turned at the thought of Evelyn being used as a commodity of negotiation between the two powerful men.

From the courtyard below, a loud horn sounded. "Oh!" yelled Lord Tallisker excitedly. "The hunting party must be ready." He moved quickly for a man of his size, rushing to look down at the courtyard. "Where is he... ah!" Lord Tallisker pointed down at the courtyard. "Lad!" he bellowed.

Harper moved to the edge of the battlements and looked down at a startled Edmond and Evelyn, their pleasant walk interrupted by Lord Tallisker's boorish behavior.

"Say your goodbyes to the lovely lady and get ready. The hunt's been called!" Lord Tallisker squared his shoulders and strode toward the stairwell. "Come, Lord Dalton, you need to see what a fine shot my lad is. He might look like a plum pudding, but mark my words..." Lord Tallisker's bluster continued as he descended the stairwell.

Harper stood on the battlements, squinting against the sun as he looked out over the courtyard. The interruption had flustered Edmond, and he was talking quickly to Evelyn. Harper's heart beat faster as Evelyn looked back at him, ignoring the commotion around her.

"Captain," called Lord Dalton behind him. Harper turned. "Best not to keep them waiting."

"Apologies, my lord." As he followed Lord Dalton down the stairs, Harper felt pleased with his work repositioning the cannon formerly aimed at the Vestal. He didn't enjoy being threatened, but always found satisfaction in returning the gesture.

Evelyn snapped her attention back to Edmond as Harper departed the battlements.

"Apologies, my lady," Edmond said. "Father can be quite... brusque at times."

Evelyn shook her head. "You don't need to apologize for his behavior. If that were our job, I would be endlessly apologizing for my parents as well."

"I suspect you might enjoy having some distance from your parents, just as I have. Being the Lord of Dunshire hasn't been without its challenges, but I must confess," he leant toward Evelyn and whispered conspiratorially in her ear, "I do enjoy the freedom."

It was the first time that Evelyn had ever heard the word freedom mentioned in relation to her future. For an instant, she felt liberated at what a life out of Airedale Keep could be. Away from her parents' political machinations and her duties at court. A life where she could choose what she wanted to do and who she wanted to be. Her hand involuntarily squeezed Edmond's as the excitement came over her.

The moment was quickly interrupted by another loud call from Lord Tallisker. "Edmond!" And with the sound of his voice came the reminder that her "freedom" would only ever stretch so far. She still had no say in where she would live out her days or who she would be married to. Edmond seemed kind enough, but if she was to be his wife, then she would always be bound to his land and his body. Thanks to Captain Harper, she knew now that she wanted more. Or at the very least…something different.

Her mind returned to the moment she had shared with him as she saw Harper make his way across the courtyard. He kept himself a respectful distance behind Lord Dalton and Lord Tallisker as they approached. As the horn sounded again, Lord Tallisker broke into a brisk trot, caught up in the excitement of the imminent hunt. Evelyn felt overcome with concern for whichever of father's horses was to be burdened with the task of carrying Lord Tallisker's immense backside.

"Come on, lad," said Tallisker to his son. "It's time to show Lord Dalton what an impressive shot you are. The horses are saddled, and the guns loaded, let's go kill something." His mustache bristled with excitement. He seemed overly eager for Edmond to show up his soon-to-be father-in-law in front of his own hunting party. Edmond surrendered and gave Evelyn a reluctant look. "I'd best go," he said sadly. "But I thoroughly enjoyed our time together. Perhaps I could see you again tomorrow."

"You'll see her at dinner tonight, boy!" exclaimed Lord Tallisker. "Stop wasting the daylight and go and find yourself a horse. Unless you intend to do your hunting on foot!"

Evelyn ignored Lord Tallisker's outburst. "It will be my pleasure to see you at dinner tonight, my lord," said Evelyn politely, making sure her eyes didn't move to Harper. She was already feeling flustered in his presence. "And I hope we find the time to walk together tomorrow as well."

Edmond turned his body faster than his head as he spun to leave, tripping over himself as he took off. He kept his back to Evelyn, hiding his scarlet cheeks as he collected himself. He looked to Harper,

"Do you think she saw that?" he whispered.

The captain shook his head no, then caught Evelyn's eye as he helped Edmond steady himself.

"Aren't you joining us?" Edmond asked the captain. He had been looking forward to the opportunity to show off to Harper.

"No, my lord. Hunting is a sport for gentlemen, and I fear too much time at sea has not given me any experience in a saddle. Enjoy your time with Lord Dalton; I suspect he is a hard man to please." Edmond nodded and headed to the stables. Harper winced as he saw the boy trip again and wondered how he'd ever made it so far in life.

With the help of the stable hands, the hunting party was saddled. Evelyn watched with amusement as two strong young men struggled to get Lord Tallisker situated. With blaring horns, the horses galloped out of the courtyard, and soon Harper was alone with Evelyn and her chaperones. "You don't hunt, Captain?" asked Lady Tallisker haughtily, as if she found the notion amusing.

"No, my lady, I do not hunt," said Harper as he approached the group. Lady Tallisker looked at him with contempt. "Not game at least. I find a more challenging prey in French frigates or Spanish galleons. I prefer an adversary that can at least hope to match me, and I find most pheasants and deer to be sorely lacking in that capacity. Though I look forward to enjoying the spoils of your son's hunt. I am sure we will eat heartily tonight." Evelyn grinned broadly at Harper's cheek. For the first time since she had met her, Lady Tallisker seemed lost for words. Evelyn watched the large woman struggle to comprehend how she had just been spoken to. Doubtless, it had been a long time since someone had given her such a blasé response.

"We were about to conclude our walk, Captain," said Lady Dalton, who also seemed amused by Harper's response. "Would you care to accompany us back to the hall?"

"Actually," said Harper, giving Evelyn a quick glance. "I was hoping someone might give me directions to the chapel? It has been some time since I last had a chance to confess."

This took Lady Dalton by surprise. "I didn't take you for a pious man, Captain."

"I like to keep a clean soul," replied Harper. "Much of the work at sea is unsavory and the quiet contemplation offered through prayer is a welcome part of my time at shore."

"I can see that one of the servants shows you the way..." began Lady Dalton.

"Actually, Mother," said Evelyn, surprised at the sound of her own voice interrupting the conversation. "I am meeting with Father Baldwin soon, so I don't mind showing Captain Harper to the chapel. Perhaps he could meet with Father Baldwin after my confession. I'm sure the father wouldn't mind?"

Lady Dalton's brow furrowed slightly as she considered this. The captain had danced with Evelyn at the feast and behaved himself well enough. He seemed to have ingratiated himself with her husband, so she relented and nodded to her daughter. Besides, Lady Dalton knew full well how many sets of eyes there were in the Keep. If Harper decided to chance anything with her daughter, she would find out about it very quickly. Probably from the sound of gunfire.

Evelyn felt her heartbeat hard in her chest as she walked with Captain Harper to the chapel. She knew the risk she was taking by even suggesting that she escort the captain about the Keep. Her blood rose with the same warmth that it had when he had first touched her.

"How do you find your husband to be?" asked Harper, when they were out of earshot from her mother and Lady Tallisker.

"He's very...polite," she replied, struggling to find the right word. In truth, she had enjoyed her walk with Edmond and had found a common ground with the young man, but she didn't feel that was the answer Harper was looking for. He smirked at her response.

"Aye, he's certainly polite," he said. As they left the garden, Evelyn noticed an area she used to play in as a child. A weeping willow formed a natural curtain that cascaded over the old stonework, and Evelyn had used it as a hiding spot whenever she was in trouble. She'd stopped once she learned the servants used it for something else entirely. She remembered watching the lovers she had caught in the middle of their fornication. Now she imagined herself and Harper in their place, the hard bark of the willow pressed against her as he explored every inch of her body.

She noticed Harper looking around cautiously as they approached the chapel. "Do you believe in God?" he asked her. She blinked at the question. She had always done all the things that people who believe in God did. But no one had ever asked her if she actually believed or not. It was just that everyone assumed she did, and so she had assumed she did as well. Now when it was put to her, she wasn't sure what her answer was.

"Yes," she said, after some hesitation.

Harper nodded and continued to look around in all directions.

"What on earth are you looking for?"

"A moment," he said. It wasn't the answer she expected, but she soon understood. As they moved toward the door of the chapel, he cast one last look around and then pulled her, gently but firmly, around the side of the old building. With his hands around her waist, he pressed her against the wall and she once again felt the rough coarseness of his facial hair against her cheek. She loved the feeling of his body against hers, but her eyes widened in panic. "Not here," she breathed in urgently. "For God's sake, someone will see us."

He stopped and stood back from her for a moment, admiring her as she exhaled heavily against the stone wall.

"I can't. Not in there," he said, nodding at the chapel. "Not if this place is holy to you."

She smiled. For the first time since he had stared at her through the crowded feast, she felt she had the upper hand on him.

"Why, Captain, how noble of you," she said mockingly. "You'd happily steal a kiss from a betrothed woman, but you won't do it in a chapel? Your morals are higher than these walls, sir."

"I'd prefer every moment you spend with me is done with a clean conscience," said Harper, knowing even as he said it how foolish he sounded.

"That's what confession is for," she said playfully. "A chance to repent my sins."

Harper laughed softly, keeping his voice down. "You'd confess this to a priest?" he said excitedly, moving in and kissing her before she could answer.

She put her hands on his chest and gently pushed him back, reluctantly breaking the kiss. "I can make peace with God," she said, her voice an urgent whisper. "But if anyone sees us out here, you'll be shot, and I'll be cast onto the streets. Inside," she said firmly.

The chapel was quiet. Rows of unattended pews leading up to a silent alter. Candles flickered to produce a low light in the otherwise dark interior. Harper knew full well that Father Baldwin had left the Keep, but he wondered if Evelyn knew as well. "We're in luck," she said softly. "Father Baldwin isn't here." She felt Harper's fingers glide over the fabric of her dress. "You didn't know he was gone?" Evelyn shook her head. "Then why did you volunteer to walk me here?" He tugged at her dress, trying to pull her closer to him, but her feet stayed planted. "I know firsthand how you treat women, Captain Harper. Do you think I could let the same fate that befell me last night be thrust onto some poor servant girl?" She turned to face him with a coy look on her face. "Or perhaps you may have taken your liberties with the Lady Tallisker now that her husband has left for the hunt. Who knows what dark desires lurk behind that cunning grin of yours." She smiled at the look of sheer repulsion that crossed the captain's face. Gently, softly, she planted a kiss on his lips. The only sound in the chapel was the soft rustling of her dress as Harper's hands ran up and down her sides.

This time, it was Harper who broke the kiss. "This morning," he said, leading her deeper into the chapel. "You were the first thing I thought of and have been on my mind ever since I woke. I could still smell you on my clothes and on my skin."

She blushed at the mention of her scent.

"But," he said hungrily," nothing my imagination can conjure compares to having you in my arms." He gripped her dress tightly and pulled her close to him again. They kissed again, harder, more passionately. She took the lead now, taking his hand and guiding them toward the confession chamber on the far wall of the chapel. As they kissed, she met the disapproving stare of a large statue of Christ crucified on the opposite wall. She pulled Harper forward as she backed against the wall, using his body to block the view. She didn't want an audience, divine or otherwise.

She felt her wrists being collected in his strong hands and before she knew it, her arms were held above her head. "Mine," he said to her quietly. She shook her head and pulled one arm free. As much as she was enjoying losing herself in the moment, she was determined not to let Harper have everything his own way.

"Yours?" she challenged. "You have no claim over me, Captain." The brazen nature of the captain was part of his allure, but she would not be so easily subdued.

Harper opened his mouth to respond, but Evelyn did not give him the chance to speak. "You were very free with yourself last night, Captain," she said, "and I can't imagine for an instant that I was your first encounter with the fairer sex."

Harper closed his mouth, knowing that anything that came out of it was only going to serve to incriminate him further. She leaned in closer to him, her voice little more than a whisper. "You stole my first kiss from me," she said. She guided his hand to her lap, felt his fingers trace over her, separated only by the material of her dress.

"Was that all I stole?" asked Harper.

"That remains to be seen," said Evelyn, resting her hand on his chest as his fingers continued to press against the fabric of her dress. "But I'm certain nothing good can come of this."

"No, it can't," said Harper. He released her other hand and gently lifted her chin to bring her mouth back to his. This kiss was softer, gentler than any they had shared. The tenderness of his touch felt like an apology, and Evelyn was only too happy to accept. "I have never felt as I did last night," she confessed. "It is my hope that you will feel like that as…" Harper stopped midsentence as the door to the chapel creaked opened.

They looked at each other in wide-eyed panic. Harper mouthed something to Evelyn that she couldn't understand before slipping into the confession booth. Evelyn straightened her hair and did her best to get her breathing under control. Without knowing what else to do, she turned to face the statue of Christ and dropped to her knees, bowing her head in a false prayer. She heard familiar footsteps walking through the chapel. "Ah, my child," came Father Baldwin's voice. "It warms my heart to see you at prayer." Evelyn kept her eyes closed as Father Baldwin approached, pretending to finish whatever prayer she was involved in, hoping that the extra time would help reduce the flush in her cheeks.

She stood, meekly, and bowed to the priest. He returned her bow with a warm smile. "I passed your mother on my way back to the chapel," he said, as he looked around the transept. "She said that you had a man with you... a, um, Captain I believe." Evelyn's eyes widened as she struggled to think of something to say. She heard a throat clear behind her as Harper emerged from the confession chamber.

"My apologies, Father," he said. "I often pray out loud and I didn't wish the noise to disturb the young lady while she was at prayer. My time at sea often has me asking for forgiveness for things I would rather not have fall on the ears of the innocent."

"Ah," said Father Baldwin enthusiastically, "You must be Captain Harper. How it gladdens me to have a wholesome man of God visit our little corner of Christendom."

Evelyn watched with a cruel sense of glee as Father Baldwin descended on the captain.

"Tell me, Captain, how long has it been since your last confession?"

Harper ran a hand awkwardly through his hair, trying to find a way of evading the inevitable fate he had delivered himself into.

"Admittedly, it has been quite some time," said Harper, looking desperately toward Evelyn.

"I think this would provide an excellent opportunity for Captain Harper to get closer to God," said Evelyn, almost too sweetly. She winked at Harper as the priest turned back to him with a smile.

"I could not agree more," said Father Baldwin with unsuppressed enthusiasm, gesturing to the confession booth. "Shall we unburden you of your sins, Captain?"

"Why not?" sighed Harper, unable to conjure an excuse. He shot Evelyn a scowl as he followed Father Baldwin into the confession chamber. Evelyn felt her body singing as she floated out of the chapel. She knew Harper would think twice before being overly presumptuous with her again.

True to his father's boasts, Edmond had proven to Lord Dalton that he was a skilled hunter. Despite his clumsiness on his own two feet, he was an accomplished rider and a skilled marksman. The massive boar he killed created a considerable amount of work for the kitchen staff. The beast was skinned and butchered and immediately the cooks began working on a feast. The hideous yellow tusked head formed the centerpiece on Lord Dalton's table. In the morning, the head would be taken to the tanner who would preserve it into a trophy. Then it would rest among the other severed heads in Lord Dalton's office.

Evelyn did not have time to speak to Edmond before the evening meal. She had seen him return to the courtyard surrounded by the other hunters, who each took turns slapping him heartily on the back and congratulating him on his kill. It had taken six men to get the boar from the stables and bring it up to the kitchen. Evelyn had seen the beast before they turned it into dinner, and she had to admit it was impressive. The tusks were thicker than her forearms and looked capable of easily giving someone a grizzly end.

The lifeless, beady eyes of the boar stared out at Evelyn as she slowly chewed her food. As tasty as the meat was, she was finding it difficult to enjoy her meal while its severed head stared at her. It was a smaller affair than the previous night, but even though Evelyn knew that Captain Harper was in attendance, she couldn't see him. There were nearly fifty people seated at the two long dining tables, and she didn't want to draw attention to herself by trying to move about. She was a lady, and her husband to-be was the hero of the evening. She needed to keep her composure and act accordingly.

"How did you find the forests around Airedale, my lord?"

Edmond looked up at her, his mouth stuffed with roast boar. He looked panicked as he furiously tried to chew and swallow as fast as he could so he could answer her. Evelyn waited patiently for him to finish his mouthful, worried that he may choke in his haste.

"Very pleasant," replied Edmond some time later.

"I've never seen game so plentiful in my own lands." Evelyn welcomed the opportunity to learn more about her potential new home. "And what are your lands like, my lord?"

"They're nothing quite so grand as Airedale," he said, loud enough for Lord Dalton to hear. "Our port is far smaller, and our manor isn't so impressive as your keep, my lady. But our people are content and not prone to riotous behavior. There are far more troublesome holds that I could have found myself placed in. Oh, and of course we are celebrated for our fine cheeses."

"It sounds…" boring, was the first word that wanted to spring from her mouth, but she forced it down, "charming." Evelyn silently congratulated herself on her lady-like choice of words.

"Oh, it is," said Edmond with a confident nod. He stuck his fork into another pink cut of boar and prepared to raise it to his mouth. Before he put the cutlery to his mouth, he nodded to Lord Dalton and Lord Tallisker farther down the table. The pair were embroiled in deep conversation. "What do you suppose they're talking about?" he asked, quickly shoveling the food into his mouth while he waited for Evelyn to answer.

Evelyn didn't need to 'suppose'. She knew. Over the course of the evening, she had caught Lord Tallisker looking over at her while he conversed with her father. Deals were being made, bargains were being struck, and a contract was taking shape. "Us," said Evelyn, looking over at her father. He was deeply engrossed in his conversation, but Lord Tallisker caught her eye as she looked down the table. Evelyn found it difficult to read his expression through his ridiculous mustache.

Edmond nodded. "I suspect you're correct." He leant forward in his chair and whispered just loud enough that only Evelyn could hear him. "I promise you that no matter what happens, I will be good to you." There was an honest sincerity in his eyes that made Evelyn trust him. She mouthed a 'thank you' to him over the noise of the feast. She watched as her father rose to his feet. Lord Dalton was not the sort of man that needed to clink a glass or clear his throat to announce his presence. The moment his rear left his chair, the room fell silent. Evelyn had admired that her father had a way of addressing a room that made each person feel as if he were speaking directly to them. He could give eye contact to twenty people at once and make each of them feel as though they were the only other people in the room.

"Last night, we gathered to welcome the Tallisker family to Airedale. Tonight, we are gathered to welcome their son to our family. Long allies, the Tallisker family have been loyal and true friends to the Daltons. Today we announce the merging of our two houses through the marriage of our only daughter, Evelyn, to Lord Tallisker's youngest son, Lord Edmond of Dunshire. This union is a happy one that will bring much prosperity to both our houses. I know that any man who is as fine and capable a hunter as Lord

Edmond will prove a worthy and suitable match for my Evelyn. So," Lord Dalton reached for his glass and raised it high, "please join me in celebrating the engagement of Lord Edmond Tallisker and Lady Evelyn Dalton."

Evelyn wasn't sure whether to reach for her own glass and instead sat frozen as she felt the gaze of dozens of guests wash over her.

"May you know nothing but happiness," said her father as he raised his glass to his lips and drank.

The rest of the room drank from their glasses and echoed her father's last words. "May you know nothing but happiness." Then followed the awkward silence that follows all such speeches.

Everyone waited for someone else to talk before deciding it was safe to do so.

For a moment Lord Tallisker looked as if he might try to stand and add words of his own, when in fact all he was doing was shifting his weight to surreptitiously pass wind. Slowly, murmurs and hushed conversation penetrated the silence and gradually rose to become lively and animated. The musicians struck up a tune and celebrations resumed. Evelyn hadn't moved since her father had stood to speak. She slowly turned over what was happening around her. She was now, apparently, officially to be wed to a man she had just met. And, as pleasant as Edmond Tallisker seemed, Evelyn could find no happiness in the contemplation of a life together with him. Her mother had said that the best she could hope for would be a man that wasn't cruel. But she knew in her heart that wasn't enough for her. She looked over at Edmond, who seemed just as unsure and uncomfortable as she did.

The plates were soon cleared away, and the wine was poured more liberally. The guests rotated in their seating, catching up with the people they actually wanted to speak to rather than those they had been seated next to. As a result, the room became louder. Guests came over in small groups, first to congratulate Evelyn on her engagement and then to congratulate Edmond on his fine hunt and thank him for their meal. She found it odd to have people she had never met before congratulating her for something she didn't want. It began to make sense when she noticed the well-wishers looking sideways to her parents, desperately hoping they were being noticed. Edmond was forced to retell the story of his hunt repeatedly, and as the evening drew on, he appeared to be struggling.

When he had first started telling the story, he had been full of pride and had gone to great lengths to tell every detail of the hunt. It was as if he was telling the story of Saint George and the Dragon with just a few subtle changes. The ride had been long and hard, the beast dangerous and ferocious, but it was the skill of man that won the day. But as the night wore on, so did his enthusiasm for storytelling. Evelyn would never have said it, but her enthusiasm for hearing the story had ended after its first telling. By the time the dancing began, and the guests were well and truly into the wine, Edmond's story had lost all its luster. "There's got to be a better way to tell a tale than that," said a familiar voice as Edmond finished telling the story for the twentieth time.

Evelyn saw Edmond's face light up as Captain Harper approached the table. "Captain!" exclaimed Edmond as he rose from his chair. "I must say, you are a sight for sore eyes."

"I hear congratulations are due all around," said Harper, looking from Edmond to Evelyn. "Congratulations on the announcement of your wedding, Lady Evelyn. I think you've found yourself quite a considerable match in your fiancé."

Evelyn didn't quite know how to respond, but any sign of Harper's true feelings for her was being very well hidden. To a casual observer, he was just another well-wishing guest. "I, well yes, thank you for your kind words, Captain." Evelyn fumbled through her response. She'd been so proud of her lady-like conduct all evening, but now her sense of propriety was quickly unravelling in the captain's presence. Thankfully, Edmond's excitement at Harper's presence gave her a moment to collect herself.

"And I understand I've you to thank for my dinner this evening, my Lord." Edmond beamed with pride at the captain's recognition of his accomplishment.

"Well, yes, I suppose so," Evelyn raised an eyebrow as she watched her new fiancé fumble almost as much as she had. It dawned on her that Edmond idolized Harper.

"But I do wish everyone would stop asking me about it."

"And why is that, my lord?" asked Harper.

"I've told the story so many times now I almost wish I hadn't killed the damned thing. Even I'm bored with hearing myself talk."

"You've fallen into a common trap there, my lord. If I may?" Harper gestured at the empty seat next to Edmond.

"Yes, yes, of course. Please join us," said Edmond eagerly.

Evelyn opened her mouth to protest but couldn't find a good enough reason. Instead, she simply sat and watched as the man who had only hours ago held her against the chapel walls now sat and conversed pleasantly with her future husband.

"You learn how to spin a good tale when you're at sea," said Captain Harper, drawing Edmond in with every word. "There's a secret to retelling a story over and over so's that it never gets boring for you. Every time you tell the tale, add something in, don't leave something out," Edmond nodded slowly as Harper spoke. "See, if you get bored with telling your own story, no one will want to listen to you or hear what you have to say. Why should they listen to you when you don't even care about what you're talking about? Look at Lord Dalton," Harper gestured over his shoulder. "I've never seen him look bored when he talks. And I can guarantee he has some dull topics to discuss in his day. He's a man who knows exactly what he wants to say and how to keep you listening to every word."

"But he isn't being asked about hunting a boar, he's being asked about important things, things that matter," protested Edmond. "He has more to say than I do."

"See, everything matters to a man like Lord Dalton. Or at least it seems to when he talks. You're the Lord of Dunshire. You have as many important things to say as he does. And when you say them, you want people to listen to you, don't you?" Edmond nodded. "So, get some practice in. Embellish, escalate, elaborate. Make your story the only story people remember after tonight. No offense, my lady," said Harper, winking at Evelyn. Edmond laughed. Evelyn did not. "If it gets too tedious for you, don't forget to mention the part where the boar turned around to face you and charged toward you. You'll never forget the horrible look in his red, fiery-red eyes as he came straight for you—"

"But that isn't what happened…" said Edmond

"And his eyes were yellow," said Evelyn, nodding at the severed head on the table.

"All irrelevant, my lord. What's relevant is making sure that whoever listens to you tell your tale will want to listen to you again the next time you have something to say. And, if you tell your story right, they'll tell it again for you. That's how legends start."

Evelyn looked at her empty glass of wine and desperately hoped someone would be along to fill it. Perhaps her mother had told the servants to make sure Evelyn's glass was empty for the rest of the night, lest her daughter cause some embarrassment. It felt odd watching Harper and Edmond bonding. She wondered if the captain was enjoying her discomfort.

"When you command a ship," said Harper as he continued with his lesson, "you need to make sure that every man on board is ready to listen to every word you say and act on them without hesitation. I would imagine it's the same for any lord on land."

"You must have some astonishing tales from your time at sea, Captain," said Edmond, eager to hear a tale of excitement and adventure that wasn't coming from his own mouth. Harper smiled and rose to his feet.

"Indeed, I do, my lord. Each taller than the last. But they shall have to wait for another day. I have a long walk back to the Vestal, and the hour is late."

"The Vestal? Nonsense, I'll have them make a room up for you here in the Keep," said Edmond.

"After a thorough and…lengthy…confession this morning, I am sure I will sleep deeply tonight. However, I find sleep scarce when I'm not at sea."

"I'd much prefer you stay and regale us with stories of your exploits, Captain."

"Well, don't distress, my lord. We will have plenty of time to talk about adventure on the high seas when we set sail. I am happy to inform you that Lord Dalton and Lord Tallisker have entrusted me with your safe passage to Dunshire. I am sure your father will inform you soon enough. It is my understanding that Lord Tallisker thinks Lady Dalton will benefit from some time in her new lands and among her new people before the wedding. He wants her to feel like a 'true Tallisker' when she weds."

Evelyn watched in dismay as Edmond and Harper had their glasses refilled. The servant blushed crimson as she stared at him and raised her glass, but he didn't make eye contact with her. Her glass left empty, Evelyn was left to contemplate what feeling like a 'true Tallisker' meant. Though the thought worried her considerably less than being aboard the Vestal. She was sure that she probably couldn't be trusted to behave like a lady aboard Harper's ship. As for Harper, she was certain that she couldn't trust him to behave himself.

"Well, that is cracking good news," said Edmond, rising to shake the captain's hand farewell. "I'm sure we couldn't be in safer hands than with you and your fine men, Captain. I know you will make sure that my bride-to-be and I arrive safely at her new home."

"Of course, my lord. And who knows," said Harper, turning to face Evelyn. "We may even create some memorable tales of our own whilst at sea. Every voyage has the potential to become an adventure." He kept his stare on her for a moment longer before bowing his head and taking his leave.

Evelyn looked at the full wineglass he had left on the table. "Didn't even drink it…" she said in disbelief.

"He's a genuine sort, isn't he," said Edmond, returning to his seat.

Evelyn nodded. "Yes. Genuine."

"He can be an intimidating character, I'll grant," said Edmond, sensing that Evelyn may have been uncomfortable. He reached for his glass and took a long sip of wine. "Give it some time, and I'm sure you'll come to like him as well. Perhaps we'll even find a wife for him when we arrive in Dunshire. Imagine that." Evelyn gave a weak smile as Edmond laughed to himself.

◆

It wasn't until the noise of the Great Hall was behind him that Harper became aware he was being followed. He kept his pace steady and his hands free at his side. He was still some distance from the front gate, and the torches that lit his way cast deep shadows in the exterior stonework of the Keep. The front gates were wide open, as most of Lord Dalton's guests were yet to depart. Four large men stood by the main gate, their hushed conversation coming to an abrupt halt as Harper approached them. Lord Dalton's guards were easily recognizable. Their breastplates were engraved with the family crest: a lion rising on its hind legs, mouth open and tongue flickering as if in mid-roar. They each wore thick blue cloaks and were armed with muskets and sabers.

Harper looked up at the barbican above the gates and saw two more guards, both with muskets in hand. No need to guess who was following him or to even bother with turning around. He was surrounded. Harper remembered the view from the battlements when he had pointed the cannons toward the gates in front of Lord Dalton. There were plenty of places for more guards to be hiding. "Evening gentlemen," he said pleasantly, not slowing his pace as he approached the gates. "Good evening, Captain Harper," came a voice from behind him. Harper sighed and turned around. A middle-aged man stood surprisingly close to him, wearing the same armor and uniform as the other guards. There were subtle differences, though. The crossbar of his sword was elaborately fashioned, his breastplate shone just a little more brightly in the torchlight, and he didn't carry a musket like the other guards. Harper did not return the greeting. He knew a threat when he saw one. His fingers twitched at his side, eager to grip his sword.

"Captain Weaver, commander of Lord Dalton's personal guard and the Airedale town watch," the man said. He was flanked on either side by two guards, bigger than the four that were guarding the gate. "I wondered if we might have a brief conversation?" Harper looked past Weaver's face and into the man's eyes. Captain Weaver was making a show that he was not a man to be trifled with. Harper's instinct, when presented with large, serious men, was to mock them. He found it unbalanced them and made it easier to learn their true intentions. It also occasionally resulted in a punch being thrown at him. He looked at Weaver's ham-sized fists and pushed back the instinct to be clever.

"Well, you have me at a disadvantage, sir," said Harper, stretching his arms out so that his hands were clearly visible and a safe distance from his sword. "By all means...let's converse."

"I find it hard to believe that a man of your reputation is ever at a disadvantage, Captain Harper." Weaver stepped forward as he spoke. "If I ordered my men to attack you right now, how confident are you that you would be able to escape and make it back to your ship?"

Harper didn't take his eyes off Weaver. "Escape would seem irrelevant as long as those cannons are pointing out to sea," said Harper, nodding at the ramparts. "I might make it as far as the harbor, but the Vestal would be naught but matchsticks by the time I got there."

"True enough."

"But I'm sure I'd give you a hell of a fight," said Harper darkly. "If that's what you're interested in finding out." He could hear the men behind him shuffling, their armor clinking softly in the night's quiet.

"Fortunately, for you, it's not your reputation as a swordsman that concerns me tonight," said Weaver. "You have other reputations that precede you, Harper."

"Is that a fact?"

"Don't think that I haven't seen you looking at Lady Evelyn. Walking alone with her."

"I wasn't aware that looking or walking were offenses in Airedale. There mustn't be much crime here if these are the matters that concern the captain of the guard," said Harper.

"Lady Dalton is not some dockyard whore for you to pursue." Weaver's face had turned red with anger and spit flew from his mouth with each word. "In two days' time, you are to make the passage from Airedale to Dunshire, and when you set sail, I will accompany you along with four of my finest men. Lord Dalton knows you're the best man to ensure his daughter's safe arrival in her new home. Just as surely as he knows, I am the best man to keep her pure and unspoiled by some foul letch with a reputation for ruining many a young woman's virtue."

Harper looked at the man seething in front of him. With a short temper and penchant for melodramatic statements, Weaver was not a man to be pushed, at least not until he could be toppled. "I shall look forward to returning the same grace and courtesy that I have received in Airedale to you and your men during your time aboard the Vestal," Harper extended a hand. Weaver did not. Harper nodded and smiled as he withdrew the gesture. "Very well then, if there's nothing else then?"

"Be on your way, Captain, I'll make sure some of my men see to your safe return to the Vestal. Wouldn't want you getting lost on the way."

"Much obliged," said Harper.

Weaver nodded, and the two guards on either side of him fell in behind Harper as he turned to leave. The walk was spent in silence. The guards were not interested in engaging in conversation, and Harper had other things on his mind. He'd already returned Lord Dalton's earlier threat, but now he had another to repay.

The next two days passed slowly for Evelyn. Everyone around her seemed to move frantically while she felt as if she were standing in place. The morning after her marriage announcement, the servants packed up her room, collecting all of her belongings to be stored aboard the Vestal. Her father and Lord Tallisker spent the days debating her dowry, the wedding arrangements, their future alliance, and all the other affairs of state that seemed to revolve around Evelyn. Though she was at the center of everything that was happening around her, she was acutely aware that she had no influence on the course of her fate.

If Captain Harper had returned to the Keep, she was not aware of it. She heard his name mentioned in passing but saw no sign of him. She was glad for the time and the distance, though he was constantly on her mind. Evelyn was unsure if she knew what love was, but she felt something stir in her chest each time she heard Harper's name mentioned. She often found herself unable to focus as her mind preoccupied itself with the encounters that might occur on the Vestal. The danger of getting caught—and everything at stake—nagged at the back of her mind.

But each night when she lay in bed, her mind wandered back to more pleasant thoughts. She ran her fingers over her body and imagined the coarse roughness of his skin in place of hers. She remembered the prickle of his short beard against her cheek and neck. The feeling of his lips pressed against hers, the way their tongues danced in their mouths. Then she would move beyond memory and escape into fantasy. She knew all too well what two people did in the heat of passion. She imagined herself and Harper in place of the servants in the garden, finding their secret spot and losing themselves in raw physical pleasure.

It wasn't until she woke on her last morning in Airedale Keep that she felt a deep sadness. Her bed was no longer her bed, nor was her room. Or her home. In the afternoon when she would board the Vestal, she would be on her way to a new home, and there was a possibility she may never return to this place. She had very few clothes left to dress herself in. Most had been collected by servants, packed into chests, and sent to the Vestal. With her melancholy weighing on her, she let herself be dressed and took a last look at herself in the mirror.

Her somber thoughts were broken by a knock at her door. "Enter," she called.

Her father stepped into her room and stretched out his arms to her. "My daughter," he said warmly. Evelyn couldn't remember the last time she had truly embraced her father. She wrapped her arms around him tightly, as she had done as a child, and felt tears well up inside her. Though there were times she felt a great distance between herself and her parents, the thought of not seeing them every day struck her hard as her father put his arms around her and held her back.

"None of that," he said, wiping a tear away from her eyes. "Today is supposed to be a happy day. A new beginning and a time of great excitement." Evelyn looked up at her father, trying to think of anything she could to convince him to let her stay. But she knew in her heart that the 'excitement' he spoke of was only partially reserved for her. The new beginning was not about her life with Edmond, but her father's new alliance with the Tallisker family.

"Thank you, Father," was all she could say.

Lord Dalton smiled. "Don't thank me just yet, my dear. I have a present for you. I couldn't send you away from your home without giving you a piece of it to take with you."

There was the sound of fabric shuffling as the door opened. Madame Bellegarde's dress was so impressively wide that she stepped sideways to enter Evelyn's bedchambers. Even stripped of most of the furniture, the room suddenly felt considerably fuller. Though her hair was slightly more silver, and her skin now showed subtle signs of age, there was no mistaking her former mentor. Evelyn had only seen her fleetingly in recent years, but she had missed the madame dearly. "It is my honor to once again have the privilege to serve you, my lady." Madame Bellegarde bowed gracefully to Evelyn, an impressive feat given the restrictions her extravagant garment placed upon her movement. Evelyn looked at her father with an excited smile. "Truly?"

"Your mother took some convincing, but I held firm that Madame Bellegarde would be the best person we could send with you. Soon you'll have children of your own. Madame Bellegarde has proven through her mentoring of my own daughter that she is capable of making sure that my grandchildren will grow up to be educated and proper as well." Even the mention of grandchildren could not break Evelyn's elation at being reunited with her old friend. Having Madame Bellegarde come with her to Dunshire was everything she needed to make the journey less intimidating. Lord Dalton looked between Evelyn and Madame Bellegarde. "I am sure that the two of you have a lot to talk about before your voyage. I'll take my leave and see you in the courtyard. Don't take too long getting her ready, madame."

"As you wish, my lord," Madame Bellegarde's tone was as perfectly respectful as always. Until the door clicked closed behind her and Lord Dalton's footsteps had disappeared. Then she turned and smiled—a smile that only Evelyn knew—and stretched her arms out. Evelyn almost tripped as she ran to embrace her. She felt guilty about how much happier and warmer she felt when she embraced her old mentor than she did with her own father.

"It is so good to see you again, my dear. I have truly missed you."

"I've missed you too," said Evelyn. She wanted to tell her everything, let all her feelings and frustrations come pouring out. She felt as though she might erupt at any second and release every secret she had kept locked away since her first encounter with Captain Harper.

"Ah, how I would love to spend all day just talking to you, my child. But your father is correct, we have little time. Your fiancé is already waiting for you on the Vestal, and there are many farewells to be said before you depart from the Keep."

Evelyn nodded. She kept her secrets locked away and swallowed deeply just to make sure they stayed as far down inside her as possible.

Madame Bellegarde took a strand of Evelyn's hair in her fingers and tutted with false anger. "And who has been looking after you? You look only half the lady you were when you were in Madame Bellegarde's care. When we arrive in Dunshire, there will be much work to be done."

Evelyn laughed. "Yes, there'll be much work to be done. You know," said Evelyn with a smile, "I'm told that Dunshire is famous across the land for the fine cheeses they produce. I'm sure you'll love it."

"Bah," spat Madame Bellegarde. "The English make horrible cheese. Tell me something good about your fancy Dunshire."

Evelyn's expression went blank. "I...I don't know anything else," sadness had crept back into her voice.

Madame Bellegarde took her by the hand and began leading her out of her room. "Then, ma belle enfant, we shall find out together."

◆

After his encounter with Captain Weaver, Harper kept busy preparing for the journey to Dunshire. He had risen the morning after the announcement of the engagement in a mood he was unaccustomed to. He felt sad. It was a feeling he didn't enjoy and, rather than let it consume him, he found that attempting to rid himself of the unwelcome feeling gave him an inordinate amount of energy. A noble wedding was a difficult adversary to meet in battle. The successful alliance of two large and important families hinged on the marriage of two of their children. In the Dalton's case, their only child. The repercussions for disrupting it could be incredibly painful and very permanent.

As soon as the sun was up, Harper called his officers into the navigation room. Each of the four men gathered held Harper's complete trust. Nicholas Webb, his First Mate and friend of his late father, was Harper's second and oversaw command of the ship in his absence. Webb was one of few men who had served on the Vestal when she had been captained by Harper's father, and he had helped a younger Finn Harper grow into the leader he'd become. The rest of his officers were younger than Webb and more recent additions to the Vestal's crew.

Harper's quartermaster, Alfred Trent, was a sharp man. Harper had a constant challenge in keeping Mr. Trent's job interesting enough, so as not have him seek a position elsewhere. His master gunner, Benjamin Clarke, had Harper's respect by doing the one job on the ship that the captain knew he could never do as well. Clarke ran the gun deck like clockwork. Even though the Vestal was only a twenty-gun ship, under Clarke's supervision, it had stood up to much more heavily armed vessels. It amazed Harper that the man wasn't deaf from all the cannon fire he had been exposed to over his career, though he did always smell of smoke and gunpowder.

Finally, Louis Duncan rounded out the last of Harper's senior officers. Technically, Duncan was the ship's boatswain, but his flair for the culinary arts meant he was also handed the position of ship's cook. Harper ran the man hard but made sure he was rewarded for it. When the old ship's cook had passed away, Duncan had volunteered to run the galley temporarily. The improvement in the morale of the men was so dramatic that Harper immediately made Duncan's cooking a ship requirement. His skill with a blade had also landed him in the infirmary more than once, stitching up wounds or removing splinters.

"Gentlemen," said Harper, "yesterday, I received word from Lord Dalton that we are to ferry Lord Edmond and his fiancée to Dunshire in two days' time. We will have our cargo hold full of Lady Evelyn's belongings and, from what I am to understand, a rather considerable dowry."

"An easy enough job, Captain," said Webb. "Naught more'n a day and a half's sail from here to Dunshire. With fair winds, of course."

"Quite so, Mr. Webb," replied the captain. "My understanding is that we are in no particular hurry, though, as the wedding is not to take place for some time. Fair winds or no, we'll be leaving in two days' time. Lord Tallisker has been quite insistent about the date."

"Well, the ship is stocked and ready to depart at your command, Captain."

"Indeed, Mr. Trent, we have all the necessary provisions. But this voyage requires a little more from this ship and her crew than we usually give." The officers exchanged glances.

"Beg your pardon, Captain, but every man jack aboard this ship gives his all whenever we set sail," said Trent defensively.

"Aye, and whenever we make port as well," said Clarke with a devious wink. The others laughed. Harper grinned broadly. "True enough, we give our all," said Harper. "But we don't always look the part. Mr. Trent?"

"Yes, Captain?"

"New uniforms for all the men, including boots. I want them looking like the King's own men when our guests come aboard. And, Mr. Clarke?"

"Sir?"

"See to it we're well stocked on ammunition, and get the men some practice on the gun deck. Don't fire off any shots, mind you. Just go through the motions. The local lord has a touch of paranoia about him, and I'd hate to give him a reason to think us a threat. That being said, I want every man ready to fight when we set sail. Two nobles and a cargo hold full of plunder might draw some unwanted attention. We'd be fools not to be ready."

Clarke gave a stern nod.

"You'll have the best dressed gun crew in these waters, Cap'n."

"Mr. Webb, go ashore. Find me the best carpenter Airedale has to offer and bring him aboard. If he is reluctant to come with you," Harper paused as he pulled a heavy coin purse from his belt and dumped it on the table in front of Webb, "give him this. Tell him there'll be more once the job is completed, to my satisfaction." Webb nodded and hefted the purse in his hands.

"What? Is he building us a new damned ship?"

"Just get him here, Webb," said Harper, ending the subject. "Mr.

Duncan, go ashore with him. I understand we're well stocked, but I want you to find the best quality vitals you can and bring them aboard. You'll be cooking a feast for our guests on their first night. Make sure we have enough to go around for the men as well."

"That'll cost a pretty penny, Captain," said Duncan.

"The cost is irrelevant, and I'll wear it from my own savings. Once we've made an impression on these nobles, we'll be seeing a lot more coin than we're used to. The Talliskers and the Daltons have deep pockets, and my understanding is they are both looking to expand their interests to the New World. Let's impress their heirs and keep ourselves in their good graces for years to come. I want the Vestal to be their favored ship for future endeavors."

"And a few more chances to look at that lovely daughter of Lord Dalton's wouldn't go unwanted either," said Clarke with a sly grin. The others laughed and joined in.

"No, Mr. Clarke," said Harper coldly. The men fell silent quickly. "I didn't care for Lord Dalton's daughter in the slightest. But..." he rose from his chair and slammed a boot down on the table, "I'd give old Lady Tallisker a buggering she'd never forget." Harper gyrated his hips as his officers roared with laughter. "Right," said Harper, "you've had your laugh and you know what needs doing, so go get it done." "Aye, Captain!" said each man.

Once he was alone again, Harper slumped back into his chair. The image of Lady Tallisker naked and aroused was doing its best to force its way to the front of his mind. He poured himself a liberal helping of rum and belted it down, shivering as he pushed the thought out of his head. His mind returned to Evelyn. He had not expected his feelings for her to be as consuming as they had become. He'd never experienced the escalation of his emotions so quickly for someone before.

He still wasn't completely sure what he felt was love. He knew the thought of her with another man was painful to him. But wasn't that envy? Jealousy, perhaps? The image of her face was burned into his mind, and the tips of his fingers could still feel the softness of her skin. But was that sense of longing and need actually love? Harper's eye narrowed. He had woken up in the morning feeling sad. Now he felt uncertain—another unwelcome emotion. He poured himself more rum and stared at the glass for a moment before setting it back down on the table and picking up the bottle instead. Taking a long, deep gulp, he slid further into his chair and tried to think.

It wasn't long before Webb returned with a nervous-looking gentleman. Harper was all too happy for the distraction from his own thoughts. "Sir," said Webb as he entered the navigation room. "This is Atticus Howell, best carpenter in Airedale, here at your request."

Harper nodded. "Excellent, thank you, Mr. Webb. That will be all."

Webb gave a quick, sloppy salute and returned to his duties.

Harper rose to his feet, quickly realizing he was considerably taller than Howell. "Please, Mr. Howell, have a seat." Harper gestured to the chair in front of him.

"Th-thank you, sir." Howell's eyes darted about the dark room, looking at the charts and equipment that spilled over every wall and surface except for the table where he sat. "It's a nice room, you have here, sir."

"You wouldn't believe what a nightmare it is to keep clean," said Harper with a disarming smile. "You hit one enormous wave and… crash" he gestured wildly in the air with his arms. "By the time you get everything back in order again, you've got more gray hairs than you can count."

Mr. Howell chuckled nervously.

"I could build you a cabinet, Captain...if that's what you're need'n me for."

"Ah, I'm sure you could, Mr. Howell," Harper reached for his glass. He waved the bottle in Howell's direction. The carpenter shook his head. Harper gestured with the bottle again, his expression changing to feign insult. Reluctantly, Howell accepted a glass and put it to his lips. His eyes squinted as the rum hit his palate. "No, I've cabinets enough on my ship already, and I've not the patience nor the inclination to teach my men how to use them effectively." He leaned in closer. "No, what I need from you is something far more private and much more important. Mr. Webb gave you the coin I'm prepared to pay you for the work?"

"Y-yes, Captain, it is a princely sum, certainly more than I've ever received for my work before."

Harper nodded. "That payment is only half for the work that I need you to do. Can you guess what the other half is for?"

Mr. Howell shook his head.

"Silence," said Harper simply. "Do you know how to be silent, Mr. Howell?"

The carpenter opened his mouth to say something but then caught the captain's eye and simply nodded his head.

"Excellent," said Harper. "You know the price I am prepared to pay for your silence. Now, I want you to imagine what the cost of breaking that silence might be."

Mr. Howell turned white. He lowered his glass to the table, his trembling hands making it clink as he let go. "I think I take your meaning, Captain."

Harper stood and leant across the table. "Well, in case there is any uncertainty, if you break my trust and betray the silence I've paid so handsomely for...you'll be broken in turn."

Mr. Howell nodded, and Harper leaned back. He didn't like

threatening the little man, but the threat had purpose. If his plan became public knowledge, Harper could safely assume he'd be killed.

"Excellent, I'm glad we understand each other. Now, won't you walk with me to my cabin, and I will explain what I need you to do and the time frame in which you have to work?" Once Harper had finished explaining the task to Howell, he sent him back to his workshop to collect any tools he would need that weren't already aboard the Vestal. He made sure he sent two of his men with the carpenter to assist with bringing back any equipment that he might need—and to make sure the man didn't get any bright ideas about absconding with the money he'd been paid and reporting Harper to Lord Dalton. Harper had men with carpentry skills aboard his ship. While he trusted their loyalty, he feared he would lose their respect if they knew the length he would go just to spend time alone with Evelyn aboard his own ship.

He watched from the quarterdeck with a sense of satisfaction as Clarke oversaw the loading of extra ammunition onto the ship. By the time the sun was setting, Webb and Trent had managed to get all of Evelyn's furniture and belongings into the cargo hold and were making a start on securing the heavy chests full of the dowry promised to Edmond Tallisker. He felt as if he could feel the Vestal sink a little deeper into the water every time his crew unloaded more cargo and ammunition. The deeper she sat in the water, the longer their trip to Dunshire would take. Harper would use that time as well as he could to determine if his feelings were genuine. The only dilemma he had now was that if he discovered he was in love with Evelyn Dalton, he did not know what his next course of action would be.

"Everything's onboard except for the animals, sir" reported Mr. Webb just as the sun was sinking over the horizon.

"What's the delay with the livestock?" asked Harper.

"Duncan says the meat tastes better when the animals aren't stressed, sir. He says they're better off staying on land as long as possible, and then we'll load them on at first light before we set sail."

"Very well, give the men their last night of shore leave. Tomorrow we sleep on board, and I want them sober and well-dressed when our nobles arrive."

"Aye, sir, easy enough to manage, I'm sure."

"Oh," said Harper, as if remembering some stray thought, "one last thing, Mr. Webb. A Captain Weaver will be joining Lady Evelyn's party…I'd like to arrange a special welcome for him when he comes aboard."

A slow smile crept over Webb's face as Harper explained his plan.

The carriage ride did not take long. Between Captain Weaver's steel breastplate and Madame Bellegarde's expansive dress, Evelyn had squashed herself into the most comfortable position possible. Her farewell to her family had been brief. Her father assured her they would see her in a month for the wedding, while her mother made a show of hugging her goodbye. And that was it. Airedale Keep was behind her as the carriage slowly descended into port. From her position Evelyn could hardly see the streets, but Madame Bellegarde commented constantly on how many people were lining up to wave farewell to their Lord's daughter.

Soon the cheering was replaced by the smells and sounds of the docks filling the cabin of the carriage. Men yelled to each other from ship to dock. The smell of the sea air was stronger than she'd ever known. Wooden ships creaked. Livestock bleated, mooed, and clucked. Bells rang. Evelyn heard the driver call to the horses as the carriage slowed to a gentle halt. "Ah," announced Madame Bellegarde excitedly. "We have arrived!"

"Indeed, we have, Madame," Captain Weaver's tone was significantly less enthused. Evelyn stayed silent as they disembarked.

Weaver stepped out of the door to the carriage and offered his hand to Evelyn. She took it, if only to prevent herself from awkwardly tripping on her dress as she made her exit. In all her years living in Airedale, she had never been down to the docks. When Evelyn was a child, Lady Dalton had told her how easily young ladies could disappear at the docks. Evelyn had nothing to fear from the citizens of Airedale, but the docks were populated by strangers. People she was told she could never trust to have her best interests at heart. She reflected that the first stranger she had met from the docks had been Harper, and their first meeting certainly hadn't been a conventional one.

She stood in stunned silence as she looked up at the Vestal. The beautiful bronze figurehead that rose proudly from the bow of the ship was taller than any statue in Airedale. The ship was larger than Evelyn had ever imagined it being, and she suddenly felt very small. She realized this was the ship she had seen from the lookout at One Tree Hill only a short time ago. It had looked so tiny on the horizon.

Behind her, she could hear Madame Bellegarde's dress erupting from the carriage like a jack in the box. Free of the limited space the carriage offered, her dress once again spilled out to its full girth. "What a fine ship," Madame Bellegarde stated. Evelyn turned to face her old governess. "Do you really think so?" she asked. "It certainly looks grand, but I've nothing to compare it to."

"Mais oui" replied Madame Bellegarde. "She is very well looked after. The sails are crisp and white, the railing is freshly painted and even the men are well dressed." Evelyn squinted against the sun to glimpse the men. Some had stopped in their duties to watch her, but quickly set back to work once she noticed them. They certainly didn't have the filthy, unwashed look she had been expecting. But their gazes made her uneasy about boarding the ship.

"She is a very lucky woman," said Madame Bellegarde.

"Who is?" asked Evelyn.

Bellegarde pointed at the bronze figurehead of the Vestal.

"To have a captain who cares so much for her." She leaned in closer to Evelyn and continued in a whisper. "You can tell what kind of lover a man is by the pride he takes in his work."

Captain Weaver cleared his throat. "Lady Evelyn, perhaps we might board without further delay?"

Evelyn nodded but waited a moment for someone else to move first and then realized that all eyes were on her. She drew herself up, let out a long breath and took her first step up the gangplank. As she did so, she heard a whistle blow loudly on deck and the frantic scrabbling of boots against the heavy wooden boards.

She looked up and felt the ship moving gently with the waves. Her head spun slightly at the sensation. Looking down didn't help much, but it was better than closing her eyes. Slowly, she put one foot in front of the other and made her way up. Behind her, she could hear Madame Bellegarde beginning her trek up the perilous piece of wood. When Evelyn was almost aboard the ship, an outstretched hand appeared to assist her. She accepted it gladly, clasping it with a vice-like grip to steady herself as she alighted from the gangplank.

"Welcome aboard, my lady," Edmond smiled as she released her tight grip on his hand.

"Thank you for your assistance, my lord," she replied, doing her best not to let her anxiety creep into her tone. She took a single deep breath out and pushed her feet into the solid decking of the Vestal. The sensation of gentle swaying hadn't stopped, but she felt better on more solid footing. Edmond gently moved her out of the way so the rest of her entourage could board.

"How long have you been aboard, my lord?" asked Evelyn as Captain Weaver and his men made their slow ascent up the gangplank.

"I came aboard early this morning," replied Edmond. "I wanted to…that is to say, it was important to me…to ensure that I was here to assist you with your boarding. I also thought I could make myself of use to Captain Harper in the event he needed any assistance getting underway," Edmond swallowed nervously.

"And did he require any assistance?" asked Evelyn, knowing the answer.

"Not as such, my lady. Though it has been an interesting exercise to watch him give orders to his men. This ship runs like a clockwork timepiece." Evelyn heard the admiration for Captain Harper come through Edmond's voice. She wondered what her fiancé would think if he knew the secrets that she kept. She couldn't imagine such a sweet and caring man to be angry, but she would be a fool to expect him to understand or accept what had already transpired between herself and the captain he admired.

The crewmen of the Vestal stood in formation, hats pressed to their chest the entire time that Evelyn and her people boarded, their eyes staring straight in front of them. Captain Weaver and his men assembled in flanking positions around Edmond and Evelyn once they had boarded. Their blue cloaks and steel breastplates stood out against the sea of beige shirts, grey jackets, and white breeches worn by the crew. Behind their clean clothes and shiny boots, Evelyn could see the telltale signs of a weathered crew that had endured a life at sea. Their skin was bronze and hardened by their labors in the full heat of the sun. Occasional tattoos, earrings, and scars caught Evelyn's attention as she scanned the ranks. Behind her, Madame Bellegarde took in an excited breath. The whistle sounded again, high pitched and loud.

Captain Finn Harper stepped out onto the quarterdeck with purpose. He wore the same captain's jacket he had worn on the night Evelyn had first met him. Like the rest of his crew, his uniform was spotless. Evelyn had never seen him look so neat and well presented. "Come aboard, sir, Lady Evelyn and her attendants," Webb bellowed out the announcement loud enough for the entire crew and half the port to hear.

"Thank you, Mr. Webb." Harper turned his attention to the crew. "All hands, report to your stations and prepare to make ready." The men dispersed with intense purpose. Captain Harper remained at the top of the stairs to the quarterdeck, the ship's wheel behind him. "Lord Edmond, before we cast off, I would like to speak with yourself and Lady Evelyn. Mr. Weaver, if you'd be good enough to join us as well. My quartermaster will see that your men are shown their berths and made aware of ship rules and regulations."

"We shall join you presently, Captain," replied Edmond cheerily.

"You too, Mr. Webb," said the captain, addressing his first mate as he turned and walked back into his quarters. Webb nodded and fell in behind his captain.

"He's got some nerve," muttered Captain Weaver. "Addressing his betters as if they were part of his crew. Does he think he can summon us like common dogs?"

"Oh, come now, Mr. Weaver," tutted Edmond, taking Evelyn by the hand and leading her toward the quarterdeck. "The captain and I have become firm friends in our time together. We needn't stand on the ceremonies or tedious rituals of court whilst at sea."

Evelyn wanted to point out that they were still in fact anchored at port and not at sea, but kept her mouth closed. She watched Weaver as his eye twitched angrily from the change in his title from 'Captain' to 'Mr.' Harper had started it, but to have it immediately echoed by the young Lord was a poor start to Weaver's voyage. Edmond led the way up the steps to the quarterdeck, describing as much of the ship as he felt qualified to as Evelyn followed closely behind. Madame Bellegarde had positioned herself behind Evelyn, leaving Weaver to trail grumpily behind the rest of the party. "That's the helm," said Edmond excitedly as he helped Evelyn up the last of the stairs. "Usually, you'll see Mr. Trent or one of his men at the wheel, but sometimes Captain Harper may prefer to be at the wheel himself." Evelyn had no doubt that a man like Harper often liked to be directly in control. She imagined he would want his own hands to be on the ship's wheel, to steer the Vestal and guide her through whatever dangers the oceans might stir up.

Harper had already positioned himself behind his desk when Edmond and Evelyn entered his cabin. Evelyn had tried to imagine what sort of place the captain lived in before she came aboard. At first, she had imagined a decadent, luxurious accommodation. The walls adorned with treasures collected from his escapades and lavish furnishings to match his daring and arrogant personality. She had always imagined an impressive bed, taking up much of the cabin's space. It was, after all, the centerpiece of many of her fantasies.

She hadn't been prepared for how humble it was. Apart from an ornate, well-polished oak desk that dominated much of the room, the rest of the captain's belongings seemed rather mundane when compared to those of Evelyn's imagination. Instead of treasures hung on the walls, there were swords. Dozens of swords meticulously arranged. The furnishings were dustier and more unloved than she would have thought. The captain's bed chamber was partitioned off from the main cabin, but Evelyn managed to steal a glimpse of the wide, flat bed and white sheets. The bed chamber seemed to be swept to the side, purely a functional area that allowed little chance for indulgences in its cramped conditions. Evelyn's stare lingered on the bed for a moment before Madame Bellegarde gave her a gentle prod with her fan, reminding her to keep moving forward.

Captain Harper remained seated as his guests entered his chamber. Mr. Webb stood behind him, a pleasant expression on his face, but Evelyn couldn't help noticing both the pistol and sword that hung from his belt. The only other person Evelyn knew who remained seated while others stood in front of him was her father. She quickly pushed the similarity out of her mind, repulsed by the idea of drawing anymore connections between her lover and her father. She did note one difference, though. Now, she found herself looking down at Captain Harper, whereas her father would always be raised higher than anyone he was addressing whilst seated.

"It looks as if you have moved some of your furniture around, Captain," said Edmond. "When I last visited the captain's quarters…" began Edmond, the smile on his face evaporating as he realized he was going to tell his fiancée a story about the time he had injured himself on one of the captain's chests in an act of pure clumsiness. "I…that is to say…was most impressed with the captain's collection of fine swords. It seems they have been…dusted since last I was here." Edmond was red in the face. Evelyn saw Captain Harper smirk—almost imperceptibly—and came to her fiancé's assistance.

"Your time at port must have been dull indeed, Captain. You found yourself with nothing to do but dust your sword?" Evelyn immediately regretted not using the plural but felt a due sense of satisfaction as the smirk disappeared from Harper's face.

"My Lady," replied the captain evenly. "If my swords," Harper emphasized the plural strongly, "are ever in need of dusting, then there is always someone to do it for me."

"I'm sure your men fall over each other for the opportunity," said Evelyn.

Harper made sure his expression didn't change. He enjoyed Evelyn's boldness, but now was not the time for jeering.

"Indeed," he said flatly. "But perhaps we might discuss the coming voyage before we disembark?"

Evelyn fell back in line with a second prod from Madame Bellegarde's fan, harder than the first.

Having recovered from his embarrassment, Edmond took another opportunity to show Evelyn that he was no stranger to naval matters. "Of course, Captain. I noted the winds seem as unfavorable today as when we arrived in Airedale."

"Quite so, my lord. However, Lord Tallisker was firm on our departure date, so we will set sail shortly. The winds are less favorable than we might like, and the Vestal has taken on considerably more weight than she was carrying when we arrived. These two things combined will slow us down. Luckily, as I understand it, we aren't in any particular hurry. The wedding isn't for a month, so..."

"A month! Mon dieu!" Madame Bellegarde's fan flew to her face to exacerbate her surprise.

Harper looked at Madame Bellegarde as if only noticing her for the first time.

"And you would be?" he asked.

"Madame Florence Bellegarde," she replied proudly, drawing herself up.

"I see no mention of a 'Madame Bellegarde' on the manifest Lord Tallisker provided me," said Harper. He picked up a piece of paper from his desk and made a show of inspecting it thoroughly. "What is your purpose here?"

Madame Bellegarde looked shocked. "I am, of course, here to attend to Lady Dalton during her voyage and to see to her ongoing needs when she makes her new home in Dunshire."

"Her passage is not negotiable, Captain," said Evelyn, before Harper had a chance to respond.

"And yet I have no space to accommodate an additional passenger, Lady Dalton."

"She can share my quarters," said Evelyn quickly.

"I'm afraid I can't allow that," said Harper, fearing his plans being unraveled by an intrusive French mother hen. "The Vestal, such as she is, has small quarters. Even for such esteemed guests as yourselves. The two of you simply couldn't share such a confined space—"

Before either Madame Bellegarde or Evelyn could answer, Webb interrupted. "She can 'ave my quarters, sir!"

Harper looked up at his first mate in disbelief.

Webb stared straight ahead, unwilling to look his captain in the eye.

For just a moment, Evelyn thought she saw Harper's jaw drop. Just a fraction. There was a long pause.

"Very well, Mr. Webb," said Harper, after some consideration. He took his quill from its inkwell and scribbled on the manifest. "Since you never make use of your berth anyway, I will assign it to Madame Florence Bellegarde."

"Thank you, monsieur," said Madame Bellegarde. She gave a polite smile to Webb, who responded by turning the deepest shade of red Evelyn had ever seen.

"The passage may take as long as two, perhaps two and a half days," said Harper, returning to the matter at hand. "Should our conditions not improve, that is. During this time, I am happy for any of our guests to have free movement about the ship, provided, of course, they are under escort of a senior crew member. This is not to place any undue restrictions on your movement, but as Lord Edmond has witnessed, life at sea can be somewhat unpredictable, and your safe passage is my principal concern. For your meals, I have arranged for the finest vitals available to be brought aboard, and I can attest to the skills of our cook personally. You will dine most heartily during our passage to Dunshire."

"Will Lady Dalton and I be dining at your table, Captain Harper?" asked Edmond politely. Weaver scoffed, just loud enough to be heard by everyone in the room but softly enough that it wasn't worth mentioning.

Harper stretched his arms out wide and smiled. "Lord Edmond, I would take it as a personal affront if I did not have the pleasure of your company at each evening meal during your time aboard the Vestal. I will arrange for some extra seats to accommodate Madame Florence Bellegarde and Mr. Weaver as well." Harper stood up and extended a hand to Edmond. "Welcome back aboard the Vestal, my lord."

Edmond shook the extended hand with vigor. "Delighted to be back on her, Captain."

"Excellent," said Harper, ignoring the awkward phrasing. He looked past Edmond, his eyes landing on Captain Weaver. "Now, my lord," said Harper, his eyes fixed on Weaver, "if you would allow Mr. Webb to assist you in showing Lady Evelyn and Madame Florence Bellegarde to their quarters, I would appreciate a moment of Mr. Weaver's time to discuss matters of security on the voyage."

"Of course," said Edmond. He turned to Evelyn and extended his hand. "I would be honored to escort you to your bedchamber." Once again, he regretted his choice of words.

Evelyn stole one last glance at Harper's bed tucked away at the back of his quarters. She sighed and came to the rescue of her fiancé for the second time. "My lord," she said in the most formal tone she could summon. "I would be honored for you to take me to my bedchamber." She gave Harper a coy look before allowing herself to be led out of his quarters and back onto the main deck.

Mr. Webb almost fell over himself to get to Madame Bellegarde. She failed to notice as he extended his hand toward her, instead turning to follow closely behind Evelyn and Edmond as they made their exit. He let his hand hover awkwardly for a moment, in case the Madame turned back, but when it was apparent that she wouldn't, he closed it and returned it to his side. He gave Harper an inelegant salute and then cast his eyes to the ground, shuffling sheepishly out of the room.

◆

Harper waited until the door to his quarters clicked closed and then returned to his seat. Ever since their first interaction, he had been waiting for the chance to respond to the subtle threats that Captain Weaver had levelled at him. When he'd first seen him, Harper had acknowledged that Weaver was a large man, but now, in the cabin's interior, he seemed positively colossal. The low ceiling and narrow walls amplified the man's presence. Harper was certain that if they ever came to trading blows, he would end up the worse of the two. He folded his outstretched hands and rested his elbows on the desk. "Now," said Harper without looking up, "we are going to need to come to an understanding about security onboard the Vestal—"

"I will have two of my men stationed outside Lady Dalton's room whenever she is in her chambers, and she will have an escort whenever she chooses to be about on deck. At each of her meals..."

Harper raised a hand until Weaver fell silent. "I am happy to leave Lady Dalton's protection in your capable hands, Mr. Weaver—"

"Captain," replied Weaver abruptly.

"Captain Weaver." Harper sighed and rose to his feet. He planted both his hands squarely on the table in front of him and looked Weaver directly in the eye.

"The Vestal has but one captain, Mr. Weaver. Should we see combat, the men need to know that there is only one man giving orders and those orders will not be coming from you. You are not a nautical man; you have no tactical knowledge of this ship and have never commanded men at sea." Harper was making some broad assumptions, but he could tell from Weaver's reaction he was correct. "When we make port at Dunshire, you may call yourself what you please. Should I hear you refer to yourself as captain again whilst you are aboard this ship, I will make sure you spend the rest of the journey in the brig. The same holds for each of your men. Failing to address me as captain will be considered insubordination, the penalty for which will be the same. A ship runs on discipline, Mr. Weaver, and I cannot afford to have your pride disrupt my authority."

"Now listen here, Harper—"

"Captain Harper."

Weaver ignored the correction and pushed on. "I am the commander of Lord Dalton's personal guard and entrusted with the safety of the citizens of Airedale—"

"On this ship," said Harper, his words slow and deliberate, "I am Lord Dalton." Weaver looked taken aback. Harper could see the anger building in the man, but it had clearly been a long time since someone had spoken to him so bluntly. Harper imagined a man of Weaver's size, temperament, and lofty position often found that people chose their words carefully when discussing delicate matters with him.

"The very idea that you would compare yourself to my Lord," scoffed Weaver. "Your insolence will be reported to both the Daltons and Talliskers."

"You are free to report whatever you would like to the Daltons and the Talliskers if you survive your journey to Dunshire. There are a lot of dangers at sea, Mr. Weaver." Harper leaned back, making a show of examining Weaver. "That breastplate, for example, would sink you like a stone should you find yourself swept overboard in a squall." Harper gave Weaver a long, calculated stare. Silence filled the room. When he was confident that his point had been made, Harper smiled. "You've nothing to fear onboard the Vestal, Mr. Weaver. You make sure that you keep Lady Dalton safe and sound, and my men and I will make sure that you and yours are kept safe in turn."

"I..." Weaver seemed lost for words. He looked as if he were chewing through his thoughts, trying to find the perfect phrasing to shift dominance back in his favor. Eventually, he seemed to deflate slightly, and the room felt calmer. "If there's nothing else?"

Harper looked at Weaver expectantly.

"Captain."

Harper felt a sense of satisfaction as Weaver spat the title.

"No, Mr. Weaver," said Harper, returning to his seat. "That will be all." Weaver turned and made his way to the door. "Close it behind you," called Harper behind him. The large man didn't turn around as he walked through the door but threw it hard behind him. The door shuddered hard on its hinges as the latch hammered home.

As he stormed onto the quarterdeck, Weaver suddenly became very aware he was being watched. From outside Harper's quarters, he had a view of the entire ship. The sound of the captain's door slamming shut had never been heard on the Vestal before. Each of Harper's men turned from their duties and stared hard at Weaver. With each step, he felt the cold, hard stares of dozens of men. He scanned the main deck, looking for a familiar face. His men had all been escorted below deck to their berths, and Edmond and Evelyn were nowhere to be seen. As he stepped forward, he became aware that some of Harper's men had positioned themselves behind him. Though each of them made a show of slowly moving about their duties, their eyes never left him.

It had been a long time since Weaver had felt alone. Longer still since he had felt intimidated. Now, as the Vestal rocked gently beneath his feet, he was acutely aware that he held no advantage here. Fear and anger boiled inside him. His breastplate, which had always protected him, felt constricting as his heart beat faster. He made the mistake of looking overboard and imaged his armor pulling him down, deep into the blue waters. His breathing became faster. He cursed Harper under his breath, infuriated that such a man could get to him.

Taking a deep breath, he gathered himself. He was the captain of Lord Dalton's personal guard. He didn't tremble at the scowls of seadogs. Traversing the narrow steps down to the gun decks, he ignored the looks from the sailors that had positioned themselves around the cannons. In the interior's gloom, the sailors looked more threatening. He pretended to briefly inspect one of the cannons, giving an unimpressed sound as he walked past. He had to show he wasn't cowed by these men. He was representing his lord.

"Mr. Weaver?"

Weaver spun around and met the bright, beady eyes of Mr. Nicholas Webb. Harper's first mate smiled politely. "Feel'n alright, sir?"

"I...yes, yes. Of course," replied Weaver. As he looked about the deck, each of the men that had been staring at him all seemed thoroughly occupied in their work. Their attention solely fixed on preparing the Vestal for her departure. A few of them had started whistling as they busied themselves. "I could have sworn..." said Weaver quietly.

"Sworn what, sir?" asked Webb cheerily.

"Never mind. Webb, isn't it?"

"Aye, sir."

"I'd like to be shown to my quarters."

Evelyn watched as the only home she'd known in her twenty years slowly slipped farther away. The journey had taken longer than she had expected to get underway. She had asked to stand on the main deck as the Vestal departed and now watched as Airedale disappeared from view. From his position at the helm, Captain Harper was doing whatever it was captains do. Evelyn was cautious not to look his way too often, but curiosity continued to turn her gaze toward him.

Edmond, meanwhile, briskly walked the deck of the ship, watching what each of the men was doing with keen interest. Evelyn could see in his eyes that all he wanted to do was run up and down the deck, asking as many questions as he could think of to as many people as he could find. She watched her fiancé as he attempted to assist one of Harper's men coiling a rope, keen to prove he was more than a mere passenger on the voyage. He had an inexhaustible thirst for knowledge, which Evelyn found charming. She had always considered herself someone who wanted to learn and was interested in how things worked and how people thought. But she had to confess to herself, she had absolutely no interest in the work being undertaken by the sailors shuffling around her. For Edmond, though, it held an intense fascination.

Since she had met him, she had not seen a hint of malice or cruelty in Edmond's eyes. By her mother's standards, that made him the ideal candidate for a husband. But he was so incredibly different from Harper. He was softer, not only in body but also in spirit. He had a sweetness that Harper lacked, but he also lacked the captain's tenacity. The entire evening they had met, she had felt Harper's eyes on her. She had felt his power as she danced with him. He had risked a kiss that could have meant his life. She couldn't imagine Edmond doing anything so bold. When he looked at her, he seemed embarrassed or shy.

That thought resonated with her for a moment as she watched Harper giving orders to his officers on the quarterdeck. He had risked death to steal a kiss from her. She had never known a man as bold or presumptuous as Harper. As she watched him, Harper caught her gaze and held it. He was still talking, too far away for her to hear, but his green eyes seemed to cut through all the distractions around him and stare straight into her. She could hear some commotion coming from behind her and, welcoming the distraction, she turned quickly to see what had happened.

In his attempts to "help," Edmond had tangled himself up, and two sailors were delicately trying to clear up the mess he'd created for himself. Though the sight of it made her smile, she felt a touch of pity for the poor sailors trying to assist her fiancé. The usual 'slap him over the back of the head and leave him to figure his own way out of the mess he's created' approach wasn't allowed when a lord did something foolish. They had to deploy a patience and understanding they were not accustomed to.

Evelyn was so caught up in watching poor Edmond struggle she missed the last sight of Airedale as it slipped out of view. When she next looked back to her home, she found nothing but unfamiliar landscapes and the sprawling flat sea. "Ah," came a familiar voice from behind her. "I know that look." Evelyn didn't turn as Madame Bellegarde sidled up next to her and took up a stance on the railing. "I had the same look when I first left Le Havre. Home...has disappeared. It's unsettling, non?"

"Yes," said Evelyn distantly. It was unsettling. She was now between worlds. One of them she knew well, and the other was, apparently, famous for cheese.

"Do you know what Le Havre means in your language?" "The Haven," said Evelyn. "You may have mentioned it once or twice during your lessons," she added playfully.

"Oui," said Madame Bellegarde. "But for me, my haven, my Le Havre, became Airedale. In a small room, with a little girl, who I grew to love. So for me, leaving this time is not so bad."

"Why?" asked Evelyn. She was still desperate to find a reason to be happy about leaving her home, now more so than ever, as it had disappeared from view.

"Because, my sweet child, the thing I loved most about that land is here with me now." Madame Bellegarde put a reassuring hand over Evelyn's.

Evelyn felt as though a rock had been thrown in a fast-flowing stream. All around her, everything was changing and moving far too quickly for her liking. But, strong and unyielding, Madame Bellegarde was making it her business to give Evelyn a sanctuary among the uncertainty.

Before Evelyn could reply, an old and weathered sailor stationed at the forecastle broke into song. It caught Evelyn by surprise, and her mouth dropped open. Madame Bellegarde quickly used her folded fan to lift Evelyn's chin.

> Come all you young sailor men,
> listen to me;
> I'll sing you a song of the fish in the
> sea, and it's...

Evelyn could almost hear the collected intake of breath from the nearby sailors as they gathered up their lungs to join in the chorus.

"Oh, Lord," she heard Madame Bellegarde mutter. "They're all going to sing."

> Windy weather boys,
> stormy weather, boys
> When the wind blows,
> we're all together, boys
> Blow ye winds westerly,
> blow ye winds, blow
> Jolly sou'wester, boys,
> steady she goes.

There was an almost imperceivable pause from the entire crew before a young sailor from across the main deck took up the next verse:

> Up jumps the eel
> with his slippery tail,
> Climbs up aloft
> and reefs the topsail,
> and it's...

The crew again erupted in chorus. Evelyn looked to the quarterdeck and saw Harper nod to Webb. She watched as the balding first mate made his way down the stairs toward her. "At least this one is about fish," muttered Madame Bellegarde. "And not..." she looked at Evelyn for a moment and then changed the word she was about to use, "ladies."

> Windy weather boys,
> stormy weather, boys
> When the wind blows,
> we're all together, boys
> Blow ye winds westerly,
> blow ye winds, blow
> Jolly sou'wester, boys,
> steady she goes.

Another crewman stole his chance to pipe up with a verse:

> Then up jumps the shark
> with his nine rows of teeth
> Saying, 'You eat the doughboys,
> and I'll eat the beef!'
> and it's...

> Windy weather boys,
> stormy weather, boys
> When the wind blows,
> we're all together, boys
> Blow ye winds westerly,
> blow ye winds, blow
> Jolly sou'wester, boys,
> steady she goes.

Mr. Webb slowly walked past Evelyn and Madame Bellegarde. He didn't look twice at Evelyn, but as he passed Madame Bellegarde, he touched the tip of his hat and bowed politely to her. Then, he took in a huge breath and took his turn at the verse.

> Up jumps the herring,
> the king of the sea,
> Saying, 'All other fishes,
> now you follow me!'
> and it's...

There was something about the way that Webb sung "and it's" that got the whole crew fired up. The men launched into the chorus louder than ever. Evelyn looked around, expecting to see the men slacking on their duties, but as they sang, they seemed to work harder and more passionately than before.

"He fancies you," said Evelyn, nodding to Webb. She didn't bother to whisper, the crew's loud singing creating enough distraction.

"Don't be a ridiculous child," replied Madame Bellegarde. "Anyone with eyes could tell that you are the only woman on this ship worth looking at."

"He only looked at you as he walked past."

"Nonsense."

Evelyn rolled her eyes dramatically. "Maybe he sees something 'that all the men' don't see. Not to mention he offered you his quarters without hesitation."

"Enough," said Madame Bellegarde sternly. "He was simply being a gentleman."

"Or perhaps he likes the thought of you sleeping in his bedchambers?" Evelyn couldn't stop the grin on her face.

Madame Bellegarde was close to giving Evelyn a smack with her fan until she spied Edmond approaching and took the opportunity to retaliate. "Oh, my Lord Edmond," called Madame Bellegarde, "how fortunate to see you here." Madame Bellegarde shot Evelyn a sharp look. "Perhaps a reminder of why it is never a good idea to tease a French lady?" she whispered quickly with a wink as Edmond strode toward them. Evelyn felt dread as she glanced between Madame Bellegarde and Edmond. He beamed as he approached.

"What a marvelous tune," he said as the chorus struck up again. "They didn't sing this one on the voyage over. I quite like it. Smacks of comradery and mateship."

"And fish," replied Madame Bellegarde.

Edmond chuckled. "Quite so, Madame Bellegarde. And fish."

"Actually, it may interest you to know, my lord, that Lady Evelyn is a very accomplished singer. When she was a child, she had the fairest voice in Airedale. When she would sing at court it was a thing of beauty."

Evelyn turned bright red. The fact that she was one of the worst singers ever to grace the court at Airedale was a long-standing sore point in the Dalton family.

Of course, no one had told Evelyn that her singing was offensive to the ears and, as a child, she had reveled in every opportunity to sing in front of her parents and their guests. Until one evening when she picked a poorly-timed fight with her mother and, in her anger, Lady Dalton had told Evelyn that she preferred the sound of cats fornicating in the gardens to Evelyn's tone-deaf attempts at singing. Evelyn had never sung in public since. But she still sang to herself, enjoying the act in solitude.

"Truly," said Edmond in a keen tone. "I would very much love to hear you sing, my lady."

"Oh, I don't think that—"

"Perhaps after we have concluded dinner this evening," said

Madame Bellegarde. "It would make a fine end to the exquisite meal the captain has promised us."

Evelyn's hands clenched tight, her knuckles turning white.

"That is an absolutely smashing idea," said Edmond. "I'm certain Captain Harper and his officers would rejoice at hearing a pure and feminine voice sing to them for a change." Evelyn caught the sideways glance of her mentor. She had a victorious look in her eyes. Evelyn took a deep breath and unclenched her hands.

"I would be delighted," she said cordially. Evelyn refused to give Madame Bellegarde the satisfaction of watching her squirm. She felt that her singing had improved with age and practice. She was determined not to be tripped up by Madame Bellegarde.

"And I am sure that we will each of us also be delighted in turn," Edmond struggled through the sentence. His attempts at sounding formal were getting away from him. It was clear he still felt nervous in Evelyn's presence, especially in such a public setting. "I had best go and prepare for the evening."

"Of course, my lord," said Madame Bellegarde. She managed a polite half bow, the most movement her dress would allow.

"I am looking forward to dining with you, my lady," he said. He extended his hand to her.

Evelyn gave him her hand and felt herself pulled forward on her feet as he clumsily pulled it to his lips and kissed it gently. "I'm looking forward to it as well, my lord."

Once Edmond had taken his leave, Evelyn glared at Madame Bellegarde. "That was very cruel, Madame Florence Bellegarde. Very cruel indeed."

"Ah," said Madame Bellegarde with a glint in her eye. "But you have learned a very important lesson. Never tease a French woman."

O nce the Vestal was underway, Harper relinquished the helm and took some time to enjoy the solitude in his quarters. The light of the day was already waning, but one of the crew had made sure the lanterns had all been lit. He sat down at his desk and removed his hat. He felt the familiar curve of the chair underneath him and closed his eyes. For a moment he let his mind wander, imagining Evelyn's hands coming over his shoulders, moving down his chest and undoing his shirt. There were very few places a man could find himself any privacy aboard a ship, and the sanctuary of his quarters was a privilege that Harper never undervalued. A privilege he yearned to share with Evelyn if she would indulge him.

He opened his eyes and pulled himself back to reality. There was more to be done if he hoped to bring his fantasies to life. He pulled the cork from the small inkwell on his desk and took a fresh piece of parchment from a drawer. His brow furrowed as his quill hovered over the blank page. Thoughts struggled to turn themselves into words. No sooner had the tip of his quill touched the parchment and formed the first letter than a loud knock came from his door. He sighed and rested the quill in the inkwell. Nicholas Webb closed the door quietly behind him.

"Pardon the intrusion, Captain. You asked to be kept informed of the men's performance on the special task you gave them today?"

"So I did." Between stolen glances with Evelyn and getting the ship underway, he had almost forgotten his earlier order.

"They waited until Lady Dalton and Lord Tallisker were out of sight. I also made sure Madame Bellegarde got safely to her quarters as well."

"And then?"

"Well, the men heard your door slam shut and each one of them gave Weaver an icy stare." Webb did his impersonation of the 'icy stare'; his chin raised, and eyes bulged threateningly. "None of his men in sight, mind, they're all down below being shown their quarters and getting situated."

"And how was he when you came across him?"

"Well, by the time I found him, he was thoroughly rattled, sir," reported Webb.

Harper smiled.

"And a might confused. Couldn't believe his eyes when they all went back to work. Looked like he was waking from a dream."

"Ah, I wish I'd had the opportunity to see it myself." Harper imagined Weaver's look of confusion and fear as the Vestal's crew had closed in around him. "Let's hope that teaches him I won't be threatened, least of all on my own damned ship. Tell the men to leave off for now, though. No need to agitate him any further if he's learned his lesson. Make sure that all the men get an extra rum ration with their evening meal. A good performance should be rewarded."

"Aye, sir."

Harper picked up his quill again and intended to begin writing once more. He was aware that the large shadow of Nicholas Webb was still casting itself over his desk. "Something else, Mr. Webb?" he asked.

"Only if you have a moment, sir." Webb shifted uncomfortably. "It's a personal matter, see."

Harper reluctantly returned the quill to the inkwell. "Of course, old friend."

"Thank you, Captain," said Webb. "Like I said, it's a personal matter—"

"For God's sake," said Harper with feigned irritation, "Take a seat and spit it out, man!"

"It's just, you've always had a way with women and I...pardon me, Captain, do you have some water? I've come on parched suddenly."

"Good Lord," said Harper, rolling his eyes. He reached for the bottom drawer of his desk and pulled out a half empty bottle of rum. "Here," he said, thrusting the bottle toward Webb. The first mate gladly accepted, pulling the cork out and taking a long, generous swig from the bottle before handing it back. Harper examined the now nearly empty bottle. "When we're through here, I expect you to replace this," he took a swig himself and placed the now empty bottle down on the desk.

"Madame Florence Bellegarde..." began Webb, hesitantly.

"The uninvited governess that you fell over yourself to give your quarters to? Yes, what of her?"

"Do you think she's...beautiful?" Webb asked nervously.

"She's a shade too old for me, Webb," replied Harper dismissively. "And decidedly far too French."

"I just wanted to make my intentions clear, Captain. I didn't want there to be any bad blood between us if we were both pursuing the same lady, is all." Webb took the bottle again, realized it was empty, and set it back on the desk.

"Bad blood?" Harper was thoroughly confused.

"Well, if you and I were both to court the Madame..."

"Webb..." Harper ran a hand over his scrunched-up face as he struggled to comprehend what was happening. "Are you suggesting that there is a possibility that you and I might end up fighting over the affections of Madame Florence Bellegarde?"

"Yes, Captain." Webb hung his head with embarrassment. "I just didn't want no confusion between us. Wanted to be upfront and honest with you."

Harper was seeing something in his first mate he had never seen before: a humble and gentle soul who wanted desperately to find someone to love. Harper took a deep breath. "Webb, not only do you not have to worry about there ever being bad blood between us, I hereby give you my most solemn vow that I will never pursue the affections of Madame Florence Bellegarde." Although he found the words ridiculous to say, he said them with sincerity, and it brought a smile to Webb's face.

"Thank you, Captain. That has been weighing on me awful fierce ever since I first laid eyes on her. She being the only woman aboard not spoke for and knowing full well that if you courted her as well that she'd be choosing you over me without any doubt."

"You honestly have nothing to worry about in that regard," said Harper, trying not to smile. "Besides, who says she'd choose me anyway?" he gave Webb a calculating look. "You're fitter than any man aboard this ship."

"Aye, but shorter'n most. An' older too. Barely a hair on me head—"

"Enough of that. You have two days, perhaps a little more, in which to get to know this woman. Don't dine or drink with the crew tonight. Sit at my table with the lords and ladies and find some common ground with Bellegarde. Find out who she really is. There's more to a woman than her hair and her dress, Webb."

"Aye, I know that," said Webb with a sly grin.

"Not like that, man! If you are truly serious about courting a woman who has spent most of her life among the nobility, then you're going to need to stop thinking with your trousers."

Webb looked worried.

"Two days, Mr. Webb. It's a longer time than you might think. Start with conversation tonight. If you look like you're in trouble, then I'll step in."

"Captain?"

"I won't let you make an arse of yourself, man," said Harper bluntly.

"And what next? After conversation?"

"Well, when you feel the time is right and you feel she might want to listen, then you tell her how you feel. It's as simple as that."

Webb nodded, "I can do that." But his tone was far less certain than his words.

"Good man." Harper picked up the empty bottle and thrust it at Webb. "Now go and get a fresh bottle from Duncan. Then scrub up as best you can. Get your whitest shirt and make sure your boots are shining."

"Aye, Captain" said Webb with tentative enthusiasm.

After he was gone, and Harper could enjoy his solitude, the quill returned to hover above the blank parchment. The letter 'D' stared back at him. He finished the word 'Dearest' and stared at it on the parchment. After a while, he scrunched the paper up and threw it over his shoulder toward his bedchamber. He took out a fresh piece of parchment and smoothed it out on the desk. "Tell her how you feel," he repeated to himself. "It's as simple as that." He took a deep breath and let the quill touchdown on the parchment as his feelings for Evelyn transcribed themselves into words on the page.

◆

Evelyn had spent little time in her quarters since arriving on the Vestal. No sooner had Edmond shown her to her room than she was back out on the deck. When the wind had chilled and the salt in the air stung her eyes, she decided it was time to retire. Now she had more time to appreciate the effort Harper had gone to in arranging her transitory home. Though the space was cramped, it was very homey.

The first thing she noticed was the smell. Bouquets of lavender and bluebells adorned the bedside table and desk in her small cabin, splashes of blue against the wooden interior. To match the color of their crest, the Dalton family had encouraged the planting of blue flowers throughout Airedale and their surrounding lands. Evelyn had grown up with the smell of lavender around her for so long that she hardly noticed anymore, but after coming in from the fresh salty air of the sea, she felt as if she were breathing in a taste of home. It was strangely calming.

A large painting hung from the wall opposite her bed. At first, she thought it was Captain Harper, the same piercing green eyes and dark red beard. But the hair was graying. The brow more creased. A plaque on the bottom of the wooden frame read "Captain Declan Harper." The Vestal was painted in the background, set in a fierce, deep blue ocean. It gave the portrait a dark and foreboding presence. Evelyn had already decided she would sleep facing the window rather than wake up each morning to her lover's father. She wondered whether Captain Harper would mind if she threw a sheet over it for the next couple of days but couldn't think of a way to ask tactfully.

Evelyn knew that Madame Bellegarde would want her to be well-dressed for dinner. No doubt she was already choosing a dress for Evelyn and would soon be present to help her squeeze into it. Evelyn took the short time afforded her to undress down to her undergarments and threw her clothes over the single chair in the room. There was ample storage to put them away properly, but Evelyn did not feel like being proper for the moment. She felt like being carefree and heedless. There were no eyes to watch her here. No one to tell her what to do or how to act. Though it was small, this cabin represented complete freedom. For as long as she was aboard the Vestal, this space was entirely hers.

As she folded the last of her clothes over the chair, she saw something else she hadn't noticed when she first entered her cabin. Among the blue flowers, a fleck of red caught her eye. An unassuming letter sealed in red wax was propped up against one of the floral arrangements on the desk. She could have sworn it hadn't been there hours ago when she'd first entered the cabin.

She sat down on her bed, preparing to read the letter, and noticed a familiar softness. These were her quilts and pillows. The bed was considerably smaller than she was accustomed to, and the bedding spilled over the sides onto the floor, but someone had done their best to make it look presentable and tidy. She was about to lie down when she heard a low growl coming from under her sheets. Slowly, carefully, she peeled the covers back.

In a flurry of claws and teeth, a hideous black shape bolted from its nest of sheets and quilts. Evelyn pulled her hand and gave a yelp of surprise. "Hells!" Resettled on the desktop, Blackbeard gave her a cold, one-eyed stare. She heard a hard knock on the door.

"Everything all right in there, my lady?" One of her father's men called to her through the solid oak door. Evelyn caught her breath before answering.

"Yes, yes, fine, thank you." Evelyn examined the creature in front of her. If she had to guess, she would have said it was a cat, but she had never seen anything quite like it before. Its missing eye was covered by an eye patch that had been fastened behind its tattered ears.

Its bristled fur flattened against its body as it got over the shock of being disturbed. Gingerly, Evelyn extended a hand toward the creature. She smiled as it nuzzled against her fingertips. Sensing she was in no immediate danger, she sat back down on the bed. In her surprise, she had dropped the letter on the floor and stood on it. As she took the crumpled parchment and prepared to open it, the grizzled black cat leapt from its perch and landed squarely in her lap, pinning her hands to her thighs. It rolled over and exposed its belly, making an affectionate gurgling sound. Evelyn supposed it sounded like a purr, if the purr were coming from a bear.

Evelyn slowly pulled one hand free and scratched the exposed belly of her furry captor while keeping the letter firmly grasped in her trapped hand. The surreal sensation of stroking the world's least attractive cat whilst under the stern gaze of Declan Harper's portrait was finally broken by the sound of singing above her.

> William Taylor was a
> brisk young sailor
> Full of heart and full of play
> Till his mind he did uncover
> To a youthful lady gay

There was no mistaking the voice. From almost directly above her, she could hear Captain Harper singing. The tune was light and playful, and the captain had a strong voice for singing. Evelyn wondered why he hadn't sung earlier with the rest of his men. The sound of his voice made her feel strangely calm, and she lay back in her bed to listen. Blackbeard curled himself around her hand, his claws flexing and unflexing as he purred. The sound of Harper's singing seemed to relax him as well.

When Edmond had shown her to her room, he had taken a long and winding route to get there. Evelyn couldn't determine whether it was because he had been eager to show off more of his knowledge of the ship or simply because he had managed to get himself lost. Now she was acutely aware that the only thing separating her quarters from Harper's was the ceiling. She scanned the ceiling, making sure there were no holes or hatches built into the woodwork, no way for the captain to sneak into her room without her father's men detecting him. She was absolutely unsure of what she would do if she found himself alone with Harper again, but she knew it would be unladylike.

> Four and twenty British sailors
> Met him on the king's highway
> As he went for to be married
> Pressed he was and sent away
>
> Folleri-de-dom, de-daerai diddero
> Folleri-de-dom, domme daerai dae
> Folleri-de-dom, de- daerai diddero
> Folleri-de-dom, domme daerai dae

Above her, she could hear Harper pacing as he sang, and she imagined him getting ready for the evening. At the sound of the captain's footsteps, Blackbeard moved from her lap and scratched at the window. His best efforts to negotiate the latch fell short, and he gave a frustrated cry. He looked at Evelyn with a forlorn, one-eyed stare until she moved to assist him. Carefully, she slipped the letter under her pillow, worried that if she opened the window, it might get blown out to sea. As she fiddled with the window latch, the ragged cat did his best to get in his way as much as possible, adding an unnecessary degree of difficulty to the task. The moment the window was free of its latch, Blackbeard shoved his head into the opening and forced it to fly open. Before Evelyn could catch him, the one-eyed cat had leapt deftly from her bedroom window and onto the outer hull of the ship.

She kept her hands firmly on the inside wall and pushed her head out of the small window, craning her neck to catch a glimpse of the escaped feline. The wind was stronger than she imagined and her hair broke free of its bonds and whirled around her face. She found her balance and pulled her hair out of her eyes with one hand. She saw the end of the beast's tail as it slipped into the open window above her head. "Ah, Blackbeard, you devious miscreant..." she heard Harper call to his pet. "Where the devil have you been, boy?" Evelyn pulled her head back in quickly and closed the window firmly behind her. She didn't want to risk another unexpected visit from Blackbeard. Above her she could hear Harper humming the chorus of his song before striking up the next verse."

> Sailor's clothing she put on
> And went to board a man-o-war
> Her pretty little fingers
> long and slender
> They were smeared with pitch and tar
>
> On the ship there was a battle
> She, amongst the rest, she did fight
> The wind blew off her silver buttons
> Breasts were bared all snowy white.

"You like that part best, don't you?" she heard Harper say. "You rotten little devil."

"Is he talking to his cat?" Evelyn asked herself in disbelief. For a moment, she found it amusing, but then she was overcome with a sense of sadness for the captain. He couldn't, or at least wouldn't, sing with the rest of his men when he was out on deck. Clearly, he had a strong enough voice to join in with his men as they sang, but perhaps he didn't think it was appropriate for a captain to sing with his crew.

Alone, in his cabin, he sang only to his cat. Seeking its feedback and input as he did so. Evelyn wondered if Harper was lonelier than he might otherwise appear. There was no woman in his life, at least none she dared imagine. No family. His crew were his responsibility, but unlikely his friends. His officers perhaps formed the closest connection to him, but still had to be kept at arm's length.

> When the captain did discover
> He said, fair maid, what brought you here
> Sir, I'm seeking William Taylor
> Pressed he was by you last year
>
> If you rise up in the morning
> Early at the break of day
> There you'll spy
> young William Taylor
> Walking with his lady gay
>
> She rose early in the morning
> Early at the break of day
> There she spied young William Taylor
> Walking with his lady gay

The song was interrupted by a loud and unabashedly intrusive knock at her door. "Lady Evelyn," came the voice of one of her father's men. "Madame Bellegarde to see you, my lady."

Evelyn sighed. She had become intrigued by the young woman in Harper's song. A woman who slipped away aboard a ship to find her true love. She had dressed as a man and fought alongside them, all in the hopes of finding young William Taylor. Evelyn had to know if the young woman was successful, if all her efforts were rewarded. She determined she would ask Harper at the next opportunity she got.

"Please allow her to enter," called Evelyn to the closed door in front of her. Above her, the singing stopped, as if the whole thing had been a private performance for her, not to be heard by other ears. Madame Bellegarde entered the room sideways, only turning once she was through the door. She wore a new dress that almost spanned the entire room. As improbable as it seemed, Madame Bellegarde had managed to find a garment even more unsuitable to sea travel than the dress she had boarded in—a brilliant gown of red and yellow, complete with extravagant bustle and a crimson stomacher that accentuated her already impressive bosom.

"Well..." said Madame Bellegarde with a disapproving head-to-toe scan of Evelyn. She paused on the wild hair and shook her head at the young woman standing in her undergarments, then tutted.

"What!?" asked Evelyn, still irritable that the Madame had organized for her to sing at dinner.

"If you wanted someone to clean the floors, I'm sure Captain Harper would have sent one of his men to do it."

Evelyn gave Bellegarde a defiant but ever so slightly perplexed look. "I beg your pardon?"

"A mop," began Bellegarde, "there was absolutely no need for you to turn your hair into a mop. I am sure Captain Harper could have provided you with one if you needed one so desperately." A thin smile cracked its way through the Madame's face.

Evelyn didn't know whether to slap her old mentor or cry. In the end, she did neither as she burst out laughing.

"I truly did forget how presumptuous you can be," said Evelyn with a smile. "Any other lady would have you thrown overboard for that comment."

"Can you imagine how traumatizing my time with your mother was?" Madame Bellegarde threw a hand across her forehead. "To contain a wit as sharp as mine for so many years. It was torturous." "You'd have definitely been tortured if you'd spoken to mother the way you speak to me!" said Evelyn was a laugh that ended in a very unladylike snort.

"Enough of this," said Madame Bellegarde, waving her hand in the air and pushing Evelyn out of her way. She tucked her dress expertly around her legs and sunk down heavily into the only chair in Evelyn's room. "Stand over there," she pointed to the one spot in the room where Evelyn couldn't be seen from the door. Evelyn shuffled into place. Madame Bellegarde clapped her hands loudly. The door swung open and two of Evelyn's father's men entered, carrying a heavy chest between them. "There," said Madame Bellegarde, pointing at the very limited floor space in the cabin. The men set the chest down with a heavy 'thunk'. "Thank you," said the Madame to the two men," you may leave now." The two men nodded and bowed.

Once the door clicked close, Madame Bellegarde rose from her chair and slid the bolt, locking it from the inside. She opened the heavy lid to the chest with surprising ease for a woman of her physique and age. Evelyn craned her neck to look inside. Dresses of almost every cut and color shone out at her. Some she recognized from her own wardrobe, others she had never seen before. "When your father told me I was to return to your service, I took the liberty of organizing a new wardrobe for you. If you are to be the Lady of Dunshire, then you are required to be the best dressed woman in all the land." Madame Bellegarde gave Evelyn a coy wink. "With one exception, of course."

"They're...exquisite," said Evelyn, trying to find the word she thought Madame Bellegarde would most approve of. She did not relish the idea of spending her entire life in constricting and impractical clothing. Her mind drifted back to the first time she had met Edmond. When his mother had sat on the edge of Evelyn's dress and squeezed the air out of her lungs.

"Which would you choose?" asked Evelyn, already afraid of the answer.

Madame Bellegarde clearly appreciated the question and eagerly rifled through the chest.

"We want to show your fiancé what an exquisite beauty he has to spend the rest of his life pleasing...Ah!" Bellegarde triumphantly pulled out a splendid red silk dress with golden embroidery. Evelyn looked at it with a raised eyebrow.

"And whose breasts were you thinking of when you chose this dress? Yours perhaps? How am I supposed to keep that from falling off?" Evelyn pointed to her slender frame and Madame Bellegarde slapped herself theatrically on the forehead.

"Zut alors! This one is for after the children have come," she said. "Madame Bellegarde plans for the future!" She returned to rummaging through the chest.

Evelyn was pleased that Madame Bellegarde's gaze was fixed on the chest and not on her. The thought of children hit her like a cold blast of air running straight through her skin. It wasn't the mention of children or even the bustier dress that made her heart freeze long enough to skip a beat. It was the knowledge that both those things came at the price of never knowing Captain Finn Harper's touch again.

"Long gloves..." Bellegarde was almost finished assembling Evelyn's evening outfit. "Et c'est parfait," she stood up and arranged the clothes on the bed so that Evelyn could give her approval. Bellegarde had selected a pale blue mantua gown with dark blue lace embroidery. The Dalton family crest had been intricately woven as a pattern through the sleeves and the bodice stood out a darker blue against the rest of the outfit. Long lace gloves would cover her arms, as the dress had very short sleeves. Evelyn approved of the lack of restriction. It made eating much more graceful when she could actually lift a fork to her mouth without draping her clothing through her food—a skill she was yet to master with some of her dresses.

"If you are only to be a Dalton for a short while longer, then I thought it appropriate you dress the part," said Madame Bellegarde, placing her hands on Evelyn's shoulders.

"It's beautiful," said Evelyn sincerely.

"Now... let's get you inside it so that you can show Lord Edmond Tallisker what a truly lucky man he is."

Edmond was grateful for Mr. Webb's company as he made his way to Evelyn's quarters. Ordinarily, Edmond would have been a fit of nerves by the time he came to knock on Evelyn's door. Oddly, Mr. Webb's state of sheer terror had a strangely calming effect on the young Lord. Edmond felt the need to be brave on Webb's behalf and, in doing so, he had found his own courage. He looked at Harper's first mate with concern. If Webb perspired any more, he would be a dried-out husk by the time they sat down to dinner.

Edmond stopped a short distance from their destination, feigning a look of pain. "Everything alright, my lord?" asked Webb with genuine concern.

"Yes, quite alright," said Edmond, reaching down and unbuckling his boot. "These damned new boots cause the most agitating blisters you could imagine. Would you mind awfully if we stopped for a moment?" Webb nodded in relief as Edmond leant against the ship's railing, lifting his foot and pretending to massage his non-existent blister.

"Dreadful things, blisters," said Webb knowingly.

"The price of wearing lavish footwear, I suppose," said Edmond thoughtlessly. "Oh, and I suspect the price of a hard life at sea as well," he added quickly.

"Aye," said Webb, relaxing a little and taking up a position next to Edmond on the railing. "But blisters can be the least of your worries on a long voyage."

"I can quite imagine," Edmond watched Webb as he relaxed. He kept up the charade of his sore foot as he tried to coax a little more conversation out of Webb. "I would imagine that cannonballs and cutlasses are far more hazardous, though." Webb smiled a well-meaning, patient smile.

"Not so much as you might think, my lord. Most voyages are awfully dull. Long days, cold nights. You've more risk of running out of potable water than you do of running into an enemy at sea. Or having rats and weevils clean out your larder. Diseases of the mind and body. Oh, aye, there's far worse things'n blisters to worry you at sea."

"I would imagine a considerable lack of female company as well?" Webb noticeably tensed.

"Certainly, my lord. The harsh life at sea is no place for a lady."

"I can imagine. And yet you and I have been charged with the task of escorting Lady Evelyn and Madame Bellegarde to the captain's table. Two very fine ladies whose safety we must ensure while they are at sea." Webb glowed crimson.

"Truthfully, my lord. I've never had the honor of escorting a lady to a dinner before. Or anywhere else for that matter."

"I had an inkling that might have been the case," replied Edmond with a considered tone. He drew himself up and held his arm out as he would if he were escorting a lady. "Hold your arm like this." Webb attempted to mimic the gesture with a modicum of success. "That's good," said Edmond encouragingly, moving to Webb and making a few adjustments to his pose. "Just don't stand so stiffly. Try to look relaxed but also in control. Take your steps slowly, especially when navigating stairs. From what I have seen, Madame Bellegarde enjoys a rather lavish wardrobe, so you'd best tread carefully, you don't want to step on her dress."

"Alright," said Webb hoarsely. "I can do this."

"Of course you can," said Edmond as he gave the first mate a reassuring slap on the back. "Take a few deep breaths, and we'll begin again."

"Much obliged, my lord. How's that blister feeling now?"

"Do you know, I'd almost completely forgotten about it," said Edmond, sliding his foot back into his boot. "How's your resolve?"

"Much improved, my lord," said Webb. "Thank you."

"I'm very happy to be of service, Mr. Webb. Though I must confess, my own knowledge of the female creature is somewhat limited as well. It's an area I am hoping to learn a lot more about over the coming month now that I have a fiancée."

"Captain Harper's been a help for me there," said Webb as they resumed their walk toward Evelyn's quarters

"Advice around conversation and the like. Good advice like yours, my lord. Between the two of you, I might just make it through the night without making a fool of myself."

"You've nothing to fear on that account," said Edmond, trying to sound reassuring. "I'm sure I'll be looking foolish enough for both of us." They stopped a respectful distance from the door to Evelyn's quarters and waited for the guards to announce their arrival.

"Just breathe," said Edmond, as he felt his own nerves returning.

"I'm doing my best, my lord," replied Webb in a loud whisper.

"I was talking to myself, Mr. Webb," said Edmond as the door slowly opened. Madame Bellegarde emanated from the confined cabin like a butterfly bursting from its chrysalis. The bright red and yellow of her dress stood out magnificently against the drab wooden exterior of the ship. From somewhere behind the impressive visage of Madame Bellegarde, Edmond caught a flash of blonde hair. He held his breath as Evelyn stepped carefully around her mentor.

Though Evelyn's dress was considerably more modest than Bellegarde's, Edmond couldn't take his eyes away from her. She smiled shyly back at him as he gazed into her beautiful green eyes. Edmond thought she looked so splendidly dressed in her Dalton colors, he felt guilty about taking the name away from her. Before he could stare at her any longer, his instinctual formality kicked in and he bowed deeply to both the ladies in front of him. Out of the corner of his eye, he could see Webb attempting to copy his movements. "Good evening, Lady Evelyn and Madame Bellegarde," he said in his best formal tone. "It is our absolute pleasure to escort you this evening to the captain's table for our evening meal."

"Thank you, my lord," replied Evelyn, for both herself and Madame Bellegarde. "We are looking forward to the evening." It felt odd to Evelyn to lead the conversation. Madame Bellegarde had made it very clear that the evening was a good opportunity for Evelyn to act as the lady of the house. For the first time in her life, she couldn't rely on someone else to direct conversation or maintain etiquette. Although Madame Bellegarde was not a noble, Evelyn had never spoken for her. Another novel sensation for her to add to her ever-growing list of new experiences.

Edmond cleared his throat and gave Webb a gentle nudge with his elbow. The first mate stepped forward and offered his arm to Madame Bellegarde. "Lady...sorry, Madame Bellegarde... I would be honored to take you... that is to escort you to the dinner at Captain Harper's table," Mr. Webb stumbled through his greeting as if he were walking on hot coals. Madame Bellegarde kept her expression pleasant and professional as she extended her hand and took hold of Webb's arm.

"It would be an honor to walk with the first officer of such a fine vessel," her voice was honey. Evelyn watched as Webb performed an awkward dance around Madame Bellegarde so that he could turn around without stepping on her dress. Each step seemed painfully considered as they slowly made their way toward the main deck.

"My Lady?" asked Edmond as he extended his own arm to her. Evelyn wrapped her gloved fingers around Edmond's arm. He waited a few moments for Webb and Bellegarde to get a small distance from them before taking his first step.

"You look..." Edmond struggled for the right word. Desirable? Ravishing? Delectable? Magnificent? Delightful? None of them seemed to do justice to what he wanted to say. "Indescribably beautiful," he said honestly.

"Thank you, my lord," said Evelyn. "Though I fear my attire pales in comparison to Madame Bellegarde's," she smiled.

"I think it suits you perfectly. You wear your family colors better than any of your ancestors could have ever hoped to." Evelyn wished her mother had been present to hear that comment.

Ahead of them, Madame Bellegarde laughed uproariously at something that Webb had said. Such a break in formality surprised both Evelyn and Edmond. "Well, he seems to have found his courage, at least," said Edmond to himself.

"Pardon me, my lord?" said Evelyn.

"The poor devil was an absolute wreck of nerves while we were making our way to you this evening. I believe he has truly fallen head over heels for the good Madame."

"Ha!" Evelyn exclaimed victoriously. "I knew it. I even told her as much this afternoon." Edmond stopped walking, pulling back ever so gently so that Evelyn stopped with him.

"Perhaps we should give them just a little more space," he said. "Let them continue to enjoy their time together."

"A lovely thought, my lord," said Evelyn. "It has been some time since I have heard Madame Bellegarde laugh that heartily at something she didn't say herself."

"I..." began Edmond hesitantly. "Do you think that when we are married, you will still call me 'my lord'?"

Evelyn considered the question. "It is your official title," said Evelyn plainly. She tried to think of a time when her parents had addressed each other by their first names in front of her. If it had ever happened, she couldn't remember it.

"Yes, but if we're to be married, shouldn't there be more freedom between us? At the very least in our private moments together? I don't want to be your 'lord'. Not when it's just the two of us."

"What would you like me to call you?" asked Evelyn

"Well...Edmond," he said. "It is my name, after all. Though I so rarely hear it spoken on its own."

"Edmond, then."

Edmond turned to look at Evelyn as she spoke, trying to read what was happening behind her emerald eyes. "I like how that sounds coming from your lips," he said. He blushed after he said it, feeling as if he had overstepped an invisible boundary between them.

"It's just your name," said Evelyn with a smile.

"It is," he said softly, "but it seems to mean more when you say it than it has ever meant before." He cleared his throat and took a deep breath. "We should probably keep moving before we fall too far behind," he said, trying to regain his formal tone.

As they continued their walk, he could have sworn he felt Evelyn's fingers tighten ever so gently around his arm.

◆

Evelyn wasn't sure what to expect from a dinner at Captain Harper's table. To get there, they had had to pass close to the crew's quarters. The sound of loud singing accompanied by fiddles and flutes met them as they walked above the lower decks of the Vestal. The stink of the crew mingling with the sumptuous bouquet of smells wafting from the galley created a unique blend of aromas. An ornate door of solid oak led to the captain's dining room, thick and heavy enough to drown out the sounds and smells of the rest of the ship.

When they arrived, Harper was standing with Mr. Weaver and two of his other officers, each with a glass of wine in hand. As soon as he heard the door open, he moved to greet Edmond and Evelyn. "Lord Edmond and Lady Evelyn, thank you for joining us." He turned to Madame Bellegarde and gave her a deep bow. "And it is my esteemed pleasure to welcome you to my table as well, Madame Florence Bellegarde."

"We are most delighted to join you, Captain," said Edmond excitedly. "I have been telling Lady Evelyn about Mr. Duncan's skills in the galley."

Harper nodded.

"He doesn't have an equal on land or at sea when it comes to the culinary arts. May I offer a drink before we take our seats?" One of Harper's crewmen silently appeared next to Evelyn with a silver tray of glasses, each filled generously with red wine.

"Upon finding out we had a French woman in our company, I ensured we had some bottles of Chateau Bourdillon on board before we left Airedale." Madame Bellegarde smiled approvingly, waiting until Edmond and Evelyn had each taken a glass before taking one herself.

"A very fine choice, Captain." Harper lifted his glass to the madame and then put it to his lips.

"I'm glad you approve, Madame. Now," he said with a hint of formality, "we have a few introductions I believe need to take place. Lord Edmond, you're familiar with my officers, of course, but for the ladies, I would like to introduce two of my finest men who will be dining with us this evening." Harper gestured for the assembled men to step forward. "Mr. Alfred Trent, the Vestal's quartermaster, and Mr. Benjamin Clarke, our master gunner. Of course, you already know the last member of our party this evening, Airedale's own commander of the guard, Mr. Weaver." Weaver raised his glass at the sound of his name, but a nonplussed expression lingered on his face. "Well," said Harper, breaking his formal tone. "Now that we're all here, I would like to propose a toast to a safe voyage for our guests and to their continued happiness after their departure."

"Aye. Here, here," said Mr. Webb as the guests raised their glasses.

Light conversation broke out among the assembled guests and Evelyn felt Edmond lean in closely to her. "It's a different kind of formality from what we're used to at court," he whispered to her.

"Indeed, it is," said Evelyn.

"Captain Harper isn't one for ceremony, but his table is warm and generous. Once you get used to it, it really is very agreeable. Though I note that the conversation is freer and the drink more generous than you may be used to."

"Thanks for the warning," said Evelyn. She took a moment to take in her surroundings.

The room was neatly decorated, but not lavish. Harper had dressed himself in a formal dinner jacket but had kept his appearance modest so as not to compete with any of the other guests. Although the etiquette seemed more relaxed than she was used to, Evelyn noted that the table had been set with meticulous care. Nothing was out of place, from the intricately folded napkins to the shining silverware. Each setting had a neatly written place card sitting above the cutlery. Before she had a chance to read where each of the guests was sitting, one of Harper's crewmen approached his captain and said something Evelyn couldn't hear.

Harper clapped his hands together. "Friends," he said, gathering everyone's attention. "I believe our first course is ready to be served. Mr. Duncan is a mild man, but I'd rather not invoke his ire by delaying him in the galley. Please be seated," he gestured to the table and each of the guests quickly found their seats.

Eight places were set at the table, with four on each side. Evelyn found it odd that Harper hadn't had the heads of the tables set for himself and Edmond. She took her seat at the center of the table, with Edmond seated to her right and Madame Bellegarde to her left. Mr. Weaver sat down on the other side of Edmond, rounding out their side of the table. Mr. Webb was seated opposite Madame Bellegarde, which made Evelyn smile. She had enjoyed watching the two of them talk. As shy as Webb was, there was no hiding his affection for her mentor.

Mr. Clarke sat opposite Mr. Weaver, and the two were already striking up a lively conversation about cannons and armaments. Edmond rose slightly from his chair to shake hands with Mr. Trent as he took his seat opposite the young Lord. Evelyn looked at the empty seat in front of her. She knew Harper would have positioned himself near her, but she wasn't expecting him to be so bold as to sit directly in front of her.

Harper gave Evelyn a knowing smile as he took his seat. "Lady Evelyn," he said, his fingers closing around the stem of his wineglass, "I trust you've found your voyage pleasing thus far?"

"Well, apart from the mercurial creature I found sleeping in my bed, it's been quite agreeable so far," replied Evelyn. She watched the captain's smile grow wider at the mention of his cat.

"Aye, our Blackbeard is a notorious scoundrel. But he keeps the rats out of our galley, which makes him a very valuable member of our crew. He's lived aboard this ship longer than anyone else, with the exception of Mr. Webb." Evelyn saw a chance to finally learn more about her captain, beyond what he could do with his hands and his lips.

"How long have you been on the Vestal?" she asked.

"This will be my sixth year as her captain," said Harper. "I inherited her from my father when he passed."

"Captain Declan Harper?" asked Evelyn.

Harper raised a brow.

"I believe he'll be watching me as I sleep tonight," she added

Realization dawned on Harper's face. "Oh, yes, I forgot he was sharing your quarters now. I've only recently moved him there." Harper leaned in closer and spoke softly to Evelyn. "I grew tired of him judging me while I was at my desk."

"He does have a degree of judgment in his eyes," agreed Evelyn. "What sort of man was he?"

"Stern," said Harper, leaning back again. "But strong. I never sailed under his command, but a few of the men still aboard did, including Mr. Webb. They speak highly of his leadership. I imagine in some ways he was more a father to those men than he was to me. Life at sea makes it hard for a father to spend time with his children." Evelyn couldn't read the expression on Harper's face, but she related to the sentiment.

"Believe it or not, Captain, it is very similar at court. You might see your parents more often, but they don't have time for you." She nodded at Madame Bellegarde, who was busying herself by teaching

Webb about the nuances of French wine. "In a lot of ways Madame Bellegarde was a truer parent to me than my own mother and father." It was the first time she had ever said it out loud or even admitted it to herself. Something about Harper sharing a piece of himself with her made her want to open up to him. She wished for a moment she could clear the room and just talk to her captain the way that any two lovers might. Even in the less formal setting of the captain's dining room, there was a code of formality she had to follow, which restricted her from asking some of her more burning questions.

Before Evelyn and Harper could continue, the first course was brought out to the table. Rich aromas filled the room as Harper's men brought in steaming bowls of spiced ox tongue broth. The slow cooked meats melted in the mouth. Evelyn could taste liberal amounts of butter, nutmeg, and salt as she lifted the spoon to her lips. She had never tasted a soup like it before, so alive with flavor and textures. "Goodness," exclaimed Edmond, "this is a truly remarkable broth. I've never experienced such intense flavor in such a humble dish." Murmurs of agreement filled the room. Even Mr. Weaver momentarily seemed to enjoy himself.

"I'm pleased that it agrees with you, my lord," said Harper politely. Before clearing the plates away, two of Harper's crew moved around the table, quietly filling up each of the wine glasses. During the brief pause in their conversation, Evelyn listened to the other guests. Webb and Madame Bellegarde still seemed to be getting along very well. Webb was asking as many questions as he could about France, which Evelyn noted was a clever tactic to keep Madame Bellegarde constantly talking excitedly.

Weaver and Clarke seemed to be kindred spirits. They had moved on from talking about artillery and were now exchanging battle stories. Clarke seemed to have the advantage in that department, as his life at sea had provided him with more tales, but Weaver seemed to be holding his own. Edmond was eager to learn more about the Vestal and life at sea, constantly asking questions of the ship's quartermaster. His enthusiasm for learning never waned, and he seemed to possess the ability to store every scrap of knowledge he was provided. Evelyn had to commend Harper. The way the room was arranged was very logical whilst still placing him as close to her as possible.

"Could the Vestal make the journey to the New World?" Edmond asked.

"Aye, we've made the voyage several times now," replied Trent. "It's a bit like returning home for the captain and I. Both of our first commissions were to the West Indies."

Edmond turned to Harper. "Truly?"

"Aye," replied Harper. "The first ship I served upon was the Tyger, a pirate hunter, when I was just a lad of sixteen." Evelyn could feel Edmond lean into her as he got sucked into the conversation. She noticed that Weaver and Clarke had also stopped talking and were now paying attention to Harper. "Have you heard of it?" asked the captain. Evelyn shook her head as Edmond nodded excitedly.

"You sailed with Captain Jonathan Barnet on the ship that captured Calico Jack Rackham? And Mary Read and Anne Bonny?!" Edmond was so far on the edge of his seat that he was practically sitting on Evelyn's lap.

"A fearsome battle, it must have been," scoffed Weaver. "Taking on a rabble of women dressed as pirates and the dandy that led them." He looked to Clarke for approval at his comment but didn't find any. "I heard they found Rackham cowering in the cargo hold instead of fighting with his men."

"As I said," said Captain Harper, "I was sixteen at the time. I could barely hold a sword or fire a pistol. I was running up and down rigging and working the sails for the most part. But..." Harper paused for effect, drawing his audience in deeper, "when we did finally catch up with Rackham and board his ship, I learned the most valuable lesson of my life." Evelyn felt Harper's boot brush against her calf, a slow but deliberate movement as he continued his story. At first, she felt she should pull away, but the sensation was so welcome that she pressed her leg back against him, strengthening the touch. Harper looked at Evelyn, their green eyes meeting across the dinner table. "Never underestimate the strength of a woman." Evelyn's eyes didn't flinch, but she felt her heart race as Harper spoke the words.

"Let me tell you something, Mr. Weaver," said Harper, turning to look down the table. "Those two women fought harder than any man on that ship, including Rackham himself. I saw Read gun down one of her own men when he abandoned his post." Harper took a long drink from his glass, drawing his audience in as silence filled the room. "If each of the men in Rackham's crew had fought as hard as Read and Bonny, then I'm sure I wouldn't be sitting here today for we'd have never won that battle." A veritable avalanche of questions descended onto Harper from across the table after he had finished his tale. He answered them each in turn, all the while keeping his foot brushing against Evelyn's leg. Occasionally, he would raise the hem of her dress slightly and she would push his foot back, readjusting her skirts under the table. When she did, he would stop for a while, but the troublesome foot would soon return, eager to resume its playful advances.

"Why do you think Read and Bonny fought harder than the rest of the crew?" asked Evelyn when there was finally a chance for her to ask a question.

"Simple," said Harper, his foot rubbing harder against her leg. "Love." Evelyn felt her entire body freeze as the word left Harper's lips. She couldn't tell if he meant what he was saying or if he intended the word just for her and was disguising it in his tale.

"Love?" asked Edmond curiously. Weaver scoffed again. Harper took his eyes off Evelyn to address Edmond, but she kept staring straight at him. She felt as if her captain had just declared his true feelings for her in front of everyone. A secret language that only she could understand.

"Yes, my lord. Love is a powerful motivator. In my opinion, a man defends what he loves with his life, no matter the cost or the danger. In my case, everything I love in the world, everything I hold dearest, is on the Vestal. And indeed, the Vestal herself. And so, it was for Bonny and Read when they were aboard the William. Everyone they held dearest, but also everything their lives represented, was part of that ship. They were fighting for everything they loved."

"But Bonny and Read weren't men," said Weaver. "You said a man defends what he loves…"

"Quite so, Mr. Weaver," said Harper. "But they spent much of their time dressed as men, living among men, fighting as men. In their case, what makes a man wasn't defined by what hung between their legs. Or perhaps the sexes aren't so different as we seem determined to pretend they are." Harper turned to Evelyn and Bellegarde. "I apologize for the crudeness ladies." Madame Bellegarde grinned broadly, a sign of how much she was enjoying the Chateau Bourdillon. "Nonsense, Captain. Far cruder things have been said at a dinner table before."

The second course came out. Followed quickly by the third. Miniature pork pies followed by roast beef. More variety of vegetables than Evelyn had ever seen in her life. Fresh bread, rich butter, thick gravy, and exotic seasonings. Harper had spared no expense to impress his distinguished guests. When the food was being cleared from the table and conversation was at its loudest, Evelyn took a moment to ask the captain a question that had been burning inside her all evening.

"Captain?" she asked politely. Harper set his wineglass down on the table as she spoke, giving her his full attention.

"Yes, my lady?" His boot returned to her calf as she spoke. She knew he was doing his best to make her break her poise. As much as she loved his touch, she was unwilling to give him the satisfaction of seeing her flustered.

"Are you familiar with the tale of William Taylor?" she asked as nonchalantly as possible. A knowing smile formed on Harper's face, and he leant forward in his chair. Beside her, Edmond was attempting to compete in tales of combat with Weaver, Trent, and Clarke by telling his boar story. Webb had a firm grasp on Madame Bellegarde's attention. It was the most private opportunity she'd had with Harper all evening, and she did not want to waste it.

"I know the song well," said Harper in a soft voice. "When did you first hear it?"

"Only recently," replied Evelyn. "But I must confess that I don't know how it ends."

"A song interrupted is a terrible thing...do you remember the last verse you heard?"

"She had just seen William walking with his new lady gay," said Evelyn with keen interest. "I need to know what happens next."

Harper tutted quietly. "It's not a happy ending," he said.

"I'd still very much like to hear it," said Evelyn.

"Very well," said Harper quietly. In a soft voice, he recited the last verse, speaking the words in an almost lyrical fashion, but he did not sing them. Not in the manner he had before.

> She procured a pair of pistols
> On the ground where she did stand
> There she shot bold William Taylor
> And the lady at his right hand

"Goodness," said Evelyn. "She killed both of them? That was not the ending that I expected."

Harper nodded.

"Jealousy. So it is with every romance in history, my lady. There can only ever be two lovers, not three. The moment there are three, romance becomes tragedy. At least for one of the party."

Evelyn's brow furrowed, and she pulled her legs free from Harpers, hooking them under her chair.

"What if two people get separated by circumstances beyond their control? What if fate doesn't let them ever be together?"

"I'd say that defines a tragedy," said Harper. "But I would imagine the brief time spent together might allow for a beautiful memory that outlasts their time together."

"Or perhaps a terrible scar that never heals," said Evelyn. She looked into Harper's eyes, trying to decipher his thoughts. Evelyn had become so lost in her conversation she had not realized Madame Bellegarde leaning in closer to her.

She could smell the wine on her breath as Madame Bellegarde whispered in her ear. "Speaking of songs...I hope you haven't forgotten that you promised to regale us with a song this evening, sweet child." Evelyn suddenly felt her earlier appetite turn against her as her stomach churned.

"Please... no..." she whispered back. But it was too late.

"My lord," began Madame Bellegarde. Edmond turned from his conversation. "I believe we spoke earlier that Lady Evelyn would love to opportunity to sing for you?"

"Oh, yes," said Edmond. "I'd quite forgotten after all the excitement of the evening."

"If you'd prefer I didn't..." began Evelyn, feeling her stomach heave.

"Nonsense!" Edmond exclaimed brightly. "I am sure we would

all enjoy a song while we digest. Wouldn't we, gentlemen?" The rest of the men all chimed in, agreeing that they would love to hear her sing. All of them except Harper, who just watched her with a strange expression.

"Very well," said Evelyn, pushing back from her chair. She took a few steps backward and drew herself up straight. The movement helped her stomach to settle. "I thought about what I should sing," she began slowly, "and I remembered some songs from my childhood. I felt that since Madame Bellegarde has only recently come back into my life, that I would sing one of the songs she used to sing me."

Though there were seven pairs of eyes on her, the only gaze she felt was Harper's. His eyes were looking straight inside her, but he wasn't smiling. He seemed to know she was uncomfortable and was trying to show his support. At least, that's how Evelyn chose to interpret his expression as she opened her mouth and began to sing. She closed her eyes but held the image of Harper watching her as she sang. It was a Christmas carol that Madame Bellegarde had sung to her as a child. The tune was somber, but she knew all the words. More importantly, she felt that singing in a different language might mask her lack of talent.

> Entre le bœuf et l'âne gris
> Dort, dort, dort le petit fils,
> Mille anges divins, mille séraphins
> Volent à l'entour de ce grand Dieu d'amour.
>
> Entre les pastoureaux jolis,
> Dort, dort, dort le petit fils,
> Mille anges divins, mille séraphins
> Volent à l'entour de ce grand Dieu d'amour.

Entre les roses et les lys,
Dort, dort, dort le petit fils,
Mille anges divins, mille séraphins
Volent à l'entour de ce grand Dieu d'amour.

Entre les deux bras de Marie,
Dort, dort, dort le petit fils,
Mille anges divins, mille séraphins
Volent à l'entour de ce grand Dieu d'amour.

Edmond was the first to rise from his chair and applaud. It was as though he was attending an opera and had just witnessed the performance of a lifetime. The others stood and applauded as well. When Evelyn opened her eyes, Harper was the first thing she saw. He gave her a polite, subtle nod as he applauded her with the others. She gave a bashful curtsy to the room and returned to her seat. Once she was seated, the rest of the party returned to their seats as well. Edmond loudly waxed lyrical to the other men about what a spectacular voice Evelyn had as Madame Bellegarde leant over and whispered to her again.

"That was magnifique, bravo child."

Evelyn gave her old mentor a dark look. "If you ever do that to me again, you'll be cleaning the latrines in Dunshire for the rest of your years." She tried to make it sound like a threat, but she knew she could never stay angry at Madame Bellegarde, and even as she said the words, a smirk tried to sneak onto her face.

"Well, this evening it is my turn to have learned a lesson," said Madame Bellegarde with her hands raised in apology.

"Oh?" asked Evelyn, reaching for her wineglass. She realized her hand was shaking as she took a long drink.

"Lady Evelyn Dalton should never be underestimated. It is just as Captain Harper said, never underestimate a woman. And you have become a brilliant, young woman." Madame Bellegarde raised her glass and clinked it to Evelyn's. "À votre santé"

"À la tienne," said Evelyn in return.

E velyn breathed a sigh of relief when the door to her room clicked closed behind her. She slid the bolt into its hinge and locked the door from the inside. She was used to having a fire lit in her room when she entered, but there were no open fireplaces on the Vestal. Instead, she felt a chill as she entered the room. Carefully, she patted every lump on her bed, making sure there were no one-eyed intruders waiting for her. Convinced she was indeed alone, she flopped down backward onto her quilts.

The dinner had been long and there seemed no end to the courses that Duncan had laboriously prepared for the captain's guests. By the time all the food had been eaten, even Weaver was enjoying himself. It struck Evelyn that he had never been allowed to sit at the table when there was a feast in Airedale. He was always working as he watched every social occasion for signs of trouble. She resolved she would invite him to dine with her in Dunshire before he had to return to Airedale, giving her an opportunity to thank the man who had been entrusted with her safety for so many years.

After her singing, Webb had taken the opportunity to sing a song of his own. Even Edmond, after enough wine had been poured, sang a song he'd learnt from his governess. She had thought about asking Harper to sing, but she also wanted to keep his performance private. Something just for her to enjoy.

Edmond had escorted her back to her room once the last course was cleared away. Harper had farewelled them as they left and said he needed to thank Mr. Duncan for his efforts before he returned to his quarters. The other guests had remained, free to finish the wine that Harper had provided for the evening. Madame Bellegarde seemed to have no contrition about staying behind and continuing to enjoy the evening, so Evelyn had simply said goodnight and left.

She felt too tired to remove her dress, even though it was uncomfortable to lie down in. She stretched her hands out behind her and felt something brush against her fingertips. The letter! She had completely forgotten about it after she had let Blackbeard out of her window. She sat bolt upright and looked down at the now scrunched parchment in her hand. She felt nervous as she broke the wax seal. With trembling hands, she unfolded the letter and held it out in front of her.

> *For my Evelyn,*
>
> *Ever since I first saw you, my waking mind has been consumed by thoughts of you. No woman has ever captured my heart and my affection so rapidly and completely as you have. You are more than my equal in wits and charm and you are more beautiful a woman than a man like me could possibly deserve. And yet I am compelled in my attempts to claim you as you have so effectively claimed me.*
>
> *I would know every inch of your body and every corner of your mind. I would spend every spare moment I have left*

in this life learning what pleases you and mastering the art of that pleasure. If you would let me discover that knowledge, and in turn discover me, I will be waiting for you each night you are aboard the Vestal.

Behind the painting on the wall opposite your bed is a small doorway. The ladder behind it leads directly to my quarters. There is a key in the top drawer of your desk. It unlocks the latch at the top of the ladder. I cannot come down to you, you can only come to me.

The choice to be with me must be yours to make. All I can promise is that if you find yourself in my quarters and in my arms, then I will give my all to see that you receive pleasure beyond your deepest desires. Everything I am and everything I have is yours,

With love,

Your Captain

Evelyn stared at the parchment in front of her long after she had finished reading its words. Her fatigue and full belly had vanished and been replaced by complete shock. She could feel Declan Harper's cold, painted eyes staring down at her from his position on the wall. She was certain that he didn't approve of being used as a secret doorway between her room and his son's. She stood up from her bed and moved to the desk. Her hands trembled as she opened the top drawer. A small key was the only occupant of the large drawer, just as the letter had stated.

If Harper had told the truth about the key, then had he told the truth about everything else he had written? Had she claimed him, even without intending to, as completely as he stated? And if that were the case, was he truly prepared to make her pleasure his life's ambition? She thought back to their first encounter, when her body had been pressed against the cold stone of the Great Hall. She remembered how her legs had trembled at his touch. She remembered the temperature of the room seeming hotter. The sounds of the celebration seeming louder. Her senses peaked in a way she had never known before or since. She wanted to feel that way again.

Though her cabin had been cold when she entered, she suddenly felt very warm. Her mind wandered back to the dinner table. She remembered feeling the touch of Captain Harper's boot running up her leg. Another secret they shared as everyone else around them conversed and ate. The feeling of him touching her again, even through their clothing, made her flush. More than his touch, she remembered his words. She had looked right at him as he said the word. 'Love.' His private declaration to her made in such a public setting.

She let her imagination dwell on the possibilities that could arise if she turned the key to the captain's quarters and joined him for the evening. She knew it would only be her that was fighting to keep her honor intact. Harper would pluck her flower with no compunction and, in so doing, would mark her as an unfit bride for Edmond Tallisker. She honestly did not know if she had the resolve to resist him once he put his hands on her again.

She took the key in her hand. It felt odd to her that such a heavy decision weighed so little. It sat neatly in the center of her palm, unassuming and simple. "Just a key," she said to herself, but she knew full well what it would unlock within her. There had been almost no sound from Harper's quarters since she had returned to hers. No singing. Not heavy boots on the floorboards. She wondered if he had even returned from the dinner. If she went to his quarters, would she be alone? The idea of being alone in Harper's quarters was almost as thrilling as the prospect of being with him. She could rummage through his affects, pry into the most secretive part of his life and learn more about him.

As she paced back and forth in her cabin, key in hand, mind racing, she heard Harper's cabin door open. There was a brief, muffled sound of conversation before she heard the door click closed and the sound of footsteps crossing the floor. She strained to hear more. The sounds of the wind and ocean and the creaking of the Vestal's hull masked more definable noises. She took a deep breath, clutched the key firmly in her hand, and took a bold step toward the portrait of Declan Harper.

"You're in my way, old man," she said defiantly. Her fingers hooked under the frame of the portrait and pulled gently. When it didn't budge, she pulled harder, her slender fingers straining as Declan Harper remained firm. She placed her foot on the wall for balance and pulled her whole weight against the frame. She could feel the Vestal pitch in the water, leaning in with her as she pulled. Clearly, the ship wanted Evelyn to go to her captain as it moved with her. Finally, reluctantly, Declan Harper gave up his defiant stand, and the portrait swung out toward her on heavy hinges. Her fingers slipped, and she tumbled backward onto the bed, her dress tangling her feet and sending her sprawling.

She looked up from her bed at the open doorway. A ladder had been built into the room behind the portrait. She stared at it for a long while, knowing full well what it would mean if she were to climb it. She took a deep breath, gathered herself up, and stepped into the small, confined space. With some degree of difficulty, she pulled her dress around her waist to give her legs more freedom. She gripped the wrung just above her head and pulled herself up. She only had to take two steps before her head was level with the ceiling. As Harper had promised, the latch was locked firmly. He clearly had no intention of stealing into her room uninvited. Above her, she heard the scratching of a quill on parchment. Awkwardly, she took one hand off the ladder and slotted the key into the lock. It clicked loudly as she turned the key and disengaged the latch. The sound of writing above her stopped suddenly. She could hear the scrape of a chair moving against the floorboards and the sound of footsteps coming toward her.

Light spilled down into the dark room as Harper lifted the trapdoor that had been built into the floor of his quarters. "My lady," he said softly, almost in disbelief. He sank to his knees and offered her his hand, helping her to make the last step of the journey. Once she was standing on solid ground, he closed the trapdoor behind her and rose back to his feet. They stood for a moment, staring at each other, neither completely sure of what to do or say first. Harper held his arms out to her, and she felt herself slowly walk toward him. She let herself be wrapped in his tight embrace. She felt the now familiar coarseness of his beard against her cheek, and he moved to kiss her. She opened her mouth to his, accepting his advance and giving into passion.

"Days between touches are far too long," said Harper, breaking their first kiss.

"I've come to agree with that," she said. "You have been on my mind constantly, the sole occupation of my waking thoughts."

"You can't imagine how that makes me feel," said Harper. He continued to hold her tightly, moving to kiss her neck. Evelyn felt a shiver run through her entire body. The room swayed around her as the ship rocked gently in the ocean, held fast only by her lover's embrace.

Her eyes fell on the display of swords Harper had on his wall, and an idea formed in her mind. "Do you truly believe that it was love that made Read and Bonny fight so strongly?" Harper stopped kissing her neck, only for as long as it took him to answer.

"Yes."

"But they knew how to hold a sword, too," she whispered into his ear. She let her hand trace down to Harper's trousers, her fingertips brushing over his firmness.

"Yes," he said hungrily.

"Will you show me how to hold a sword?" she asked coyly.

"Oh, God, yes," he said.

She stepped back from him, watching as he breathed heavily with lust and desire. She made a show of looking at the swords on the wall behind him. He turned around, then turned back to her. A puzzled look on his face.

"I want to be able to fight as passionately as Read and Bonny," she said. "I want to be able to fight for what I love."

Harper looked back at the swords mounted on the wall and sighed. "You want me to teach you swordplay?" he said, his entire body deflating as she nodded. "Right now?" he asked. She nodded again.

"Yes, right now," she said sweetly. "I may never get another chance to learn from you."

"There are many other things we may never get a chance to do as well, my lady," said Harper, desperation clinging to the edge of his voice. Evelyn just nodded again toward the swords. Harper sighed, giving in to her. He took one of the shorter blades from the wall and delicately handed it to her. She drew the blade eagerly.

"Show me how it works."

Harper came and stood behind her. She could feel his body pressing into hers. Even through the fabric of her dress, she could feel his hardness against her backside. Harper put his arms around her, trailing them up from her waist, over her breasts, and then down her arms. "This is a defensive stance," he said softly into her ear as he manipulated her arms. "If you are ever charged," he positioned her hands just to the left of her waist and tilted her hands until the sword was pointing upwards. Evelyn felt she was being shown a position that allowed Harper the most convenient ways to touch her. She felt his foot come between her legs, gently guiding her feet to find the right stance. "Keep your knees bent, spread your feet like this…" he pushed against her feet slightly until she shifted them.

He let go of her, his fingers dragging across her body as he lowered his hands. "The point of the blade should be aimed at your opponent's chest or neck," he said as he walked around to stand in front of her. "I'm a little taller than you, so you might find it easier to point at my chest." Evelyn nodded and gripped the hilt of the sword tightly in her hands. "If an enemy is dashing toward you, keep your sword up like this and let them do the work for you." She nodded and let the tip of the blade hover less than an inch away from Harper's chest. Their eyes met and he smiled. "I don't think I've told you how beautiful your eyes are," he said.

Evelyn said nothing but let the tip of the blade rest against his chest. She could feel his body stiffen as the point pressed into the fabric of his shirt, but his expression didn't change. He was still dressed in his evening attire, though he had removed his jacket. Now nothing, save the thin white garment, stood between the blade and his heart. With the utmost care, she cut a line through the shirt, lowering the sword down to his waist until she had opened it up completely. He gave her a cool, unyielding look as she stepped toward him.

She dropped the sword, letting it clank to the floor and placed her hand through the opening she had cut in his shirt. She stretched her hand over his firm chest, feeling the soft hair between her fingertips. She leant in, clenching her hand slightly, pulling at his chest hair. "Mine," she said to him, trying to replicate the same tone he had used in the chapel.

He stretched out a hand and lifted her chin so that her eyes met his again. "Yes," he said. "Yours." He leant down to kiss her. It was as if she had lit a fire inside him. She felt his passion grow as their tongues danced, his hands moving over every inch of her body, pulling at her clothes. Her hands began to wander his body, exploring him more fully than she had before. Suddenly, he broke the kiss. "Enough of this," he said sternly. "I need to taste you."

He kissed her again, his spare hand trailing through her soft hair and brushing at her cheek. She felt his hands grip her firmly around her waist before he lifted her roughly and planted her on his desk. Once she was sitting in front of him, he traced his hands up the fabric of her dress and back down her bare arms, finally stopping as they grasped her wrists. He nuzzled his chin against hers, lifting her lips to meet his as he kissed her deeply again. She was at his mercy, completely his. He kept her held firmly to his desk as he breathed a groan of pleasure into her lips while kissing her. His was a soft, deep rumble born from desire. She kissed back harder than she ever had, spurred on by the sounds of his pleasure. He released her hands, and she felt her entire body sigh. He stared into her eyes as he placed a hand on each of her shoulders and pushed her back. She let herself sink backward onto his desk.

She closed her eyes as his hands moved to her dress, lifting it up and sprawling it over the desk. She breathed in deeply as he exposed her bare legs, his warm hands running over her soft thighs. She gasped as he dropped to his knees in front of her. "I will master the art of your pleasure," he said, reciting his letter to her.

"Yes," she breathed, letting her head lie back on the desk as she reveled in the sensation.

His hands locked around her rear, squeezing her soft flesh. She gasped again, loudly, as she felt the warmth of his tongue trace up her thigh and kiss her tenderly between her legs. She almost felt her entire body rise off the desk as he began to pleasure her. "You…" was all she could muster before another sharp gasp escaped her mouth. She felt her captain rise, her knees falling over his shoulders. At first, she thought it was so he could better angle himself for her pleasure, but she soon felt fingers pressing gently against her lips. In her ecstasy, she had forgotten where she was and how loud her moan had been. She moaned her next breath of pleasure into Harper's hand, and she felt his body stiffen as she did.

She couldn't tell how long they stayed like this. His tongue was like a sword as it artfully danced around her. A thrust deep inside her, a parry across her, a lunge as he brought her whole body forward into his face. Her hands fell to his shoulders, and he reveled in the feeling of her firm grasp as she writhed in front of him. In the dim candlelight of Harper's quarters, she felt herself explode. Her entire body lit up as his tongue traced circles around her. She bit down on his hand to stop herself from screaming so loud the entire ship would hear. Reluctantly, Harper withdrew himself from her skirts and rose back to his feet. He looked down at her with a broad smile, pleased with his accomplishment. She propped herself up on her elbows so that she could look back at him. "I have never felt like that before," she said through long, deep breaths.

"If I had my way, my lady, you would never stop feeling like that."

Evelyn remained silent for a moment.

"What is it?" asked Harper.

"I…" she began, the last of her resistance fading as she finished her sentence. "I want to make you feel like that as well," she said.

Edmond had woken early in the morning. Though his head felt slightly groggy from the wine, he rose feeling happier than he had in a long time. Dining with Evelyn had been a pleasurable experience. Indeed, with each exchange he shared with her, he grew more comfortable with the idea that she would soon be his wife. He was impressed by how capable she was at holding herself in conversation, even against seasoned veterans like Madame Bellegarde and Captain Harper. His thoughts remained of Evelyn as he dressed and readied himself for the day ahead.

It was cold on the deck of the Vestal. The sun had not yet fully made its way over the horizon and the chill of the night lingered. A heavy fog had rolled in from the coast, and Edmond struggled to make out any signs of land. He knew the Vestal would remain close to the coast for the entire journey, as it had done when they sailed to Airedale. This was the first time that Edmond had not been able to see any sign of land in his life.

The soft lapping sounds of the waves against the hull reminded him of his very full bladder and he walked toward the bow of the Vestal. As much as he was trying to adjust to life at sea, he was still uncomfortable with passing water over the side of the ship in plain sight of dozens of men. He preferred, when possible, to find a private moment at the front of the ship. With his back to the foremast, he felt shielded from prying eyes as he undid his trousers and relieved himself.

Most of the crew were still sleeping and, in the morning's quiet, he was acutely aware of the loud splashing he was making. He stared straight forward, eyes not straying, looking deep into the fog as his cheeks flushed red with embarrassment. To distract himself from his own bashfulness, he focused on trying to make out the shapes of the mountains hidden under their thick white blankets. The fog ran down the slopes like a river until it spilled out from the land and over the ocean. He strained his eyes as he tried to see deeper into the mist. Something caught his eye, sitting high above the waves. A shape that disappeared too quickly for him to make out.

He became nervous. Had the Vestal drifted too close to land? Were they in danger of running aground? He looked back over his shoulder, making sure someone was still manning the helm. Mr. Trent was at the ship's wheel with both hands firmly gripped on the handles. Reassured, Edmond turned back to the task of fastening his trousers. His task complete, he took one last look back at the fog. He squinted hard against the gloom of the early morning. Slow, subtle movement caught his eye again. There was no mistaking it this time. Almost perfectly camouflaged in the fog, Edmond could see the rippling of sailcloth and the faint outline of a mast.

When Harper had transported him from Dunshire to Airedale, they had passed several ships with no cause for alarm or concern, but something felt cold at the bottom of Edmond's stomach. He scanned the deck for the nearest crewman and walked briskly toward him. "I say," he called. The young crewman looked up from his work and gave a polite nod to Edmond.

"Good morning, my lord."

"Yes, yes, a fine morning to you as well," said Edmond hurriedly. He was nervous, but there was no call to avoid being polite. "Would you mind coming with me for a moment?" The crewman looked at Edmond uncertainly. "I believe I see a ship out there," Edmond pointed to the fog. The crewman looked out in the direction that Edmond was pointing.

"From the west? Unlikely my lord, there's no ports nearby and we're close to land..." he stopped in mid-sentence.

"There, you see it?!" Edmond waved his arm more dramatically.

"Aye... I see it," something about the change in the crewman's tone made Edmond feel nauseous. The cold feeling in the pit of his stomach seemed to be rising up toward his throat. "And she's coming straight toward us.

The sails disappeared behind the thick fog again, and Edmond felt a firm grip on his shoulder. "I'll raise the alarm below deck, my lord. Get to the quarterdeck and tell Mr. Trent. We best wake the captain!" Edmond watched as the crewman sprinted toward the steps down to the gun deck. His own feet felt heavier than they should as he ran toward the quarterdeck. Any lingering effects of his hangover quickly subsided, as fear and panic pulsed through his body. His heart pounded in his chest as he ran harder than he had ever run in his life.

He was almost breathless by the time he reached the stairs leading to the quarterdeck. "Morning, my lord," called Mr. Trent from the helm. The quartermaster looked down at Edmond as he clumsily, urgently, made his way up the steps. "What's got you in such a fluster?"

"Another...ship" panted Edmond, pointing out to the fog. Mr. Trent's eyes narrowed. "Heading toward us."

"You sure, my lord?" Mr. Trent took out his spyglass and

extended it to its full length. As he scanned, Edmond could hear the alarm bell ring from below the main deck.

Edmond counted only four rings of the bell before Captain Harper stormed onto the quarterdeck. Harper, dressed only in his nightshirt and breeches, had a wild look about him.

"Report," he barked coarsely.

"Lord Tallisker says he spied a ship converging on us from the fog, Captain," said Mr. Trent, lowering the spyglass. "Can't say I can make it out myself."

"Glass," commanded Harper with an outstretched hand. Edmond held his breath as Harper held the spyglass to his eye. "Alter course, Mr. Trent," he said, without lowering the spyglass. "Take us out to sea and away from this damned fog."

"Aye, Captain," Mr. Trent grabbed the wheel of the ship and began to spin it quickly. Harper lowered the spyglass.

"You've a hunter's eye, Lord Edmond," said Harper. His dry throat gave his tone a particularly grave cadence. He handed Edmond the glass. "Keep your eye on those sails and don't lose sight of them."

Edmond nodded. "I can do that, Captain."

Harper turned his attention to the main deck as his crew started to scramble about. He caught sight of Mr. Webb as he made his way blearily up the steps from the gun deck.

"Mr. Webb," called Harper. "Have the crew report to their stations and then join me on the bridge."

"Aye, sir," replied Webb with a quick salute.

Edmond could hear whistles piping and drums beating as Webb and Harper barked commands to the crew. He kept his attention focused firmly on the fog. Occasionally, he caught glimpses of the sails, but they quickly disappeared in the fog. As the Vestal slowly turned away from the coast, he struggled to keep his eye trained on the target. Edmond kept one hand firmly on the railing as he leant forward. His hand was trembling, so he pushed the eyeglass harder against his skull to keep it steady. "Anything, Lord Edmond?"

"They're following us, Captain, but I can't get a clear view of them. They seem to be all over the place... almost as if..." Edmond didn't like where his thoughts were taking him.

"There is more than one ship," Harper finished Edmond's thought for him.

"I can't be sure though," said Edmond, lowering the spyglass and handing it to Harper.

Harper took it and placed it to his eye.

"Yes, my lord. I think you're right. Two ships, close together, trying to hide that fact from us until it's too late. They've got a cunning commander leading them.

Webb had made his way to the quarterdeck, closely followed by Weaver. "The crew have reported to their stations, Captain, awaiting your orders." Webb stood to one side as Weaver pushed his way toward Harper.

"What the bloody hell is going on, Captain?" Weaver sounded flustered.

"We appear to have attracted some attention, Mr. Weaver," replied Harper.

"Attention? What kind of attention? Speak plainly, man."

"An ambush, I suspect." Harper's tone was flat. He was stating a fact without the slightest hint of emotion. "We're a considerable distance from any ports. The ships have likely been here overnight, counting on the morning fog to conceal them. Their bearing suggests they sighted us, possibly a scout with enough elevation saw the lights of our lanterns... though the 'how' is irrelevant now."

Edmond could see the outlines of the ships forming more clearly as they reached the edge of the fog. "The Vestal is a fast ship, though. I remember you saying you've never met her equal in speed,

Captain." Edmond looked desperately at Harper, Trent, and Webb. Their expressions didn't reassure him.

"Aye, she's fast," answered Webb. "But we're fully loaded with provisions and ammunition. Not to mention Lady Evelyn's personal effects and her dowry—"

Weaver turned angrily to Webb. "You're saying Lady Evelyn is the cause of this—"

"Nobody is saying that, Mr. Weaver," said Trent reassuringly. "The point is the Vestal isn't as fast as she might normally be."

"And though Lady Evelyn does not have any of the blame for this situation, she is most assuredly the target. Along with her dowry," said Captain Harper.

Minutes dragged like hours as the Vestal gathered every scrap of wind the crew could harness to outrun her pursuers. Edmond stayed on the quarterdeck alongside the captain and his officers. The Vestal had pulled far enough away from the fog to draw her ambushers out of their concealment. Mr. Webb had joined Edmond at the railing, his eyes fixed on the approaching ships. There was no doubt they were gaining on the Vestal. "The Roseline and the Juniper, Captain," called Webb, lowering his spyglass. "Bloody, pack rats," he muttered with disgust.

"I'm sorry?" said Edmond. "I've never heard that term before, Mr. Webb."

"They're packet ships, my lord," explained Webb. He pointed out toward the two ships. "Mostly used for transport, they stuff as many men into them as possible and they don't much care where they find their crews. Mostly criminals and ne'er-do-wells that find their way onto them. Closest thing we've got to pirates in these waters."

"How awful," said Edmond. He remembered his first conversation with Evelyn, telling her how he had longed for excitement and adventure at sea. The reality of his situation was far less exhilarating than he had hoped for.

"See how high they sit in the water, my lord?" Edmond nodded, pretending he could see what Webb meant. "They've stripped their cannons right back, taken the weight out to give them more speed. Just a couple of guns on the bow to give chase to us. They'll try for our mast and sails with them. Means they're looking to board us, rather than scuttle us."

Harper overheard his first mate talking and glanced back at the ships. They were sitting higher in the water than he would have expected. He knew full well the reason the Vestal was slower than normal was because he had loaded her with extra ammunition and supplies for surplus to his needs. He had wanted a longer voyage so that he could extend what little time he had with Evelyn. Harper cursed himself, knowing his lust for Evelyn had endangered not only his men, but also the woman he loved. He was confident that the Vestal would overcome the odds facing her, but not without some losses to her crew. "How many men do you think those ships could hold?" Edmond asked Webb nervously.

"I'd guess a hundred men or more to each ship. Maybe two hundred and fifty between them..." Edmond's heart sank. The Vestal boasted a complement of sixty men. Sixty-five with Weaver and his men aboard. They'd be outnumbered four to one if they were boarded.

"My lord," called Captain Harper. Edmond and Webb turned to face him. "I think now would be an appropriate time for you to secure yourself in your quarters. Your keen eye brought us the time we needed to draw our enemy out, but your part in this fight is over." Edmond swallowed, aware he was about to say something that would put his life in danger.

"Captain," he said carefully. "I will stand and fight with the rest of your men if these 'pack rats' come anywhere near Lady Evelyn."

"No man here is judging your courage, my lord, but I cannot risk your life in the coming battle." Harper's tone was stern. He disliked being argued with on his own bridge.

"If these men are here to claim Lady Evelyn and I do not stand to fight for her, then I am not fit to be her husband," Edmond stared Harper in the eye with a fierce determination.

Harper seemed to consider this for a moment, and Edmond used the silence to push his point further. "You told me that a man defends what he loves with his life, no matter the cost or the danger."

"So I did," said Harper, recalling his words from the previous evening. He had wanted to show Evelyn how much he cared for her, but he also seemed to have unwittingly stirred something inside of Edmond.

"Well, Captain, I will defend what I love, and I do not care about the cost or the danger." Harper smiled approvingly. For a moment, he stopped seeing Edmond as a clumsy and pompous boy and saw the man that was underneath.

"Very well, my lord. How do you intend to join the fight?"

"I'm the finest shot onboard this ship. Give me Mr. Weaver and his men, along with those of your crew who can fire a musket. If those pack rats try to board us, I'll defend the railing." Harper looked at Edmond. "The finest shot onboard this ship, are you?"

"Have you heard the story of the boar I killed in Lord Dalton's forest?" said Edmond evenly.

"I heard it was the start of legend," said Harper.

"The next chapter of that legend is written on this ship, Captain." Harper couldn't help but feel a sense of pride as Edmond stood his ground. It was a strange feeling to gain respect for the young

Lord while he pursued Evelyn's affections with complete abandon. He'd seen Edmond grow in confidence considerably since their first encounter. Now he saw a young man that was eager to prove himself worthy of both the title he held and the woman he was to marry. A man who was prepared to risk death to prove that worth. Harper pushed his own conflict to one side and got on with the task of readying his ship for battle. "Very well then. Mr. Webb will accompany you to round up the men and get you armed." Edmond nodded and left with the first mate to prepare. Harper watched them as they moved with purpose, rounding up men and heading to the armory. The prospect of action seemed to cure Edmond of his usual clumsiness. He was ready for a fight, and he seemed determined not to fall behind.

"This is far too reckless a move, Captain," Weaver stood over Harper, using his height to press his point. "If anything happens to that young Lord, you and I won't live to see another dawn on land..."

Harper nodded. It was reckless. But Edmond was a lord, and he was entitled to partake in the combat if he chose to. Harper briefly considered what might happen if Edmond were killed in battle. It would certainly remove one complication from his relationship with Evelyn, though it would likely introduce a bigger problem. Harper may find it hard to continue his affair with Evelyn if Lord Tallisker had him executed for losing his son. "I'll make sure they don't get the opportunity to board us," said Harper, though he knew his chances of sinking both vessels before they closed the distance on the Vestal were slim. Weaver nodded.

"What's your first move then?"

Harper looked down at himself, still dressed in his night clothes. "I am going to command a ship in battle, and I'd rather be dressed for the occasion. I can't think of a single captain who won a battle in his nightshirt."

"Do you truly think you can keep them at bay?"

"Let me worry about those ships. You just concentrate on keeping Edmond Tallisker safe if it comes down to a close quarters fight, Mr. Weaver. You're quite right, of course..." added Harper dryly. "We'll both likely end up swinging from the gallows if that young man comes to harm."

Evelyn woke feeling like she had hardly even closed her eyes. Dinner had concluded late, but her encounter with Harper had seemed to last an eternity. She had no idea what time it was when she had made her way back down the ladder to her quarters and slid the lock back across the trapdoor. Through her small window, she had seen the first signs of day beginning as the night sky turned pale, but there was still no sign of the sun. Now it was in its ascension as light spilled into her cabin, forcing her to wake. Her tired mind raced as she lay in her bed and listened to the sounds of the crew about the deck beginning their day. Bells and whistles seemed to be commonplace in shipboard life. Though she couldn't make out the words, she could hear Harper's voice over the background noise as he bellowed his commands. She wondered how anyone ever slept aboard the Vestal. There rarely seemed to be a moment of absolute silence. Her hand moved under her pillow and retrieved the crumpled-up letter. It surprised her how well Harper had captured his passion for her in his written words. She had never thought he would be as bold on paper as he was in person. Her eyes lingered over one sentence, reading the words over and over. 'I am compelled in my attempts to claim you as you have so effectively claimed me...'

He certainly had been compelled, as he had held her body down on his desk and pleasured her with his tongue. She felt her body react to the memory. Her hand brushing over her breasts before tracing down her stomach. Her fingers tentatively brushed against the fabric of her nightgown, not yet ready to explore further. Her mind wandered back to her own actions of the previous night. "I want to make you feel like that as well," she said to herself.

Her legs felt weak when she rose from Harper's desk, but she was determined to return the gift he had given her. She placed a hand on his chest as she rose to meet him. The cut she had run through the garment made access to his body easier, and she leant in and placed a kiss softly on his sternum. She felt she had become familiar with the softness of his lips, so she turned her attention to the unexplored contours of his body. She pulled at his shirt, exposing more of his chest as she kissed down toward his nipple, her tongue enjoying the salty taste of his skin.

Her free hand brushed against his trousers, and she could hear his excited breath in her ear as her fingers brushed against him. She traced soft circles around him, unsure of what her next move should be. His hand reached out for her face, stroking the soft strands of hair that fell over her cheeks as she kissed his bare chest. She thought back to the gardens at Airedale Keep and the fornicating servants she had witnessed when she was younger. She remembered a woman on her knees, in front of one of the guards. He had his eyes closed but a look of pure rapture on his face as she manipulated him with her mouth. Just as Harper had done with Evelyn. She wanted to return that favor, for him to know the pleasure that he had caused within her.

Delicately, she lowered her hands to his belt. The moment she did, though, all her fingers seemed to transform into thumbs. Her digits fumbled hopelessly with Harper's elaborate belt buckle, and she could feel her cheeks turning red with embarrassment as she failed in her task. She could hear Harper's breath in her ear and knew from the sound that he was smiling. "Would you like some assistance, my lady?" he asked. Evelyn ignored the overture of smugness in his tone and pressed onward, finally unhinging the belt from its irksome buckle.

"Are you in a hurry, Captain Harper? Is there somewhere else you would rather be?"

Harper put his hands on her shoulders and pushed her back slightly, just enough so that he could look her in the eyes. "There is nowhere on this Earth or any other that I would rather be."

Evelyn looked into his eyes. "Good," she said. "Then don't think to rush me." She tugged hard on his belt, ripping it through the loops. "See?" she said triumphantly. "No assistance required." She pushed Harper back until he was up against the wall of his cabin. She chose her destination carefully, making sure that she didn't push him backward onto a sword or into a cabinet. Harper, for his part, allowed her to push him wherever she pleased, enjoying the feeling of her lust powering her actions.

"Does it feel familiar?" Evelyn whispered the question into his ear as her hands return to undressing him.

"I don't recall ever being pressed against a wall in such a fashion," replied Harper playfully.

"Perhaps you've always been too eager to be the one doing the pressing," said Evelyn. She breathed in deeply as she lowered herself to her knees. She could feel the seams of her dress stretch as she knelt before Harper, its designer never having intended the garment for such an action.

Evelyn hooked her fingers under Harper's trousers, closed her eyes, and pulled them down. She kept her eyes closed as her nostrils filled with a musky, sweaty aroma. She was unsure if she found the smell pleasant or nauseating but didn't dwell on the thought. When she opened her eyes, she almost wished she hadn't. She had seen one before, though never this close, and even then, she had found it unsettling to look at. She reached out with her fingers and gently wrapped them around Harper. She could practically feel him melting into the wall at her slightest touch. She knew she couldn't be the first woman to handle him. At his age, Harper was likely to have had several lovers before her. But she was determined to be the best, the most memorable.

She stroked him for a short while, watching with a bemused expression as he grew longer and harder in her hands. She was glad that Harper had thrown his head back and closed his eyes, as she was sure her curious expression would likely have caused him some concern. After some trepidation, she leant forward so that her forehead was resting on Harper's hip and gave a gentle kiss on his waist. She turned her head slightly, kissing him at the base of his shaft while her fingers continued to stroke him. She kissed him just as she had kissed his lips, tenderly and softly. Slowly, she lowered her hand as she mouthed soft kisses down his length. When she reached the end of her journey, she looked up at him, watching him as she watched him. Slowly, deliberately, she took him into her mouth and began to mimic the actions she had witnessed in the gardens of Airedale. He only held eye contact with her for a moment before his head rolled back in pleasure. He groaned and gasped as she found her pace. Her tongue now felt like an obstacle as she tried to fit him inside her mouth and struggled to find a place for it to settle. She soon realized that the movement of her tongue was pleasing to him and listened to his breathing to work out how best she could use it to her advantage. It took him longer than her to reach his climax. Her tongue and jaw felt fatigued as she relentlessly pursued Harper's pleasure. Her knees, only ever used previously for praying, ached against the hard wooden floorboards. Her back, pulled taught by her restrictive garment, caused her to fidget uncomfortably. But she pushed through all the distractions, her sole focus on achieving her captain's climax. She could tell he was close as his body tightened. She could feel every muscle inside of him tensing as she ran her mouth up and down his seemingly ever hardening manhood.

He gave a gentle push on her shoulders, indicating she should release him. She smiled around him, unwilling to release him, willing him to reach his climax in her mouth as she had in his. She felt powerful as he gave an almost inhuman, guttural grunt and arched back, pressing his body into hers. Her eyes opened wide as an unexpected bolt hit the back of her throat. With Harper still pulsating inside her mouth, she had no choice but to swallow the unknown substance as he continued to explode inside her. Later, he explained he had hoped to spare her from that. But now, as she lay alone in her cabin, she was glad that she had experienced him, tasted him. She was so lost in her memories that she had barely noticed the sounds of the crew were getting louder. Now it was all she could hear. Men were yelling frantically at each other, and she could feel the ship start to turn. Above her, she heard Harper's door shut loudly and the sound of heavy footfall crossing the floor. Only one set of footsteps, she noted as she sat up in bed. She wanted to go to him and embrace him, but she also wanted to find the cause for the commotion on deck.

For a moment, Evelyn considered changing from her nightgown into something more appropriate. Above her, Harper's footsteps sounded frantic, as if he were dashing from one end of his quarters to the other. She decided she did not have time to get changed. She could feel a rising sense of fear in her stomach, a horrible feeling that something was not right.

With more resolve than the previous evening, she pulled Declan Harper's portrait out of her way, keeping her feet steady as she made her way into her secret room. As she climbed the ladder, she wondered how Harper would explain it if it ever got discovered. The climb was considerably easier in the freedom of her nightgown, and she made the steps quickly, unlocking the trapdoor and knocking against it. Seconds felt like minutes as she waited in the cramped, dark interior of the secret passage. She knocked again, more forcefully, and was rewarded by the sound of approaching footsteps. She squinted against the light as Harper opened the trapdoor. "I was worried you were going to leave me in here," said Evelyn indignantly.

"I thought it best to lock the door before letting you into my quarters..." said Harper, looking down at her. "Especially in your nightgown," there was a tone of approval in his voice. He lowered himself so that he could help her make the last steps into his cabin. "I didn't dare think I'd ever be so lucky as to see you like this." He let one hand trace longingly down Evelyn's side. "And if I were able, I would take every advantage I could of this moment."

"Why can't you?" asked Evelyn as Harper moved away from her and made his way with purpose to his desk. She followed him uncertainly.

"We're under attack," said Harper bluntly, opening one of his drawers and withdrawing a pair of pistols. He tucked each into a holster strapped to his chest and then withdrew a second pair. "You will probably never hear me say this to you again, but I want you to return to your chambers and lock the door behind you." Harper turned his attention back to his pistols, placing them in the empty holsters on his belt.

"But I want to fight..." said Evelyn quietly.

Harper pretended not to hear her and made his way to his bedchamber. He flung his wardrobe open and rummaged around for a moment before pulling out a heavy-breasted black jacket. His arms were only halfway inside his jacket before he was heading toward the collection of swords that hung from the wall.

"Did you hear me?" asked Evelyn, her voice finding its strength. "I want to fight with you."

Harper stood with his back to her, looking at the swords in front of him.

"No," he said. There was no malice or anger in his voice, but Evelyn knew that tone. She had heard it from her father. It was a tone that demanded obedience.

"You said that a man defends what he loves with his life, no matter the cost or the danger..." Evelyn hoped that Harper's own words would soften him, but they seemed to have the opposite effect. "You said that the sexes weren't so different, so why can't I—"

"You two..." he cut her off, still not turning. Evelyn's brow furrowed as she tried to comprehend who the captain was referring to. "I don't think anyone has ever listened to every word I've said so keenly. Your damned fiancé just tried the same tactic," said Harper, finally turning. "Now him, I have to listen to, because he's a lord and he gets to choose what battles he wants to fight in. And if he wants to fight for something he loves..." Harper stopped as he saw Evelyn's expression.

"Something he loves?" she asked.

Harper ignored her and pushed on. "He gets to choose his battles. You do not."

Evelyn felt a swarm of rebuttals building up inside her. "What about Anne Bonny or Mary Read? What about William Taylor's lady fair?" she asked. She could feel the tears pricking at the back of her eyes, but she refused to let them surface. She put a hand on his chest. "I want to fight for what I love, just like they did."

"If you think I like saying no to you, then you're mistaken," said

Harper, taking her hand in his. "If you step out onto that deck, you put yourself in danger. I don't think I can command this ship in battle and worry about you in combat at the same time…"

"But…" protested Evelyn.

"If something were to happen to you, I don't know what would happen to me," he leant in to kiss her on the forehead. "I need to know you're as safe as can be when the cannons start to fire. Everything I am about to do is to keep you safe." Evelyn nodded slowly and took a step back from Harper.

"Then please promise that you will come back to me." She looked him up and down, realizing that if the danger they were in was as real as it seemed, there was a chance she may not see him again.

Harper turned away from her, selected a sword, and made his way to the door. "I can only promise you one thing," he said, his hand on the latch. "I will fight harder than I have ever fought before just for the chance to see your face again."

Evelyn's mouth opened, but she couldn't find the words she wanted.

"Go back to your quarters. Stay safe." Harper opened and closed the door in one swift movement. The door shook on its hinges as it slammed closed behind him.

Evelyn didn't move for a moment as the strange sensation of being alone in the captain's quarters washed over her. Harper's inadvertent words were still ringing in her ears. Edmond had said that he loved her and wanted to fight for her. She knew that Edmond had expressed a fondness for her, and she did have a genuine affection for him as well. But love? She couldn't fathom how he had leapt to the conclusion so quickly. They hadn't shared the experiences that she had shared with Harper. There hadn't been any burning passion between them. No stolen moments. She didn't know how it made her feel. The inevitability that she would marry Edmond had never left the back of her mind, and hearing that he felt strongly about her should have made her feel safer about the prospect of a life together with him. But his declaration of love unsettled her. It was something that she couldn't return. Something she felt she didn't deserve. She had already given herself so completely to Harper that to even try to return Edmond's love would be the very definition of deceitful.

She looked at Harper's sword collection. Resting on the wall was the short blade that she had used to slice her lover's shirt open. She moved to it, delicately picked it up from its display hooks, and removed it from its sheath. It didn't feel as heavy as it had the first time she had held it. She swung it through the air, her blood rushing as she did so. She imagined Mary Read slashing her way through the crew of the Tyger as they boarded her ship. Defending what she loved. She moved about the cabin, experimenting with different thrusts and swings. Each time she moved the sword, she was rewarded with the satisfying sound of the honed blade cutting through the air. She stopped as she caught a reflection of herself in Harper's dress mirror. She moved closer to it, examining the girl standing before her in the glass. Her hair, tussled from her movements, gave her a wild look. Her night dress clung tight to her slender frame and revealed her long and delicate arms. Her eyes rested on the blade in her hand. She liked the way she looked holding it. She gave it flourish, watching herself in the mirror as she inexpertly tried to spin the blade in her hand.

A thunderous blast rang through the air, and she dropped the sword in surprise. The point of the blade drove itself hard into the wooden floorboard inches from her bare feet. She didn't have time to look down to check if she had cut herself before she heard a colossal splash. She watched through the rear facing windows of Harper's quarters as water rushed upward over the glass. "Ranging shot, sir!" she heard one man yell over the sound of whistles and alarm bells. Slowly, carefully, Evelyn walked toward the rear of Harper's quarters. She peered around the partition to his bedchambers. His sheets were sprawled over the floor, as if he had erupted from his bed with great urgency. Even with the overwhelming sense of danger, Evelyn wondered what his bed smelled like. How soft it was? What would it feel like to wrap herself in his sheets? She looked up from the bed, through the thick glass of the windows and out to sea. Though the view was blurred from the water running down the panes, she could see two ships with white sails bearing toward the Vestal. She held her breath and watched carefully as she tried to determine how quickly they were gaining.

"Ready on that sail! Prepare to come about!" Harper's voice called out loud against the rest of the noise. A puff of smoke blasted out from the lead ship. The same thunderous roar rang out, followed by the splintering of wood above her. She put a hand to her mouth to stifle her surprised gasp and sat down on Harper's bed to steady herself. She could feel the ship start to turn. The Vestal's captain was turning to fight.

"And he won't fight alone," said Evelyn, drawing herself up. A calm determination came over her as she looked around Harper's cabin. She moved to the dresser, opened the drawers, and rummaged through Harper's clothes. At the bottom of a drawer, she found a pair of black trousers she hoped might fit her. She lifted her nightgown and pulled them up to her waist. She held them with one hand as she fished around for one of Harper's belts. While searching, she stepped on something sharp. The irksome belt buckle that had caused her such trouble the previous evening pointed up at her. "At least it will be secure," she mused as she picked the belt up and wrapped it tightly around her waist. Her fingers turned to thumbs again as she tried desperately to secure the belt through the buckle. Another explosion sounded in the distance. Evelyn heard the loud splash as the cannonball hit the water. She looked down at the perfectly threaded belt. In her panic, instinct had taken over and completed the task for her. She gave the pants a firm tug to check that they wouldn't fall down. Satisfied, she pulled one of Harper's white shirts from the dresser and held it against her. The chest was far broader than her own, but she figured she could stuff the excess material into her trousers. She looked around quickly, checking to make sure she was absolutely, completely alone. She hastily pulled her nightgown over her head and let it fall to the floor before punching her arms through the sleeves of the shirt and tugging it down over her bare chest. The linen of Harper's shirt was considerably courser than the silk of her nightgown; her nipples itched against the fabric. She thought of William Taylor's fair lady, her snowy breasts exposed as her shirt blew open during a fight. "No thank you," said Evelyn, tucking the shirt deep into her trousers. She found a leather sash with two empty holsters on it and threw it over her shoulder, pulling the straps tight against her chest to pin the billowy garment into place. There was a plethora of hats to choose from. Some were gaudy, lined with golden lace, and clearly worn for special occasions. Some seemed more practical, worn for shade when the Vestal ventured to warmer waters. She chose a plain brown leather tricorn. Nondescript and not so large as to fall over her eyes. Carefully, she bundled up her long blonde hair and stowed it away safely in the confines of her hat. She returned to the mirror and gave herself another look. Something was missing. She looked down at her feet and realized they were still bare. She didn't relish the idea of fighting pirates barefoot, but she knew that all of Harper's boots would be ludicrously too large for her. She also knew her own footwear was completely impractical for battle. Poking out from underneath Harper's bed, she spied two brown bed slippers. She slid her feet into them and stepped down hard, testing the soles. They were loose but, given her options, they'd suffice. Satisfied, she took a deep breath, drew herself up, then pulled the sword free from the floorboards and looked back at the mirror. She hefted the sword and gave the stranger looking back at her a defiant nod. She didn't know who the person in the mirror was, but it wasn't Evelyn Dalton, not anymore. Out there, on the decks of the Vestal, were two men who loved her, and she was not ready to just sit back and learn their fates after the battle. She was going to help decide their outcome.

Nicholas Webb knocked again at the door to his own quarters. He could hear the sounds of movement from within, but no answer had come when he called out. As he raised his hand to knock for a third time, the door creaked open an inch. "Oui..." came the croaky voice of Madame Bellegarde. "Madame Florence Bellegarde..." began Webb.

"What time is it?"

"It's early, Madame, very early." said Webb apologetically. "I need to speak with you." The door opened wider. It was clear from her face that Madame Bellegarde had not enjoyed a good night's rest. Her makeup was smeared across her face, her hair tussled, and her eyes hung heavy in her head. Her nightgown was almost as extravagant as the rest of her wardrobe, black with a gold lace pattern. Even in her disheveled and exhausted state, Webb still found her beautiful, and his words quickly failed him as he stood staring at her.

Bellegarde fixed Webb with a look of pure impatience and motioned for him to continue. "I regret to inform you, Madame, that we are under attack." Her expression changed immediately.

"Evelyn..."

"She's under the guard of Lord Dalton's men, she'll be kept safe."

"I should be with her," Madame Bellegarde put a hand on Webb's shoulder to move him out of her way, but the first mate held firm.

"During a battle, the standing orders on the Vestal are for all passengers to return to their cabins and lock the doors. It's so we know where to find you if we need to get to you quickly. Captain would have me strung up if I let you out on the decks now."

Madame Bellegarde tried to push her way through Webb for a second time, but he stood firm. She gave him a long stare, and he shuffled nervously at her gaze. She could tell he was not enjoying the position he was in, and with a dramatic sigh, she relented. "Very well," she said, gathering herself up and clearing her throat. "Thank you for informing me. I will remain here until I am told I can come out." She attempted to slam the door, but Webb stuck his boot in the opening, wincing as his foot took the brunt of her rage. "And now you want to stop me from locking my door as instructed?" she asked haughtily.

"No," replied Webb. He pulled a whistle from his jacket pocket and held it to her through the opening in the doorway. "Please take this. If anything happens to you, anything at all, blow on this whistle and I will come for you. I promise."

Madame Bellegarde opened the door a little wider and took the whistle. "Merci," she said simply. She could see an honest concern for her safety in Webb's eyes. She couldn't remember the last time someone had looked at her like that. She was a servant. A high ranked servant, but a servant, nonetheless. It was her job to show concern for others and rarely in her life had she felt it was reciprocated. She knew that Evelyn loved her the same way a child loves a parent. In their relationship, Madame Bellegarde had always been the protector and comforter. She had never needed Evelyn to show concern for her because it was not her place to do so. Looking into Webb's eyes, she realized that having that connection with someone in her life was something she had been missing for a long time.

"Oh," said Webb, as if remembering something important. "Take this as well." He pulled his pistol from his belt and held it out to her. Madame Bellegarde shook her head.

"No, no, no."

"I'd feel a might better going into this battle if you did have it," said Webb. "I don't want you to have to use it, but if we get boarded and I know you're holding onto it, then it'll be a great comfort to me." Madame Bellegarde hesitated, then held out her hand, taking the weapon from Webb, holding it between her thumb and forefinger and keeping it at arm's length, as if it might explode at any moment.

"It's loaded and ready to fire," said Webb. "If anyone tries to come through that door without announcing themselves, you point that pistol at them and pull the trigger. Don't think twice about it, neither."

Madame Bellegarde nodded. "Thank you, Monsieur Webb. I will pray that I won't need to use it."

"I..." Webb hesitated.

"Go on. Please."

"I very much enjoyed sitting with you last night, Madame Florence Bellegarde. I know we talked about a great many things, but there's still a lot more I want to hear you say. And also, there's a lot more I want to say to you. If it comes to a fight today, then I'll be fighting for the chance to share another meal with you. If you'd have me at your table."

Madame Bellegarde felt her chest tighten at his words. It had been many years since a man had spoken so sweetly to her. "I will make sure I am better dressed for the occasion than I am now," she said with a smile.

Webb smiled weakly back at her. "You look perfect to me just the way you are." He didn't give her a chance to reply as he gave her a quick, but polite bow and hurried to leave before she could see how crimson his face was. Webb felt a sense of relief wash over him when he heard the door to his quarters click shut. Madame Bellegarde was as safe as she could be, given the circumstances. He didn't know what he would do if he heard the sound of her whistle blowing during the battle. Would he drop everything and rush to save her? Abandon his post to be her hero? He didn't know the answers to the questions rising up inside him. He hoped they would stay unanswered for as long as possible.

Fortunately for Nicholas Webb a distraction from his thoughts soon presented itself as Captain Harper burst forth from his quarters and stormed onto the quarterdeck. "All hands, clear for action!" Webb picked up a brisk pace as he made his way to the quarterdeck to join the captain. Around him, the crew flew into a frenzy, each man moving with a well-trained purpose.

"Nick," Mr. Clarke gave a salute to his first mate as they crossed paths.

"Ben," replied Webb, returning the salute.

"Fine mess, this one," said Clarke, turning his head as he continued making his way to the gun deck.

"Just be ready to have those guns blazing, Mr. Clarke."

"No worries on that count, sir. We'll be ready for the bastards!"

"I hope you're right, mate," said Webb under his breath. "By God I hope you're right."

By the time Webb had made it to the quarterdeck, Captain Finn Harper was in his element. He had taken control of the helm from Mr. Trent and his hands were firmly gripped on the ship's wheel. He had a cold, calm look on his face. "Lord Edmond and Mr. Weaver are armed and ready, Captain."

"Good man," said Harper, not taking his eyes off the open ocean in front of them. "Where's your pistol?" Webb's mouth fell open. He was sure Harper hadn't even glanced at him since he had returned to the quarterdeck. Webb said nothing. "You're about to go into battle man, go and get your bloody pistol."

"I..."

Damn it, man, have you lost it again?" said Harper. "You would lose your head if your neck wasn't doing you the service of holding onto it for you."

"I left it with Madame Bellegarde, Captain," said Webb. He spoke the words as quickly as he could, hoping Harper might mishear him. He was ready for Harper to be furious and to send him back down to his quarters to retrieve his weapon from the madame. Instead, the captain pulled one of his own pistols free from his belt and handed it to Webb.

"Well, mate, I'd say that qualifies as telling her how you feel about her."

Webb took the pistol with a nod and stashed it in his belt. "Thank you, Captain. I'll make sure you get it back."

"Clean it first," said Harper. His tone was flat, but there was a smirk on his face.

"Aye, sir."

"She means so much to you that you'd go into battle unarmed?"

"I've got my sword, Captain," said Webb defensively.

"I've seen you swing a sword, Webb," said Harper, shaking his head. "Unarmed seems accurate."

"Well, then I suppose she does mean that much to me."

Harper nodded.

"Good. That means you'll fight all the harder for it."

Webb moved to the railing and looked back at the two ships, now closer than ever. "They'll run us down before too long."

"Aye, I know," said Harper. "We can't face them without our guns ready, though, I'm buying all the time I can until we're ready."

"Clarke's getting the gun deck cleared for action as we speak, Cap—"

The boom of cannon fire bellowed from the stern. A loud splash sounded seconds later, and water erupted over the back of the Vestal.

"Ranging shot, sir!" yelled one of the crew from the rigging. "Not more than twenty yards off our stern!"

"I'd say they have us ranged then," said Harper dryly. "Ready on that sail! Prepare to come about!"

"Come about, sir?" asked Webb uncertainly. "We should keep our distance, let them taste our broadside…" A second blast sounded, cutting him off before he could finish. The sickening sound of splintering wood at sea rang through every pair of ears aboard.

"Report!" yelled Harper.

"Caught the railing on the starboard quarter, sir! Glancing shot!"

"Captain, what's your thinking?" asked Webb desperately as he watched Harper's hands move quickly as they turned the ship's wheel.

"Think about where they're shooting, Webb. One stray shot through Lady Evelyn's quarters, and we can knot our own nooses. I won't risk another shot to stern. Get down to Lord Edmond and Mr. Weaver, tell them to prepare their men for a fight. Once we've come about, we'll run out the guns." Webb was halfway down the stairs to the main deck as he felt the ground shift underneath him. The Vestal lifted in the water as she strained to turn as quickly as her captain demanded. Harper was quick on the wheel, straightening his ship back up as the two enemy vessels came to view in front of him.

Webb made his way to Edmond and Weaver as they tried to steady themselves. Some of Lord Dalton's men looked as though they might be ill. With her sails full and the wind now at their back, the Vestal was pitching and crashing higher in the water. He worried for a moment about Madame Bellegarde, alone in her room, with no warning that the ship was turning. He wanted to rush back to reassure her that everything was going to be alright.

"Mr. Webb," called Edmond, "we appear to have turned." He was putting on a brave front for the men, but Webb could see the fear in the young man's eyes.

"Aye, my Lord. Captain Harper intends to face the enemy rather than let them take another shot at our stern."

"Worried he might get a hole in his bedroom?" asked Weaver darkly.

"No..." said Edmond, looking up at Harper as he gripped the ship's wheel. "It's Lady Evelyn. He won't risk a shot hitting her quarters."

Webb watched as the fear disappeared in Edmond's eyes. Something had lit a fire inside him.

"He's doing his part to keep her safe and we'll do ours." Edmond hefted his musket and pointed it toward the lead ship. "The second one of those blighters comes into my range, I'll see he never steps foot on this ship."

Webb put his hand on the musket and lowered it gently. "A fine sentiment, my lord, but they're a long way out of musket range yet. Captain'll try to sink them before they get closer, but now we've turned, there's a good chance they'll close the distance. You'll get your shot yet." He looked at the two advancing ships. The Roseline had started to turn in the water while the Juniper continued on a direct course for the Vestal. He pulled his spyglass from his jacket and handed it to Edmond. "Look up and down the railing of the Roseline, my lord." Webb did his best to guide Edmond's view.

"Do you see any small cannons—they'd be mounted to the railing."

"Aye, " said Edmond, very nautically. "I see two of them."

"Swivel guns," explained Webb, taking the spyglass from Edmond and handing it to Weaver. "They'll be loaded with case shot, designed to tear through flesh and bone. Not powerful enough to sink the Vestal, but they'll turn her crew to mince."

"Christ almighty..." muttered Weaver. "I'm going to get my breastplate." Webb watched as the large guardsmen took off toward his berth.

"Took my bloody spyglass with him and all," muttered Webb. "So you're the best shot on board, my lord?"

Edmond nodded.

"Well, you can prove it by making sure that any man who gets close to those swivel cannons don't get a chance to fire them. You'll keep a lot of our lads alive if you can keep those bastards away from those guns."

"I can do that," said Edmond nodding.

"You've said that a few times this morning, my lord. Keep this up and who knows what you'll be capable of by the time the sun goes down."

"At this point, I'm just hoping I'm going to be here to watch the sun go down." They stood in silence for a moment, watching as the enemy ships drew ever closer.

"Run out the guns!" Harper's command bellowed forth from the quarterdeck. Beneath his feet, Webb could hear the cannons being wheeled out as the gun portholes opened. He looked at Edmond. He wanted to return the favor the young Lord had shown him the night before when his nerves had taken control of him.

"Don't worry, lad," he said with a smile. "This ship, her crew, and her captain are the best in these waters. No harm is going to come to your lady fair, so long as she keeps her head down and stays out of trouble."

Edmond smiled back. "Well, her father's men have her under lock and key. There's no chance for her to get up to any mischief."

"Plenty of time for mischief once the two of you are safe in Dunshire," Webb gave Edmond a cheeky wink.

"Well, I suppose that's something to look forward to after all this is behind us," said Edmond, blushing brightly.

Cannon fire sounded again, louder than before. The cannonball screamed above their heads as it ripped through sails and blasted apart rigging. "Are you scared?" Edmond asked the first mate.

Webb gave him an honest look. "I'd be a fool not to be." Webb picked up a musket of his own. "There's someone on this ship that means the world to me. It burns me to my core to think of her coming to harm."

"Madame Bellegarde," said Edmond. "I feel the same way about Ev... Lady Evelyn."

"Well, I plan on using every scrap of fear that's bubbling up inside of me to fight like hell today. Because it is my absolute intention that I sit down to dinner with her again this evening and have her tell me more of her delightful stories."

"So that's what you're fighting for, Mr. Webb? A hot meal and a story?" asked Weaver, re-joining them adorned in his brightly polished breast plate.

Webb considered the question for a moment. "No, Mr. Weaver. I believe I'm fighting for love, sir."

Harper had been watching the approaching ships with such ferocious intensity that he didn't notice as the door to his quarters opened and closed quietly behind him. The Vestal had picked up enough speed that the roar of the water smashing against the hull drowned out all but the loudest sounds around him. His crew yelled back and forth up the deck as his commands were followed. The guns were ready to be fired; the men prepared to do their duty. This was the moment he had been waiting for.

He had been patient, waiting until the ships were so close that he could count the number of men on each of them. Webb had been accurate in his assessment. The enemy vessels had stripped their cannons so that they could cram on as many men as possible. Harper had been watching carefully as the two ships distanced themselves from each other. The Roseline turned in the water. It was proving to be the faster of the two ships, her captain clearly having designs to out-maneuver the Vestal. Sitting heavier in the water, the Juniper was making its course directly for the Vestal. The Roseline had the greater chance of a successful boarding, but the Juniper had the larger complement of men. If her crew boarded the Vestal, the fight would be over. He had his target.

"Mr. Trent," yelled Harper to his quartermaster. "Inform Mr. Clarke that we're about to engage the enemy. Tell him to hold fire until all our cannons have the Juniper in sight. I want to cripple her with our first volley."

"Aye, Captain!" Trent made his way to the gun deck at an impressive pace. Harper took in a deep breath. There was a part of him, a part he preferred no one ever knew about, that loved the moments before the battle. He knew the men would be scared, and they had every right to be. But he loved putting the Vestal to the test. Putting himself to the test. Showing the world that his ship and her captain were a force to be reckoned with.

He clenched his jaw as he turned the Vestal to deliver her first broadside. He knew he would have one chance to make the shot he needed. If he over-steered, his crew would miss their opportunity. He felt the coolness of the wind on his back and pull of the sea beneath his ship. He kept his eyes fixed on his target as the wheel moved through his hands. The Juniper attempted to turn with the Vestal. Harper knew the Roseline would use this moment to close as much distance as possible. He had little more than a thin shred of hope that he would be able to turn the Vestal around fast enough to fire on the Roseline after crippling the Juniper. Everything depended on the speed and skill of Benjamin Clarke and his gun crew.

Harper let a faint smile cross his face as Juniper failed to outmaneuver the Vestal. Robbed of the advantage the wind had provided, the Juniper was sluggish in the water. "She's ours now," he said to himself. "Fire as she bears!" he yelled. He heard Trent, then Clarke, echo the order down the gun deck. The timber shook beneath his boots as Harper watched the smoke rise from the gun deck as all ten starboard cannons fired. Clarke was already giving the order to reload before the cannonballs had hit their target. One by one, the solid iron balls smashed through the hull of the packet ship.

The Vestal was close enough that the screams of her victims could be heard. Harper pulled his spyglass from his jacket and extended it to its full length. Every single shot had hit the enemy, but the mainmast still stood strong. He watched as the Juniper's crew rushed to assist their bloodied and injured comrades. At least they had succeeded in shaking their enemy's morale.

Clarke had already given the order to reload, but Harper knew that even on their best day, it would take his crew at least a minute and a half to complete the task. Ninety seconds for the enemy to continue their gain before the Vestal could fire again. Each second dragged on. Harper heard the blast of cannon fire, but this time, it wasn't from below him. It came from the bow of the Roseline, the chase cannons now pointed directly at the Vestal as she bared down on Harper and his crew. He heard the whirring sound of a chain shot tearing through rope, sail, and wood. He looked up to a shower of splinters raining down on him as the Vestal's main sail tore and fell loose from its rigging.

No screams, though. He had that to be thankful. It was far too early in the battle for the Vestal to lose any of her men. Mercifully, the mast had remained undamaged, but without her mainsail intact, the Vestal would soon be slowed to a crawl. There was spare sailcloth and rigging in the hold, but no time to secure it and make repairs. He gripped the wheel and turned the ship again, using the last of the Vestals' speed to give his gun crew any advantage he could. "Fire!" he yelled down the deck. As the command was echoed down to the gun deck, all ten cannons fired as their crews took aim at the Juniper. Again, Harper heard the order to reload even before the cannonballs had found their mark. Clarke was proving his worth.

This time, one shot tore straight into the mainmast of the Juniper, followed swiftly by a second. Harper watched with a due sense of satisfaction as the heavy mast collapsed onto the deck, tearing away at the ship's rigging and sails as it plummeted down. A few of the Vestal's shots hit the water, but the rest slammed heavily into the hull. Now their enemy was likely taking water. He heard a cheer go up from the crew on the gun deck. A premature celebration, but Harper allowed them to enjoy their success. It was important to keep high spirits raised for as long as possible.

Ordinarily, this would have been the moment to press the attack and finish his adversary off, but that was no longer a luxury Harper could afford. The second broadside from the Vestal was followed by another blast from the Roseline. Every man on the deck held their breath as the whirring chain shot slipped through masts and sails, missing its intended target and splashed loudly into the ocean as it passed through the Vestal. The Roseline was close enough that Harper could hear her crew hurling abuse and obscenities. The ship cast a shadow over the main deck of the Vestal. There was nothing for it now, a boarding was inevitable.

"Take the helm," said Harper to his closest crewman. He saw the man's hands trembling as he took the wheel from his captain. "Keep her turning as best you can," said Harper, placing a hand on the crewman's shoulder. "Don't make it easy for them." The sailor nodded desperately.

"Aye, Captain!"

"All hands, prepare to be boarded!" yelled Harper. "Mr. Trent, get your division set to repairing those sails. Mr. Webb, get your marksmen in position. The rest of you are with me. Let's show these scum how the men of the Vestal make war!" A yell went up from the crew as each man went about his assigned task.

Harper drew his sword as he made his way to the main deck. Those of his crew that weren't on the gun deck or trying to repair the rigging assembled around him. Edmond, Webb, and Weaver had taken up positions along the railing with the rest of the sharpshooters.

He looked around at his crew. He had purchased their new uniforms and polished boots just to make the right impression with Evelyn, but now he was happy he had done so. As the enemy ship bore down on them, he could see a few of their crew hanging over the railing. Dirty clothes. Mismatched outfits. At least it would be easy to tell friend from foe when swords clashed.

As he turned back to his men, something caught his eye. One of his own hats seemed to have found its way onto one of his crew members. Not just any hat, his father's old brown tricorn. It sat at about shoulder height among the rest of the men; the wearer hidden by their short stature among the strong-arms and broad chests of the rest of the sailors. Before he could open his mouth to say anything, he heard the first grappling hook hitting the deck. He turned and watched as the rope was pulled fast and the hook bit heavily into the wooden railing of the Vestal. "Axes!" he yelled to his crew as they surged into action. "Don't let a single line hold, boys!" More hooks flew through the air and were pulled taught. "Fire," Harper heard Edmond make the call as the muskets sounded. Several screams rang out from the Roseline. One sailor keeled over the railing and plummeted into the ocean, falling between the narrowing gap as the two ships were pulled closer together.

More hooks flew through the air, coming in faster than the crew could handle. The hooks and lines slowly sewing the Vestal and the Roseline closer together like a terribly stitched wound. Finally, Harper heard the sound he had been dreading. A loud crash rang through the air as the hulls of the two ships slammed together. Anything that wasn't bolted down in the Vestal was flung about, including her crew. Glass shattered and wood splintered.

From below him, Harper heard Clarke give the order to fire. The Vestal lurched in the water, straining against her bonds as the cannons blasted the enemy. Some ropes snapped as the Vestal pitched, but enough remained secure that the enemy crew could now shimmy across. A few of the braver ones were even jumping the distance between the two ships. Harper calmly drew one of the pistols holstered to his chest as the first pack rat leapt from the Roseline. The musket ball hit the man square in the head, flinging his neck backward. He was dead before his body hit the planks, landing at Harper's feet. Harper looked up coldly as a dozen more men followed the first. Each desperate to claim their share of the Vestal's prize.

Looking down the railing, Harper watched as Edmond took aim and fired, shooting a man square between the eyes before he could deploy one of the swivel cannons. "A fine shot, my lord," called Webb as he aimed his own musket and followed suit. Harper flourished his sword and turned his attention back to the boarding party. Many of the men were being cut down as soon as they made it onto the deck, but a few were holding their ground, proving themselves more capable than the rest. These were the men Harper targeted as he cut his way through the enemy. The ones who threatened his crew more than the rest.

Through the thick of the battle, Harper caught a second glimpse of his father's tricorn hat. Its wearer seemed to have backed himself into a corner as two large assailants advanced with swords drawn. Harper sheathed his sword and stepped up onto the narrow railing, dashing nimbly through the surrounding mayhem. When he was close enough, he leapt from the railing and drew his remaining two pistols, firing into the two men advancing on the thief. Harper dropped both his pistols as the two men fell to the floor, dead. He drew his sword and advanced on the young man in front of him. The boy kept his eyes on the ground, but held his sword out in front of him, pointed straight at Harper's chest. "That belongs to me, lad," said Harper, raising his sword to tip the tricorn hat upward.

A single strand of golden hair fell across the youth's face as Harper lifted the hat. His heart froze in chest. Green eyes rose to meet his as Evelyn looked up from her feet. Behind him, the sounds of battle faded as Harper looked at Evelyn. She was clutching the same sword he had put in her hands the night before, though now it was caked in blood. Her shirt, he quickly realized, was actually his shirt, and had bloodstains splashed across it. He didn't know whether to be proud or furious.

He was so in shock that he did not notice the large axe-wielding man approaching from behind, but he saw Evelyn's eyes turn wild as she pushed him out of the way and thrust her sword forward. Harper turned and watched the surprised look on his attacker's face as he fell to his knees. Evelyn wrenched her sword free before pushing it deep into the man's chest for a second time. She was breathing heavily, strained gasps of air, as she stepped back and watched the man fall forward and impale himself on her sword.

"Are you injured?" Harper asked sternly. Evelyn shook her head. "Alright...good." He wanted to pull her close and hold her tight, but he could not imagine a worse time to do so. His mind raced as he tried to think of what to do. The battle raged across the deck of the Vestal. He was cut off from the quarterdeck, unable to get Evelyn safely back to either her quarters or his. "What in God's name were you thinking, Evelyn!" he did his best to curb the anger in his voice, but the seriousness of their situation was weighing on his temper.

"You said you were going to fight harder than you've ever fought before just to see my face again—"

"You need to stop using my own words..."

"Well, I want to see your face again, too!" said Evelyn. She regretted how childish she sounded as she said it, but she managed to stun Harper back into silence. "You said love is what makes people fight their hardest."

Wood shattered around them as a musket ball buried itself in a nearby beam. Harper dove forward, pulling Evelyn behind cover as a rain of gunfire erupted around them. "Love won't save you from the muskets or swords," said Harper. He looked down and realized his hand was firmly around one of her breasts. Evelyn looked back up at him, half pinned under his body, her breathing calmed as she inhaled his scent. Through the thin fabric of his shirt, Harper could feel every curve of her soft breast in his hands. Instinctively, his hand closed ever so gently around her.

"I don't think now is the time, my captain."

"Quite right," said Harper, regaining control of himself. He looked back at the axe that his attacker had dropped. Evelyn's sword was now irretrievable, but the axe looked sharp and serviceable. "Do you think you could lift that? Swing it?"

Evelyn nodded firmly.

"Aright," said Harper. "In a moment, we're going to join the action. First, grab that axe. Then we run to the railing and you cut every rope you can see. I won't ever be more than arm's length from you, keeping you safe. If anyone comes near you, I'll stop them. If I yell for you to 'duck', get as flat as you can because it means someone is shooting at us. Understand?"

Evelyn nodded again. "Yes, I understand," she said.

"And thank you," said Harper.

"For what?" asked Evelyn.

"You saved my life," said Harper, nodding at the dead sailor in front of them. "He'd have killed me sure and true." Evelyn looked down at the man she had killed with her own two hands.

"No one is allowed to take you away from me," said Evelyn. "Not yet."

He lifted her chin and stared into her eyes. He wanted nothing more than to kiss her in that moment, but knew that if he did, he would lose control of his senses. "I love you." He lifted her hat and gently placed her golden hair back into its hiding place.

"I love you, too," said Evelyn. It felt bizarre to speak the words among the blasts of gunfire, the clashes of steel and the screams of men, but Evelyn felt it was a very real possibility that if she didn't say them now, she may never get another chance. It was the first time they had said it to each other so plainly. A simple statement of fact as opposed to convoluted words or passionate actions.

"Ready?" asked Harper, raising to his haunches as he prepared to sprint off.

"I'm ready," said Evelyn. She could feel her resolve taking control. She felt ready to fight beside her captain. Ready to prove that her love was as strong as anything ever felt by Mary Read or Anne Bonny.

"Now!" said Harper. He dashed out ahead of her, covering her as she made a grab for the axe. She hefted it in both hands, feeling its weight. Maybe it was the adrenaline in her veins, but it wasn't as heavy as she imagined it would be. Harper moved close to her as she advanced on the railing.

Though the pack rats had a significant advantage in numbers, they were finding it difficult to get onto the Vestal. Harper's crew were giving their all to repel the boarders, sending many of them down into the depths before they ever set foot on the deck. Dressed as she was, Evelyn didn't seem like much of a threat, and she was small enough to duck and weave her way through the fight. Harper had a harder time of it. His coat identified him as the ship's captain, so he drew more attention. He fought like a man possessed, making sure no one stopped him from being close to Evelyn.

Evelyn felt the men rally around Harper as they joined the fight. Shouts of support came as the crew of the Vestal watched their captain pushing the advancing enemy back against the rails. She lifted her axe, the first swing clumsily missing the rope, burying the head deep into the polished wood of the Vestal's railing. Harper winced as she pulled the axe free and revealed the hacked woodwork underneath it. Evelyn's second swing was more accurate, and the axe cleaved through its target. The rope snapped just as one of the pack rats made his descent to board the Vestal. He fell backward into the Roseline, hitting the back of his head hard against the hull before plummeting into the water.

Evelyn looked down the railing, catching sight of Edmond. He was deep in concentration, firing his musket with deadly accuracy. Next to him, Mr. Webb, Mr. Weaver, and half a dozen other men were also brandishing firearms. With each puff of smoke from their weapons, she could hear screams from the Roseline. She couldn't make out what he was saying, but it was clear that Edmond was issuing commands. He did not seem the same awkward young man she had first met just days earlier. Something had changed. Harper said that Edmond had confessed his love for Evelyn. Was that driving him? She realized how much love had changed her as she looked down at her blood-stained disguise. Here she stood, dressed as a man, taking lives and fighting alongside the crew of the Vestal rather than staying locked in her quarters. All because she wanted to protect the man she loved.

Just as she turned her attention back to cutting the lines between the Roseline and the Vestal, she heard a terrible cry of pain from Edmond's direction. Harper and Evelyn looked down the railing to watch as a grappling hook missed the railing and instead bit deep into Weaver's flank. It pierced straight through his breastplate, causing him to convulse with such pain that he dropped his musket. Evelyn gripped the axe firmly in her hand and made a dash for Weaver, determined to cut the line before it could be pulled taught. She used her light frame to slip through the battle, dodging past men as they hacked and slashed at each other. Harper followed, stepping up onto the railing and dashing nimbly across, cutting and kicking his way through the battle.

Evelyn watched in horror as the grappling line was pulled tight, the hook biting even deeper into Weaver's body. She saw the pained look on his face in the moment before his body was pulled over the railing. She was too late. She let the axe fall to the ground. The hull of the Vestal slammed against the Roseline as the ships collided in the water. Evelyn took a deep breath and looked over the side of the railing. Through the thin gap between the ships, she could see Weaver thrashing about in the water. He was still alive. "Good lord," said Edmond from just behind her. Evelyn hadn't been aware of how close she was standing to him.

"There's naught for it, my lord," said Webb grimly. "Best we can do now is honor him by getting through this alive."

"But he's still alive!" protested Evelyn, doing her best to disguise her voice.

Webb shook his head solemnly. "He won't survive the ocean with that wound, lad."

Evelyn glanced back down. Weaver was slipping below the surface. She wasn't the most accomplished swimmer, but she had learned at a young age. A determined look crossed her face as she decided she could save Mr. Weaver. She took a step back from the railing and rolled up her sleeves. Her feet moved quickly as she stepped up to the railing and prepared to dive.

She felt a hand fly out and catch the collar of her shirt, pulling her back down and throwing her hard onto the decking. "What do you think you're doing...lad?" asked Harper. He stood over her, blocking her from getting to the railing.

"I can save him," said Evelyn, staring defiantly back up at Harper.

"No, you can't," said Harper evenly. "A man his size, drowning. He'd pull you down to the depths with him."

Evelyn ignored him, pushing herself up to her feet and trying to push past him.

Harper knocked her back down again. He hated doing it, but he saw the determination in her eyes and knew she wouldn't be stopped. He looked down at the gap between the two ships. Weaver had sunk beneath the surface.

Evelyn saw Harper look away and struggled back to her feet, making her way to the railing.

He thrust his hand in front of her to stop her, looking at her with an expression she couldn't read. He looked over to the deck of the Roseline and then back down at Weaver.

Evelyn wished she could see inside his mind as he turned back to her with a solemn look. "Mr. Webb," he called.

"Aye, Captain?"

"Do everything in your power to get the Vestal to safety. I'll give you the opening you need to escape. Do not wait for me to return." Disbelief formed on the first mate's face.

"Captain..."

"The ship is yours, Mr. Webb." Harper turned and looked at Evelyn, the realization of what was happening dawning on her face. "Keep her safe."

Before Evelyn could open her mouth to say anything, Harper was gone.

The Vestal and Roseline collided as Evelyn rushed to the railing. She steadied herself as the entire deck shook from the impact. There was no sign of Harper or Weaver below her. She couldn't even see the water between the two ships as the curved hulls ground against each other.

"Hells," said Webb from behind her. "I never thought I'd see him abandon her in battle. What's in his head…"

"What now?" asked Edmond, frantically reloading his musket. "We can't hold them back forever."

"We need more men," said Webb. "You, lad," he called to Evelyn

She kept her head down, hoping neither Edmond nor Webb would recognize her. "Run down the gun decks, get Clarke and his men…"

Evelyn heard the shot. She looked up to see Webb drop his musket and place both hands on his chest. "No…" she cried as the Vestal's first mate dropped to his knees. Edmond returned fire, killing Webb's shooter with a shot to the head. Evelyn rushed to Webb, pushing her shoulders into his chest to stop him from falling forward. She could hear his labored breathing in her ear. "He's alive," she called to Edmond. She tore at her loose sleeve until the material ripped free. Bunching the fabric tightly in her hand, she placed it firmly on to Webb's chest, doing her best to stop the blood flow.

"Thank God for that," said Edmond.

Webb groaned loudly as Evelyn tried to support his weight.

Edmond pointed to one of Harper's crew. "You there, give the lad a hand. Get Mr. Webb down to the infirmary at once! Then find Clarke and tell him to get his men up here!"

"Yes, my lord," said the crewman as he bent down to help Evelyn shoulder Webb's weight.

"I can fight," said Webb, trying to stand up on his own. He gave a cry of pain and slumped back into Evelyn as she struggled to support him.

"You're in no condition to fight, Mr. Webb," said Edmond gravely. "Get him below please." Evelyn nodded, keeping her head low as she shifted her weight and prepared to help carry Webb away.

Webb gave a sharp intake of breath as the two of them lifted him over their shoulders.

Evelyn took his blood-soaked hand and placed it over the makeshift bandage she had made. "Hold it firmly," she whispered softly to Webb. She felt his hand close around the bandage and push down on his chest. She was straining under his weight but promised herself that she would not falter. Edmond was already reloading his musket, his attention now focused on clearing a path to the gun deck.

"Give them cover, gentlemen," he said to his remaining men. With Webb and Harper out of the fight, Edmond seemed to be slipping into the role of command. Evelyn looked down the deck at the fighting. She could see the stairwell to the gun deck, a short enough distance from where she was standing.

Since she had no idea where the infirmary was, Evelyn did her best to be led by the crewman as they hauled Webb over their shoulders. She imagined she was following a gentleman's lead in a dance, trying to anticipate the moves before they happened and making sure she didn't miss a beat. It was the first time in her life she was glad of the dance lessons she had endured in her youth. Though Webb's weight made the dance more complicated, she soon found her rhythm as they headed for the stairs.

Two men advanced on her with swords drawn. She was now completely defenseless. The only way to fight was to drop Webb on the deck. Before she had to make the choice, shots rang out behind her and both men fell flat on the deck. She turned back. Edmond gave her a firm nod. He was covering her, protecting her, even though he did not know who she was. She turned back, taking her next steps forward with more confidence. "Reload!" she heard Edmond give the command. When she was almost at the top of the stairs, a loud crash came from across the deck. A gangplank had landed heavily on the Vestal and now the Roseline's crew were descending in droves.

Striding down the gangplank was a thin man dressed in a faded red jacket. His hair was long and black, barely contained under his unnecessarily large hat. He had a long ducktail beard, clearly meticulously maintained. No sooner had his boots touched the deck of the Vestal than he drew two pistols. He barely took aim as he fired into the two nearest crewmen. "Take the ship, lads! When you find the little lord and his bonny bride, bring them to me," he bellowed. Evelyn felt her grip around Webb's arm tighten with rage as she saw the man stride confidently up to another of Harper's men and run his sword through the man's back.

"To me men," yelled Edmond as Evelyn descended the chairs. "Don't give them an inch!"

"Come on, lad," said the crewman assisting her. "The sooner we get Mr. Webb some aid, the sooner we can make these bastards pay."

"Just leave me, Swanson," said Webb, his pain present in every word. "I can make it on me own." Evelyn looked at the crewman helping her carry Webb. Swanson, as Webb had referred to him, was probably the same age as her, maybe younger.

"We'll not be leaving you, sir," replied Swanson firmly as they navigated the stairs. "You'd do the same for every man aboard and we know it. No one's leaving you behind today."

"Aye," agreed Evelyn coarsely. She had kept her eyes fixed on the red-coated man until he disappeared from her view, watching him as he moved about the Vestal with undeserved confidence.

It took a moment to adjust to the dim interior of the gun deck. Smoke filled the area from the recent cannon fire and the smell of gunpowder hung heavy in the air. Clarke rushed over as soon as he saw them. "Nick," he said to Webb, "can ya hear me?"

"Aye, mate," replied Webb hoarsely, "I'm not dead yet."

"I've been trying to get enough elevation on the guns to sink the bastards, but we're just too damned close to them. Just blast'n holes straight through 'em" spat Clarke. "Best we can hope for is to shake free."

Webb shook his head wearily. "You need to get your lads up there, Ben. Captain's overboard. Young Tallisker's giving his all, but he needs more men. Get your lads forward, set up a barricade and keep Lord Edmond alive."

 Clarke nodded.

"What about Lady Evelyn?" he said, pulling his sword from its scabbard. Evelyn stared at the ground, doing her best to hide her face.

Webb gave a grim look. "We're cut off from the quarterdeck. Can't get to her quarters unless you can cut your way through forty men. We'll have to trust her father's men can keep her safe until we can get to her."

"Alright, you heard Mr. Webb, lads. Draw ya blades and follow me!" Clarke charged up the stairs with a bloodcurdling battle cry, his men falling in behind him as Evelyn shuffled out of their way.

"Keep moving, lad." Evelyn felt Webb's arm move around her shoulder as Swanson started moving again.

Down another flight of stairs. Deeper into the ship than Evelyn had been. The crew quarters were empty. Securely tied hammocks lined the deck and a very human smell filled Evelyn's nostrils. "Nearly there, mate," Evelyn heard Swanson trying to reassure Webb as they headed toward the stern. Evelyn made out a small room at the end of the deck and figured it was their destination. Movement was hindered by the hammocks and storage chests, not built with enough space for three men to pass through at the same time. Evelyn did her best not to trip on the obstacles. Each step out of place seemed to cause Webb more pain.

Above them, she could hear loud footsteps. "She wasn't in her quarters, sir! Not the Captain's either," she heard a gruff voice yell out.

"She must be hiding somewhere else then," Evelyn recognized the voice. The captain of the Roseline, the man in the red coat. "Spread out, search every crevice. You men, come with me. Let's find out what sort of dowry Lord Dalton's little bitch is worth."

Evelyn felt her blood boil again. She could hear footsteps coming down the stairs behind her. She almost wanted them to find her, to give her the chance to fight them. "Let me down, lads," said Webb. Evelyn gently took his weight off her shoulders, letting Webb find his feet under his own strength. "I don't think we're going to make it to the infirmary." Webb drew and cocked the pistol that Harper had given him and pointed it at the stairwell. Evelyn looked around for something to defend herself with. Before she could spy anything to arm herself with, she heard Webb's pistol go off right next to her.

Her ears rang loudly as she watched a man stumble and fall down the last of the steps leading to the crew quarters.

Webb started to reload the pistol as two more men came down the stairs. Swanson fired his pistol, missing his target. He spat in disgust, throwing the gun to the ground before drawing his blade. He moved in front of Webb, protecting his senior officer as the two men advanced on him. Swords met in the air as Swanson tried to repel the attackers. He wasn't as skilled a swordsman as Harper, but the young crewman was proving his worth as he held his enemies back. Evelyn watched as he used the cluttered confines of the crew quarters to his advantage. He waited until his enemies unbalanced themselves, blundering through the storage chests and hammocks before he struck.

Swanson's sword carved its way through one man's neck, and Evelyn watched in morbid fascination as blood splattered across the white hammocks. Webb seized the opportunity to fire his pistol, killing the second man as he swiped at Swanson, only barely missing. "Thank you, Mr. Webb," said Swanson, breathing in deeply. Webb nodded, one hand clutching his pistol as the other kept his makeshift bandage firmly in place. None of them heard the soft sound of footsteps coming down the stairs. Evelyn turned, just in time to see the red-coated captain raise his pistol and fire.

Swanson didn't even see what hit him. The side of his head caved inward as the musket ball traveled through his skull. His body fell awkwardly forward into one of the hammocks, suspending him as his lifeless arms stretched out in front of him. Evelyn saw his sword roll out from underneath him, only a few feet away from her. "Bastard..." said Webb under his breath.

"Captain, actually," said the red-coated man as he calmly stepped over the dead body of one of his men. "Captain Brendon Leighton." Evelyn tried to inch herself closer to Swanson's body, hoping to get within arm's reach of his sword. She heard the click of a pistol being cocked and looked up at Leighton, aiming his gun straight at her.

"Stand fast there, lad," he said to Evelyn. "I don't enjoy killing children, but if you take one step closer to that blade, I will end you. Understand?" Evelyn said nothing as she stared back fiercely into Leighton's eyes. They were cold. Unflinching and uncaring. His gaze was more frightening than the weapon he pointed at her.

"Leave the lad alone," said Webb, drawing himself up to his full height. Leighton gave him a calculating look.

"Old, fat, and short. You must be Nicholas Webb, Harper's chief lapdog. That wound looks bad, mate. Best you run off and get it seen to."

"Aye," said Webb through gritted teeth, "I'm Webb."

"But where is the renowned Captain Harper," asked Leighton. "Don't tell me my men killed him already. One of the only reasons I took this damned commission was so that I could prove myself against a man of his reputation. Never mind, if anyone asks, I'll just say it was me who killed him."

Webb was still gripping his pistol firmly. "Aye, the Captain's not here," Evelyn watched as Webb subtly shifted his grip on his weapon. "Which you'd best be happy about." "Oh?" asked Leighton, almost cheerily. "And why is that?"

"Cause even his lapdog's more'n a match for you," Webb threw his pistol forward, striking Leighton's gun pointed at Evelyn. The hit knocked the gun off target as it fired. Evelyn winced as the bullet struck a nearby beam inches from her head. Webb dropped his bandage and charged for Leighton, drawing a knife from his belt. Leighton had just enough to draw his sword before Webb hit him with his full weight.

The two men tumbled backward over on the hammocks. Evelyn lost sight of them, but she heard Webb groan with pain as they crashed to the floor. She darted across the floor, grabbing Swanson's sword from the ground and rose back up to her feet. The blade was heavier than the one Harper had given her. Less evenly balanced and much broader. But she had seen how well it could cut and knew that it would serve her purpose. Leighton gave a howl of pain as he rose to his feet, pulled Webb's knife from his flank, and threw it to the ground. Webb, still on the ground, tried to get up as Leighton advanced on him, sword drawn.

"Stop!" called Evelyn. There was no more disguising her voice. She stood defiantly, her weapon held out in front of her. Leighton stopped and turned, looking at Evelyn with cold bemusement. "You're here for Lord Dalton's daughter, aren't you?" Leighton stared at her as she removed her hat and let her hair fall free. "Well," said Evelyn, no hint of a tremor or fear in her voice, "you've found her." Leighton didn't seem surprised. Instead, a thin smile crossed over his face as he took slow steps toward her.

"I had heard you were a troublesome child," he said, raising his sword. Evelyn noticed the subtle wince he gave as he did so. The thick red coat had softened Webb's attack, but the blade had still found its mark.

Evelyn looked around at her surroundings as Leighton closed the distance between her. She had watched Swanson's footwork as he had fought Leighton's men. He had almost danced between the surrounding obstacles, using the terrain to his advantage. She discreetly slid her feet out of Harper's slippers and planted her bare feet firmly on the cold hardwood floor. There was no doubt that Leighton was the superior swordsman between the two of them. If she hoped to defeat him, she would need to surprise him. "You won't find this troublesome child easy prey, Captain." Leighton scoffed.

"The Vestal is all but taken. Her Captain has fallen. Her best soldiers are dead or dying. Like you, she is a pure and chaste lady, now alone at the mercy of her captors. This fight will be over quickly, my lady. I offer you one chance to surrender yourself to me and I promise you won't be harmed." He was close enough now that their swords met. He ran his blade along hers and smiled sadistically. Looking her up and down, he smirked. "If you make it difficult, I will make sure my men are rewarded for their efforts today with unfettered access to your body."

Evelyn gripped her sword tightly, ignoring the threat. "You won't be the first man to die by my hand today, Captain Leighton. But you are the only one it will give me pleasure to kill." She thrust her sword forward. Leighton took a step backward, deflecting her attack with ease. She pushed forward, yelling as she thrust again, aiming her sword square at his heart. He blocked her effortlessly again, an expression of feigned boredom on his face. Evelyn took a step back as he swung his sword forward. The blade narrowly missed her face, cutting several strands of her hair as she pulled backward. He was toying with her, the way a cat toys with a mouse once it's been caught. Leighton advanced on her, stepping forward quickly. She put her foot out behind her, her toes closing on one of the crew's storage chests.

As he knocked her blade aside and moved in toward her, his free hand stretched out to grab at her. Evelyn looked down, trying to remember which of Leighton's flanks Webb had stabbed. It was hard to tell under the thick red coat, but she could just make out a trace of blood around his left ribs. As his hand clasped around her shoulder, she kicked back off the chest, rising her knee and striking hard into Leighton's wound. He gave an angry yell of pain and stumbled back, giving Evelyn the chance to adjust her grip and pull her sword back up. She watched as Leighton stumbled back before gathering himself up. She realized he was in more pain than he was letting on. "If you surrender yourself to me," said Evelyn coldly, "I will see you returned to your ship unharmed." Leighton shook his head in disbelief and drew himself up.

"You must be joking, girl," he said with a snarl. "I am Captain Brendon Leighton; my name is feared in these waters. I've eluded His Majesty's navy at every turn. I send men to their deaths, I—"

"You are boring me, Captain" said Evelyn, keeping her sword pointed forward.

"My apologies," sneered Leighton as he swung his sword out in front of him. The movement lacked his prior finesse. Evelyn could tell that his anger and his pain were getting the better of him. But his anger was a soothing balm for her; she drew strength from it as he moved toward her.

She weaved backward, slipping between the hammocks as Leighton advanced on her. He tried to move as she did, but the pain at his side was limiting him. "You clearly never had dance lessons," she teased, as her feet slipped between the low-lying obstacles. Leighton lost sight of her momentarily. Something flew at him, and he slashed his sword out in front of him, resulting in a shower of straw as he cleaved through a pillow. Evelyn ducked underneath his extended blade, cutting Leighton just under his right arm. He gave a furious growl and slashed in her direction, but Evelyn kept moving. She darted away from him, ducking out of view again.

She watched him from behind the cover of a large chest as he scanned the room for her. Blood was running down his arm and over his hand. He winced with the pain of keeping his sword arm raised. "I rescind my earlier offer, Lady Evelyn. After I take you back to my ship, I will have you myself." He walked forward as he spoke, searching for her. "And then I will watch as each of my men enjoys his time with you. My contract only requires you to be kept alive.

'Unsullied' was merely implied. We will take our time breaking you until..." His boot stepped into Evelyn's reach. She took a deep breath and held it only a moment before striking out with her blade, slicing through the back of Leighton's knee. He stumbled and fell backward, slamming his head against a beam. Evelyn heard the crack of bone as his body hit the ground, his sword falling from his grasp

She stood over him, her sword pointed at his chest.

"No..." he gurgled.

"No?" she asked, "What would you have me do? Spare your life?"

Leighton nodded. "Puh...lease…" he managed. His eyes rolled about in his head, unable to keep their focus.

"You should have surrendered," said Evelyn, pushing the blade through his chest. She bent down and picked up his sword. It was light and beautifully made. She doubted a man like Leighton had earned such a blade—more likely it had been stolen from its previous owner. As much as she wanted to keep it, she knew she would already have too much to explain once she was discovered by the crew. Carefully, she lay the blade back down on the ground.

She heard Webb groan from the other side of the room and moved to help him, forgetting to stow her hair back away under her hat. "Lady Evelyn…" said Webb vaguely. "I must be dreaming..."

"I wish you were, Mr. Webb." She offered him her hand. "We must get you to the infirmary." Carefully, she helped him to his feet and tried to shoulder his weight. Without Swanson to help her, it was considerably more difficult.

"Leighton?" asked Webb.

"He took a fall after you stabbed him," said Evelyn. "You saved my life, Mr. Webb. I'm forever in your debt." Webb nodded, barely conscious. He slumped forward and Evelyn struggled to keep him upright.

"Madame Bellegarde will be so happy to hear that you're safe," she said as she struggled to get him moving again. It seemed to work. He pulled himself together and took a few more steps forward. Evelyn helped him maneuver over Leighton's body. But as she stepped over the dead captain, she very deliberately trod down on his privates. Just to make sure he was completely deceased. But also because it felt extremely cathartic.

Harper kept his body as taught and streamline as possible as he dove between the two hulls of the ships. He could see the gap between the vessels closing as the water rushed up to meet him. The moment his body hit the water, he kicked furiously to get as deep as he could. Above, he heard the dulled crash of the two vessels slamming into each other. The reality of what a brash choice he had just made sunk in as he looked up and saw that the gap between the two ships was now completely sealed. Had he been a moment later in his timing, he would be little more than a smear of unsavory red jam sandwiched between two colossal pieces of bread.

Even with the shadow of the ships above him, it wasn't hard to make out Weaver's brightly polished breastplate and the struggling man encased within it. The grappling hook that had pulled him overboard was still lodged in his flank. Harper couldn't tell how much of the impact Weaver's armor had absorbed, but it was clear the man was in pain. Suddenly the rope snapped taught, and Weaver let out a silent scream. Air bubbles spewed from Weaver's mouth as the rope hauled him back to the surface.

Harper pulled his knife free from his belt and swam with every ounce of strength he could summon. When he was close enough, he reached out and grasped onto the rope, cutting frantically as it pulled upward. The moment the rope was severed, it disappeared in a flash up to the surface. Harper imagined the men pulling on the other end of the rope were now scattered about the deck, falling over themselves as the weight they were pulling against had disappeared. Luckily for Harper, in their efforts to reclaim their lost grappling hook, the pack rats had done most of his work for him. Weaver was now considerably closer to the surface, and Harper had little trouble grabbing onto him and pulling him up the rest of the way.

As they broke the surface, both men took in a huge gulp of air. Weaver was still thrashing about, desperately trying to keep himself above the water and fighting against the increased weight of his breastplate. Harper felt large hands pressing down on his back, pushing him back under the water as Weaver feverously tried to keep afloat. Again, and then again, Harper surfaced for air only to have Weaver push him back down. Harper knew never to grab onto a drowning man, but without rope or driftwood to offer, he was running out of options. As he was pushed under water for a third time, he could feel water entering his lungs and knew he would have to take more drastic measures.

He grabbed onto Weaver's shoulder with his left hand, bunched his right into a fist, and kicked out of the water. The punch didn't connect with a lot of force, but it was enough to get Weaver's attention. "Damn it, man," yelled Harper. "Just be still a moment." Harper reached around Weaver and felt where the grappling hook had bitten through the breastplate. Weaver gave a sharp intake of breath as Harper moved the hook slightly.

"Careful!" he hissed.

"There's nothing for it, mate. The whole bloody thing's going to have to come off," said Harper. He awkwardly pulled Weaver in close to him, kicking his legs to keep them both afloat. "You'd do us both a favor if you kept those legs kicking," said Harper as he cut into one of the thick leather shoulder straps.

The straps on the side of the breastplate proved trickier to cut away. The side with the grappling hook piercing it proved particularly challenging, but Harper pushed on aggressively. Already, in the time since they had surfaced, the Vestal had drifted farther away. The Roseline still had her firmly in its clutches, dozens of lines pulling the hulls together. "Careful, I said!" barked Weaver as Harper pricked him with his knife.

"Sorry," said Harper, turning his attention back to the task at hand. The straps were all cut, but the breastplate still clung to Weaver's chest. Harper felt around the large man's frame until he found the grappling hook.

"Alright," he said grimly. "The straps are clear, but I can't get you out of this contraption until we pull the hook out." Weaver nodded. "Do what you have to do, Captain."

"On three," said Harper. "One..." Weaver took a deep breath in, "Two..."

"Hurry up and pull it out, man," spat Weaver through gritted teeth.

"Three!"

"ARGH!"

Harper let the hook and breastplate fall from his hands and sink down into the depths below them. He gave Weaver a moment or two to catch hold of his breath and collect himself.

"Can you swim?" asked Harper.

"I think so," said Weaver, pushing away from Harper and keeping himself afloat. He winced as he moved his arms, but Harper was impressed by his ability to push through the pain.

"Then follow me," said Harper darkly as he swam toward the Roseline.

"Have you lost your senses, Harper?! That's not the Vestal," yelled Weaver.

"We're not going back to the Vestal," called Harper over his shoulder as he continued to swim. "Now keep up."

The distance was made longer by the boats slowly drifting away from them. Harper checked over his shoulder periodically to make sure Weaver hadn't sunk, but the guardsman was keeping pace. The sounds of the fight rang out across the sea, and as Harper drew closer to the Roseline, he saw dozens of dead bodies floating on the surface of the water. Some of them, he had to assume, were his own men. He doubted he would get the chance to reclaim any of his fallen crew from the water. They would be denied their last rites on the deck of the Vestal, so he mouthed a silent prayer for them as he swam. Though he wasn't a religious man, he did hold that everyone deserved to have someone read over them and remember them when their lives came to an end. Especially at sea, where life so often ended so far away from friends and family.

No one noticed as they drew closer to the Roseline. With the battle commanding everyone's attention, it was easy for two swimmers to make a stealthy approach. Harper quickly spied what he had been looking for. A small ladder that ran down from the deck and underneath the water line on the ship. His access point to the Roseline. He waited until Weaver had caught up with him. "Well, Mr. Weaver, if the swim didn't kill you, then the climb well might." Harper reached out and grabbed the first rung, hauling his body out of the cold water.

"Don't worry about me, Harper," Weaver gave a pained grunt as he gripped the first rung, "You won't be rid of me that easily."

Harper peered over the top of the railing. With the Roseline's crew facing the Vestal, it would be easy enough to climb aboard unnoticed. As quickly as he could, he clambered over the railing and then reached back to assist Weaver. There was just enough room behind the staircase leading to the quarterdeck for them to hide from view. Harper was grateful that Weaver was no longer wearing his breastplate as they shared their confined hiding place. "Careful not to bleed on me," said Harper.

"I'll do my best," said Weaver.

Harper looked at the wound. It was difficult to tell how bad it was underneath Weaver's clothes, but there was a lot of blood around his flank.

"Don't worry," said Harper, trying to sound reassuring, "the water always makes it look like there's more blood than there really is."

"Blood doesn't worry me, Captain."

"Well, it will if you run out of it," said Harper.

Harper risked a peek down the length of the deck. Scores of men were practically climbing over each other to try and board the Vestal. There were at least three officers among them, trying to bring order to the chaos. In the heat of battle, the Roseline's crew were displaying a lack of discipline.

"Harper..." Weaver's voice sounded urgent.

Harper raised a hand, signaling Weaver to be quiet as he continued to study the battle.

"Quiet, I'm thinking." Weaver remained silent, but only for a moment.

"Captain..." the guardsman changed tactics, hoping the use of title would get the attention he sought. When no response came for a second time, Weaver grabbed Harper by the shoulder and physically turned him.

"Damn it, man..." Harper stopped when he saw what Weaver had been trying to point out.

The Juniper had launched longboats to assist the Roseline in the battle. Harper counted six boats, each crewed by roughly twenty men. Though the boats were still some distance away, their crews were rowing hard and making impressive speed. It wouldn't take them long to join the battle. If they were cunning, they could row around to the other side of the Vestal and flank Harper's crew as they boarded. Either way, Harper knew if they reach the Vestal, then the battle would be over. "Well, that changes things," said Harper. "If we're to alter the course of this battle, then we need to act fast, Mr. Weaver.

"What exactly do you propose?" asked Weaver, "There's too many for us to fight alone."

"Far too many," replied Harper. "But we don't need to fight them all. We just need to free the Vestal and give her a chance to get away."

"With us on board?" asked Weaver hesitantly.

"Ideally," said Harper, "but let's remember why we're here. Lord Edmond and Lady Evelyn's safe arrival in Dunshire doesn't depend on our survival, Weaver. Just our action." He drew his sword and nodded for Weaver to do the same. "We need to take the bridge. There shouldn't be too many of them up there now. If we're quiet, it might take them awhile to notice."

"And once we have?"

"First, look for anything that might start a fire. A lantern, a fuse, anything..."

"And where am I supposed to go after I've set this fire?"

"Get yourself overboard and make your way to the Vestal. I'll be close behind."

Harper turned to leave, but Weaver called out to him. "Wait!" he hissed gruffly. "Where do I start the fire?"

Harper grinned, stepping backward out of their hiding place. He stretched his arms out and gestured around him. "She's made of wood and sail, man. Anywhere'll do, just make it big." Harper charged the flight of stairs, his sword finding its first victim before Weaver had made it halfway up the steps behind him. He had been correct in his assumption. With most of the men assigned to the boarding party, the bridge was barely defended. Clearly the Roseline's captain hadn't considered the possibility of a counterattack.

Harper moved quickly to dispatch his foes, not wanting to risk them calling out an alarm to their comrades on the main deck. His sword was swift and coldly deliberate as he cut swathes through his unsuspecting foes. Weaver fought with considerably less panache. The intense pain from the tear in his flank seemed only to fuel his strength as he hammered through his foes. Harper couldn't remember the last time he had fought with a man of Weaver's size and strength. Half drowned and bleeding, Weaver was still more than a match for any of the Roseline's crew. After seeing him in action, Harper's doubts about how he'd fare in a fight with the large guardsman were confirmed.

They secured the bridge quickly and efficiently. Each of the men died with a surprised look on their face, never expecting to have been ambushed from behind on their own quarterdeck. "Excellent work, Mr. Weaver" confessed Harper. He hadn't expected to ever find himself paying the man a compliment, but he knew that Weaver's strength had been the key to their success. Though Evelyn had played an unwitting part in their action as well. If she had not been so brave as to attempt jumping after Weaver, Harper would have let the man drown. Instead, a desperate plan had formed in his head which kept Evelyn aboard the Vestal and gave them a chance to free her.

The crew of the Roseline still hadn't noticed them. Harper looked down as swarms of men climbed over each other, each trying to make his way onto the Vestal. There seemed to be no order to their movements, no one commanding them. Realization dawned on Harper. "Her captain is on the Vestal," he said.

"How can you be sure?" called Weaver, as he searched the quarterdeck for something flammable.

"There's no order to their movements, no discipline. This is the same ship that ambushed us, wreaked havoc with our sails and boarded us. She has a skilled captain for sure, but the crew is a mindless rabble without him here to command them. I wish I had the chance to face him myself." Behind him, Harper could hear Weaver pulling at something.

"I'm sure between your crew and my men, this rabble's captain will meet his end. We've some fine men aboard the Vestal."

"Indeed," said Harper distantly. He watched the deck of the Vestal, trying to catch sight of Evelyn.

Weaver came over to Harper, brandishing an oil lantern in each of his large hands. "So 'anywhere'll do, ey?" Harper nodded.

"Light her up, Mr. Weaver."

Weaver lowered one of the lanterns on to the deck and placed the free hand over his open wound. With a roar, he launched the first lantern high into the sails and rigging of the Roseline. It hit the rigging, tumbling through rope and bounced off sailcloth until it slammed against the hard wood of the mast. Oil and flame spewed forth, catching onto every surface it touched. The movement caught the attention of the Roseline's crew. Harper looked down as the men at the rear of the boarding party turned to advance toward them. Weaver fell forward, the pain overcoming him. His fist punched into the deck beneath him, trying to steady himself.

"Get overboard, Mr. Weaver, I'll see that you make it over safely."

Weaver shook his head. "I can throw...the other one," he said.

Harper watched the large guardsman struggle to get to his feet. The enemy was approaching, swords and axes at the ready. Too many for Harper to fight on his own. His eyes darted around, looking for something to help him. Across the deck, mounted to the railing, was a loaded swivel cannon, the fuse still ready to be lit. Around the cannon, slumped over the railing or crumpled on the deck, were half a dozen dead bodies. Someone on the Vestal had done their best to make sure the gun had not been fired.

Harper didn't waste any time. He grabbed the second lantern from the deck, opened it up, and exposed the naked flame to the fuse. He knew he had only seconds to aim the swivel cannon before it fired and quickly turned it away from the Vestal, pointing it down the staircase leading to the quarterdeck. He heard a shot somewhere in the distance as he held onto the cannon. It felt like someone had just punched him extremely hard in the forehead as his brain rattled in his skull. He touched his forehead and his vision blurred as he stared at the blood on his fingertips.

Harper fell heavily onto the deck and heard the swivel cannon fire above him. Scores of grape-sized bullets shredded through the flesh and bones of the men advancing on the quarterdeck. Horrid, deafening screams from the survivors wailed out from the Roseline to the Vestal. Harper laid on his back, gazing up at the orange flames and black smoke that were enveloping the Roseline's sails. He closed his eyes, still able to see the fire from behind his eyelids. Screams of agony filled his ears as darkness nearly overcame him.

For a moment, he let himself drift. The surrounding noise seemed to soften. He thought of Evelyn. For the first time since he had laid eyes on her, he couldn't picture her face. But he could hear her voice. Softly singing to him in the darkness. The sounds of battle faded away completely until all he could hear was a lilting French

Christmas carol. Evelyn's voice singing just as she had at his table. He felt his lips turn upward in a smile as he thought about her voice being the last sound he might ever hear.

"Captain!" Harper felt a shock as a large hand struck him across the face. He looked up into Weaver's grizzled face. "Am I dead?" he asked vaguely. "If I am, you've got to be the most hideous angel I've ever seen."

Weaver offered Harper a hand and helped him to his feet. "I'm no angel," he grunted as he tried to take some of Harper's weight, "and you've not left us yet, Harper."

"The hell happened?" said Harper, regaining his senses.

"You were shot, clipped the side of your head," said Weaver.

"Not a bad one, but enough to knock you cold for a moment."

"A moment?" asked Harper. "How long?"

"A few seconds, I think," said Weaver, his voice sounding faint.

"If I'm being honest, Captain, I don't think I'm all here myself right now."

Harper looked around. The deck of the Roseline was in absolute chaos. Weaver and Harper seemed all but forgotten as the crew tried to split their attention between putting out the fire and continuing the assault on the Vestal. "Get me to the wheel," said Harper, nodding toward the large ship's wheel. As Weaver set their pace, Harper leant down to retrieve the lantern. They limped slowly toward the ship's wheel, each of them staining the deck with the blood with every step. Harper stood on his own feet as he turned the wheel, pulling the Roseline away from the Vestal. There was still enough integrity in the sails to slowly turn the ship. The grappling lines strained and snapped one by one as the Roseline lurched away from her prey. Harper heard a cheer go up from the Vestal as the Roseline's gangplank fell into the sea, along with the men traversing it.

Harper waited until he had a line of sight on the Juniper's long boats paddling toward the Vestal and then set the course. He knew they would have plenty of time to steer out of the way, but he hoped the sight of their ally's flaming ship headed straight for them would put enough fear in them to keep them away from the Vestal. He took a step back, hefted the lantern, and then brought it down on the center of the wheel. He watched with satisfaction as the flames spread.

"It'll take a determined soul to take a hold of that," said Weaver approvingly.

"Aye," said Harper. He looked back at the Vestal, now free of her bonds and slowly escaping the Roseline's capture. "Fancy another swim, Mr. Weaver?"

"Might be the last we take," said Weaver. "Think there's more of our blood on the deck than in our bodies now."

"Blood doesn't worry me, Mr. Weaver," said Harper, echoing the guardsman's earlier bravado. "Shall we?"

They didn't so much jump as topple over the side of the railing as they made their escape from the Roseline. Harper felt the sting of the salt water across his forehead as he hit the sea, but the cold shock was enough to snap him to his senses. He rose quickly to the surface among the debris of battle. Driftwood and corpses littered the surrounding water. The smell of gunpowder, blood, and saltwater filled his nostrils. Nearby, Weaver burst from the water like some huge leviathan, taking an enormous breath of air as he breached the surface. "Ahoy! Vestal!" Harper yelled out from the water. "Throw a line!"

"Captain's in the water!" Harper heard a cheer go up from his crew. "Throw a line, lads! Get him up!" Harper and Weaver let the men on the deck do most of the work as they pulled them back to the ship and helped them reach safety. Harper felt several pairs of hands pull him over the rails. He flopped down onto the blood-soaked deck, exhausted. "We'll need a few more hands here, lads," yelled one of the crewmen helping Weaver. Two more men rushed over to help pulled the guardsman back onto the deck. Harper looked up to see Benjamin Clarke standing above him. "Bloody well done, Captain," he said, offering his hand to Harper. Harper took it and rose unsteadily to his feet. "It was a fool's gambit, Mr. Clarke," said Harper, looking back at the Roseline. The flames had all but consumed the sails, spreading through the rigging and down the mast. "And a hard decision to make." Beyond the Roseline, Harper could make out the longboats still pressing forward for the Vestal. "Better get your men back down to the gun deck, Mr. Clarke. Either give those longboats a reason to turn around or send them to join the rest of their friends in hell. Then, on my command, we send the Roseline to the depths."

"Aye, Captain. What about the Juniper, sir?"

"She's taking water and out of range. Once her longboats are turned about, she won't pose a threat to us anymore."

Harper watched Clarke round up what men he could and lead them back down to the gun deck.

Some of the crew were doing their best to help Weaver back up on his feet. "Get him down to the infirmary," said Harper. "Make sure he's looked after."

"Aye, Captain," replied one of his crew. Weaver gave Harper a firm nod as three men lifted him and carried down to the infirmary. Harper returned the nod, watching as the men struggled under the weight of the enormous guardsman. He smiled to himself, realizing that only a few hours ago, he would have happily let Weaver sink to the bottom of the ocean in his ridiculous breastplate. Now Harper owed him his life and his ship. He turned back to watch the flames consuming the Roseline just as he heard Clarke give the order to fire.

The cannon fire shook the deck as the gun crew unleashed their fury on the approaching longboats.

The longboats were smaller targets than the Roseline, but Clarke's crew were well trained and hungry for revenge. The water turned red as neither boat nor body was spared from the Vestal's vengeance. Wood, bone, and blood erupted as three of the longboats were blasted to pieces. Harper watched as the men in the remaining three boats tried to assist the survivors. "A minute and a half..." said Harper to himself as he turned away from the carnage, "that's all you bastards have left." He didn't watch the next volley as Clarke gave the command for a second time. He knew that any man that hadn't been killed wouldn't be fool enough to risk a third.

Harper walked to the top of the stairs leading down to the gun deck. He watched with pride as the crew reloaded the cannons as swiftly and expertly as ever. "Mr. Clarke," he called down. Clarke looked back up at him, his face blacked from the smoke and power. "The Roseline is a flaming wreck. I hope your men are feeling kind spirited enough to supply her with enough water to quench her flames!" A roar went up from the gun crew. "You heard the captain," yelled Clarke, "show these bastards what happens to those what dare attack our fair maiden!"

Harper moved back to the railing, settling in to watch the Roseline meet its fate. "Captain," Alfred Trent stood a respectful distance behind Harper.

"Mr. Trent, you're just in time..."

"Sir, I need to speak with you quite urgently," said Trent. Harper ignored the quartermaster. He just stood perfectly still as he watched the flames consuming the Roseline. "Have someone fetch Mr. Webb, he'll want to see this as well," said Harper. "And Lord Edmond, I daresay he'd enjoy—"

"I regret to inform you that Mr. Webb is indisposed."

"Indisposed?"

Before Trent could answer, the deck shook again as the Vestal unleashed her final volley against the Roseline. Every shot hammered through the charred and fragile wood as the hull was torn asunder. Harper waited until the sound of cannon fire and the cheers of his men had subsided. "Where is he?" he asked quietly.

◆

Evelyn's disguise was well and truly unveiled by the time she got Webb to the infirmary. The smell of the room was potent. The light was dim. That part Evelyn was thankful for. Half a dozen men lay in cots close to the walls, each with serious and bloody injuries. The low light spared Evelyn the genuine horrors of their wounds, but her ears filled with the low moans of pain and the shallow, labored breathing of men close to their deaths.

She had arrived just in time to watch as a large splinter was being pulled from a sailor's leg. Blood pumped from the open wound as the man screamed. Two men held him down firmly as Louis Duncan quickly stitched and bandaged the wound. Evelyn watched, still shouldering Webb's weight, as Duncan poured the contents of a small brown bottle into a glass and gave it to the wounded man. "Drink this, never mind the taste." Evelyn read the bottle as Duncan set it down: LAUDANUM. The man scrunched his face up as the liquid hit his tongue, but quickly drifted into a calm repose.

Duncan turned to face Evelyn and Webb. If he was surprised to see her in the infirmary, dressed as a man and covered in blood, he didn't show it. His eyes were tired beyond exhaustion. "Help her get him on the table," said Duncan to the room at large. The nearest able-bodied man came to Evelyn's assistance, taking most of Webb's weight from her. She watched as Webb was laid out on the operating table. "You'd best return to your quarters, Lady Evelyn," said Duncan as he looked over Webb's injuries. "This is no place for you."

"I'd like to stay with him," said Evelyn.

Duncan fetched a long, thin pair of scissors. Evelyn noticed that rather than blades, the scissors ended into toothed prongs.

"He wouldn't want you to see him like this," said Duncan, placing the tools down next to Webb and reaching again for the bottle of laudanum. "And I'll work better without the distraction."

Evelyn took a few steps back until she was standing in the doorway. "Will he live?" she asked. She felt rude for being so blunt, but she had to know. She couldn't leave the room without an answer.

"That remains to be seen," said Duncan, still examining Webb closely. Evelyn opened her mouth to say something, but she couldn't summon any words. Her throat felt completely parched as she watched Duncan pour a measure of laudanum and speak softly to Webb. His tone was gentle and caring. A well of anger bubbled inside her, furious that Harper's men, his family, would be put in this position. All so that one man could attempt to claim her as a prize.

Evelyn heard heavy boots pounding toward the infirmary and stepped out of the entrance and into the shadows. Harper stormed in with a grim look on his face. Mr. Trent and a few other crewmen followed close behind as they rushed past her. It was the first time since their eyes had first met in the Great Hall of Airedale Keep that Harper had seemed not to notice her. One side of his face was covered in blood from a head wound he had sustained in the battle, but it didn't seem to slow him down.

She watched as he pushed through the group of men gathering around Duncan. The stony silence that filled the infirmary spilled out into the main cabin. Evelyn felt her blood turn cold as she caught sight of Harper's expression. His face was stern, but she knew it well enough now to recognize the pain it was bearing. She wanted to go to him. She wanted to hold him, show him she was there for him. But she knew it wasn't her place. Harper needed to be with his men now more than ever, and she needed to find a way to explain why she had ended up in the crew quarters, dressed in sailor's clothes.

A few men had come down from the main deck and were giving her puzzled looks as they caught sight of her. She stepped slowly away from the infirmary and kept her head down as she passed through the crew quarters, feeling the eyes on her. She knew that each of the men staring at her had lost friends in the battle. She knew that a part of them would blame her, her presence on their ship, for those deaths. Her pace quickened as an overwhelming sense of guilt rose up inside her.

She stopped as she reached the stairs. Her hand gripped the railing, but as she took her first step back toward her quarters, she heard a faint sob coming from below. She looked down the stairs that lead to the hold and listened. She heard another stifled cry, barely audible over the rest of the background noise of the Vestal. There was something familiar about the sound, even though she had never heard it before. It struck her that she hadn't seen any of Harper's men cry after the battle. They all wore stern and sorry faces, but none of them had shed any tears that she had seen.

Against her better judgement, Evelyn descended the stairs into the cargo hold. All she wanted to do was get out of her blood-stained clothes and fall into her bed, but something about the sound of the cries kept her moving. She heard another sob from deeper in the hold and quietly moved in the direction it originated. Each time she heard the noise, tears pricked up behind her own eyes. The moment she had some solitude, she was going to need to cry, just to let her mind move past the events of the day. She had seen more blood in one morning than she had in her entire life. Hearing the screams of men as they died were sounds she would never forget. She had learned what it felt like to hold a life in her hands and take it. She had never imagined that as Lord Dalton's daughter, she would have learned such terrible things about the world.

It wasn't hard to find Edmond. The hold had been packed so tightly with her dowry and her possessions that there were few places a full-grown man could hide. When she found him, he was sitting on the floor with his knees close to his face and his back pressed against a large wooden crate. Evelyn approached so quietly that he didn't notice as she stood near him. His face was buried in his hands as he tried to soften the sound of his cries. She looked down at him, still dressed in his crisp white shirt, and felt a wave of relief wash over her. There were no bloodstains on his clothes. His cries didn't seem to be caused by any injuries his body had suffered.

She hovered over him, uncertain of how best to announce her presence. Just as she was about to say something, Edmond sniffed loudly and looked up from his hands. "My lady!" he exclaimed as he saw her. His gaze shifted wildly, scanning the bloodstains on her clothes. Clothes that were not hers. "Are you hurt? Who did this to you?"

"I'm unharmed, my lord," said Evelyn, doing her best to sound soothing. "It isn't my blood. Just a disguise to help me escape from my would-be captors."

Edmond's legs scrambled frantically underneath him as he tried to rise to his feet. Evelyn moved closer to him and put a hand on his shoulder to prevent him from standing. Instead, she pressed her back against the crate and slowly slid down it until she was sitting next to him. They didn't say anything for a moment, both staring forward at the beams of the ship. The creaking of wood and gentle sounds of the sea were the only sounds that filled the hold. "I wouldn't have you see me like this..." said Edmond sullenly.

"I'd prefer you not see me dressed in the blood-soaked clothes of a sailor," said Evelyn, still staring forward. "But if someone had to see you as you are, my lord, then I'm glad it was me."

Edmond sniffed again and nodded. "I suppose, in a way, I am glad it was you as well."

Silence filled the room again.

"I heard you were very brave in the battle," said Evelyn. In truth, she hadn't heard it, but had witnessed it with her own eyes. He truly had slipped into a different persona once the fighting had started.

Edmond gave an odd sigh. "I've never been more terrified in my entire life," he confessed.

"Neither have I," said Evelyn sincerely. She brushed her hand over Edmond's until it opened, and she could lock her fingers between his.

"I should have died in that fight," said Edmond.

"Don't say that," said Evelyn. She turned to look at him, but his gaze remained fixed on the beams in front of them.

"Before Weaver and Harper set fire to the Roseline," Edmond began, then gulped, his words faltering for a moment before he could find them again. "Mr. Webb told me to keep my eye on the enemy swivel guns. So I did. I shot down every man who got close to them." Evelyn opened her mouth to say something, but as she watched Edmond, she realized it was important for him to get through whatever it was he wanted to tell her. "I killed...perhaps eight men or more, so determined not to let a single one of them fire a shot from those guns. So focused that I didn't realize how close the enemy had come to our position."

Evelyn watched as tears formed again in Edmond's eyes. "I didn't even have time to draw my sword before they were upon me. One of Harper's men grabbed my shoulder and pulled me back out of the way. He defended me, gave me a chance to reload while he drove them back. Before I could help him...he was dead. Cut down trying to keep me alive." Evelyn thought about Swanson. Remembering how bravely he had fought protecting her and Webb in his last moments.

"I didn't even know his name," said Edmond sadly. He turned and looked at Evelyn for the first time since she had sat down next to him. "Why did he do that?" he asked. Evelyn looked back at him. The confusion and sorrow on his face were enough to rend her heart. But she didn't have an answer for him.

"I don't know..." she said softly.

"He died so that I could live. As if my life was somehow worth more than his. But it isn't!" She could tell Edmond hated the concept. That his station was what had kept him alive through the battle. That men had died to protect him just because he was a lord.

"He knew you had an important part to play in the battle," said Evelyn reassuringly. "He knew that you were keeping the rest of the men safe from those guns. His duty was to make sure you could do yours. Did you let them fire even a single time?" The question seemed to stir up an even deeper sorrow in Edmond. "One of them fired once," said Edmond. "At their own crew. When Captain Harper turned their own gun against them when he boarded. But not before I shot him."

Evelyn needed a moment to comprehend what Edmond had just said to her. "You shot Captain Harper?" she asked in disbelief.

"When he made his attempt to take the swivel gun, I couldn't tell it was him. I just saw someone about to fire the cannon and knew I had to stop them from attacking our men." Evelyn recalled the head wound she had seen on Harper as he had passed her. "I think I killed him!"

"No. No, you didn't," said Evelyn, giving his hand a squeeze. "I just passed him on his way to the infirmary, and he was strong as a bull."

Edmond gave a deep sigh of relief. At least one burden seemed to have been lifted from his shoulders. "Though it may be a while before I get invited back to his table for a meal."

Evelyn gave him a faint smile.

Edmond tilted his head back, thumping it against the wooden crate behind him, and breathed out again. "I really did think I'd killed him."

"He's tending to Mr. Webb as we speak," said Evelyn reassuringly.

"Alive and as well as can be expected, given the events of the morning."

"It was...quite a morning," said Edmond.

Evelyn nodded.

"Not the adventure that I think either of us were expecting."

"No," said Evelyn. Indeed, nothing had been as she expected from the moment she had set foot on the Vestal.

"I thought only of you throughout the entire battle," said Edmond. "I wondered where you were. If you were safe. What must have been going through your mind. I imagined you barricaded in your quarters..." Evelyn turned away from Edmond as he gave her a strange look, "but that obviously isn't where you were."

She didn't say anything for a moment, contemplating how truthful she should be. "How did you come to be in those blood-stained clothes, my lady?" Evelyn could feel her heart beat faster. When she had come to comfort Edmond she hadn't considered her own story in the battle. She hadn't yet had time to fabricate one.

"I escaped my quarters when I heard men attempting to break through the door. Though Captain Harper had done a fine job making my quarters feel homey, there were some old clothes that I found in my dresser. I presume from the gentleman who used my cabin last. I changed quickly and made my escape through the porthole in my cabin..."

"Extraordinary," said Edmond. "You escaped on the outside of the ship, during a pitched battle?!"

Evelyn felt guilty as Edmond swallowed her lies whole. His earnest trust in her couldn't fathom the possibility that she would take any commodity with the truth.

"Thankfully, my cabin was on the side of the ship not engaged in battle," said Evelyn quickly, trying to make her story sound more believable. "I was able to get down to the gun decks and slip through one of the...cannon holes." Her naval vocabulary was failing her.

"Gunports," said Edmond, even now eager for the opportunity to show off his knowledge of the ship.

Evelyn nodded. "With Clarke and his crew focused on the battle, it was easy for me to slip down below to the crew quarters and find a hiding spot."

"And I'm so very glad you were able to, my lady," said Edmond. He paused for a moment, giving her a slow, calculated look. "But that doesn't explain the blood."

Evelyn thought about how best to answer him. It did her soul no good to continue lying to him, and if she was to spend the rest of her life with this man, she wanted as few secrets between them as possible.

"It's Captain Leighton's blood," she said. She knew that was hardly an explanation, but she used Edmond's surprise to buy herself a few more seconds to craft the closest story she could to the truth. "When Mr. Swanson was taking Mr. Webb to the infirmary, they came across me hiding in the crew quarters. Mr. Swanson offered to escort me back to my quarters after he had delivered Mr. Webb to the infirmary, but he never got the chance..." Evelyn retold the rest of the story, almost as it had happened. She left out certain parts of the story. She didn't tell Edmond that she challenged Leighton directly. Nor did she tell him she pushed her sword through his chest as he begged for mercy. There were some details that he did not need to be burdened with. She played up how lucky she was—that it was simply a matter of Leighton's wound from Mr. Webb that allowed her the slightest chance of victory.

Edmond listened to the account with astonishment, his own worries and sorrows evaporated as Evelyn told her tale of the battle. She looked at him after she had finished speaking, unable to gauge the expression on his face. "Are you angry, my lord?" Edmond shook his head but didn't respond. Evelyn suddenly felt very uncomfortable in the silence. "Please say something..." she said softly, as he continued to stare at her. Then Edmond did something that surprised them both. He squeezed her hand firmly and leaned in toward her. It wasn't a kiss like she had shared with Harper. It became apparent to Evelyn very quickly that this was Edmond's first kiss.

His lips were soft and tasted of salt from his tears. He pressed his face into hers, his inexperience showing in his eagerness as his tongue desperately tried to find hers. Evelyn's eyes were wide with surprise as she attempted to match Edmond's enthusiasm. It dawned on her, as their tongues thrashed about, that this would have been her first kiss. Had she never met Harper, she and Edmond would have taken their first steps toward intimacy together. She doubted very much that the location would have been the same, but the experience would have been.

Harper had been just as passionate and eager when he had first kissed her, but he had done so with the skill of a well-practiced lover. He had held her with such certainty as they shared their first intimate moment. Edmond's smooth skin was a stark contrast to Harper's. Soft and uncertain hands touched her face as they kissed, and she pressed her face against his touch. It was the first intimate moment she had shared with someone on an equal footing. Despite her time with Harper, Evelyn knew she was still inexperienced.

He broke the kiss almost as suddenly as he had initiated it and turned his head away from her. "I'm sorry," he said quickly. "I shouldn't have done that."

"Please don't be sorry," said Evelyn.

"I should have had more self-control," said Edmond, turning bright red. "I just felt overwhelmed. You could have been killed today. We both could have been killed today."

"But we weren't," said Evelyn, "and we owe it to the men who gave their lives for us to keep going." Evelyn swallowed before she continued to speak, a dry lump formed in her throat trying to choke her next word. "Together." She wasn't sure why she said it. Maybe it was because she thought it was what Edmond needed to hear, or maybe it was because that's how she felt in that moment. She felt guilt return as she held onto Edmond's hand, knowing that Harper would also be grieving immensely and that there was nothing she could do to comfort him.

They stayed in the hold for a long time. All the while she held onto Edmond, she thought of Harper and what he must be going through. Above her, she could hear the sounds of the Vestal's repairs being undertaken, and she knew that her time with the captain was rapidly growing to a close. She squeezed Edmond tighter, knowing that she was going to betray him one last time before she left the Vestal. Because if she didn't, she'd spend the rest of her life regretting it.

Harper stared into the cold, dead eyes of Robert Swanson as he threaded the needle through the burial shroud. There had been enough old sail cloth aboard to wrap up the fallen members of his crew, a task he made sure he was present for. Five other men helped him gather the bodies and begin stitching together their canvas coffins. The fallen crew of the Roseline were given no such honor. As soon as he had returned from the infirmary, Harper had ordered the bodies of his enemies cast overboard and that no prayers be read as their corpses were thrown into the cold depths of the sea. He had done the same with the injured survivors, though made sure neither Evelyn nor Edmond were nearby to hear him give the command.

Most of his crew were engaged in repairing the rigging and getting the Vestal ready to sail again. Mr. Trent and Mr. Clarke were overseeing the repairs, a duty that Mr. Webb would normally have performed. Harper threaded another stitch, pulling the canvas tight as he thought about his first mate lying in the infirmary. "The shot pulled some of his shirt in with it," Mr. Duncan had stated as he pulled the musket ball free from Webb's chest. "I'll need to get it out as well or it'll infect the wound." Harper didn't look away as Duncan struggled to extract the bloodied piece of cloth from Webb's wound. It took far too long for Harper's liking. The troublesome material seemed to have knitted itself into Webb's flesh. With each labored breath, the cloth pulled deeper into his body.

With a final, brutal tug, the scrap of shirt came free, and Duncan breathed a sigh of relief. "Give me a hand to close him back up, Captain." Harper hadn't lingered long after Webb had been laid out on one of the sick beds. As much as he wanted to stay and watch over his dear friend, the battle had left the Vestal broken and in desperate need of her captain's attention. Harper had gathered every able-bodied crew member he had left and set about getting his ship underway.

He gave himself the task of wrapping the dead members of his crew. He wanted his men to know that their captain mourned the deaths of their fallen comrades every bit as much as they did. But it was more than that. He bore responsibility for the deaths of these men. Every thread he stitched through their shrouds stabbed at his soul. He had overloaded his cargo hold to slow the journey. He had wanted his time with Evelyn to last for as long as possible. It had cost the Vestal her speed and her chance to escape from her enemies. And now it had cost the lives of his men.

He pulled the canvas closed and watched as Swanson's face disappeared under his shroud. Pulling the thread tight, he readied himself for the final stitch, then pushed the needle through Swanson's nose, hoping desperately to hear a scream from under the shroud. No sound came. Just as it hadn't with any of the others. Swanson was as dead as the other twenty-three men who had lost their lives in the battle with the Roseline. Harper touched the wound on his forehead, remembering how close he had been to facing his own death.

He felt a shadow fall over him and turned to see Mr. Weaver

standing nearby, his large frame blocking the sun. "Ah," said Harper, sitting back on the deck, "Mr. Weaver. Come to provide me with some shade while I work?" Apart from the sling around his arm and the occasional expression of discomfort, Weaver looked considerably healthier than he had any right to.

"I understand you requested the bodies of my men be kept below in the cargo hold for transport back to Airedale."

"Aye," said Harper, rising unsteadily to his feet. "I did. When we make port in Dunshire, I'll make arrangements with a caravan to take them back home."

"Thank you," said Weaver. "It means a lot to me that'd you'd make the effort, Captain."

"Those men gave their lives protecting what I love most in this world, Mr. Weaver," said Harper earnestly. "The least I can do is make sure they're buried at home."

Harper moved to the railing, getting some distance from the smell of the dead bodies and inhaling the fresh sea breeze.

Weaver joined him, resting uncomfortably against the railing next to the captain. "Meaning the Vestal?" he said, after a long pause.

"Sorry?" said Harper distantly, as he rested against the railing.

"The thing you love most in this world," said Weaver. "You meant the Vestal?" Weaver asked as if he already knew the answer.

Harper didn't appreciate the line of inquiry. "What else would I have meant?" he said.

"Long before I was the Captain of Lord Dalton's guard, I served as a guardsman in the Keep. I've watched over his family for over two decades. I trained hard, every day, to make sure that I was worthy of a place on my lord's guard, and, in time, I became one of his most trusted men. It's the reason he saw fit to send me with his daughter and ensure her safety on this voyage."

Harper said nothing as Weaver spoke. His hand instinctively

moved to his waist, reaching for the hilt of a sword that wasn't there. With nothing to grip, his fingers curled tightly by his side as he waited for the threat he was certain Weaver was going to issue.

"I remember the day Lady Evelyn was born. Over the years, I watched her turn from a girl into the woman she is today. And over those years, I've kept her safe. As she grew older and more beautiful, she began to draw a lot of attention. Not always from suitors or noblemen. Other men, with darker purposes in mind, would often come to the Keep looking for the right moment to steal Lady Evelyn away. She had no idea they ever got close to her. I made sure those who attempted to lay unwanted hands upon her were met with a swift and fatal punishment." Harper's expression hadn't changed.

"And you did your job well," he said plainly.

Weaver nodded.

"The suitors were a different matter. Most were men accustomed to their station providing them with the privilege of acting however they saw fit. Some of them even thought that privilege extended to Airedale Keep and Lord Dalton's daughter. Their lessons weren't so fatal, but I made sure they were taken to heart."

"I can imagine there was a certain amount of satisfaction in instructing your social betters about the folly of being too forward with the lady under your protection."

"I got good at reading their faces. You can tell a lot about a man from his eyes. Especially when he isn't looking at you. When he's looking at something he wants, something he desires, it's so much easier to read his intentions." Harper turned to face Weaver, staring straight into his eyes. "I've seen your face, Captain."

"Is that so?" he said evenly.

"I'm sure you have your own way of reading people around you. You're an astute man. I doubt there's much you miss. But don't underestimate me."

"I make a point never to underestimate someone who could crush my skull with his bare hands," replied Harper as he looked out to sea.

"I don't imagine you've encountered many women you can't seduce, Captain," continued Weaver. "You're a handsome fellow with no small degree of charm. You captain your own ship and have a host of stories both interesting and fanciful." He took a deep breath. "I've seen the way you look at Lady Evelyn, the same way I've seen countless other men look at her."

"Oh, have you..." said Harper, his patience fading as his tone grew sharp.

"I don't blame you, of course," said Weaver, almost reassuringly. "She's a beautiful woman, by any man's standard. Of course, if you were ever brazen enough to lay a finger on her, I'd have to cut you down. But I'd understand why you took the risk."

Harper pushed himself up from the railing. "I believe I warned you about threatening me on my own ship—"

"I don't mean to threaten, Captain," said Weaver, quickly raising his one free hand. "You saved my life today, as well as the lives of Lord Edmond, Lady Evelyn, and three of my men. I'm in your debt."

"You have an odd way of showing gratitude, Mr. Weaver."

"You saved me. Now let me try to save you."

"Save me?" asked Harper incredulously. "And how are you going to do that?"

Weaver gave a sincere, apologetic look. "By telling you the truth, Captain. You overcame incredible odds today, just as the reputation that precedes you suggested you would. But this battle," Weaver pushed a finger against Harper's heart, "this is a battle you cannot hope to win. There isn't a talent you possess that will help you to overcome the odds stacked against you. Even if she is the thing you love most in this world, and we both know that she is, there's nothing you can do to make her yours." He sighed deeply, as if considering whether to continue or not. "I've watched her as carefully as I've watched you, Harper. She's never looked at another man the way she looks at you."

Harper didn't say anything. If Weaver was as good at reading faces as he claimed, he needed to keep himself calm.

"She is a lady, betrothed to a lord and soon to be married. Nothing will change those facts now. She is a higher station than you or I. She's untouchable. She will never be yours. And, as sad as it is, she has no say in that matter."

Harper almost had to smile at the word 'untouchable.' He alone knew what Evelyn's soft skin felt like, the taste of her lips and the sound she made when she breathed her climax. But he kept his expression reserved. "You're right, of course." Harper tried his best to make it sound as if he were defeated. "After all this is done, I will be required to simply sail away and leave her to her new life."

"It brings me no joy to tell you this, Captain. We may not have seen eye to eye at first, but you've proven your bravery and loyalty to the Dalton family. I felt I owed it to you to spare you from any further heartache you will surely bring upon yourself. And…any further heartache you'll bring to her."

Harper nodded sincerely. "Thank you, Mr. Weaver. Though I have to say, if this is how you reward your friends, then I do feel sorry for your enemies."

Harper caught sight of Edmond leading Evelyn by the hand toward them. Even though he knew he had shared so much with Evelyn, seeing her hand in hand with another man almost made him wish he had been killed in the battle. A horrible blend of fear, jealousy, and pain came over him as he watched them walk together. Behind Evelyn, Madame Bellegarde, dressed in black and wearing a veil, kept a steady pace. The fact that Madame Bellegarde had bothered to pack a black veil in her belongings surprised Harper. She truly was a woman who was prepared for every occasion.

"Captain," called Mr. Trent from down the main deck. "We're ready to begin, sir." Harper nodded and moved to join the rest of the men.

Weaver winced as he drew himself up off the railing. "If you have no objections, I'd like to join you in paying respect to your men."

Harper nodded.

"Of course, Captain Weaver." He didn't turn to watch Weaver's expression. He didn't need to. It was time to repay respect in kind.

Benjamin Clarke sounded one long, high-pitched blare from his whistle as a hush fell over the deck. The only sound was the creaking of the Vestal's hull. Every man on Harper's crew knew better than to expect a bible reading from him. Usually, on the rare occasion there was a reading over the dead, he would say a few words, and then Mr. Webb would speak from the bible. Today, that honor had fallen to Mr. Trent. Harper watched as his young quartermaster fumbled with the bible he was holding, trying to find the right page. Harper cleared his throat. "We are gathered today to acknowledge the bravery and service of some of the finest men to serve aboard this ship. The sacrifice of each of these men helped achieve the victory that we, the survivors, were able to claim. Without them, the Vestal, her crew, and her passengers would have been taken by our enemies." Harper paused and looked down at the row of bodies. "But that is a heavy price to pay for victory. These men were friends and family to us all. They were brothers." Harper caught Evelyn's gaze. Her green eyes framed red from her tears as she held onto Edmond's arm. "I would have gladly given my own life today if it meant keeping the Vestal and the souls aboard her safe." Harper took a step back.

"We will now hear a reading from Mr. Trent before we commit our fallen brothers to the sea."

Alfred Trent stepped forward, taking the place of his captain. "The grace of our Lord Jesus Christ, and the love of God, and the fellowship of the Holy Ghost, be with us all evermore, Amen."

"Amen," responded everyone except Harper. Mr. Trent spoke the words slowly, deliberately taking his time to show the respect his deceased crewmates deserved.

"We therefore commit these bodies to the deep, to be turned into corruption, looking for the resurrection of the body, when the sea shall give up her dead, and the life of the world to come, through our Lord Jesus Christ; who at his coming shall change our vile body, that it may be like his glorious body, according to the mighty working whereby he is able to subdue all things unto himself."

As the prayer was read, Harper's thoughts turned to Weaver's words. "She will never be yours," he had said. Harper didn't agree with the statement, but the entire day had felt like a crushing defeat to him. He was a planner, a schemer. But now he found himself without a compass or a heading, simply heading blindly into whatever fate had in store for him next. He had shared many secrets with Evelyn in their short time together and seeing her now holding Edmond's hand only made his mind clearer on one subject. He was not ready for her to leave his life.

When he spoke of the sacrifice his men had made, he alone knew that they had also laid their lives down because their captain had chosen to slow the ship down. The most selfish act Harper had ever made in his entire life had cost him in blood. He knew he would never make peace with himself for that decision. He would regret that choice for the rest of his days. But now that it was done, and the cost had been counted, he couldn't simply give up.

His thoughts of self-loathing and sadness were interrupted as Trent finished his prayer. "We now commit the bodies of..." Harper snapped back to his senses, aware he still had one last duty to perform for his men.

"Jonathon Myers," said Harper firmly. Four crew men picked up the body of Jonathon Myers and slid it down a smooth plank. Harper felt his heart tighten in his chest as the body splashed loudly into the ocean. "Matthew Jones," said Harper. The men repeated the process. Again. And again, as Harper called each of the names in turn.

With every splash of a body hitting the water, Harper felt the weight of his decision crushing down on him. "Robert Swanson," he called the last name. Evelyn gave a sharp, single cry as the name was called and the body committed to the water. The sound Evelyn made cut through Harper deeper than any blade ever could. It pierced his heart and froze his blood in his veins. In that moment, he would have given everything he had to keep her from ever feeling that pain again.

As the last body hit the water, Mr. Clarke sounded his whistle again, a long, piercing noise that concluded the ceremony. The crew begun to slowly shuffle back to their stations, each man silently returning to his work. Harper felt Mr. Trent give him a pat on the shoulder. "You spoke well, Captain. Did the men proud." Harper nodded but didn't respond. He watched as Edmond led Evelyn and Madame Bellegarde back to their quarters. Weaver moved painfully back in the direction of the infirmary. Mr. Trent and Mr. Clarke went back to overseeing the repairs. One by one, each member of the assembly peeled away until Harper was left standing on his own.

The sun was shining its last light over Airedale Keep when Lord Tallisker made it up the stairwell to his guest chambers. By the time he had reached his room, his face was the same color as the crimson sunset. He knew now why all the members of the Dalton family kept such slender figures. There were too many damned stairs in the old Keep. He shrugged his heavy coat off his shoulders and let it fall in a heap on the floor. One of Lord Dalton's servants had already lit the fire in his room and the warmth was stifling. He stood by the window, letting the evening breeze cool the sweat on his clammy skin.

He stared out at the ocean and thought about his son's beautiful new fiancée. He curled his fingers through his mustache as he remembered the way Evelyn's slender hips had felt in his large hands as they had danced at the feast. A smile formed under the thick facial hair as he remembered seeing how she had behaved with Captain Harper. Unknowingly watched by Lord Tallisker as she stole away into the shadows for a secret liaison. The flushed look on her face as she had returned to her parents. The girl clearly had a mischievous streak. A thought that had kept Lord Tallisker's mind active through the chilly nights he had endured at Airedale Keep.

He remembered the frame his wife has used to carry before a life of luxury and several pregnancies had taken their toll. Though he himself was a large and heavy-set man, he found his own wife displeasing to his eye. And it only seemed to get worse as she aged. Now she was repulsive to him, a reminder that he was getting older. If he had his way, he would spend the last of his years with a younger, far more desirable woman. A woman who could make him feel alive in a way he hadn't for years.

He imagined his whelp of a son with a woman like Evelyn and gave an audible scoff. The boy was wetter than a haddock and about half as smart. Edmond could shoot and ride as well as any man Lord Tallisker had ever met, but he worried about the future of his family name once his legacy passed to his sons. Especially Edmond. Tallisker spent his evenings in Airedale Keep imagining siring a child with Evelyn after he had made her his bride. There was strength behind those fierce green eyes that was lacking in his own bloodline. Though his best years were behind him, Lord Tallisker was convinced he had enough time left to start again.

By now the Roseline and the Juniper would have engaged the Vestal. The service of the two vessels and their crews purchased for a fraction of Evelyn's dowry. He knew that once the inbred rabble of sailors and criminals were done boarding the Vestal most of the dowry would be gone. Trinkets and baubles squirreled away for lesser men to claim as their own. Lord Tallisker had no thirst for gold or silver anymore. His desires were far more primal.

During his negotiations with Lord Dalton, he had made sure that rather than be overly greedy on the price of the dowry that he secured heavy objects to help slow the Vestal. Large items of furniture, statues, and other oversized items that Lord Tallisker claimed 'would add the Airedale charm to the drab interior of Dunshire manor'. A passable enough reason to bring so many weighty objects on the voyage. A father-in-law's gift to his new daughter. Transporting part of her old home to her new home.

By now, Lord Tallisker assumed most of the statues and furniture would be sinking to the bottom of the ocean along with the Vestal. Evelyn would be secure on Leighton's ship, restrained and unspoiled as agreed. As he watched the sunset over the ocean, he wondered for a moment if his son had died fighting or cowering. He doubted Edmond would have had the stomach for combat. He tugged at his mustache as anger filled him, imaging his blubbering offspring dying a coward's death on the deck of the Vestal. This was why he had to start again. Cleanse his own line so that he could begin something better. Something stronger.

Lord Tallisker looked up as he heard a soft knock at his door. "Enter," he called gruffly. The door creaked ajar, and a timid young man stepped through the small opening. Tallisker recognized him as one of Lord Dalton's servants.

"My lord, there is a messenger in the courtyard requesting an urgent audience with you." Tallisker smiled. The bearer of good news, no doubt. Long before the Vestal had departed, Tallisker had sent scouts along the coast to report back to him should anything happen on the voyage. As far as his men knew, this was the concerned gesture of a parent worried about his son at sea. Nobody knew that the Roseline and Juniper had been dispatched to intercept the Vestal. Nobody knew what news Lord Tallisker secretly wanted to hear.

"Send him up presently," said Lord Tallisker, "I shall receive him here in my chambers." There was no chance that he was going to exert himself on any more steps than necessary. Already the thought of descending the long flight of stone steps again filled him with a cold dread. It was made all the worse knowing that soon he would need to traverse them for the evening meal. The journey back to his room after dinner had upset his bowels terribly every evening that he had stayed at Airedale Keep.

Tallisker didn't have to wait long for the messenger to present himself. He spent the time trying to suppress the growing sense of glee he was feeling. The thought of Evelyn becoming his soon excited him far too much, and the news he was about to hear was supposed to be tragic. He needed to play the part of a bereaved parent. A knock sounded at his door. Tallisker took a long, deep breath and wondered if he would be able to cry. It seemed easier to pretend to be furious. Anger was an emotion that came naturally to him.

The door opened and Lord Dalton's servant introduced the messenger.

"Leave us," Lord Tallisker addressed the servant. He didn't want word reaching Lord Dalton from any lips other than his own. He would control how the story of poor Evelyn and Edmond's demise was told. He waited until the door clicked closed behind the servant before turning to the messenger with a concerned look on his face. "You requested an audience with me, lad?"

The young man nodded. "Yes, my lord. I bring word from the coast."

Lord Tallisker watched the young man carefully. He didn't seem nervous at all.

"Out with it then," huffed Tallisker.

Lord Tallisker listened to the report. Anger rose in him as the messenger excitedly relayed the news of the battle to him. "The men who saw it said it was a spectacular account, my Lord. The Vestal left naught but blood and flames in the water when she blew apart her attackers." Tallisker nodded distantly as his mind raged like a maelstrom. 'HOW!?' he screamed internally. It wasn't possible.

"Once the smoke was cleared from the battle, your men watched the Vestal for as long as it took. My lord," the messenger was almost at the point of tears, "your son is alive. Your scouts confirmed he was on deck with the crew shortly after the fighting. Lady Evelyn as well."

Though Tallisker was pleased to hear Evelyn was alive, this provided him with a new problem that he hadn't anticipated. Had she "died" at sea in a tragic pirate raid and then been handed over to Tallisker, she could have lived out her days as his secret prize. Her family would never have needed to know of her survival. Lady Tallisker would have inevitably "fallen ill," and then he could have married Evelyn secretly in his own chapel. Then she was to be his. Night after night, willing or no, until she gave him a son. And then another. As many as she could produce. That was the plan.

"That is good news," said Tallisker slowly, as if waking from a trance. "Very good news," he said, a false enthusiasm finding its way into his words. "Have you told anyone else of this yet?"

"No, my lord, only those that know are the men who saw it. They passed it onto me when their horses needed resting. We all rode as fast and as hard as we could to get this news to you."

Tallisker smiled brightly.

"And you did a fine job." He moved closer to the young man and lowered his voice. "But I worry that news like this might upset Lord and Lady Dalton. The thought of their daughter in danger would cause such unnecessary stress upon them after only yesterday saying farewell to her."

Lord Tallisker pulled a small pouch from his belt. The telltale clink of coins rubbing together filled the silence in the room. "Not a word of this to anyone," said Tallisker, holding the pouch out to the messenger but keeping it firmly grasped in his fingers. "Let me be the one to tell Lord and Lady Dalton and assure them of their daughter's continued safety at her new home."

"Aye, my lord. Not a word," repeated the messenger. His eyes shifted down to the pouch as Lord Tallisker relaxed his grip on it.

"Ride back out and share that with the men who brought you the report. Tell them exactly what I told you. Not a word of this to anyone."

The messenger nodded as the pouch fell into his eager hands.

"Now go." Tallisker knew the news of the Vestal's battle would spread quickly, but he hoped to buy himself as much time as possible before it reached the ears of anyone noteworthy.

He waited until the door was closed and the sound of hurried footsteps on the stonework had died away. Rage boiled up until he couldn't contain it any longer. He threw his fist down hard on the desk. Despite being overweight, he wasn't a weak man. The old wood creaked ominously as the rage passed from his fist into desktop. He took a deep breath. He wanted to yell. He wanted so badly to bellow his fury out across the cold stone walls of Airedale Keep. But he needed to keep himself composed.

He used the last light of day and hurriedly scrawled a letter to Captain Moore, the head of his own guardsmen. He then summoned one of Lord Dalton's servants and gave him instructions to deliver the letter immediately to Moore. There was nothing written on the page that would cause alarm to anyone who read it, but he knew Moore would understand what needed to be done. All wasn't lost. Plans had changed, as they often did, but Lord Tallisker had not forsaken his prize.

Slowly, calmly, he dressed himself for dinner and made his way to Lady Tallisker's chambers. He smiled at her as they descended the stairs together for their evening meal with Lord and Lady Dalton, then greeted his hosts warmly, made a display of enjoying his meal, drank his wine merrily, and applauded the minstrels as they played. He had endured so many similar evenings throughout his life that he barely even had to focus on what he was saying or how he was acting. Instead, his mind fixated on how he would change his fortune. With Leighton presumably dead, and Evelyn now resumed on her passage to Dunshire, his method for securing her into his possession would be considerably more complicated.

As the last of the plates were cleared from the table, Lord Tallisker was approached by one of his own servants. "My Lord," said the servant in a hushed tone. "My apologies for the intrusion, but Captain Moore is waiting for you." Captain Moore stood smartly by the large doors to the Great Hall, dressed in his full uniform with his hands behind his back. Lord Tallisker made a show of reluctantly rising from his chair and rolled his eyes dramatically as he caught Lord Dalton's stare. "Affairs of state," he mumbled as he strode across the room.

Tallisker had a hushed conversation with Captain Moore as Lord Dalton watched with interest. Knowing he was being watched, Lord Tallisker threw his hand up before pacing back and forth. Captain Moore continued the theatre, nodding stiffly and marching out of the Great Hall with purpose. "A problem, my lord?" asked Lord Dalton as Tallisker returned to the table.

"Regrettably so," said Lord Tallisker. He leaned forward, lowering his voice so that only Lord Dalton could hear him. "I am required to return to my hold. Apparently, there have been murmurs of insurrection among the lower classes. My presence is required to put things back in order." He turned to Lady Tallisker. "I should only be gone a week, my love."

He made the rest of his apologies quickly, making overtures to Lord Dalton for allowing Lady Tallisker to continue her stay while he saw to his affairs. Once he was in the courtyard, he smiled a thin smile. Captain Moore had arranged for three carriages to be ready for him. Two were full of his men, armed and ready to execute any order their lord gave them. The lead carriage was his personal carriage. At speed, he could be in Dunshire by the following evening.

He slumped back into the cushioned interior of his carriage and let himself be rocked gently to sleep as the journey began. His last waking thoughts on conquering Evelyn Dalton once he'd removed his son and her protectors out of his way.

Harper's head was pounding as he closed the door to his chamber and locked it behind him. He couldn't remember a time when he had been more exhausted. Without the energy to entertain, he had arranged for his guests to eat in their rooms. Besides, he couldn't justify a lavish meal while the men were still mourning. Not to mention, Duncan had his hands full in the infirmary. Harper hadn't eaten since the previous evening. While he was sure his body needed food after the day he had endured, he found he had no appetite. Instead, he poured himself a large glass of wine and leaned on the edge of his desk as he drank.

He looked at the swords that hung from the wall of his chambers, noting that one was still missing. Probably now at the bottom of the ocean, still stuck in some brute's chest. As he reclined against his desk, he contemplated the absent blade. Evelyn had taken the one sword she had ever held, with barely an inkling as to how to use it and had stormed out from his cabin to face her enemy head on. He couldn't think of anyone braver than she had been at that moment. He hadn't had the chance to speak with her alone since he had discovered her during the peak of battle. He remembered the words he'd spoken to her as the battle erupted around them. "I love you."

He couldn't remember the last time he'd said those words to anyone. He was sure he had before, but the recollection escaped him as he continued to stare at the empty spot on the wall. If he had ever said them, he mused, it hadn't meant as much as when he had said them to Evelyn. Even among the sounds of battle, the blast of cannon fire and screams of men being cut down, his feelings had overwhelmed him. Those feelings had powered him through the entire battle. He could have died over a dozen times, but his desire to see her again had fueled him through the fight.

He was so caught up in his thoughts that he didn't hear the soft shuffle of footsteps coming from his bed chambers. He closed his eyes and ran his hand across the wound on his head; the pain brought back a darker memory with it. He remembered the way Evelyn held Edmond's hand during the funeral service. The sound she made as Robert Swanson's body hit the ocean. His mind created images of Evelyn and Edmond kissing passionately. Her hands roaming over his body the same way they had roamed over his.

He knew, deep down, that nothing would be happening below him in Evelyn's bed chambers. That he was still the only man that had held her, tasted her, pleasured her in the way that he had. But the fear brought with it a certainty. He would not always be the only man that knew Evelyn the way he did. He wouldn't always be the last man to kiss her or hold her. He wouldn't be the only man to make her moan softly in his ear or feel her body tremble in pleasure from his touch. He hated the thought of her being with anyone else almost as much as knowing there was nothing he could do to prevent it.

He was so lost in his downward spiral that he missed the sound of Evelyn clearing her throat behind him. Instead, he just stared bleakly at the wall in front of him. Tomorrow, as the sun rose, the Vestal would arrive at Dunshire. And even though he was the captain, there was nothing he could do to stop the Vestal from making the journey. Evelyn would disembark. She would begin her new life with a young Lord. A young man that claimed to love her. But Harper knew Edmond would never love her the same way that he did. His love was born out of a pure desire that grew into something far more. Edmond didn't have to risk his life to steal a kiss from Evelyn. He was simply given her as his wife because of his station.

A strange feeling came over him as he realized he was jealous of Edmond. Harper would have given up everything he owned and everything he was if it meant a life with Evelyn. Edmond simply had to be born to the right parents and she would be his. He had done nothing more remarkable than being unmarried at a time his father wanted to broker an arrangement with Evelyn's. For that, his reward was that he got to share his life with the most courageous and captivating woman Harper had ever met.

With that melancholy thought bouncing around in his exhausted mind, he rose to his feet. As he turned to his bedchamber, he felt his breath hitch. Shock ran through his body. The glass of wine slipped from his hand and shattered as it hit the floor. His jaw dropped and his hands fell limp at his side as his brain struggled to comprehend what he was seeing. Jealously and sorrow were banished to the furthest recesses of his mind. Now he didn't know what he felt. For a moment, he considered he might in fact be luckiest man alive.

Evelyn stood in front of him; a soft, nervous smile on her face as she studied his reaction. He didn't know how long she had been standing there or how long she had waited for him. She was wrapped in his bedsheet. The thin white sheet was very clearly the only thing that covered her body. The soft candlelight behind her caught her hair, the long blonde strands forming a golden aura around her face. Harper took a deep breath in as he looked at her, his eyes staring straight into hers as he stood perfectly still. "Captain..." she began softly, "I don't like the thought of this being our last night together."

Harper felt his heartbeat in his throat as he slowly took a step forward. "In fact, I hate it," said Evelyn, her green eyes staring back into his. "I might spend my life hoping for more moments with you, but this feels like the only one that I can control. I don't know what will happen tomorrow, or the next day, or in years to come. All I know is that if I don't share this night with you, then I will spend the rest of my days regretting that decision.

"I..." began Harper, his brain slowly allowing him to regain control of his words.

"Yes?" she asked.

"I can't explain what those words mean to me. There is nothing I want more in this world than to be with you, Lady Evelyn. I've never met anyone braver than you. I saw a strength in your eyes the first time I looked into them, but even then, I never truly understood how strong you are. And now..." he took another step forward, "I have you here, in front of me, wrapped in my own sheets...I'd never have dreamt I'd be so fortunate as to see you like this."

"I'm certain you've managed to dream much more than this, Captain," said Evelyn softly. She turned away from him and blew out the candle behind her. As she stood with her back to him, she released her grip on the bedsheet and let it fall to the floor.

With the candle flame extinguished, Harper could only make out the silhouette of her slender figure. She stood with her back to him as he slowly approached. His gaze ran from her small shoulders down to the soft curves of her buttocks. He reached out a hand to touch her, his fingertips tracing the small of her back. He felt her inhale, a nervous and excited breath, as he traced a line up her bare spine and rested a hand on her shoulder. Slowly, gently, he pulled her in to his chest. She could feel him, even through his trousers, pressing against her naked cheeks. She felt her body flush as he pulled her even closer to him. His fingers traced the bottom of her chin as he half turned her and lifted her face to meet his.

There were no sounds but the soft lapping of the sea against the hull of the Vestal and the gentle creaking of the hull as the ship moved through the moonlit water. With every passing moment, the Vestal pushed closer to her destination and both the lovers felt it as their hands roamed urgently across their bodies and their kissing grew more passionate. Evelyn's fingers loosened several of the buttons on Harper's shirt, and her cold hands moved under the fabric, exploring his chest. As she rose to kiss him again, she pulled at the short, wiry hairs on his chest. She felt his hands move down, caressing her rear gently at first, but then firmly gripping her flesh as she pulled at his hair. Evelyn broke their kiss, looking up at Harper as she finished removing his shirt. She felt his warmth as they embraced and kissed again, her breasts pressed against his warm chest.

Evelyn heard the sounds of Harper kicking off his boots. His hands hadn't strayed from her body since he'd first touched her back, but slowly he was managing to undress himself. She lowered her hands to his belt. Only yesterday her fingers had fumbled with the buckle as she had blundered her way through undressing her lover. This time, she didn't falter. These were not the same hands she had boarded the Vestal with. These hands had swung swords and ended lives. She kissed Harper's neck as she pulled the belt free. He gave a groan of sheer pleasure as she did and the sound he made lit a fire inside her. In turn, a small purr left her lips as she gently bit down on his neck.

Free of the belt, Harper's trousers were easily enough removed, and once he had stepped out of them, he stood. Now completely naked, both lovers looked over each other's bodies. The first time they had been stripped bare in front of each other. The moment hung in the air for what seemed like hours. "You're beautiful," said Harper, simply but earnestly.

"So are you," replied Evelyn.

Harper smiled. "I think that's the first time anyone's said that to me."

"Maybe it's because no one gets to see you like this," said Evelyn. She looked down at Harper. His body was ready, she could almost smell the arousal rising off him. "The way that only I get to see you."

Harper held his hand out to her and guided to his bed. They sat on the edge of the timber frame, his hand brushing the hair from her face before he kissed her one final time before pulling her down onto the sheets with him. Evelyn wrapped her legs around Harper's as they fell into the bed, pressing herself against him as she let herself be claimed by the moment. She felt his fingers slide from her belly down between her legs. She felt that wonderful, exhilarating feeling she had experienced on the night they first met. This time, there was no fear of being caught. Locked doors, warm sheets, and an ocean around them meant that no one could disturb her as she lost herself to the touch of her lover.

He kissed her neck as his fingers traced small, delicate circles around her. She let a stifled moan escape into his ear as he focused on pleasuring her. She could feel her entire body flush and just as she began to feel her body respond to his touch, his fingers ceased their work and returned to her belly. Frustrated, she bit his ear, urging him to keep going. He turned to her, so they were both lying on their sides. His fingers resumed their work as he stared into her eyes. The same movements. The same pleasure. He waited until her breathing increased, until the soft moans returned on the breath. And then, he stopped again.

He moved his arm across her and then rose up above her. She took a deep breath as he lowered himself down. Her chest rose to meet his, and she felt the coarseness of his chest hair against her bare breasts. He locked her lips in a kiss as she felt his hardness press between her. Instinctively, she opened her legs, rising her hips toward him as they continued to kiss. She felt his fingers run down her body, trace momentarily over her thigh and then guide himself into her. Her eyes opened wide as she felt herself start to open.

Harper broke their kiss, looking down at her. He kept his body still as he looked into her eyes. She bit down on her bottom lip and nodded, closing her eyes as she felt him enter deeper into her. Every muscle in her body flexed as Harper slowly made love to her. It felt so different from his fingers or his lips. The small touches he had given over the surface of her body had been a very different sense of pleasure than what she was feeling now. Slowly she felt her body begin to accommodate his, changing to allow her lover to join with her in the most intimate way she had ever known.

They stayed in this slow, rhythmic state for a long time. Evelyn closed her eyes and listened to the sound of the ocean lapping against the hull as Harper moved in and out of her. The sound of the waves seemed timed to Harper's movements as he gently thrust in and out of her. Harper lowered himself back down to kiss her, and as he did, she felt his fingers return. The same slow circles that had brought her so close to her climax. Harper's other hand now moved to her breast, teasing her nipple between his fingers as he continued to stimulate her. She could feel the fire building up inside. Every vein in her body felt a surge of heat as Harper continued to rub and thrust. This time, he did not stop as she screamed her pleasure into their kiss. Her body tightened around his as wave after wave of pleasure cascaded through her.

Her hips left the bed as she writhed underneath her lover. Harper broke their kiss as he let out a moan of his own. She remembered the sound, the same sound he had made the night before when she had knelt before him and taken him in her mouth. She knew what came next. She felt him twitch inside her for a moment before he exploded. His warmth spread through her as he reached the peak of his ecstasy. He kissed her neck before he lowered himself completely onto her. She wrapped her legs around him, keeping him in place for as long as she could, savoring every moment of their time together.

"I don't want this to end," said Evelyn, digging her fingers gently into Harper's back as he propped himself back up.

"Nor do I," he said softly. "I'd stop time right at the moment if I could."

"Is it... always like that?" asked Evelyn. She felt foolish for asking it, knowing she probably didn't want to know the answer, but her curiosity got the best of her.

"No," said Harper earnestly. "It's never like that."

Evelyn's face wrinkled in the darkness. "Is that good or bad?" she asked playfully, suspecting she knew the answer.

"Being with you is like nothing I've ever experienced," said Harper. "I don't think I've ever known so much pleasure in a single moment."

Evelyn ran a hand through Harper's hair. "Do you think we have time to have more moments of pleasure?" As she said it, Harper hardened inside her, and his fingers gripped tightly around her arms, as if overtaken by his most basic urges. "There are still many more hours left before the sun rises, my lady." Lost in their pleasure, he grabbed her by the arms and pulled her over him.

The waters around Dunshire were draped in morning fog as the Vestal quietly crept into dock. Evelyn was woken by the sounds of the crew calling to each other as they unloaded the hold. Despite her desires, she had chosen to sleep in her own bed rather than risk being discovered in Harper's quarters. She had slept deeply once her head hit the pillows, and despite an evening of using her body in new and exciting ways, she felt surprisingly energetic. She breathed in deeply, inhaling the scent of lavender that filled her room. It smelt like home, just as Harper had intended it to. She knew as she lay there that no matter what her future had in store, a part of her soul would always belong to him. She felt assured that as much as she was his; she had fully captured his heart as well.

It took her a moment to realize the Vestal was almost completely still, barely moving against the water. She heard the gangplank being lowered and the loud thud as it hit the dock. She knew the sound signaled the end of her time aboard the Vestal. When she came aboard, she had dreaded the inevitable arrival at Dunshire, but now that she had arrived, she felt strangely calm. She enjoyed the feeling, unsure of where it had come from, but lingered happily in her bed as she listened to the sounds of the crew.

In the few short days aboard the Vestal, she had seen more adversity and experienced more change than the entire rest of her life. Even though her feelings for Edmond and Harper remained in conflict, she felt prepared for whatever life was about to throw at her. After all, it had been less than a day ago that she had driven her sword through the heart of a man who meant her harm. She reasoned that her survival of the voyage alone made her more than equal to any challenges she might encounter in Dunshire.

She sat up in bed and opened her window, taking in her first view of her new home. Beyond the low-lying fog that covered the docks, she could make out rolling hills and wide meadows. While Airedale was made of stone and steel, cobbled streets and tiled rooftops, Dunshire was far more provincial. The buildings were wood and thatch and much shorter than she was used to. Dunshire was tiny by comparison to Airedale. From her small vantage point, she felt like the entire town would have been able to squeeze inside the walls of her father's keep and still have room for livestock.

The streets she could see weren't paved in the same way as Airedale. The roads were mostly hard packed dirt or flagstone. She was surprised to find she didn't dislike what she saw, as her eyes eagerly took in as much as they could. At first, she thought maybe it was because she was so prepared to hate Dunshire that it was simply enough that it wasn't on fire. But as she looked on, she realized it was more than that. She felt genuinely excited looking at the rolling hills and charming cottages. She wanted to get on the back of a horse and explore these new lands. She would be riding somewhere new for the first time since she was a child.

A knock at the door made her head turn. "Lady Evelyn, Madame Bellegarde has arrived to assist with your departure," called a voice from the other side of her door.

"Please let her in." Evelyn rose to her feet and quickly ran a hand through her hair in a vain attempt to make it appear she was already up and moving.

Madame Bellegarde entered with less aplomb than Evelyn was accustomed to. Though she was fully dressed and looked ready to face the day, there was an unmistakable sadness behind her eyes. Evelyn thought of Mr. Webb and wondered about his condition.

Few words passed between them as Madame Bellegarde selected a dress for Evelyn and helped her change into it. She sat silently, like a doll, as Madame Bellegarde brushed her long blonde strands and transformed chaos into order. She hated this. It felt like a return to how she was treated as a child. She tried to think of what she could say to comfort someone who had been her teacher and a caregiver for so long. What could she say to someone who had been comforting her for her entire life? She knew that Webb's injuries would weigh heavily on Madame Bellegarde but wasn't sure how to broach the subject.

Suddenly it dawned on Evelyn that for the first time in her life she knew something Madame Bellegarde did not know. While the Vestal was under siege, Evelyn had been among the men, fighting and surviving side by side with the crew. She recalled the fight with Captain Leighton as she felt the comb pass through her hair and remembered how Webb had fought.

"He was very brave," said Evelyn. The brush stopped midway through her hair for a moment. "During the battle," added Evelyn. She took a deep breath. No more secrets, not from the one person she knew she could trust above all others. This wasn't like with Edmond or even Harper. This was someone she knew she could be completely honest with. She let the story come out naturally, paying particular detail when it came to Nicholas Webb and the actions he took in saving her life. She also went into every detail about her own actions. She let everything out, from putting on Declan Harper's hat to making love to his son. From killing her first man to saving a man she loved to sitting in the cargo hold and holding her fiancé as he wept. The brush didn't move through her hair until she stopped speaking. Madame Bellegarde's expression was impossible to read. "Please say something," pleaded Evelyn. There was a long pause. "Anything…"

"Vous ne cessez jamais de m'étonner," said Madame Bellegarde quietly. Evelyn turned around and rose to her feet.

"J'ai appris des meilleurs," said Evelyn. As the tears welled up in Madame Bellegarde's eyes, Evelyn moved forward and grabbed her in a strong embrace. As she hugged her mentor tightly and let her freshly donned dress soak up the tears, she felt an immense gratitude for the woman in her arms. "Merci pour tout, Florence," whispered Evelyn. She felt Madame Bellegarde's hands tighten around her as she used her first name for the first time.

"I don't know what will happen next for you," said Madame Bellegarde solemnly. "But whatever happens, I am here with you," she continued gently. "Everything happens a pointe nommé."

"I haven't heard you say that before," said Evelyn. "What does it mean?"

"The right time, the right place. Never before. If this is how things are meant to be for you, if Captain Harper is who you are meant to be with, then it will happen…but only when it is meant to happen."

Evelyn could feel the tears building up and knew she had to change the subject.

"I owe a lot to Mr. Webb. Before we leave, we will go and see him. I would like to check on him, to see him with my own eyes."

"I would like that very much, sweet child." They stayed holding each other for as long as they needed to be until they were both ready to leave the small cabin for the last time.

♦

Harper closed the lid on the chest. It wasn't locked. If he locked it, it would never be opened again. And that wasn't the intention. It hadn't been easy to find all the objects he wanted to place in it. After Evelyn had returned to her chambers, he hadn't been able to sleep. He had a sole occupation, his last attempt to change the course of his fate. He carefully placed the chest among the small collection of furniture and clothing that was destined for Evelyn's bedchamber in Dunshire. He smiled at the thought of Evelyn opening it, hoping that she would appreciate the small tokens of his love he was sending her.

By the time he was ready to return to his cabin, he heard the call from the main deck. "Land, ho!" All thoughts of returning to bed and getting any sleep quickly vanished. The captain took over from the lover as Harper prepared the ship for dock. Dunshire was a quiet port and the calm seas made for an easy dock, despite the heavy fog. The crew seemed to visibly relax as the anchor was cast and the docking lines secured. The journey had been unpredictably perilous, and the respite offered from a port was welcome.

Harper watched grimly as Nicholas Webb was carefully moved on a stretcher down the gangplank. Normally the crew would have organized a crane for such a delicate procedure, but Duncan was eager Webb be moved as swiftly as possible. Edmond had assured both Harper and Duncan that there was a competent physician in Dunshire who could attend to Webb as soon as the docking was complete. He had even offered Dunshire Manor as the hospice for Webb's recovery and had sent word ahead to get everything prepared.

Duncan had agreed before Harper could open his mouth and the matter was settled.

As much as his mind wanted to linger on the pleasurable thoughts of Evelyn, the day was already promising not to give him any moments of solitude. The battle, his injuries, and an evening of passionate sex had drained him, and he had wandered the deck half-awake as the crew unloaded the cargo hold. They had arrived earlier than expected. Harper's tortured mind wondered if the weight reduction from the deceased crew had sped the journey, though rationally he knew it would have made little or no difference. Nevertheless, as the sun rose on a new day, the deaths of his men weighed heavily on his mind.

Duncan joined Harper at the railing as they watched Webb being loaded onto a cart and slowly driven away. "I'll see him situated, Captain." Harper turned to Duncan, probably the only man aboard more sleep-deprived than he was. He looked almost skeletal, his clothes still caked in a mixture of blood and bodily fluids. Harper felt a few extra pounds added to the load of his guilt. But then the weight got even heavier. "We lost two more in the night."

"Damn," said Harper. "How many left injured?"

"Enough that we can't make a long voyage any time soon. We might need to hug the coast for a while." Duncan looked out over Dunshire. "Reckon you and Mr. Clarke'll need to do some recruiting. Might be able to find a few lads here that would likely trade pushing a plough for a life at sea."

"I'll speak to Lord Edmond first," said Harper dryly. "Make sure he feels comfortable about us taking some Dunshire men on board before we pitch up."

Duncan hesitated a moment. "You'll need a new First Mate," he said. Harper could hear the pain in his voice.

"That bad?"

"Aye, that bad. If he makes it through, he'll need a long recovery. Even if he wanted to return to sea, he'd be in no way fit to resume duty. Least not for a few months…" Duncan trailed off.

Harper knew he wanted him to finish the thought. "Which is far longer than we can stay. Can't feed and pay the crew if the Vestal isn't moving. Lord Dalton is looking to the New World for trade. We need a full complement before we can make that journey." Duncan nodded. There was a pause. "I'll go and talk to Lord Tallisker."

"I'll see Webb situated." Duncan gave a salute and took his leave, heading for the docks.

Edmond wasn't hard to find. Even when he was trying to fit in with the crew, he stood out for miles. Harper found him attempting to assist Mr. Trent with unloading the cargo hold. As usual, his well-placed intentions served more as a hinderance than any known definition of "helpful." This morning there was a determination about the young man, something more serious in his eyes. Battle seemed to have hardened some of his soft edges. Just like Evelyn, Edmond was going to be a different person when he stepped off the Vestal.

"My Lord," called Harper as he approached.

"Ah, Captain, I had hoped to see you up and about this morning. How fares your wound?"

Harper instinctively touched the scab on his head. Now that Edmond mentioned it, he felt his headache come rushing back.

"It gave me no trouble overnight, my lord. Seems to be healing well."

"Jolly good," said Edmond. "Very glad to hear that." He visibly relaxed, as if all the tension held in his muscles released and he could finally stand at ease.

"I wondered if I might trouble you with a proposition, my lord," asked Harper.

He explained the need for more men; the timing required to repair the Vestal, and the intention to leave as soon as the ship was able. Edmond seemed to genuinely enjoy taking part in discussing the business of running a ship and nodded eagerly as Harper spoke. "I don't see any issues with 'pitching up,' as you put it, Captain, but I think you may find your chances of recruitment here…somewhat challenging. The people here are slow to trust and slower still to embrace change. But I daresay given your propensity for charm and phraseology that you'll have an easier time winning their hearts than I ever did."

"Thank you, my lord. I assume there is a tavern or public house that we can set ourselves up in?"

"Oh, yes, quite. The Golden Swan is the local favorite. Though I believe there are several taverns in the township. I've never been to any, you see." There was a twinge of disappointment in the last sentence.

"Understood, thank you again, my lord." Harper paused for a moment. "There is one other matter I would speak to you about."

"Of course, anything."

"Mr. Webb's convalescence. Duncan expects his recovery to be… protracted. I have the means to pay for his ongoing support along with any costs that may be associated with a physician, treatments, and such. He will, of course, have his own funds, but I would see that…"

Edmond rose a hand, politely indicating for Harper to stop talking. "Captain," he began with a deep breath. "Nicholas Webb saved the life of Lady Evelyn with no thought of the danger it posed to himself, after already receiving an injury during battle. The man is a bally hero in my book, and it would be my personal honor to see to his full recovery at Dunshire Manor. I cannot accept your coin to support a man who acted in such a way to protect my love. The very least I can do for both Mr. Webb and yourself is to see to his comfort and support. While he is close to Lady Evelyn and I, he is among friends."

Harper was at a loss for words. "Does that meet with your approval, Captain?" asked Edmond searchingly.

"Very much so, my lord." Harper accepted Edmond's hand as he extended it and shook it gratefully. "I suspect if you continue to show the same generosity and nobility as you have in your time aboard the Vestal, then you will serve the people of Dunshire very well."

"Thank you, Captain," said Edmond. "As I have answered your favor, I hoped you might answer one of mine as well?"

"Of course."

"If you're recovered enough, I hope Lady Evelyn and I can count on you to join us for dinner this evening at Dunshire Manor. I've not discussed the matter with her, but I can only assume your presence at the evening meal would help her to settle into her first night in a new home. I'd like Mr. Weaver to attend as well, if he's able." Harper was hardly able to refuse given what Edmond had offered, so he graciously accepted and said his farewell.

He found Clarke eating his breakfast in relative solitude, his face still caked in a mix of sweat, smoke, and gunpowder. "Morning, Cap'n," said Clarke, looking up from his bowl only for as long as it was polite before rising his fork back to his mouth.

"Mr. Clarke," said Harper, taking a seat. "How are the good men of your division today?"

Clarke nodded as he chewed. "As good as can be expected, Cap'n. Everyone on board lost a friend yesterday, but none of them are talking about dissertation. No anger, just sorrow."

"Well…that's something," said Harper dryly. His presence had been noticed by one of the crew, who placed a small bowl of stew and a spoon in front of him.

"Eat up," said Clarke. "You look like you're about to waste away."

They ate in silence for a few minutes. The moment food hit his empty stomach Harper felt immediately better. "How is he?" asked Clarke once his bowl was finished.

"On land for a few months to recover…with some rough days ahead."

Clarke nodded. "We'll miss his leadership, sure and true. Any ideas on succession?" asked Clarke.

Harper shook his head. "Just dealing with the news as it comes for now. Two more overnight. I don't even have their names yet." Harper rubbed at his brow, willing the headache away.

"Hawthorne and Tolman," said Clarke flatly.

Harper recalled the faces. Both were far too young to see an end to their lives. "Well," said Harper, drawing in a long breath and rising to his feet. "We've got a lot of work to do. Have a wash and find a clean shirt, Mr. Clarke. You and I are on recruitment duty."

Apart from the views she'd had of both towns, Evelyn's only other way to judge the difference in size between Airedale and Dunshire was the length of the carriage ride to Dunshire Manor. The seat was still cold beneath her buttocks as she rose to disembark from the carriage. She had thought Edmond would make the journey with her, but as she'd left the Vestal, she was informed he was already at the manor, preparing for her arrival. She did have the customary farewell from the ship's one-eyed feline. Blackbeard let out a strange, baleful call as she took her first steps down the gangplank. She wondered if, like his master, the ancient cat didn't want to see her leave.

The carriage moved slowly through the mud as it approached Dunshire Manor. A line of carts had formed all the way up to the entrance of the manor as the Vestal's crew saw to the delivery of her possessions. And her dowry. It was the first time Evelyn had seen the full size of her dowry. Judging from the size of the loads and the sheer volume of carts, it was clear her father had placed a lot of value in his alliance with the Talliskers.

The fog had cleared for the most part, but as Evelyn soon discovered, the ground was still treacherously damp. Madame Bellegarde's attempts to encourage patience failed as Evelyn flung the doors open and took her first, squelchy footstep onto the grounds of Dunshire Manor. She soon realized, as she saw the servants rushing out to the carriage with a length of carpet to protect against the mud, that perhaps patience would have made for a more graceful first impression.

The coach driver stood tensely next to her. To his credit, he had barely made a noise as the carriage door flung out and caught him by surprise. "Oh, I'm terribly sorry."

"Think nothing of it, milady," said the driver, surreptitiously rubbing his bruised ribs under his jacket. Edmond was making his way through the mud toward her. Evelyn examined his filthy boots and decided that if Edmond didn't care about the state of his footwear, then she didn't either. She took awkward steps toward her fiancé, ignoring the carpet being rolled out for her.

"Welcome home, my lady," said Edmond, stretching an arm toward the manor.

Evelyn steadied herself as she sized up the building in front of her. The stone and wood of the exterior mirrored the rest of the town, but the similarities ended there. The main building was only two stories tall, but the roof was dramatically vaulted, nearly twice the height of the structure it capped. Both the east and west sides of the manor had turrets that Evelyn guessed were spiral stairwells, similar to the towers of Airedale Keep, only much smaller. Every balcony and window was taken up with flowers of more color and variety than Evelyn had ever seen. They looked so theatrical that Evelyn had to assume they were for her benefit and not the usual presentation.

"It looks lovely," said Evelyn. Words were coming with a degree of difficulty, but her sentiment was sincere. "I really didn't know quite what to expect, but it is very beautiful."

"The flowers aren't always there," Edmond confessed, confirming Evelyn's suspicion. "But the staff are very excited to welcome you to Dunshire. As am I, of course." He offered her his hand, and she took it, squeezing tightly as they traversed the mud and made their way toward the paved entrance to the house. Behind them, the carpet had been rolled out and Madame Bellegarde alighted from the carriage. "All this will be paved soon," said Edmond, gesturing broadly at the grounds around them. "It's still very much a provincial township, and the manor is…old, but I have every intention of bringing more of the modern world to Dunshire."

The doors were opened for them as they stepped into the parlor. Edmond guided Evelyn and Madame Bellegarde through room after room of the house, commenting on each portrait or interesting vase they passed. While Madame Bellegarde listened intently and commented at every opportunity, Evelyn simply let herself be moved through the tour as her eyes took in the unfamiliar sights of her new home. The first thing she noticed was that the servants seemed happier than she expected. Airedale keep was as cold as her parents were and the servants wore a permanent expression of banality.

Occasionally, Evelyn managed to sneak glimpses of the view behind the manor, but it wasn't until they ascended the stairwell that she truly got an understanding of the lands surrounding them. The sweeping green hillsides and tall forests reminded her of the country she used to ride in, but there was more farmland and livestock than she had ever seen. Just like the buildings in the township, the hills were smaller than she was used to, but no less picturesque for it. "Are there stables?" asked Evelyn, catching Edmond between breaths. She could see multiple herds of cattle and sheep, but no horses among them.

"Of course," Edmond smiled. "I take a daily ride whenever I'm able. Father made sure we had horses for you to choose from when you arrived here. He sent some of his finest stock to Dunshire months ago and the staff have been looking after them and keeping them in condition." Evelyn stopped for a moment. It was the first time she had been given an indication that the marriage had been in planning for months. "Perhaps this afternoon you could choose a horse and we could go for a ride together?" Edmond's face turned red.

"I'd like that," said Evelyn, though truthfully, she was longing for her own company after spending so much time around men, but being back on a horse and feeling the wind through her hair was too appealing to pass up.

They arrived in front of an ornate wooden door, and Edmond stood proudly next to it. "And finally," he said, "this is to be your bedchamber." Evelyn stared at the thick wooden door as Edmond opened it for her and let her take the first steps inside. "The servants haven't finished unpacking everything yet, but I thought you might enjoy a moment of respite. I've arranged sometime this afternoon for some formal introductions to the house staff. Can't have you wandering the halls as a stranger in your own house, can we? Until then, you're free to rest at your leisure."

Evelyn nodded as she stepped into her new bedroom. She hadn't thought about Harper since leaving the Vestal, but the moment she looked at the large bed dominating the center of the room, her mind wandered back to the night before and she felt her body flush. She didn't know much about how married life was meant to work. She assumed she would go to Edmond's chambers whenever they were… intimate. She hadn't thought about the practicalities of her married sex life before. She was certain there would be less rules and more passion in a relationship with Harper.

The rest of the room was still in a state of being prepared. Chests and furniture were spread across the floor in neat piles. The fire was lit, and the room had a warmth to it. "I'll leave you to get settled in," said Edmond, still hovering at the doorway. "No doubt you'll want to get some rest. I need to catch up on affairs since my departure, but I'll see you this afternoon for our ride?"

Evelyn nodded. "I look forward to it, my lord."

Edmond closed the heavy door gently behind him.

"Come, Madame Bellegarde, your own quarters are only a few rooms down the hall. We've arranged for a very comfortable room next to the nursery.

"Actually, my lord, if I could make a request before we…" Madame Bellegarde's voice trailed off, leaving Evelyn to wonder what the request might be.

Silence filled the room. No creaking or splashing. No sounds of the crew or bells and whistles. Only the occasional gentle crackle from the fire as it flickered in the hearth. Evelyn released a deep breath as she let herself fall backward onto the bed. She stared at the unfamiliar ceiling as her mind replayed the last two days over and over. Memories of pure pleasure and sheer terror surfaced and sank as her mind roiled. She could feel herself drifting into a light sleep. Just as her eyes closed, and she felt herself fully relax, a loud knock at the door pulled her back to reality.

"Enter," she called as she sat up. Two servants entered the room carrying several more chests between them. "Good lord," she exclaimed. "How much more can there possibly be?"

"This is the last of it, my lady," replied one of the servants politely. Evelyn watched as they meekly stacked three chests in a neat pile. Something inside one of the chests rattled as they set them down. "Lord Edmond has asked that we finish the unpacking while you're enjoying your ride this afternoon, so as not to disturb you any further, my lady." Evelyn nodded vaguely. Her eyes fell on a long, rather flat chest that sat on the top of the recently arrived collection. It was older and more weathered than the rest.

"Thank you," she said vaguely, as the servants bowed and left. She waited until she heard the door click closed before she moved to the chest to investigate it further. Two brass latches kept it closed. They sprung open easily as she flicked her thumbs under them. Her eyes widened as she looked at the contents. There was no mistaking Declan Harper's brown tricorn hat, but it was what was underneath it that most delighted her.

Underneath the hat was a sword, sheathed in a plain leather scabbard. Carefully, she lifted it out of the chest and pulled the blade free. She looked at the elaborate scabbard and realized it was the same sword carried by Captain Leighton when he'd boarded the Vestal. She hadn't mentioned to Harper that she had wanted to keep it for herself, but somehow, he had known. She pulled it free from the scabbard and gave it a few swings. She caught her reflection in the dress mirror and then reached for the hat and put it carefully on. She liked the way she looked much more than when she had disguised herself on the vestal. Now, in her elegant dress, mud on her boots, tricorn hat on her head and sword in hand, she felt like she looked more like 'Evelyn Dalton' than ever before. A woman in between worlds.

The last item in the chest was a carefully folded piece of parchment. She placed the sword gently down on a nearby table before opening it. The first time she had opened a letter from Harper, her hands had been trembling. Now she found herself quite calm and composed as she unfolded the crumbled parchment.

For my Evelyn,

There may never come another opportunity for me to state my feelings or intentions to you. I know that what I am about to ask is a fool's request, but if I do not ask it, I will spend the rest of my life regretting my inaction. If you would have me, I would be yours. Though I know that asking you to be with me means forsaking a life of servants, safety, and luxury, I feel in my soul a life at sea would suit you well. I don't care what conventions are held, nor do I care what the crew may feel about a woman on board.

I never told you this, but every sword that hangs on the walls of my quarters is the sword of a captain the Vestal has defeated in combat. Some claimed by my father, others by myself. Captain Leighton's sword is yours by right, the victor in a battle you should never have been a part of. This weapon can hang proudly in Dunshire Manor as a memento of your bravery or it can be worn at your side, to be drawn again when the time is right. As for the hat, if he knew how proudly you wore it in defense of the Vestal, my father would want you to have it.

The choice is yours to make. Should you choose a life with me, then I will do everything I can to ensure your happiness and pleasure for the rest of your days. But it will not be an easy life. There will be consequences to this decision for both of us. I do not have all the answers, only the knowledge that I want to spend the rest of my waking moments by your side and to know what it feels like to wake up in a bed next to you each morning.

I will be waiting at the Dunshire church from dusk until dawn for you should you choose a life with me. I cannot tell you what will happen the day after that, other than I will spend

every free moment I have in pursuit of your happiness.
    As always, everything I am and everything I have is yours.
    With love,
    Your Captain

Evelyn folded the letter and put it back in the chest, closing the lid and fastening the latches. For a moment, she considered whether it would be more prudent to burn the parchment, but she knew she would want to read those words again. She looked out her window. The sun was high in the sky, but it wasn't yet midday. She had less than a day to decide, knowing that whichever path she chose would mean crushing the heart of a man who cared deeply for her. Now that she had the power to choose, the freedom to decide, Evelyn found that she felt very trapped. She wished, just for a moment, she was back in Airedale, in a time before she had met Harper or Edmond.

But that was the child in her talking. The woman she was now didn't simper or scurry away from her problems. She had a dilemma, and she would deal with it. While a big part of her wanted nothing more than to be with Harper and have a life with him, a smaller but far more rational and convincing part of her knew how dangerous and foolish that choice was. In that moment, what she truly wanted more than anything was to be on horseback, moving as fast as she possibly could.

There was a small clock hanging above the fireplace. Evelyn listened as the seconds clicked painstakingly slowly. It would likely be hours until Edmond was ready for them to go riding. It dawned on her that, despite having only just arrived, she was one of the most powerful people in the house. If she wanted to go riding, then shouldn't she be able to make that happen? She could always go for a second ride with Edmond in the afternoon when he was ready. Besides, there wasn't anything to do in her room other than sleep. She was "free to rest," as Edmond had put it, which didn't feel like any kind of freedom at all. She looked out her window at the inviting meadows and rolling green hills and decided it was time to test her theory. She summoned the servants. A gentle knock came at the door.

"I should like to go riding, please," she said, trying her best to sound authoritarian and polite at the same time. "Can you arrange for two horses to be readied and have Madame Bellegarde meet me at the stables?"

"Yes, milady," came a meek response through the door. Evelyn nodded to herself in satisfaction. There wasn't a problem in the world that couldn't be solved by a ride with Madame Bellegarde.

◆

Madame Bellegarde dabbed a damp cloth against Mr. Webb's head as Doctor Forsythe, the Dunshire physician, continued his examinations. "I'll say this," he said, lifting the bandage on Webb's chest, "whoever stitched him up at sea did a damn fine job." He sniffed the wound deeply as Madame Bellegarde did her best not to be disgusted. "No visible or olfactory signs of infection," continued Forsythe. "Nor leakage of any kind. Some minor bruising from his fall, but nothing that warrants any concern." He caught Madame Bellegarde's expression and gave a reassuring smile. "I suspect he will live, madame." Madame Bellegarde's shoulders relaxed. Her entire body had felt like a clenched fist since she had first entered the guest bedroom that had become Webb's makeshift infirmary. Now, finally, she felt the tension release.

"I'll leave notes with the staff for his ongoing care, and I'll be back daily to change his dressings," said Forsythe as he collected his instruments. "Make sure he drinks as much water as you can get inside him, even if he doesn't seem thirsty. He lost a lot of blood, and it takes time for the body to replace it. Keep him as still as possible while he heals," Forsythe placed a small bottle on the bedside table next to Webb, "and give him a spoonful of this for the pain when he needs it. The staff can see to facilitating his bodily movements."

"Merci, doctor."

Forsythe smiled. "I'll be back tomorrow morning."

"I will be here," said Madame Bellegarde, rising to stand as the doctor left.

Forsythe hovered by the door a moment. "I suspect it might be helpful for him, calming even, if he hears the voice of someone familiar. It would do no harm to talk to him as he recovers, even if he doesn't seem responsive."

Once the doctor had left, she resumed her seat next to Webb and picked the damp cloth up again. If someone had asked a younger Florence Bellegarde what her ideal man looked like, the description would likely have been the complete opposite of the man in front of her now. She had imagined herself with some barrel-chested, striking gentleman with thick black hair and a deep, sensual voice. Her life as a court servant provided her with little personal time, and the men she met fell far from her expectations. She'd had relationships in the past, sometimes with very attractive or very influential men, but none of them had ever held her attention for very long. The relationships usually lasted as long as it took her to realize there was very little depth to the heads or hearts of the men she encountered.

And then there was this strange, balding man lying wounded in front her. A man who had needed to summon more courage to talk to her than it took him to march into battle. A man who was fascinated by her words and her wit and just wanted to listen to her talk for as long as she was able. He had given her his only pistol to protect herself, showing her he would willingly put her safety above his own.

She felt a rising attraction to Nicholas Webb that surprised her. She wondered when it was that what she found desirable in a man had changed. There was an honesty, a sincerity about Webb that attracted her more than any physical attribute a man could possess. Instinctively, she reached out for his hand and gave it a gentle squeeze. She felt herself miss a breath when her squeeze was returned. She watched Webb's eyes flutter behind their lids and felt herself choke up.

"Didn't know…there was an angel watch'n over me…" His words were labored through his heavy breathing, but they brought a smile to Madame Bellegarde's lips.

"Not an angel, monsieur Webb. Only someone who wants to know you better." She remembered the doctor's advice as he left the room. "Perhaps you would like to hear another of my stories. Where to begin?" Madame Bellegarde suddenly felt she could be more honest and freer with her conversation than ever before. She began to talk to Webb about the first stories that came to mind.

She talked without pausing for a long time until she was interrupted by a knock at the door.

"Lady Evelyn requests your presence, Madame."

"One moment," she called back, giving Webb's hand a farewell squeeze. "I will be back when I can and we can continue our stories," she said gently. She placed a soft kiss on Webb's forehead before she got up to leave.

A young serving girl was standing attentively in the corridor. "Lady Evelyn requests your company for a ride," said the servant politely.

Madame Bellegarde nodded. "Of course, please show me the way."

The servant looked unsure. "Wouldn't you like to change first, Madame?"

Bellegarde looked down at her expansive dress. "Oh," she said, her haughty tone returning, "I am accustomed to riding in such clothes. I am sure there is a strong and capable stable boy who can assist me with getting into the saddle?"

"Of course, Madame," said the girl uncertainly.

If she was being honest with herself, the absolute last thing she felt like doing was getting on the back of a horse, but Madame Bellegarde knew Evelyn needed her. Her own feelings and fatigue needed to be put aside. After all, that was part of the life of being a servant—no matter how favored you might be, you were never an equal to your betters. You did what was required of you when it was asked.

The stables were clean but had the unmistakable smell that came with housing large animals together. Evelyn smiled brightly as Madame Bellegarde swept up her dress and made her way toward the horses. "There you are!" she said excitedly. "I had to send people out looking for you. No one knew where to find you."

"I was attending to monsieur Webb," said Madame Bellegarde.

Evelyn's smiled quickly evaporated. "Oh, I'm so sorry. If I'd known I never would have asked—"

"Hush, child, do not concern yourself with that," she said gently. "He is doing much better now. He is resting comfortably."

"I'm so happy to hear that," said Evelyn earnestly. "Do you want to return to him? I understand if you—"

Madame Bellegarde shook her head. Although she did want to go back to Mr. Webb and continue watching over him, she was aware there were a lot of eyes watching them. Madame Bellegarde was not eager to make a show of putting her own needs over Evelyn's in front of the Dunshire servants. To do so would set a precedent for Evelyn's authority. "No, my lady, I am, of course, happy to serve you. Let us ride together and explore your new home." Evelyn's eyes shifted from side to side. She took a few steps closer to Madame Bellegarde.

"Are you alright?" she whispered.

"Of course, sweet child," said Madame Bellegarde assumingly. "But we can't have you looking weak in front of your new servants. Come, let us ride."

With considerable assistance from two stable hands, Bellegarde was lifted onto her horse.

Evelyn refused assistance, looking profoundly unladylike as she swung herself up effortlessly onto her horse. "I had hoped we would be riding alone," said Evelyn as they trotted out of the stables, closely followed by two guardsmen.

"Then you were naive to think so," said Madame Bellegarde. "Just because you are the lady of the house doesn't mean you are free to travel without a chaperone."

Evelyn pouted at the comment.

"Were there things you wanted to discuss with me that you don't want others to hear?" asked Madame Bellegarde knowingly.

Evelyn nodded.

"I see." Madame Bellegarde motioned for one of the chaperones to ride closer. "Is there somewhere Lady Evelyn can ride her horse a little…faster?"

"There's an open field behind that hill," said the guardsmen, pointing to a nearby hillside. "That's where Lord Edmond does a lot of his riding."

"Perfect," said Madame Bellegarde, gesturing in front of her, "lead the way, s'il vous plait." She turned back to Evelyn as the chaperones took the lead. "Instead of a conversation today, you may have to settle instead for catharsis."

"Thank you," said Evelyn softly.

"Just stay where you can be seen," said Madame Bellegarde. "No adventures. This is a strange land to us."

Evelyn nodded as a broad grin came across her face. It didn't take long for them to reach the top of the hill. In front of them, just as promised, was an extensive field.

"Go," whispered Madame Bellegarde.

Evelyn didn't need telling twice. She dug her heels into her horse and sped off down the hill, catching her chaperones completely by surprise as she flew past them.

Madame Bellegarde smiled and watched from the top of the hill as Evelyn pushed her horse to go as fast as possible. "You won't catch her," she called out as one of the chaperones tried to keep pace with her. From the top of the hill, Madame Bellegarde had a commanding view of the land surrounding the Dunshire township. She had to admit that, in its own way, it was a beautiful part of the world. It lacked any proper sense of the modern world, but that was a big part of its appeal. A simple place from a simpler time. For the most part, Dunshire was just a sleepy collection of farmsteads surrounding the manor and the township. The town itself, as far as Madame Bellegarde could tell from her vantage point, consisted of the small dockyard, a collection of taverns, a few stores, and a church.

She spent a long time scanning the landscape as Evelyn tore up and down the fields below her. The stillness of the landscape was interrupted by movement on the horizon. Madame Bellegarde squinted against the sun as she looked out to one of the roads leading into the township. She could make out a number of horsemen riding ahead of three large carriages. They were moving fast toward Dunshire. Something about the way they moved made her feel uneasy. "Is that something we should be concerned about?" she called out to the chaperone who had remained close to her. He looked in the direction she was pointing.

"Oh," he said, slightly puzzled. "Those are the Tallisker banners. Looks like his lordship's personal carriage, if I'm not mistaken. Haven't seen it in these parts for months. I thought he was in Airedale."

"So did I," said Madame Bellegarde slowly. "Tell your friend to fetch Lady Evelyn. I think it's time we conclude our ride."

It was before noon when Harper and Clarke entered the Golden Swan. Despite the early hour, some of the locals were already well ensconced in their usual haunts. Harper imagined this was the sort of establishment that had very clear unspoken rules about who sat where. He let Clarke negotiate terms with the innkeeper while he prepared himself for the day ahead. Several other crewmen were out in the streets, talking loudly about the promise of adventure and fortune as people passed by. There was a considerable advantage to being the only ship in port. The Vestal certainly stood out and gave the locals something to talk about. The arrival of the local lord's new bride-to-be, the tales of battle and adventure on the voyage from Airedale, and the crew looking for places to spend their coin would be the talk of the town.

Harper approached the barman, who gave him an uninterested look. A small amount of coin could buy a lot of friendship, and it was time to generate a little goodwill among the locals. "Morning, sir," said Harper pleasantly as he leant against the bar counter.

"Morning friend," replied the barkeeper without looking up from the tankard he was cleaning. The tone didn't convey an ounce of friendship. "What's your pleasure this morning?"

Harper made a show of looking around the tavern. "I'm not sure," he said. "What do folk like to drink around these parts?"

"Scrumpy is the usual favorite," said the innkeeper.

"Very well, then," said Harper, loudly spilling the contents of a small coin purse onto the bar. "A pint of scrumpy for me and my companion. Oh, and please serve the rest of these fine gentlemen another round, courtesy of Captain Harper of the Vestal."

The innkeeper's eyes widened at the coins as a cheer went up from the locals.

Harper left the change on the bar as he collected his drinks.

"Not even midday and they'll be drunk as lords," said Clarke as Harper joined him at their corner table.

"Aye, nothing but the sounds of merriment and laughter coming from the Golden Swan today, Mr. Clarke." Harper looked down at the pint of scrumpy in front of him. There were 'bits' in it. He took the tankard in hand, clinked it against Clarke's and both men took a swig.

"Christ," spat Clarke.

"Aye," said Harper, fighting to keep his eyes from watering. He looked around at the assembled locals, eagerly taking advantage of Harper's generosity and drinking heartily.

"It's a wonder they haven't all gone blind," whispered Clarke.

Harper nodded. He had seen Clarke drink a bottle of rum like it was water. For his own part, Harper felt he was no slouch when it came to consumption, and yet the drink in front of him was showing all the promise of giving him the fight of his life.

"Strong backs and broad shoulders," said Harper, scanning the room. "Exactly what the Vestal needs. All we need to do is convince them that life at sea holds more promise than tilling fields and planting seeds." Clarke laid out the contracts in front of him on the table.

"Reckon twenty men would be a good round number, Captain." Harper nodded again.

"Ambitious but not impossible, Mr. Clarke."

It didn't take long before their first potential convert joined them at their table. He wasn't much older than Harper, solidly built with a beard that meant business. He looked like he knew what a hard day's work was. "Hear it's you I have to thank for the pint, Captain."

"Aye, hearty compliments from me and my crew for putting up with us while we make our repairs," said Harper congenially. He motioned to the empty chair across the table. "Have a seat and share a drink with us, friend."

"Reckon I will, Captain. Name's Morgan." Harper raised his glass and took a swig, his face barely contorting as he swallowed the lumpy, vaguely apple tasting liquid.

"Captain Harper," said Harper. "And my Master Gunner, Mr. Clarke."

And it was as simple as that. A few minutes of conversing, a crude joke, a childhood memory of how a life at sea had always seemed appealing and before too long, Harper had his first signed contract. Morgan made his way back to his friends, loudly telling them he was signing up with the Vestal. This naturally encouraged more men to seek out Harper and Clarke. As the hours passed, the Golden Swan grew noticeably busier. Harper continued to sponsor and encourage the drinking and frivolity as the number of signatures grew.

In the late afternoon, Harper noticed Weaver and his remaining men make their way into the tavern. They were each dressed in their full regalia, sporting the brilliant blue of the Dalton family.

He imagined they would be drinking to missing comrades and making their arrangements to return to Airedale. With Evelyn successfully delivered to Dunshire and Edmond's people now in charge of her protection, there was nothing keeping Weaver from returning to Airedale. Harper gave a polite nod and raised his glass to Weaver before returning to his recruitment duties.

As the shadows in the tavern lengthened, Harper dimly recalled he had made a promise to attend a dinner at Dunshire Manor. Even though he desperately wanted to see Evelyn again, the thought of trading the warmth and frivolity of the tavern for an evening of stilted conversation and formality sounded unappealing. Here, surrounded by the stink of the tavern and the sounds of raucous laughter, Harper felt more like himself than he had in weeks. He wasn't sure if that feeling should comfort him or make him feel incredibly depressed. He was still mulling over whether to attend the dinner when the tavern doors were flung aggressively open.

A nervous silence fell over the tavern as ten men sauntered in with a grim and entitled purpose. They were all armed, and each wore a mustard-yellow sash across their chests. Harper recognized the color from Lord Tallisker's banners, although he hadn't seen it since arriving in Dunshire. He watched with interest as the men positioned themselves at the bar, taking up most of the service space and making their presence felt. Eventually the sounds of conversation and consumption grew from hushed whispers to low murmurs, but the previous gusto had been knocked out of the room. Harper could smell the tension and fear in the air.

While Edmond had never struck Harper as a cruel man and his interactions with Lord Tallisker had been fleeting, it was clear now that the Tallisker guardsmen intimidated the local populace. It was likely men dressed exactly as these that collected taxes and locked away troublemakers. Harper watched as the Tallisker men found a table close to where Weaver and his men were seated. He noticed each of them carried two pints of scrumpy with them and, no sooner had they taken their seats, they began to drink heavily. Harper nudged Clarke and gestured at the men. "Aye," said Clarke grimly, watching as the Tallisker men drained their first pint. "There's trouble brewing there."

Harper noticed one of the Tallisker men staring at him intently. They were the eyes of a man who wished him harm. The second pint was drained within minutes, and the men called for more drinks to be brought to their table. And more drinks followed. "Six," said Clarke to Harper, as they finished collecting another signature. "In less'n an hour."

"I think we best conclude our business here, Mr. Clarke. I'm due to meet Lord Edmond at his manor and I can't see us getting much more business done with this lot here."

"Everyone!" The man who had been staring at Harper rose shakily to his feet and called out to the room in a voice slurred with scrumpy, "Raise a tankard to our young Lord Edmond Tallisker," He turned around the room with his tankard raised until his eyes fell on Weaver and his men, "and the very fine young lady he's going to share a bed with. Lucky's the boy who gets those thighs wrapped him, lads." Harper watched Weaver carefully. His knuckles turned white as they clenched hard around his tankard, but his expression remained cool. There was a general, nervous cheer from some of the locals as they raised their drinks.

"No, no, lads," continued the Tallisker man, "if you've not seen Lady Evelyn yet, then you can't fathom just how lucky our young Lord is. We spent a long time talking about what we'd do with her if we had the chance, didn't we lads?" There was a roar from the table of Tallisker men.

Weaver rose from his chair, his head nearly touching the ceiling as his massive hands came down hard on the table in front of him. "You want to keep those words to yourself, friend. Else I'll drag you by the ear to Airedale Keep, so you can speak to Lord Dalton. I'm sure he'd be very interested to hear what you and your men would like to do to his daughter." Cries of mocked fear came from the Tallisker men.

"Piss on Lord Dalton," said the man, stumbling slightly as he took a step toward Weaver. The room fell deadly silent. "And piss on you." He was close enough now that specks of spit were hitting Weaver as he spoke.

Weaver wiped his face and rose to his feet slowly. As he did so, his men rose with him. "Last warning," said Weaver. "Apologize and sit back down."

The man's eyes rolled drunkenly around in his head as he gestured to the rest of the Tallisker men. "It's ten against four, and you've only got one good arm," he said with a grin, "why should we listen to—"

"How about we even those odds a little," called Harper, rising to his feet. "Apologize for your remarks, take a seat, and I'll buy you and your men their next round."

"Oh, this will end well…" he heard Clarke mumble as he rose to his feet as well. Harper smiled as several of the recently enlisted crew also stood. He looked around the room and spoke to the lead Tallisker man.

"That seems a little more even, wouldn't you say?" He had hoped that would be enough to make the drunkard reconsider his actions and sit down.

"Oh," said the man, spinning around drunkenly to face Harper, "you must be Captain Harper. Heard you had a soft spot for Lady Evelyn…" he put a hand to his chin and stroked it. "Or was it that I heard you found her soft spot?" The laughter that came from the

Tallisker table was cut short as Weaver's enormous fist slammed down hard on the back of the man's head. He was unconscious before he hit the ground. Weaver turned to the table of Tallisker men.

"Anyone else got something to say?"

There was an audible pause before the entire tavern erupted in one loud roar. Harper watched the explosion of limbs flail outward from the Tallisker table as nine men drunkenly launched themselves in all directions, hitting the first thing they encountered.

Harper finished his pint before launching the tankard at the head of one of Weaver's assailants. He smiled at the satisfying sound it made as the pewter connected with the man's skull. "Alright then, come on, ya bastards," yelled Clarke as he threw his first punch into the brawl. Harper ducked and dodged his way through the fight, trying to get closer to Weaver and his men as the Tallisker men overwhelmed them. A few of the Tallisker men had stumbled out onto the street after taking some hits from Weaver and his men, but the fight was escalating quickly.

Then the moment came that Harper had been dreading. The sound of steel sliding out of a scabbard as the first sword was drawn. Harper scanned the room for the flash of the blade, drawing his own sword and dashing to meet the assailant. Swords met inches away from Weaver as Harper moved in to defend him. The tavern doors burst open and more Tallisker men entered. "They must have been waiting just outside," said Harper to Weaver as the men moved toward them, drawing their weapons. These men were decidedly more sober and looked far more dangerous than the drunken rabble they had been brawling with.

"Someone's going to get killed at this rate," said Weaver, picking up one of the drunks with one hand and throwing him toward the advancing guardsmen.

"Aye," said Harper, deflecting a sloppy attack and pushing his assailant backward. "Not a good look for either of us if that happens."

"I get the feeling that was the intention, Captain…" said Weaver.

The sound of a musket firing brought the entire tavern to a standstill. Lord Tallisker pushed his way into the crowded interior, two of his guardsmen preceding him with firearms drawn. "What the blazes is going on here!" he demanded. "I've got men bleeding out on the street! I'll see the man responsible hung for this!" His beady eyes scanned the room as his mustache bristled with rage. He fixed his eyes on Weaver, who was holding an unconscious Tallisker man by his shirt. "You! Anything to say, Captain?"

"With respect, my lord, your men—"

"My men? MY men!? Damn your impudence, sir! Outside, now! And bring the rest of your men with you." Talliskers' eyes fixed on Harper. "And you, Harper. I should have known you'd somehow be mixed up in this—man of your reputation. Outside, I'll deal with the both of you myself!" Lord Tallisker turned as his men fell in behind him.

"Out the back door, Mr. Clarke. Get back to the Vestal," whispered Harper, turning so Tallisker couldn't see him. "Load the guns and keep the men ready. If you hear any gunfire, you fire a ranging shot past the town."

"Captain?" whispered Clarke, uncertainly.

"If he means to hang me, he'll take the Vestal as his. You make sure he thinks twice about sending his men anywhere near her. You get word that I'm captured or killed, you set sail and don't look back. He'll not take the Vestal, understand?" Clarke nodded. "Good man," said Harper as he sheathed his sword and raised his hands.

Out on the street, Lord Tallisker was already berating Weaver and his men. Harper counted a total of twenty Tallisker men, many now sporting injuries of some kind—all of them armed, with those closest to Lord Tallisker sporting raised musket rifles. The sun was low in the sky, casting long shadows across the small township. The longest of which was cast by the mainmast of the Vestal. A long, thin shadow cut down the center of the street as the sun fell behind the ship. Harper stole a quick glance down the street, watching as Clarke made his way through the gathering crowd of locals in the direction of the ship.

Lord Tallisker gave no quarter in his verbal onslaught, not allowing more than a word at a time to escape Weaver's lips before cutting him off. "I have never in my life seen such low born behavior from someone who commands your station, Captain Weaver. Were you one of my men I'd have you publicly flogged."

"My lord…" Weaver was doing his best to sound pleading, but his teeth were gritted as he spoke.

"Oh, 'My lord'," said Tallisker, imitating Weaver's tone. "Don't embarrass yourself further by adding misplaced supplication to your blunders! Do you think such behavior is fitting of one of Lord Dalton's men?"

"No, but—"

"No, indeed!" Lord Tallisker interrupted. "An example must be made." He feigned a deep sigh of regret. "I shall write Lord Dalton this evening and we can await his response concerning a suitable punishment. In the meantime, you are to be stripped of your armor. My men will find you a cell for you to contemplate the full stupidity of your actions." Two of Lord Tallisker's men approached Weaver, tearing the blue sash from his breastplate, and then doing the same to each of his men. "Get them out of my sight," spat Lord Tallisker. Harper watched as Weaver and his men were escorted down the street at gunpoint.

"Now," said Lord Tallisker, turning to address Harper for the first time. "What am I going to do with you, Captain Harper?"

Harper didn't say anything, aware that Tallisker was looking for an opportunity to cut him off. The two stared at each other as the silence hung heavy in the street. "I think some time in a cell while—"

"No," said Harper. He took a few steps into the middle of the street until he was standing in shadow.

"No?!" said Lord Tallisker, disbelief curled around the word. Harper shook his head. The sun was fully behind the Vestal now, throwing her shadow across the docks and streets of Dunshire.

"A firing squad then?" Lord Tallisker raised a hand and Harper watched as four guns were pointed at him. "I regret the need for bloodshed, Captain, but I must set an example. I simply can't have an ill-bred seafarer openly fighting with Tallisker men in my own lands."

"I understand the need to set examples, my lord," said Harper, his hand moved to the pistol holster at his waist. "You once challenged me on the readiness of my ship for combat. I distinctly recall you asking me about how many guns she had…" Harper gestured to the ship behind him. "And speaking of guns," Harper continued, pulling one of his pistols free and pointing it toward the sky, "each man on my crew is trained to hear the exact, distinct sound this pistol makes as it fires." Lord Tallisker's mustache bristled. "And my crew have orders to open fire on my position if they should ever hear this pistol fire when I'm ashore." That was a lie, but Harper took the view that Lord Tallisker wasn't in a position to be anything but cautious. He held his pistol raised above his head and pointed in the air. "I doubt your men could kill me before I got a shot off. Put simply, my lord, you're outgunned."

Lord Tallisker considered this for a moment. "You're bluffing," he said, but there was an uncontrolled waver to his voice. "Your men would never risk firing on English soil just to save their captain."

Harper cocked his pistol. "You're welcome to find out, my lord."

Tallisker glowered.

"Of course, my men won't know who they're firing at, but if I command them open-fire then there'll be no one left to tell the tale. And who's to say the Vestal didn't discover a cell of dissidents plotting against his majesty operating here in Dunshire and took the necessary steps to eradicate them?"

Lord Tallisker remained silent for a long time.

"They'll have plenty of time to work on their story before our corpses are ever discovered."

"Very well, Captain, you will be spared the dungeon. Instead, you are to confine yourself to your ship and you will depart as swiftly as you are able. My men will stand guard over the docks to make sure that you and your compatriots stay put."

"Our repairs are nearly complete," said Harper evenly. "We can be gone shortly after dawn."

"See that you are." Tallisker's eye narrowed.

Harper walked the rest of the way back in the shadow of the Vestal. He kept his pistol drawn, aware that some of Talliskers men were following him. He wondered if shots were fired, whether Mr. Clarke would actually fire the Vestal's guns. He hoped he wouldn't have to find out.

When Edmond heard the servants opening doors, he assumed it was his guests arriving for the evening meal. His attention had been required for longer than he had hoped, and the day had been lost to work. Though he had been disappointed he didn't have time to see Evelyn during the day, he was relieved to hear that she managed to take a ride without him. And now, he was hoping that with Harper and Weaver's company at dinner, her first day in Dunshire would be a warm and welcoming experience. Edmond was particularly looking forward to the opportunity to put the finest food and wine Dunshire could provide in front of his guests, secretly hoping that they would outshine Harper's efforts aboard the Vestal.

He was understandably surprised as he made his way down the stairs to find that his servants had not opened the door for his guests, but instead found his father surging forth from the parlor. "Father?"

"Ah, boy. There you are," Lord Tallisker put his arms on Edmond's shoulders, "when I heard about the battle, I feared the worst." Edmond looked awkwardly at the hands on his shoulders, unfamiliar with an intimate touch from his father.

"I…well, thank you," said Edmond. "Obviously no harm came to me. Or Lady Evelyn, thank God."

"Damned good news, lad. I can't tell you how I worried when news first reached Airedale." Edmond was trying to work through the arithmetic of how his father had heard the news and made the journey to Dunshire so quickly when Evelyn appeared at the top of the staircase. "And there she is," Lord Tallisker exclaimed, taking his arms off of Edmond and holding them out wide, "my daughter-in-law, safely arrived in her new home."

Edmond watched his fiancée with pride as she descended the stairs, Madame Bellegarde trailing close behind her. Even in the dim lighting of the entranceway, Evelyn looked radiant. Edmond was sure he had Madame Bellegarde to thank for that. The last time he had seen the results of Evelyn dressing herself, she looked decidedly less glamourous. Though her costume aboard the Vestal was more practical for descending stairs, Edmond thought, as he watched her very slow and careful descent.

"Lord Tallisker," said Evelyn, once her feet were both planted on the floor, "I hadn't expected to see you again so soon."

"When I heard the news, I came as quickly as I was able," said Lord Tallisker as he moved forward to embrace Evelyn.

Edmond caught her eye over her father's shoulder and gave her a bewildered shrug. He watched as his father held his fiancée tightly for an inappropriately long time. Evelyn looked at him uncomfortably as she kept her arms to her side. Edmond cleared his throat loudly. Lord Tallisker released Evelyn and turned back to his son. "We should have a libation. Get your servants to bring us some wine so that we can toast your safe arrival after that dreadful battle." Edmond nodded to one of his servants.

"We are actually expecting company shortly for the evening meal. Perhaps you would like to join us, Father?"

Lord Tallisker looked at Edmond. "Oh? What company is this?" he said, glancing between Evelyn and Edmond. "I wasn't aware there were other gentry in the area suitable to dine at a lord's table?"

"Actually, we are expecting Captain Weaver and Captain Harper..." began Evelyn.

"Those two reprobates?!"

Edmond heard the familiar blunt anger return to his father's tone. Apparently, his ability to remain cordial had a very short time limit.

"Quite impossible!—Ah... excellent!" he said, as the glasses of wine were presented.

"Impossible?" said Edmond.

"Well, yes," said Lord Tallisker, sniffing the wine before taking his first sip. "When I was coming through town, I caught the both of them drunk and brawling in the streets with our guardsmen. Several of your own men, Edmond, have ended up injured because of those two ingrates."

"Captain Harper and Captain Weaver?" asked Evelyn incredulously. "Drunk in the streets?"

"Mmm, quite so," said Tallisker, taking another sip. "Locked Weaver and his men up. I'll let your good father decide their fates."

"And Captain Harper?" asked Evelyn. "Where is he now?"

"Confined to his ship, the devil. Do you know he threatened to open fire on the entire town if we didn't let him go?" Edmond couldn't believe what he was hearing.

"Now really, Father, I simply don't..."

"Don't what, lad? Believe your own father? After I've ridden day and night to be here for you. Why don't you ask any of the men who rode with me about how Harper threatened to turn this town to matchwood if we tried to arrest him. After he'd drawn a sword on your own men. Edmond, Edmond, Edmond," tutted Lord Tallisker. "You've always been soft in the head."

Edmond looked at Evelyn again, who was staring at him in disbelief and shaking her head. "Enough of this," Lord Tallisker raised his glass, "let's talk no further about those thugs and their poor decisions. Instead, let us toast," he raised his glass and waited sternly for Edmond and Evelyn to do the same. "To the health and happiness of Lady Evelyn Dalton and her safety here in Dunshire." He took a generous swig of his glass.

"Hear, hear," said Edmond uncomfortably, as he and Evelyn each took a sip from their glasses.

"No, no. Not like that," Tallisker tutted at Evelyn. "When we toast, Lady Evelyn, we take a deep drink from our glasses. It's a sign of respect. Come, come. Drink up, you two. Today is a special day after all." Edmond and Evelyn exchanged another nervous glance before both taking a larger sip from their glasses. Lord Tallisker sniffed the air. "Something smells quite delightful. Surely dinner must be close to being served. After riding for so long, I daresay I could eat a whole boar!" Lord Tallisker strode off in the direction of the dining room, with Evelyn and Edmond falling in meekly behind him.

"I don't believe what he said," whispered Evelyn carefully as she walked next to Edmond.

"I'm not sure I do either," said Edmond. "But I don't think there's much we can do about it now…"

"What the blazes are you two whispering about back there?" called Lord Tallisker. "No secrets in these walls between family!"

"I was just complimenting my lady on her fine choice of dress this evening," said Edmond quickly.

Lord Tallisker turned and grinned. "Yes, she does look… ravishing, doesn't she?"

Silence filled the rest of the short walk to the dining room. The table had been set for five guests, neatly set out with Edmond's seat at the head of the table. Edmond swallowed as Lord Tallisker took the head seat for himself and plonked his glass down firmly on the table. The glass was already nearly empty.

"Who was the fifth seat for?" asked Tallisker gruffly, as he finished his glass.

"Madame Bellegarde will also be joining us," said Edmond as he pulled a chair out for Evelyn.

"A servant?!" Lord Tallisker rose back to his feet. "For heaven's sake, Edmond! Servants do not dine at the lord's table. You," he said, pointing at Madame Bellegarde. Edmond watched in horror as she recoiled from the extended finger. "Go and eat in the galley with the rest of the maids and tell the cellar master to bring us another bottle! And tell him if I see any empty glasses at this table tonight, I'll have him thrown out on the street!"

Madame Bellegarde hesitated for a moment, looking to Evelyn who had turned as white as a sheet.

"Go!" yelled Tallisker, sending Madame Bellegarde hurriedly out of the room. He sat back down, rubbing his forehead frustratedly. The anger and exertion had caused him to sweat.

Edmond gently ushered Evelyn to her chair before taking his seat opposite her. More wine was quickly poured as Lord Tallisker lectured them both about proper dining etiquette. Of course, Edmond knew it was unconventional to have a servant, even one as senior as Madame Bellegarde, dine with them. But at Harper's table, she had added an extra element to the enjoyment of the evening that he had hoped to replicate. He felt a deep sadness knowing that Evelyn's first meal in her new home had now been spoiled by his father's brutish behavior. Deep down, Edmond had always thought that underneath his father's loud and aggressive nature, there was a man who truly cared about him. After all, he had ridden a full day and night to be with his son after hearing about the Vestal's battle.

Again, the mathematics of the timing played in Edmond's mind, and he soon realized they were bothering Evelyn as well.

"How did you come to hear of our misfortunes at sea?" asked Evelyn, as the first dishes were put in front of them. It was the first time she had spoken since taking her seat, and Edmond could recognize from her tone that shock had been replaced with apprehension. She was watching Lord Tallisker very carefully.

"There are many men in my service, my dear." He looked at her wineglass. "You've scarcely touched your wine," he waited until Evelyn took another sip before he continued. "Very little happens in these lands that I am not informed of. Word of the battle reached me within hours of its conclusion, so naturally I sped myself here as quickly as I was able so that I…"

"Does my father know of it," asked Evelyn sharply. Edmond watched his father's eyes narrow as he was interrupted and felt a puff of pride as his fiancée held her ground.

"Regrettably, he was hunting when I departed, so I did not have the opportunity to convey the news to him. I thought it best, given the seriousness of the situation, that I not worry your parents until I had ascertained all the facts." He raised his glass again, encouraging Edmond and Evelyn to do the same. "And now that I can confirm your safety, I shall write to him early on the morrow and assure him of his only daughter's safe arrival. To your health, Lady Evelyn."

Edmond watched as another bottle was brought up from the cellar before the first course had been cleared. He knew his father was a seasoned drinker, but he worried for Evelyn, and indeed for himself, as more wine was liberally poured. Not consuming it didn't seem to be an option as Lord Tallisker brought forward more and more reasons to toast and celebrate throughout the evening. Several times in the evening, Edmond noticed Evelyn sit up suddenly and move uncomfortably in her chair. When he asked her if she was alright, she simply nodded and looked away.

By the time the desserts were served, Edmond's appetite had long since left him. The entire evening had drained him and now he just watched as his father greedily devoured the small cakes and chocolates that had been laboriously prepared for them. Edmond's mind felt clouded from the wine, and he wished the evening would end, if only so that Evelyn could be spared any further time in Lord Tallisker's presence. It had become painfully clear throughout the evening that he made her uncomfortable. But what was worse was that Lord Tallisker seemed to enjoy her discomfort and even prey upon it. Edmond could feel anger smoldering inside of him. The wine now only added to his rage as he continued to drink at his father's pace.

He watched again as Evelyn moved uncomfortably in her seat and decided it was time to remove her from the situation. A plan, of sorts, began to form in his mind. It didn't feel right to him, but he took a leaf from his father's book. "I believe, now that the hour is late, that Lady Evelyn should retire to her bedchambers. The day has wearied my fiancée, and I think it proper she excuse herself for the evening." Lord Tallisker opened his mouth to protest, but Edmond stood up abruptly. "Thank you for your company this evening, Lady Evelyn. I shall look forward to seeing you in the morning for our ride." Evelyn stood up.

"Yes, our…ride," she said. "I look forward to it also, my lord." Edmond watched as she took a deep breath in. "Thank you for your concern for my welfare, Lord Tallisker. Your presence here is," Evelyn swallowed mid-sentence, "most welcome."

"Oh, it is you who are most welcome, my dear," said Lord

Tallisker, rising to his feet. He reached out a hand to her, but Evelyn turned swiftly to Edmond, pretending not to notice.

"Thank you," she said earnestly as she turned to leave.

Edmond watched as one of the servants made moves to escort Evelyn back to her chambers.

"The fire is lit in the hall," said Edmond. "Let's enjoy a drink there." Lord Tallisker grunted an approval as they moved from the dining room. Edmond turned to the cellar master as his father left the room. "Fetch the strongest brandy we have," he said quietly. "I want to make sure my father has a deep sleep after a hard day on the road."

Harper waited until the night had grown darkest before climbing down the side of the Vestal and making the leap down to the docks. Lord Tallisker's men were easy enough to slip past as he kept to the shadows and moved quickly through the streets of Dunshire. The evening had turned cold as Harper approached the church. The only sounds he could hear were his own breathing and his cautious footsteps. He looked around for a comfortable place to wait for Evelyn. There was no light coming from the church, but he didn't take that as a sign to relax. He looked in the direction of Dunshire Manor, faintly lit by its interior lights. If she was going to join him, that would be the direction Evelyn would be coming from.

The church was skirted by a well-maintained garden, and Harper found a worn wooden bench to sit on as he waited. It was a long time until dawn, but his heart raced in his chest as he imagined Evelyn walking down the path toward him. He was certain that she felt the same way for him as he did her, and there was no doubt that she was incredibly brave. Even still, he was asking her to take an enormous risk by eloping with him. He didn't dare to assume that she would make the journey to be with him. It was still a gamble of long odds.

He had no doubt that both Lord Tallisker and Lord Dalton would bring their full might down upon him if she chose a life on the Vestal. Beyond that, there were a number of other complications Harper hadn't begun to fully work through. He hadn't yet decided how he would tell the crew that Evelyn would be joining them or how he would retain their loyalty should Evelyn's presence put their lives in danger. Evelyn had convincingly passed herself off as a young man during battle, but under closer scrutiny, she would be discovered. And even if she could fool the crew, what kind of life would that be for her? Having to hide who she was every waking moment just so she could spend her evenings with Harper wasn't an existence he wanted for her.

An alternative plan was beginning to form at the edges of Harper's mind, but he didn't like where his thoughts were taking him. There was a simpler way that he could be with Evelyn, and all it required was for him to give up everything he had. If Evelyn was prepared to leave her life of nobility and privilege, then a life together required an equally large sacrifice from him. The Vestal would be the last obstacle on the path to their happiness. For as long as he was bound to his ship, Evelyn would suffer. Perhaps not at first, as the novelty of a life of adventure at sea was fresh, but it wouldn't be long before she resented Harper for asking her to choose it.

He thought hard for a moment about what he was considering. A few short weeks ago, there was nothing in the world he would have traded for the Vestal, and now he was genuinely considering abandoning her. Were the Vestal and his captaincy worth giving up for anything or anyone? Could he truly say he loved Evelyn if he wasn't prepared to make the same level of commitment that she was? Could he be happy aboard the Vestal if it meant a life without Evelyn? It wasn't the questions that bothered him as much as knowing what the answers were. Deep down, he knew what he would have to do if

Evelyn chose him. He would need to choose her as well.

There were a lot of places in the New World that two people could slip away to. He could engage the Vestal for one last voyage across the Atlantic and from there, they could find a place to call home. They would have to leave their names behind, but he had enough wealth saved that he could afford for them to start over comfortably. Evelyn, for her part, would likely only have the clothes she was wearing. It wouldn't be easy, but with the Vestal removed from consideration, a life together started to seem possible.

Hours passed without Harper noticing as he sorted through the details of how their new life would begin. His eyes stayed fixed in the direction of Dunshire Manor as he ironed out all of his next moves once Evelyn joined him. A light coming from the church broke his thoughts. The first sign that day was beginning to break. The clouds were thick, but the first subtle changes in light were chasing the night away. His heart tightened in his chest as the minutes rolled by.

"She's not coming, Harper."

"Christ!" said Harper, jumping to his feet and drawing his sword. He relaxed, only a little, as Weaver stepped toward him. "You scared me half to death."

"Hardly fitting language for a church, Captain," said Weaver.

"What are you even doing here?" asked Harper, sheathing his blade. "I thought they locked you in a dungeon?"

"They did," said Weaver. He moved to the bench Harper had been sitting on and lowered himself painfully onto it. It creaked ominously under his weight.

"Why are you here?" asked Harper.

Weaver considered the question for a moment. "I suppose, in a way, I was hoping I'd be wrong." Weaver stared at Dunshire Manor, avoiding Harper's stern eyes. "I read your letter," said Weaver, as if predicting Harper's next question. "That's how I knew you'd be here.

And I must admit, Captain, after reading your words, I genuinely believe you love her as much as any man could."

"By what right…" began Harper angrily.

"By the right of being the man charged with Lady Evelyn's safety and wellbeing from the day she first entered the world, Captain. Don't lose your temper at me. For a man with a reputation of being sharp and cunning, your passion certainly seems to have made you clumsy. In what world did you imagine an unmarked chest, clearly not from Airedale Keep, sitting atop the items destined for Lady Evelyn's bedchambers would not warrant investigation. You're just lucky it was me that discovered it."

Harper kept silent, but his eyes remained furious. "If I'd wanted to, I could have tossed your letter into the sea and that would have been the last Lady Evelyn ever heard from you."

"Why didn't you?" asked Harper. He sat back down on the bench and joined Weaver in looking out at Dunshire Manor.

"You wrote in your letter that she had earned Captain Leighton's sword."

"Aye. She killed him," said Harper, uncertain as to the meaning of Weaver's statement.

"She is a remarkable young woman, Captain. I've watched her my entire life, and even I couldn't have guessed at just how strong she truly is. While you were pulling me out of the ocean, she was onboard the Vestal fighting as hard as any man onboard." Weaver paused for a moment. "I owe both of you a debt I can't repay other than by allowing your words to reach her and to see if she truly feels the same way you do."

"What will you do now?" asked Harper as the low light of dawn reintroduced color to the world.

"Well, I can't go back to Airedale. As much loyalty as I have for Lord Dalton, he wouldn't risk an alliance over my job. He'd just as likely send me back to the Talliskers as a show of good will."

"That's a raw deal, mate."

"It strikes me," said Weaver after a short pause, "that no matter what happens next, the Vestal will need a new first mate. Someone who knows how to lead men. Someone who knows how to watch her captain's back in a fight and notices when he's being…clumsy."

"Know you of such a man?" asked Harper.

"There is one name that leaps to mind, Captain."

"Tell him to report to my quarters at two bells on the fore-noon watch. If he's nautical enough to work out when that is and presents himself on time, then I'll see if he's up to the Vestal's standards."

Weaver rose to his feet and turned to leave. "How did you escape?" asked Harper without turning.

"Let us simply say if you're going to lock up the man who oversees the Airedale dungeons, then you should station more than two guards at his cell."

"And your men?" asked Harper.

"The same fate awaits them that would await me should they return to Airedale."

"Tell them to report in with your candidate for first mate," said Harper.

"Thank you, Captain. That means a lot. When will you be returning to the ship?"

Harper looked at Dunshire Manor. "I'll give it a bit more time yet. The sun still has a way to climb before it's dawn."

"Of course," said Weaver. There was a hint of sadness in his voice.

Harper listened to the heavy footsteps until they had faded away. Somewhere nearby, a songbird was making its first call of the new day as it hailed the rising sun. He could feel an unfamiliar choke on his throat and the prick of tears behind his eyes. Harper couldn't remember the last time he had cried. He bit down hard on his bottom lip as the first tear rolled down his face. He looked down at his feet, his head in his hands as a feeling of complete and utter defeat washed over him.

♦ 310 ♦

Evelyn kept herself composed as she walked back to her bedchambers. Madame Bellegarde's earlier lesson on first impressions hadn't been lost on her and now it was taking everything she had to hide her emotions from the servants. This was supposed to be her house and within seconds of entering it, Lord Tallisker had quickly established that she and Edmond held no authority with him. Edmond's attempts to deflect conversation and even ultimately remove her from the situation seemed all he was capable of to alleviate her humiliation.

Throughout the evening, Lord Tallisker had run his foot up against her leg and every time she had tried to move away from him, he seemed to enjoy it. A stark difference to the experience she had enjoyed with Harper onboard the Vestal. This was a violation. The most unwelcome touch she had ever experienced. From the moment he had put his arms around her in the parlor, Lord Tallisker had made her feel uncomfortable in her own home. She realized her hands were clenched as she reached the top of the stairs and surreptitiously unfurled her fingers and took a deep, calming breath.

Before she reached the door to her bedchamber, she turned to the servant escorting her. "Please show me to Madame Bellegarde's room." As it turned out, it was only two doors down from her own. Before knocking, Evelyn dismissed the servant and waited until her footsteps had faded away.

"I'm so sorry…" began Evelyn. Madame Bellegarde looked at her, as strong and resolute as ever.

"You can't start apologizing for that man's behavior now; otherwise, you'll never be able to stop."

"He was wrong to yell at you," said Evelyn firmly. "No one will ever yell at you again."

Madame Bellegarde shrugged. "But he was right about the dinner. It isn't my place to sit at the table with lords and ladies," Madame Bellegarde seemed less upset about the matter than Evelyn.

"He may be right about conventions, but that does not excuse his behavior. No one, not Lord Tallisker or anyone else, will ever speak to you that way again in my house. And you will sit at my table when I request it because I enjoy your company and wit. Tomorrow morning, I will petition him for the release of Captain Harper and Captain Weaver, and he will apologize for how he spoke to you."

"No, sweet child," said Madame Bellegarde, shaking her head. "Do not make a scene on my behalf. All it will do is cause trouble for us both. He is a part of your family now and we need to respect that." She looked down to the corridor to make sure they were alone. "No matter how much we might hate him for it. Go to bed, sleep. Tomorrow we will find our strength again."

Evelyn felt her anger grow hotter as she made her way back to her room. Once the door was closed behind her, she let out a loud and angry yell. Not a scream, not a cry. She bellowed her rage against every corner of her bedchambers until her mouth was hoarse. She fell to her knees and choked back a sob. She had never cried from anger before. She felt as if she couldn't breathe as she took large, furious gulps of air. A soft knock came at the door. "Go away!" she yelled. She heard footsteps scamper down the corridor at the sound of her voice.

She picked herself and looked at the chest Harper had given her, knowing full well what it contained. She wondered for a moment what Harper would have done if he were at dinner instead of Edmond. "Likely something stupid," she said to herself as she stared at the chest. She smiled as she imagined Harper launching himself across the table and punching Lord Tallisker. She imagined it wouldn't be a single punch either, as she pictured the two toppling over, Harper beating Tallisker over and over again. Evelyn had seen firsthand what men looked like when they were torn apart in battle. She doubted many ladies her age knew just how fragile the human body was. Now she imagined Lord Tallisker's body sundered by battle. She looked at the chest again, feeling the wine steer her decisions as she stepped toward it.

When she opened the chest and reached for the sword, her fingers touched against the folded parchment of Harper's letter. She picked it up carefully and reopened it. She read the words, 'the choice is yours to make' and suddenly felt a sense of calm and clarity come over her. She had the power to leave. There was a man waiting for her who loved her unconditionally, only a short walk away from the manor. She had seen the church on the carriage ride to the manor. She had the means to protect herself if anyone decided to stop her. She could do it. She could leave.

She looked at the clock. It would be hours yet before she could leave. She decided two in the morning would be the best time. Everyone would be asleep, and the night would be darkest. Her mind began to race about how she would make the journey. She knew she wouldn't be able to scale the walls, so she would have to go through the manor. The front door would likely be locked, and she didn't have keys, so she would need to find a window or a servant's entrance she could slip through.

She would have to somehow arrange to send for Madame Bellegarde once she was safely out of Dunshire. She didn't like the thought of leaving her behind, but Evelyn knew she had to make the journey on her own. Then she remembered the other person she would be leaving behind. She looked around her unfamiliar bed chambers. There was a small desk in the corner and after a quick rummage, Evelyn found everything she needed to write. She sat at the desk and smoothed a piece of parchment out. She wasn't exactly sure what she wanted to write, but as she picked up the quill, she found the words came easily. A sadness began to well in her as her heart wrote itself across the page.

> *My dear Edmond,*
>
> *I know that as you read this, you will be feeling many things. Sadness, as you realize that by leaving, I have shown you that the love you have given me has not been returned. Anger, that I have chosen another person to share my love with and that he loves me back in turn. You may hate me for my choice, but I hope that isn't the case. A heart as good and pure as yours should never contain hatred. I truly do have nothing but warmth and affection for you, but I know that I have given myself fully to another.*
>
> *To stay would be a lie, one that I couldn't ever be happy living. I believe in time, when your heart is healed, you will understand that my leaving was the best for both of us. I couldn't bear for us to live a lie, for the years to mount up on us only to realize that we were never meant to be together. I have already been disloyal to you with my heart and with my*

body, and I know that if I stayed, my thoughts would always be of another man and another life.

I know one day you will find someone who is worthy of your love. Someone who can be yours completely and who will give you all of her heart. But I know that person cannot be me and for that I am deeply sorry. You deserve better.

Love,

Evelyn

By the time she had signed her name, tears were streaming down her face and splashing down onto the letter. A collection of tears formed at her chin and fell heavily into the wet ink. She dabbed at it carefully, trying to keep the words in their original shape. Her head was beginning to ache from the combined effects of the wine, rage, and sorrow. She sat back and breathed deeply as she waited for the parchment to dry. Once it was ready, she neatly folded the letter and placed it in the middle of the desk. On the outside she neatly printed: For Lord Edmond Tallisker. She took a candle and poured a small droplet of wax across the fold.

She got up and looked at the clock. It was approaching midnight, still hours before she planned to elope. She awkwardly untied the back of her dress and stepped out of it. Now that the servants had finished unpacking her belongings, her dresses had all been arranged neatly in her wardrobe. There was one in particular she was looking for, an old beige and blue dress that her mother said made Evelyn look like a maid. She remembered it for being more comfortable and practical than her other garments. For a moment, she worried it might not have been packed with the rest of her belongings. Perhaps Madame Bellegarde hadn't deemed it glamourous enough for her new wardrobe. But then she found it, hiding nonchalantly behind the brilliant colors of her newer dresses.

It was rare that she ever dressed herself, but she managed the process without any complications. She grabbed a dark blue woolen shawl and wrapped it neatly about her shoulders. Finally, she returned to the chest Harper had given her and placed Declan Harper's hat firmly on her head. She looked at the sword, uncertain of where it would attach itself to her dress and wondered if she had a sash somewhere that would secure it to her waist.

Her thoughts were interrupted by a heavy knock at her door. Her eyes narrowed as she checked the clock. She couldn't imagine who would be at her door at this hour. The knock came again. She felt a cold shiver come over her as she watched the latch slowly turn. She hadn't thought to lock the door behind when she entered and now it swung open with no resistance. Lord Tallisker didn't wait to be invited in. "Good evening, Lady Evelyn," he said with a slur. Evelyn could smell the spirt on his breath from across the room.

"You are not welcome here, sir," said Evelyn coldly. "Please leave."

Tallisker's face turned into a sly smile. "Speaking of leaving, where are you heading at this late hour, Lady Evelyn?" He tilted his head as he examined her. "Dressed for a cold night meeting your lover, perhaps?" Evelyn couldn't hide the shock on her face, but she wasn't about to admit anything to Lord Tallisker.

"I do not know where Lord Edmond is," she said. She knew it was a weak lie, but it was the only one she could think of. "But I do know he would not approve of your presence here. And neither do I."

"Edmond," tutted Lord Tallisker. "I think that poor lad thought he could drink me into a stupor and have me put to bed. Don't worry, my dear. I put something in his brandy to help him sleep. He won't interrupt us. No…" he began, closing the door behind him. "I wasn't referring to Edmond as your lover." Fear came over her as the door clicked closed. "I saw you, you know? Thinking you were both so careful as you slipped away at the feast." He took a few more steps toward her as she backed away. "Saw what a little whore Lord Dalton's daughter actually is. Imagine how my heart ached when I saw the betrothed of my Edmond with her arms wrapped around an ill-bred seafarer."

"One has to have a heart in order for it ache, Lord Tallisker," Evelyn couldn't hide the tremble in her voice. She knew she only had a few steps left before she hit the wall behind her. "Take another step toward me and I'll scream."

"You already screamed loud enough to send the servants running scared from you. Luckily, I sent the staff to their quarters and made sure they were asleep before I came to visit you. The lights are out. The doors are closed. You are alone, my lady."

Evelyn's eyes darted to the chest containing Harper's final gift.

Tallisker followed her gaze. "There's nothing in there, or anywhere else, that can help you now, little girl," he said, stepping in front of the chest and taking another step toward her. "It would have been much easier if Leighton had managed to secure you, much less to clean up." Her anger resurfaced and burned the fear away as Evelyn listened. "You'd already be safely stashed away. Ready to be the bearer of a new line of Talliskers once we were able to be…together." His eyes gleamed with lust as he reached out to grab Evelyn.

Her forearm came up fast and knocked his hand away as she stepped back quickly. "Do not touch me," she spat.

"There's a carriage waiting to take you away downstairs," breathed Tallisker as he turned to face her and lunged forward again. "But I think after waiting so long it's only fitting I take you here first." One hand unfastened the neck button of his shirt as he lumbered forward. With his other hand, he latched around her shawl and pulled hard.

Evelyn spun and freed herself from the garment, ducking under the fat fingers as they grasped for her again. He laughed as the garment fell to the floor and undid another of his shirt buttons.

Evelyn shifted her position again. Now Lord Tallisker's back was to the wall. She took a step back, her hand reaching for the table she knew was somewhere behind her. Lord Tallisker looked at her like a starving animal, his teeth bared as he stepped toward her again. "So much spirit. What fine children you will bear," he said, licking his lips, "and what joy I'll take in the process."

"A joy you'll never know and one I am only too happy to deny you." Evelyn's hand fell behind her as she moved backward, not daring to take her eyes off Lord Tallisker. "Perhaps you'd like to know what happened to the last man who threatened me with violence?" Her fingers curled around the corner of the table and then ran upwards until they found the lid of the chest.

"Did the 'brave and noble' Captain Harper come to save you?" mocked Tallisker. He reached out and grabbed her shoulder, pulling her close to him.

"No," said Evelyn, as the sword slid free from its scabbard. Lord Tallisker's eyes widened at the sound. "I killed him." She pulled the blade upward, moving it between their bodies, the tip of the sword pressing against Tallisker's throat. She felt his hand release her shoulder. "Step back." Evelyn pressed the blade until she felt Lord Tallisker take a step backward. "I spent this evening imagining your face beaten to a pulp just for rubbing your leg against me. So imagine…"

"You should put that down, right now…" said a suddenly very sober Lord Tallisker, stepping back until the blade was a safe distance from his throat.

"So imagine," snarled Evelyn, "what I might do to you if I found out you were responsible for the attack on the Vestal." She laughed.

Not a funny laugh. A cold laugh that had an edge of insanity to it. "Imagine if I learned that you were responsible for Mr. Webb lying broken in this house. Or the deaths of men who you could never hope to measure up to. Imagine if I learned you almost had me stolen away from my family so that you could rape me over and over again. Imagine…what I might do then." She took a step forward and pressed the blade back against his chest. "I wonder, would Edmond be sad if I ran you through right now or would he thank me?" Lord Tallisker knocked the blade away with the back of his hand, but Evelyn quickly pointed it back at his chest as he continued to retreat. "I've only known you a few short weeks, and I already want to murder you. I can only imagine how it's been for him."

"Put that damned thing away," huffed Tallisker as he moved for the door.

"Why?" asked Evelyn, "so you can 'take me here first' before you take me away to whatever god-awful life you had in store for me."

"You will be mine," hissed Lord Tallisker. "My men are just downstairs and when I return with them, we will take you by force. I'll burn this whole house to the ground if anyone tries to stop me from claiming what is mine."

The word 'mine' shot through Evelyn like a bolt and she arced the blade out in front of her.

Tallisker opened the door and tripped backward, the blade missing him as he fell unceremoniously to the floor.

"Then we are at an impasse, Lord Tallisker," said Evelyn, stepping out into the corridor and following him as he clambered back to his feet. "Because I will never be yours and I can't let you leave to summon your men."

Tallisker pulled himself up on a nearby curtain and regained his balance, just in time to dodge another lunge from Evelyn. She was close enough now that he could reach for her, and he grabbed her sword arm, squeezing hard as he pulled her toward him. Evelyn winced at the pain, but her grip tightened around the blade. She knew if she let go of the sword, the fight was over.

With his body between her and the blade, Lord Tallisker's confidence returned. He grabbed her by her hair, knocking her hat off as he pulled her head back. Taking advantage of his position, he ran his tongue against her face.

Evelyn closed her eyes as her face contorted. She could feel his nostrils inhaling deeply as she struggled against him. She brought her knee up hard, hoping to strike his groin but finding only the thick, defensive fat of his stomach.

The force was enough to separate them, but Tallisker kept his grip on her hair as he pulled at her. He pushed his feet against the wall, trying to overpower her and drag her back to her room. She shifted her grip on her sword, desperately trying to strike him as he leaned his body into hers. He moved his faced in close to hers again and this time she was ready for it. She launched her forehead at his nose and heard the satisfying crunch as she hammered it flat into his face. She felt her hair freed as Tallisker brought his hand to his face, blood streaming from his nose.

Evelyn wrenched her sword arm free and darted backward, giving herself enough room to raise her weapon.

"You will pay for that," snarled Tallisker.

"I already have," said Evelyn. "Any sin I've ever committed has been repaid a thousand times by your violations." She wiped the slobber from her cheek and then spat at him in disgust. "But I don't think you've paid enough for your sins yet, sir." She lunged for him and cut through his shirt. She was sure she'd cut him because he winced as he stepped back from her. He rose his hands defensively as the blade came at him again and he yelped as it cut across his fingers.

"The coach is ready," Tallisker sniffed deeply through his bloodied nose. "You will be on it and you will be mine. I have more to offer you than any other man, you will—"

"You have NOTHING to offer me." The sword slashed forward again, the blade humming as it whipped through the air.

Lord Tallisker stepped back, one step too far. Evelyn saw the look of surprise on his face as his foot failed to find the ground behind it. She watched as his large body fell backward down the spiral staircase and disappeared from view. As he fell, it sounded as if the corner of every step connected with each of the bones in his body. She breathed deeply as the realism of what had just happened cascaded over her. She took slow, careful steps down the stairwell as she traversed them in the dark. At the bottom of the stairwell, in a large heap of broken bones and pooling blood, lay the late Lord Tallisker.

"Evelyn?" came a weak voice in the dark.

She turned to see Edmond, silhouetted in a nearby doorway.

"What have you done?"

"**P**repare to make ready," said Harper, quietly.

"Prepare to make ready!" bellowed Weaver in a voice that carried to every corner of the ship.

"Well done, Mr. Weaver. You've just issued your first command on the Vestal." Harper leaned against the ship's wheel as he watched the crew. The new Dunshire recruits had been partnered into teams with the more experience sailors. It was hard not to be affected by the excitement coming from the new sailors as they made ready for their first voyage.

"Thank you, Captain," said Weaver. He stood firmly at attention, just a few feet behind Harper.

"At ease, man," said Harper. "This isn't His Majesty's Navy."

"Aye," grinned Mr. Clarke as he joined them on the quarterdeck. "We shoot straighter and drink harder."

"That we do, Mr. Clarke," said Harper approvingly.

"All the men have reported into their stations, Captain. Ready on your command."

As the crew climbed the rigging and readied the sails, Harper felt a lump in his throat. "Mr. Weaver," he began. "Please join Mr. Trent on the main deck and issue the command to make sail."

"All hands, cast off and prepare to make sail," bellowed Weaver.

"He's learn'n fast," said Clarke once Weaver was out of earshot. "He'll do Webb proud as first mate."

"Aye," said Harper distantly. As he watched Weaver descend the stairs, he pondered the hand fate had dealt him. He had imagined Evelyn's slender figure joining him aboard the Vestal. Instead, he'd been given a large, hairy man who'd once threatened him. It was a consolation he would need time to come to terms with. Still, he had to agree with Clarke. Weaver was a natural leader. He would command respect and ensure discipline from the crew.

Since returning to the Vestal, Harper hadn't looked to land once. It was unconscious, his mind trying to protect him from any further reminders of what he'd just lost. He had taken the biggest gamble of his life and lost. He'd never felt more exposed or vulnerable as he'd let himself become with Evelyn. He'd paid the price for that vulnerability as he learned he was alone in his feelings. As much as he wanted to hope Evelyn loved him, it felt easier to believe that she didn't. That her feelings for him had been fleeting and easily put aside. He could already feel his heart starting to harden as he built his emotional defenses.

His fingers curled around the handles of the ship's wheel. He watched as Trent and Weaver gave the order to make sail. He listened to the sails flapping in the wind as they unfurled. Fresh sails since the battle, crisp and white against the dark and cloudy sky. "What's our heading, Captain?" asked Clarke. Harper felt the cold air blowing down from the hills of Dunshire against his back.

"Clearer skies and warmer waters, Mr. Clarke," said Harper as he felt the ship start to respond to wheel. "I feel like chasing horizons."

"Pretty little town," said Clarke, as he looked back at Dunshire. "I'm sure they'll be very happy here."

"Yes, I'm sure she will," said Harper as he turned the wheel. "Safe and where she belongs."

Something brushed against his leg, and he looked down. He knelt to pick up Blackbeard and gave him an affectionate scratch behind a tattered ear. He was rewarded with a deep rumbling purr. "And I'm where I belong," he said, looking into Blackbeard's one good eye. He could feel the hull of the Vestal moving through the water as he kept one hand on the wheel. Every part of this ship, from her timber to her sails, was a part of him. And he never felt that more than he did the moment he turned the Vestal away from Dunshire and back out to the open ocean.

◆

Evelyn felt her heart sink as she watched the Vestal's sails unfurl. It had been Edmond's idea to be away from Dunshire Manor before the body was discovered. The sight of his father's broken corpse at the bottom of the stairwell had sobered him up quickly, but his priority had been protecting Evelyn. They realized there was no moving the body as between Edmond and Evelyn they had failed Lord Tallisker's dead weight. "We'll go for a ride," said Edmond, when they realized no one was coming to investigate, "as soon as the sun is up. When he's discovered, we make sure we're not in the manor." Evelyn wasn't sure if that would make them look more or less suspicious, but she didn't have a better plan.

She'd gone back to her room and immediately been sick in her bedpan. It wasn't that Lord Tallisker was dead. That didn't bother her at all. It was what his death meant for her life. She had lost her one window of freedom, her agency disappearing as the fat man fell to his death. Only hours ago, she'd had a clear course of action for her future. To meet with Harper and to elope with him. Now she knew that was impossible. It was one thing to run away with Harper and incur all the danger that went along with it, but if she went to him now, she would be implicating him in the murder of a lord. Lord Tallisker dead, Evelyn and the Vestal gone. The world would be sent to hunt them down, and she knew Harper would hang for it.

She cried like she'd never cried before. Harper would be waiting for her at the church, completely unaware of her intentions to be with him. She knew how much not going to him would hurt him. But a broken heart would mend much more easily than a broken neck. She tried desperately to think of a way to go to Harper that wouldn't link him to Tallisker's death. But she couldn't. She sat for hours, wracking her brain as she tried to think of a plan. But nothing came to her, and hope slipped further away as the clock ticked.

When Edmond came to collect her, he hugged her tightly and kissed her forehead. The same forehead she had used to break his father's nose a few hours ago. He held her hand, squeezing tightly, as he guided her to the stables. While Evelyn had been crying, Edmond had readied the horses and made the preparations for them to leave. "If anyone asks, we had arranged for a ride at dawn because we missed our ride yesterday." He'd been talking quickly, almost babbling as they quietly trotted away from the manor. "The servants heard me say to you at the dining table…that we would ride together. It's believable…They'll believe us."

Edmond had taken them to his favorite lookout, a tall hill on the outskirts of town. The air was bitterly cold, and the wind whipped Evelyn's hair about her face. "Where did you get the sword?" asked Edmond as they watched the Vestal's sails catch the wind.

"It was a wedding gift," said Evelyn, her eyes fixed on the Vestal, "from Captain Harper. He gave it to me when I left the Vestal."

Edmond considered this for a moment. "Well, I'm glad he did. Without it, who knows what would have happened."

Evelyn was quite certain they both knew what would have happened as they watched in silence.

"I wish he was staying," said Edmond as the Vestal steered away from the docks and out to sea.

"Me too."

"I'm sure he'd have some brilliant plan for us. He'd know what to do next."

"I'm sure he would," replied Evelyn. "But we have to trust ourselves now." She took a deep breath. "I'm sure we can get through this…together."

"He used to hit me, you know. My father, that is. When I was younger, and his ire was up." He turned in his saddle to face her. "For so many years, I wished I had possessed the strength to hit him back. I don't blame you for what happened. I just wish I'd taken action against him years ago so that he never had the chance to…"

"What happened wasn't your fault," Evelyn said quickly. She was in no mood for misplaced blame. "His actions were his own, and he paid the price for them. Just like Captain Leighton and his crew." The wind howled.

"We should head back," said Edmond, "I don't want you to catch a chill on top of everything else." Evelyn nodded. They rode back slowly, with Edmond detailing the plan for their return to the manor.

As expected, they were greeted with terrible news from the servants. Edmond played the part of a shocked and distressed son perfectly, but Evelyn didn't feel like acting. She wondered if her coldness would be perceived as shock, though she honestly didn't care what anyone thought anymore. Her thoughts were on the Vestal and her captain as they sailed away. Edmond would never know how much she was giving up by staying in Dunshire.

Evelyn gave a long, hard stare to Lord Tallisker's men, who were assembled outside of the manor. "I suppose they report to you now?" she asked. They made their way to the entrance. Edmond nodded. "Before the day is through, I want them looking for new work," said Evelyn, loud enough for the men to hear as she walked past them. "And I don't want them in my sight again."

"The first of many changes we will need to make," agreed Edmond as he opened the doors to the manor.

Doctor Forsythe was waiting for them in the parlor. He bowed his head respectfully as they entered. "My lord, I am most terribly sorry for your loss. By the time I arrived there was nothing that could be done."

"Thank you, doctor. I truly don't have any words…" Edmond called out to the nearest servant. "Please, escort Lady Evelyn back to her chambers. There is no need for her to endure any further distress today." Evelyn let herself be silently led away as Edmond continued speaking to the doctor. As she reached the top of the stairs, she hovered for a moment, straining to hear the hushed conversation.

"… consistent with a sharp edge, a blade of some kind…" she heard the doctor say.

"It was the fall that killed him, doctor," said Edmond firmly. "You said so yourself."

"Yes, but these cuts, very peculiar, my lord," Forsythe pressed on. "I suspect we could be dealing with foul play here."

"Nonsense," Edmond spoke more loudly. "The cuts are superficial. My father drank far too heavily last night and likely unsheathed his blade as he often did, then lost his footing climbing the stairs to his bedchamber and the blade tumbled along with him. I won't be distressed further by any other theories…"

"Of course," said Forsythe quickly. "I meant no disrespect, my lord…" He looked up the staircase and saw Evelyn looking down at them. "Perhaps we might continue this discussion another time. Would you care to accompany me to examine the body?"

Evelyn turned and resumed her walk back to her bedchamber.

The fire had been lit in her room, and she was grateful for the warmth. She looked at her corner desk, the carefully folded and sealed letter to Edmond still sitting where she had left it. With a heavy heart, she picked it up and broke the seal. She reread her words, pausing at where her tears had caused the ink to run across the words 'another man and another life'. She wondered for a moment if it was a life she could still have? She knew where the horses were kept. She had the means to protect herself. If she left now, she could make one last attempt at reclaiming her freedom before it slipped away forever.

She sighed, crumpling the letter in her hand before tossing it into the flames, and watched as the paper caught. Her words, so strongly felt and ready to be acted on, turned to ash in seconds. "Everything happens a pointe nommé," Madame Bellegarde's words echoed through her mind. "The right time, the right place. Never before." She looked into the fire and felt her strength rise up inside her. She wasn't defeated. Losing one battle didn't mean that the war was over, and now she knew what she was fighting for. Even as the Vestal sailed away, she knew that the fight for her freedom, the life she wanted, and the man she loved, was far from over.

Her search for the right time and the right place had only just begun.

ACKNOWLEDGEMENTS

Firstly, and most importantly, I need to thank my partner. Her love, support, patience, and inspiration have been the driving forces behind my creativity. In what can only be described as the most challenging and stressful year of our lives we've also managed to find time to grow, learn, and laugh.

My family, most especially my parents and my grandparents have been overwhelmingly supportive, not just of my creative endeavours but of every stage of my life. My mother, a life-long book lover, librarian and teacher, deserves the credit for developing my passion of stories and storytelling. During a time when I have been completely displaced from a normal life and travelling across countries during the pandemic it has been incredibly comforting to know there's still support and love thousands of miles away.

The writing community and aspiring authors who have answered questions and been part of the many discussions I've participated in as I embarked on this journey. Most notably, Felicity George who is a subject matter expert in all things Victorian era and provided me with such incredible feedback and suggestions after reading my first complete draft. I hope to be reading her published works in the very near future.

Finally, a very genuine and heartfelt thanks to anyone who purchased this novel and enjoyed the story. Content and creativity are as infinite as the collective imaginations of everyone on the planet, so to choose one author's work over the millions of entertainment options available is no small thing.

ABOUT THE AUTHOR

J D Easterling left his home country of Australia as soon as he finished school and set off to teach English across southern and southeast Asia. He used stories and music in his classes, including Indigenous Australian dreamtime stories, the stories that sparked his creativity as a child.

Returning to his motherland, he paid his way through university cooking and found he had a deep passion for food. Even now he enjoys challenging himself in the kitchen and keeps food at the centre of all his travel plans.

Graduating with honours in History and English, he quickly learned that the only work in his field was staying in academia and… microfiche. So instead, he worked in the food and wine industry across Australia. Eventually, he followed his heart and moved to the United States to be with his partner.

Through the turbulence of the global pandemic and visa renewals, he ended up in a small beach town in Mexico and there, with a view of the ocean greeting him each morning, he finished his first novel.

READ MORE

To learn more visit:
JDEasterling.com

He can also be found:
Tweeting @jd_easterling
& on Instagram @jd.easterling

To leave a Goodreads review, please visit
Goodreads.com and search for
The Path of the Vestal by J D Easterling.